# Dedication

To my children: Joe, Emily, and James

# The Woman and the Witch

Amanda Larkman

First paperback edition April 2020
Cover design: Jem Butcher
ISBN: 9798625919920
ASIN: B086KYFWW8

# CONTENTS

# PROLOGUE: ANGIE, TODAY

*A*s *I hack away at a thorny hedge, watching the scratches of blood scribbling across my arms, I realise, with a pulse of shock, that I'm now the same age Mrs B was when I met her - almost fifty years ago.*

*The thought is staggering. Great oceans of time surge beneath my feet, making me dizzy. A cyclone of memories threatens to overwhelm, throwing brightly coloured snatches of my past into my face; I blink and rub my skin to remove them.*

*I stumble and reach for the wall. The bricks radiate the heat of the sun and I lower myself to the ground to rest my back. It's a beautiful May afternoon; birds sing the colour of the sky.*

*I stretch my arms out in front of me to flex my aching wrists. The twisted, bony length of them is still a surprise, even after all these years. I miss the bulk I carried for most of my life.*

*Strange. I used to loathe the fat as a younger woman. Now the loss of it makes me feel insubstantial, as if a gust of wind could blow me away, leaving nothing but scraps and a pile of crumpled clothes. I examine the bones rising out of my skin. My hundred-year-*

*old skin. Not that it looks it. I'd picked up enough tricks from Mrs B.*

*They don't know I'm here, but they tend not to look around this side of the house, the secret side, as I like to call it. I have time.*

*I poke at the undergrowth curling up the side of the gate leading to the orchard. Where can it possibly be? I've found three but the fourth eludes me. I worry someone has stolen it; Mrs B, Frieda, wouldn't be happy if she knew I was missing one of her precious statues.*

*I fling out a few sparks with my hand. They float into the air spreading into glittering parachutes before dropping into the twist of weeds and leaves. Nothing.*

*There is a little more time. I sigh and close my eyes, letting the memories come. Mrs B, Charlie, Gary. Their beloved faces appear before me as I remember the day I arrived at this house, not knowing that at fifty, my life was only just beginning.*

# CHAPTER 1: FRIEDA, A BEGINNING

I knew I'd never die young. Illness, suicide, murder: none could touch me. Old age was something I expected. But this old? No. I must be over a century by now. What is a surprise, apart from the obvious horrors of skin swinging from joints and my once fiery eyes disappearing into floury flaps, is that I've mellowed. I'm not quite the evil bitch I used to be. I don't seem to enjoy inflicting the little cruelties that were such a pleasure when I was young. The mean-spirited jabs I'd dole out to people who had upset me are few and far between nowadays.

I still have a good go every now and then - that fool Andy didn't realise it was me who, with a flick of my fingers, forced his toolbox to crash to the floor. Spanners spun, clattering across my flagstones, one smashing into his elbow. A wince squeezed flat the puffed smuggery of his face, and I enjoyed watching him struggle to maintain the facade of the affable handyman. Good old Andy, here to help poor old Mrs B who lived up the hill. Poor old Mrs B my backside.

He comes because he's discovered my habit of slipping notes between the pages of books. Since he started working at the house, my *Wuthering Heights* is £50 lighter, *Beloved* has lost a twenty and my complete Shakespeare has been picked clean. Greasy fingers, more used to prying apart the pallid thighs of local tarts, have been inserting themselves between the pages of my books and milking them dry.

Firing him would be tedious. Besides, I quite like flexing the old muscles and torturing him, just a little: the sour slime clinging to the edges of the cup of tea I make with a smile, the fragment of glass I spit into his boots so he walks with a grimace. Sadly, I find as I age my powers have more of a cost; they are strong as ever, but inflicting pain leaves me with a hangover, no matter how justified the punishment.

Ha! The irony. It is almost as if a deity in which I don't believe has decided to make me a better person as I grow closer to death - good deeds seem to make my hair curl and my step lighter - bad ones give me indigestion and a headache. A shame, as I always wanted to be the girl from whose mouth toads leap, not the insipid moron who spills forth diamonds and pearls.

With irritation, I watch Andy washing his hands in the kitchen sink, splashing arcs of water that puddle on my wooden counters. His position at the window means I can admire the spreading bald patch, which he takes such pains to conceal. I wonder if he has to hold his wife's hands down in bed in case she tugs at his failing follicles in a moment of passion. I snort at the thought of the poor woman being inspired to passion by this goblin of a man.

'Something funny, Mrs B?' Andy asks, drying his hands and turning to me where I sit, crooked as a sixpence, at the kitchen table.

'No nothing, dear,' I reply, squinting up at him and attempting a smile; he looks nervous. He often does when he works up here. He finds the way I watch him unsettling; It means he can't get away with the little tricks of which I know he is fond. Even now, I see his restless eyes scanning the kitchen, looking for jobs he could offer to fix - at a cost, of course. 'What do I owe you, Mr Cartwright?' I say.

As expected, he begins to pack up, throwing over his shoulder he would get Angie to send up an invoice, his words disappearing in the clatter of his retreat as he slams the door.

Contemptuous little shit. Andy has no balls. His eye-watering bills must be paid as he's the only plumber in the village. He should have a house as big as mine with what he charges but he pisses it away. Gambling. Hence the light-fingered petty thieving he does on the side. I watch as he climbs into his van. He looks different. I can't work out how. Thinner perhaps. The wind thrashes a handful of rain against the windowpane and I blink, re-focus and smile. With a pass of my hand, the paint on his doors begins to peel.

The headache starts, sharp and sudden and I groan with the pain. Bloody thing. I draw a line across my forehead and though the pain eases, it doesn't go away. Stumping up the stairs, I shiver in the cold before reaching the bedroom and easing into bed. With an effort, I let all thoughts of the idiot recede and lie back to survey the ceiling.

Familiar landscapes shift and twist before my eyes as I drift. Faces form and dissolve, skies and sunsets pass. Every minute of my years lies heavy in my bones.

Dreaming about Charlie was always an irritation, but I didn't seem to be able to help it. Dear God! You'd think I'd have forgotten all about him by now - it's been years. I was sixteen when I fell in love, twenty when he died and now, here he is, over eighty years later haunting my dreams. My powers were raw when I was a girl, though the shine could be seen in my hair, my eyes - men flocked to my gloss and charm. I was such an idiot, I had no idea. I thought it was the size of my breasts, the hand span of my waist, the depth of my painted smile.

I wonder why it's Charlie, of all of them, whom I keep seeing. Not just in my dreams, but out of the corner of my eye as I walk through the wood, or in the smoke of the fire in the morning. Charlie's face peers at me, his mouth working but I hear nothing. Ach, I don't know what he wants and don't care much. With a strong bend of will I wrench the dream away from Charlie's face and slip with relief into a memory of sinking under water in the Indian Ocean over seventy years ago. I watch the rising stream of bubbles and feel the corrugated curves of white sand under my feet.

Waking is an abrupt and disorienting plunge back into the realities of my age, and I don't need to glance at my grandmother's clock to know it is a few minutes past four in the morning. The witching hour, I grunt to myself and open the door to let in Eldritch who has been waiting for me.

I draw some comfort from the hard push of her skull as she rubs her head against my knuckles; I pull her eyelids back, stroking the soft darkness of her fur. She knows me so well, I think, as she leaps onto the arm of my chair by the now cold fire. I have no time for her during the day, but at night, when my ghosts follow me, she knows her presence is welcome.

Sighing, I settle in my chair and catch sight of my face in the window. The black mirror shows my folds and lines, and my eyes are hollow. I know with a bit of fire, some words and a pass of my hand I could, for a while, tighten my skin and darken my hair, but it is too exhausting to consider and so I empty my head, and stroke the damn cat, avoiding my reflection as dawn begins to spread across the wood.

*

I must have dozed off in the chair as I wake that morning stiff and cold. I shake my head to throw off the shreds and threads of voices clinging to my ears and mouth. I don't eat much nowadays; food makes me heavy and sluggish, so a pot of tea seems to be enough. A few Dickinson stanzas feed me well, warming my old bones as I read of certain slants of light on winter afternoons.

Today, my walk to the village is hampered by damp rain that falls as I wrestle the gate shut behind me. Neighbours nod as they drive past; I see their mouths move as they talk to each other. I can almost hear their words. 'There goes Mrs B. Look at her! Over a hundred and still walking!' Oh, their vacuous inanities grate and I long to show them something worth their admiration.

I dream of spreading my arms like flames and rising into the air as their mouths drop open, the disgusting chewing gum falling unnoticed as I disappear into billows of steam and smoke. Instead, I smile and twinkle, as they expect me to do, and continue my walk along the green tunnels of the lane that twist down into Witchford.

Oh, look at me in this fag-end of a village! I, who have danced naked with Picasso, flirted with Beckett and helped Orton to hide bodies. I, who have watched the sun set over Indian mountains, seen the dawn slide across the dunes of the Sahara, reduced to this damp speck of an English village where I fulfil the fantasies of weekend tourists hoping to find Miss Fucking Marple.

I am in too bad a mood to acknowledge my role in the journey that has led me here. At least I know I am safe, mostly. Besides, I was growing weary of running, nobody would think to

7

look for me here. The wood protects and shelters the house, and the secrets hidden within it.

The rain sizzles on my skin and I breathe deep to rein in the irascibility that's fizzing at the tips of my fingers. The green moss of the air fills my lungs and slides its energy into my bones and muscles, so my legs grow stronger and my arms loosen. My back straightens and I stride down the path. There is a strange alchemy with which I have become familiar in the air; the greens of the wood blur and as I move I hear the caw of seagulls and then I am there again, sixteen, running down the sand, breathless and hot under a blazing blue-glass sky.

In my hands two lemon ices melt and I lap at the delicious coolness, sticky on my fingers. I tumble to the ground almost into Charlie's lap and he laughs, taking the ices from me. His skin is hot, the sun dazzles my eyes and then - with a sickening lurch - I am back in the wood, my chest heaving.

With a shaking hand, I reach for the nearest tree for support and sink to the ground. This was happening more and more often, and the effects were unpleasant. And why the memories of Charlie? I have years and years at my disposal and yet this strange form of time travel seems inextricably linked with a boy about whom I haven't thought for decades. Why wasn't I getting the chance to revisit marvellous adventures travelling around the world? Or torrid love affairs with unsuitable men? Why Charlie on Margate sands of all places?

With a tsk of annoyance, I pull myself up and recover the basket that has rolled away. I will not let these incidents affect me. I will not let myself be troubled by something that happened so long ago with someone so long dead.

My energy has left me. When I reach the shop I am in bad spirits. Mrs Gray, the owner, is a sour-faced, interfering old biddy who never recovered from the shock of losing her husband to the local vicar. From what I hear, the two of them are living together on the other side of Redbury but his name is never mentioned, and to Mrs Gray he is dead and buried. Standing by the meat slicer, arms folded across her blue bust, white hair pinned close to her skull she flashes me a saccharine smile.

'Mrs B, how nice to see you. Can I help at all?'

'I'm fine,' I grunt. 'I can find what I need.' I sense her raising her eyebrows behind my back at Maeve, the Doctor's wife who has just come in, and I clench my hands into fists before my fingers start working some mischief beyond my control. How I loathe their poking and prying.

I need tea and something for the cat, but I find Maeve in front of me, blocking my way. She's a good-looking woman, perhaps a little blowsy for my taste, but her skin is clear, and she has fine red hair and kind eyes. I have known her a long time, she would call me a friend. But she and her husband worry about me. They fester and fuss about me living on my own in Pagan's Reach. They visit often and poke about – Maeve has even tried to get a regular cleaner in, but I soon saw her off. She didn't even get through the door.

'Frieda! I was just talking to Michael about you, how are you, are you well?'

'Perfectly well thank you, if you'd just excuse me...' I try to push past but she stands firm. I knew she would.

'Yes, Mike was saying he hadn't seen you for a while and you know how he likes to keep his eyes on the village elders!' She laughs and I want to kill her.

'As I said, I'm fine.' I glare, then show my teeth in a smile. 'Do send my regards to Michael. And I hope Will is feeling better?'

I cock my head to one side in faux sympathy and enjoy Maeve's expression flittering through bewilderment to fear as she processes what I said. Hah! She must be wondering... what do I know? How do I know? Maeve and Michael's dirty little secret, the golden boy who seems not to be quite so golden after all. I see her eyes widen and her pupils dilate. If I look closely enough, I would see in her glossy irises a tiny upside-down image of her boy being carried away on a stretcher, vomit crusting his lips.

Maeve jerks away from me and turns so I can pass. Mrs Gray looks over, eyes alive with curiosity but Maeve's ashen face shuts her up and she bustles to the till.

I decide to cut across the Green on the way home. The sky has cleared, and the breeze is fresh helping to lighten the headache crawling around my temples. Unfair, I thought. I hadn't been mean, just unkind. Still, wouldn't hurt to... I see the new playground sitting at the bottom of the hill. Children crawl and squirm across all manner of wooden buildings made up of ladders and slides and poles. A few mothers are dotted about, smoking and blank faced.

A little girl sits on a bench crying as if her heart would break. I can see nobody to whom she belongs. I settle next to her, taking care to make myself as inconspicuous as possible.

'Hello, dearie,' I say in my most comfortable Grandma voice. 'What's wrong?' She's been crying for so long her yellow hair is stuck to her face with tears. Her cheeks are as red as apples. She can't have been much older than four and I look again to see who was with her. Still no one. I give her my best twinkle and she calms down enough to hold out her hands.

A ruined doll gazes at me, features smeared by a rough hand. I suspect the group of boys screaming around nearby. I hold the toy with exaggerated care. The arms have been wrenched loose and dangle. Meeting the girl's eyes, I hold a finger to my lips and pass my hand over the doll, whispering words that ripple and spin from my lips. I close my eyes until I hear the girl gasp. I feel a surge of pleasure as I return the restored doll and the girl's face, bright as a star, looks at me in astonishment.

I am still chuckling, albeit breathlessly, as I climb the hill. Playing Mary Poppins can be as fun as playing Medusa, sometimes. The children are as tiny as ants from where I stand, but I can still see the little girl, a pink dot on the bench. She waves a tiny hand at me high up in the woods.

The garden is getting so overgrown there are areas I haven't been able to explore for years. To reach all four statues is becoming a struggle but I push through the long grass, feeling the brambles scratching at my clothes. The smiling little shapes gleam through the undergrowth.

I feel the cool jade under my hand and carefully remove its covering of leaves. I can't see their features in the dimming light, but my fingers feel for their faces, slipping over familiar dips and curves, reassured nothing has changed. I know nothing can happen to them, nobody knows they are here, but I cannot help checking them every day, nonetheless. The thought of what could happen if they were destroyed is too horrifying to contemplate.

It takes a good half an hour to get round to all of them and it is cold and late by the time I finish. How I long for the start of spring. I hate these grey skies that weigh heavy on my shoulders. I feel older in the winter and being trapped here with no chance of escape is a sore punishment indeed. The house looks forbidding and bleak and even Eldritch, curling round my legs and purring as I open the door doesn't cheer me up. I feed the stupid creature and look in my cupboards, but no inspiration comes, so I settle for liquorice root tea and a heel of bread.

The fire takes ages to take, so I end up having to use an impatient flick of my fingers; it is so cold, and I am so tired. Eldritch and I watch the flames and I allow my eyes to droop in the heat that traces my face. This time the shift was more like a dream as I sit in the chair by the fire.

The warmth on my cheeks turns into tight sunburn, and the smell of hot cat is replaced by charred sausages. The chair against my back becomes Charlie's chest and I lie dreaming in his arms looking up at the sky. I turn to look at his sleepy features and say to myself - with all the fierceness and certainty of youth - I will make you love me. I will.

Charlie again! Pulling up with a start, I re-settle myself in the chair and poke at the fire. Funny, I had forgotten that night when I thought the world would end if I couldn't make Charlie love me.

I had told the story to myself so many times the truth of it had changed under my hand, like glass worn smooth by the endless movement of the sea. Now, all those years later it rested, like a pebble at the bottom of a pool of deep water, looking nothing like the jagged, grisly black rock it once was.

I sigh. I don't like these odd flashbacks, violent as they are. My memory wants to assault me, mug me, so that I remember things as they were, not as I want them to be. I don't want to remember Charlie like that; I want him to return to the faded photograph of a distant dream.

I throw the rest of my tea towards the guttering fire and pour wine into a heavy glass, admiring its red velvet depths before swigging back a gulp, making me splutter. Eldritch jumps and shakes her fur before stalking away with an irritable twitch of her shoulders.

Something in the air shifts, there are sparks of energy behind me and I stiffen, not wanting to turn. I take another gulp and put my glass down.

'What do you want?'

I hear nothing, and still I don't turn around. Another crackle in the air, a touch on my shoulder and a whisper. Then, still.

I swig back the last of the wine, gathering my strength, and stand.

A scream erupts from my throat before I know what I am looking at. The noise reverberates the bones of my skull. I drop the glass and it smashes into a million pieces sending glittering fragments far and wide.

Charlie is sitting by the window. I don't mean some white-sheeted corpse is propped up against the sill but it is him. And he is smoking, one leg tossed over the other. Maybe this was it, I'd had a stroke and I am hallucinating. Clearing my throat, I try to speak but can only manage a croak. Sitting down, I try again.

'Charlie.'

He nods with a faint smile and exhales a silvery-blue skein of smoke, making me cough. I wave my hand in front of my face. If you'd asked me yesterday what Charlie looked like, I would have had trouble remembering his features. Just a blur of blond hair, that he was tall, and olive-skinned. But looking at him now he is shockingly familiar.

'You haven't changed a bit,' I manage. 'I wish I could say the same.' I look down at my hands, lumpen, and twisted with veins.

I can't help it. My vanity is stronger than my sense. I close my eyes and pull down youth like a cloak, allowing it to settle around my shoulders. My skin plumps as the blood rushes to the surface, the leathery patchwork of liver spots disappear and the pearl white damask of my childhood returns, just for a moment.

Even though my strength is draining like water, I hold on as long as I can. I want to face him as the girl I was, not the crone I had become.

His voice, when it comes is clear but with a strange distance to it, it has a crackle like static; the sound of an ill-tuned radio.

'It's been a long time.'

'Over eighty years,' I agree. 'A lifetime. So is this it? Have I reached the end? You've come to take me away?'

'No, I'm not the Grim Reaper come to spirit you to a better place,' he chuckles.

'So why are you here?'

'Call me your conscience,' he says. 'You've left it very late and there are things you need to do.'

'Like what?' I protest. 'I have no idea what you're talking about.'

'Well, first, you never took on an apprentice.'

'Rubbish!' I say. 'Who says I had to?'

'You know that's part of the deal,' Charlie continues, 'but there's more.'

'What?'

Reaching into his jacket pocket Charlie pulls something out and throws it onto the table. A box of gold and jade. I take a sharp breath and sit back.

'How did you?' I stutter. 'That's mine!' My hands jump to my throat and, feeling the familiar weight of the gold that rests there, I sigh with relief. I reach for the box, change my mind, and sit still. The box can't be real, or maybe it's empty.

'He's coming for it, you know. He will find you. You must get ready.' Charlie's voice is implacable.

'That's not true!' I say. Anger and fear rise like snakes from my belly, twining and knotting in my throat. 'I've made sure of it. I am safe here.'

'For now,' he says, spinning the box so it glitters in the light. 'But you can't face him alone, Frieda. Time is running out. You can't live forever, powers or no. Don't you see? You must play the role Lilith played, not only because it is the right thing to do, but because you can't face that monster on your own. Besides,' he glanced at me with his wicked eyes, 'I'm going to keep haunting you if you don't.'

I let my rage give way. 'Just leave me alone. I don't want any of this. You can haunt me all you like, you little shit, it won't make any difference.' I lunge for the box and gulp when my hand passes through it. It is still safe, then. I need to get away from Charlie, he wants me to face things that are unfaceabale.

I turn and stumble from my room out into the corridor and down to the landing. As I reach the stairs, Eldritch streaks across the floor and I fall, spiralling in slow motion. I land with a thud in the darkness and groan as my poor old bones snap like twigs.

# CHAPTER 2: ANGIE

Andy's got a personal trainer,' I said to Vicky, we were panting as we ran down the street, already late for the new Weight Watchers' class.

'Ridiculous! Man of his age,' she replied, trying to light the end of her fag. It was starting to spit with rain so she gave up, pulling a vape from her sleeve and taking a deep drag. 'They all go mad at 50,' she went on. 'Look at my Dan. He had the same thing, but wiv 'im it was that obsession with his family history. Even did a DNA test. Don't bother! I said, they'll all be scavengers and thieves! Cost a bloody fortune, what a waste of time, most exciting thing he discovered was he had a French great-great- grandma, and what did he do? Wanted to start learning French, kept buying cheese...'

I stopped to catch my breath; Vik's cherry flavoured cloud nearly choked me. My heart thundered in my ears and chest. 'Christ I'm so unfit.'

'Maybe you should get Andy to take you out for a run,' said Vicky with a grin.

'Ha! Fat chance!' I said. The thought of joining Andy on one of his insane workouts was so ludicrous it made me uneasy. The awareness of how far apart we were growing was the reason I had allowed Vicky to persuade me to go to the stupid meeting. Perhaps if I lost some weight Andy would be less embarrassed about me coming along with him to the gym.

To be honest, Andy's behaviour was starting to bother me. I never thought he'd keep it up as long as he had. While he'd dwindled away to a beef jerky strip, I'd ballooned, comfort eating chips as Andy cycled grimly up hills in lycra.

Behind Vicky I could see my reflection in the dark shop window. An hour before I had stood in front of the bedroom mirror in despair. My flesh spilled over the waist band of my size 22-bought-in-an-emergency-online jeans, a denim fist squeezing a cling-filmed bag of porridge until it was on the verge of exploding.

'Come on, let's get this over with,' I said.

I could see the church before me as we wound down the street. It was a clear, bright evening with the moon rising just behind the steeple, picking out the big house up the top. I couldn't get my head around the fact it was only four o'clock. The only good thing about winter was it gave you an excuse to cover up the flab.

Tuning out Vicky's chatter, I slid my hand in my pocket to retrieve the Mars bar hidden there, soft and pliant from the heat of my body. Making sure not to let the wrapper crackle I pulled out a chunk of chocolate and shoved it in my mouth; if Vicky saw it, she would demand half. I nearly choked when a great white fluffy sheep of a thing bounded out at me from the alley, making us jump out of our skin.

'Sorry, Angie my dear! She's a bit over excited. Hello Vicky.' It was Doc Lockwood with Dolly, his bonkers labradoodle.

Like a kid, I found myself crumpling up the Mars wrapper and sliding it in my pocket. The Doc clocked the move and lifted his eyebrow. I could feel the chocolate cloying around my lips but didn't dare draw his attention by licking them.

'Evening, Doc!' I said, wondering if I could get away with wiping my mouth on my sleeve.

'What's that you got there, Angie?' he said, leaning forward. 'Now what have I said to you about cutting back on the sweets and cakes? With your family history you know you have to be careful – especially at your age.'

Especially at my age, bloody cheek. He was only about five or so years older than me, his Dad had been our family Doctor too – we knew each other well.

'Blimey Doc, you make me sound a hundred years old, besides, it's my last Mars bar, we're off to a meeting now.'

'Ah! You're joining Maeve's Weight Watchers' group. That's wonderful news. Well done you.' He looked delighted. 'Well I'd better get Dolly off before she does something beastly on the pavement. Good luck, both of you!'

He disappeared up the path towards the woods, jaunty in his red toff trousers. Dolly nudged me when she went past, and I admired her dopey, laughing face giving her shoulder a quick pat. I waved at the Doc. Andy always took the piss but I liked him. He was a good man and had always been kind to me, especially when Dad died.

I hadn't been to Weight Watchers for years, but it was as grim as ever. Cheap plastic seats creaking and groaning beneath our weight, and the obligatory bloke we all hated because men always lost tons of weight just by cutting back on the beer. It was John, who worked up at the hospital.

He was enormous – in every sense of the word – he must have been near on six and a half feet and took up three chairs. He was genial enough, and we exchanged smiles. I used to see him a lot when I was visiting Dad.

After registering with the sour faced Laurie, who ran the village shop, I'd sat down, glad to get the weight off my feet. Vicky was gassing with a group of mates from work. A woman in a purple jumper, probably a few years younger than me, drew her handbag away as if I was going to steal it. She looked a bit posh. I didn't recognise her but decided to be friendly and gave her a smile.

'You don't need to be here!' I exclaimed, giving her a nudge. 'You're only tiny!' I reckoned she was a shade under ten stone.

'Yes, well, better to come when you've only got a little bit of weight to lose, rather than leaving it and then finding out you're five stone overweight,' she said primly, giving me a pointed look.

'Very sensible,' I said. 'Wish I'd thought of that – ha ha!' I gave a laugh, but it died away when I saw she had turned her back and was watching Maeve with exaggerated interest.

'Skinny bitch,' Vicky whispered in my ear as she bounced down next to me. I chuckled, but as we sat and listened to Maeve introducing the programme, extolling how well it had worked for her, I shifted uncomfortably on my chair. It was hurtful, but what that woman had said was right.

'Do you know what, Vicky?' I said in an undertone. 'I've been coming to Weight Watchers on and off for over thirty years and I'm fatter than I've ever been.'

'Me too, love,' she said. 'Me too!'

The thing was, Vicky was overweight, sure. She and I have worked together for God knows how long, and we'd been on diets the whole time. The difference being she's put on about a stone or two, I'd turned into a hump-backed whale.

'Come on, we're up.'

Nudged from my thoughts by Vicky's elbow digging into my side I looked up. The interminable lecture had finished, and everyone was lining up for the Great Ritual of the Weigh In. One by one women took off their shoes, earrings, coats and jumpers before disappearing behind a yellowing screen to be weighed. Amateurs, I thought. Everyone knows you put on as many things as possible for your first weigh in, then, when you turn up in your summer dress and flip flops the following week, the pounds will have fallen off.

Vicky bustled over, I smiled at the extravagant wiggle in her walk, her bum was big enough to send chairs flying, but in her neon-pink body-con dress she still managed to look gorgeous.

She had that magnetic ability to snag men's eyes; like me, she was nearly 50 and more than well covered – but I knew men saw someone who'd eat them alive, a tiger in the sack. Vicky was always going on about Dan pouncing on her for a shag round the back of the pub, or dragging her into the woods for some afternoon delight.

I couldn't remember the last time Andy and I had sex like that. We didn't even kiss any more. It was even more difficult recently as I worried I'd squash him, or swallow him up into my marshmallow flesh – would he ever be found again? Fifty was about to hit me like a sledgehammer. I hadn't really stopped stuffing my face since I hit my 40s.

As I stood in the queue, I listened to the women. As always, the chat was about food. Endless recitations of what they had eaten, what they were going to eat, and what food they were going to miss. Despite my enormous lunch my stomach growled.

I thought about Andy. We hadn't had dinner together for ages – he would chuck his gym bag in the car and shoot off straight after work. He didn't seem to like sitting down to eat at the table, he would perch on the settee, nibbling away on a nut bar like a fat squirrel. Though not so fat anymore, I thought.

Andy and I had both loved our food and we'd look forward to our regular takeaways: Indian on Saturdays, Chinese on Wednesdays, and fish and chips the evenings we couldn't be bothered to pull something from the freezer. And who cared if we got more and more tubby? We loved each other, didn't we? What was the point in getting all skinny and fit if you'd already found your one?

Well, all that indulgent eating had stopped sharpish after he turned fifty. He'd asked for a bike for his present – I didn't even know he could ride one! We'd been together since we were teenagers and I don't think I'd ever seen him cycling. And you should see the clothes he bought to go with it. Awful, dungaree type things made of Lycra.

He'd looked ridiculous when he first tried them on, I had to leave the room and go into the kitchen so he wouldn't see me snorting with laughter. Imagine a middle-aged bean bag squeezed into a tiny pair of green and yellow tights, and you'll get the picture.

Of course, I'd assumed it was a fad – just like the kung fu classes, miniature golf obsession, and star gazing – all hobbies he'd been briefly obsessed with through the course of our marriage. But this one seemed to have stuck. A few years past his fiftieth birthday and he was still exercising like mad and twitching with revulsion whenever he saw a carbohydrate.

All this discipline and body worship made me go the other way. I'd started eating more than I ever had because I couldn't break the habit of cooking for two, so I kept on consuming large meals. I think part of me was hoping he'd be tempted back into eating like he used to. Didn't work.

Truth be told, I hated this other life he had created. He couldn't have found a better way to exclude me. Sure, to begin with he tried to get me to go along, but I just couldn't face it. I was always so tired, at the end of the day all I wanted to do was sit on the settee, watch TV and eat pork scratchings. Nothing wrong with that!

Trouble is I found his disapproval so wearing I ended up craving junk food more than ever and was driven to smuggling in food and hiding it in the airing cupboard. I've probably put on all the weight he's lost, and I wasn't skinny to start with.

I missed the camaraderie we used to have as we shared takeaways in front of the telly, arguing over which box set to watch (I liked romantic comedies, he liked science fiction and documentaries.) We ordered so often from the nearby Chinese takeaway we didn't even have to say what we wanted, we always had the same thing. And it included a whole host of carbs. Mmmm, the thought of lemon chicken and egg fried rice made my mouth water.

But no! I reminded myself. It was time for a change. My smuggling in junk food had to stop. It really did, because last week was the final straw. I couldn't fit into any of my clothes.

None of them. Not one thing fitted me. The horror! Even my trusty leggings, so stretched by their vain attempt to cover my arse and bulging calves they were rendered completely see through – there was no way I was going to wear them out of the house and end up on some awful internet gallery of fat fools in transparent leggings. The only thing I could get into (and they were a bit tighter than I would have liked) was the giant pair of old jeans I'd bought in a size 22 by mistake and never sent back, and my ratty old jumper.

My feet were aching. How long was this queue going to take? Purple jumpered woman was earnestly interrogating the Doc's wife about the programme. I rolled my eyes. It would be lovely to get off a bit of weight and buy nice clothes, I thought. Shame we never seemed to have any money. I couldn't understand it.

Andy was the only plumber in the village and I often had to turn people away because he was so busy. I did his accounts, so I knew money was coming in, but I never saw sign of it. It must all be going on protein bars and new tracksuits, I thought bitterly. I had asked Gary at work if I could do a few more hours cleaning at the school, the overtime rates were good, but he didn't have anything.

I averted my gaze as Vicky, next up on the scales, had a brief but intense altercation with Maeve insisting the scales were 'at least a stone out'. Her temper was legendary, and it took all of Maeve's patience to calm her down.

For extra weight I was wearing my Dad's old pea coat. I liked to imagine it still smelled of him, I found the roughness of the cloth comforting, and rubbed my cheek against the collar. I had forgotten I still had it, shoved at the back of the wardrobe.

My mood dropped as I remembered Jonathan's box, falling from the high shelf as I dragged Dad's coat out. I had caught it and found it in my hands before I recognised what it was. It was as if I had been punched in the chest. It had been a struggle to pull in a breath. The arrow of grief came less often but was as sharp as ever.

I must have stared at the smooth white surface bisected by a pale blue ribbon for ages. The corners of the box were sharp. It looked as new as the day I put it in there, thirty years ago. I had sat back on my heels, running my fingers over the box.

I knew exactly what was inside; I didn't need to open it. With an effort, I slammed a door on the memories that were picking their way towards me. I knew the gasp of pain they would bring, and I couldn't cope with it right then.

I put the box right at the back of the top shelf and pulled some cases in front of it. Andy couldn't understand why I kept it when I never looked at it, but I couldn't bring myself to throw it away.

I rubbed my face, settling myself as Maeve called me over. She gave me a big smile as I approached.

'So lovely to see you Angie, I know Michael will be very pleased you're here.' She looked a little puzzled. 'Do you want to take off your coat? You look awfully hot!'

'No I'm fine! Honestly!' Memories fled and reluctantly, I was very much in the present, about to be weighed. My brain was chattering away. It had been about three years since I last weighed in. I hadn't weighed myself at home, despite Andy's nagging.

I was heavier than Vik, but then she was about six foot and I was only five and a half. Maybe sixteen stone? Sixteen and a bit? Although I think that's what I was last time I went, and I'd put on since then. I stepped up, feeling the give of the scales beneath my boots. My stomach lurched. I squeezed my eyes shut. Maybe seventeen? Please let it not be more than seventeen.

'Twenty stone and three pounds!' Maeve said brightly. She bent her head and scribbled the figures into my new card.

My head reeled. I swallowed to keep lunch from vomiting itself out of my mouth.

My brain couldn't make sense of those numbers.

That couldn't be right. My cheeks burned a mortified red. I couldn't even look at Maeve. Twenty fucking stone! How had that happened? My brain swiftly offered me fat maths – that's two of that purple jumper woman, it told me... Three or four good sized children... The average weight of a giant panda.

I barely heard Maeve's soothing words as she waffled on about taking it one day at a time, and how the points diet was the best yet. She was a bit of a busy body but a kind-hearted one - the sort who bustled about the village in a knee length skirt and little jumpers, Maeve wore low-heeled loafer things with gold tassels on the front. I was envious of her thick red hair, which was lovely and curly, like mine used to be about a hundred years ago, but she wore it rammed under a hideous Alice band for some reason, which emphasised her beaky nose.

I focused on her weird shoes until my eyes went funny, trying to think about anything except how much I weighed. I was failing. My brain, still in fat maths mode, tried to calculate how long it would take me to get it off. I wanted to be about nine stone, that's 11 stone to get rid of... 11 times 14... 2 lbs a week... I felt sick. It would take about a million years.

I walked out of the hall in a daze, clutching my card to my chest. I would burn it before I got home; there was no way I was letting Andy see how much I weighed.

Vicky was waiting for me. 'So, come on, what's the damage?'

Wordlessly I held out my card.

'Fuck me!' she said. 'And I thought I was bad.'

'Thanks, Vicky!' I yelped, I wanted to sound like I was joking but she could hear the tears in my voice.

Looking back now it seems laughable how winded I was by the amount of weight I'd put on. Then it had seemed like the end of the world. Of course, I had no idea what was coming for me.

'Aw Angie, don't worry about it, you'll lose it soon enough.' Vicky reached round and gave me a hug. 'Besides, I reckon ten stone of that is this fucking horrible jumper and coat.' She prodded me again. 'Knock the carbs on the head, don't wear that,' she looked down at my feet, 'or those boots, and next time you'll have lost loads. It'll fall off you.'

I nodded but I didn't believe her. I started to walk back up the hill out of the village.

'Oi! Where are you going?' Vik asked.

'Back home?' I replied. 'Where else?'

'Don't be stupid, it's weigh-in day, everything you eat today doesn't count. Chinese? Just a quick one?'

I laughed. 'Really?'

'Yes, come on, the Golden Bowl is calling our names, can you hear it?'

She looked so funny standing there, her head cocked, her make up all mad. I couldn't help laughing. At six-foot-tall she stuck out like a sore thumb and I loved that she did absolutely nothing to hide her height.

Vicky was the sort of woman who would read articles headlined 'Things to never wear over 40,' and see them as a challenge. She would absorb them before going out and buying skinny jeans, short skirts, and cleavage revealing tops, every item the fashion editors had dictated were unsuitable for a 15 stone, six-foot-tall, 49-year-old woman.

'Listen! Chicken chow mein...' she whispered, holding her hand to her ear, 'prawn crackers... crispy beef stir fry...' she licked her lips. 'Come on, it would be rude not to.'

Looping her arm through mine she dragged me back into the village. She had got me salivating and we started to bolt down the street, giggling as we knocked each other out of the way.

Luckily, the Golden Bowl was still open, so after putting in our order we waited outside in the cool night air while Vicky smoked, blowing away from me and waving her hand to disperse the fug of nicotine.

I looked around the village. This bit of it was so pretty, little houses in rows, tucked up together and leaning at funny angles. So much nicer than our estate, which was a featureless square of cheap council flats. The only colour to be found was in the graffiti on the walls and the faded blue stripes marking each front door.

In the village, the buildings were all old, beautifully weathered and cosy. Many had chimneys puffing out fragrant wood smoke. My Mum and Dad had owned one of these cottages, but by the time Andy and I were looking to buy, they cost over £250,000. I regretted again my stupidity in not doing more to stop us losing the house when Dad died.

I sighed and watched a young lad, hood up and hands in his pockets, slouching up the street. Looked like the Doc's son. He looked miserable. Where was he off to? I thought. I'd heard some funny rumours about him, that he'd dropped out of university and got himself into a bit of trouble.

I kept watch as he walked past the church. It pointed its steeple towards the hills and my eye was drawn past it towards the big house that had frowned down over the village for centuries. It was completely dark except for one light in the top window, which shone out across the valley. I squinted. I could just make out a figure in the lighted rectangle.

'Look!' I whispered to Vicky. 'There's a light up there.'

She shivered. 'Gives me the creeps that house. Dunno how she can live up there all on her own. Funny old woman she is.'

'Do you know her to speak to?'

'Nah, not really, just seen her around the village. She looks about a thousand years old. Dan always said that house has a witch in. My Dad remembers the old bat before her, she was there in my grandad's time. Never known it not to have old women up there.'

I rubbed my arms, they felt cold, even with layers and layers of wool. 'Andy goes up there quite a bit, says it's amazing. Full of all sorts of stuff.' I peered through the darkness to make out the shape of the house. 'It looks massive. I'd love to see what it looks like inside.'

'Probably haunted,' Vicky said dismissively. 'Come on, let's get our food. Looks like it's ready. I'm starving!'

I took one last look at the house. Even when I was a kid it fascinated me. Something about the figure in the window made me curious. Was that the old lady? I felt like she was watching me. I wanted to wave but felt silly. When was the last time I had seen her? I thought. Mrs B, as she was known in the village, was a tiny little thing, skinny, and bent almost double – it looked like her spine had fallen in on itself –but she could be terribly fierce.

Vicky swung out from the Chinese holding a brown bag stained with blotches of grease. Steam billowed, and she was stuffing a prawn cracker into her gob.

'I couldn't wait any longer. What are you daydreaming about, anyway?' she said, spraying white crumbs.

'I was just thinking about that old lady. Hasn't she got any family at all?'

Vicky shook her head and passed me a prawn cracker. 'Nah, she's always been on her own as far as I know. The only people I see visit her are the Doc and his wife, I think they're quite close. She keeps herself to herself, don't she? God only knows how old she is. Come on, I'm freezing my tits off.' She clasped the takeaway to her chest like a hot water bottle. 'Let's go back to mine and get rid of this lot. I'm famished.'

She started to trot away back up the hill towards the estate. Dad was still sitting on the wall by the pub. I knew he was there but hadn't looked at him. I could feel his eyes on me. I thought he'd have stopped by now, but he had been about more than ever. The temptation to turn my head towards him was unbearable but I couldn't. I was too frightened.

I kept walking, following Vicky and her fragrant brown bag. I didn't look back.

# CHAPTER 3: FRIEDA FALLS

*Sicknesses cleave my bones;*
*Consuming agues dwell in ev'ry vein,*
*And tune my breath to groans.*

The pain. Christ. The pain. My old bones liquefy with an ache of fire. I can't move, my hands seem bound to my sides. I twist my head as a burning white light flashes on and off above me. Even with my eyes screwed tight shut I can still see the flashing continue: on off, on off.

The pain weighs heavy in my blood, like iron. I can picture it, snaking thick and solid along my veins. It's seeping into the pores of my bones. I use every atom of strength I have to will it away, tugging at the strands of it with my mind, desperate to uproot them from my body and cast them aside.

It's not enough. It's not enough. I am shocked to see my mother's face, pin sharp, leaning down to me… then nothing. Darkness. Breathing.

I will myself away from this place. I force myself to feel warmth. To replace the cold darkness with heat and light. There. A dark head bent at my breast. An image flickers then steadies.

Cicadas. The sun stretching long fingers across the silent room. Dust sparkles lazily in the sweltering heat. I taste bread dipped in golden pools of olive oil. Wine is in my mouth, warm as blood, flavours bold and strong. I am naked. My body is stretched, limp in the heat. A powerful arm lifts me and I open my eyes to see. He hovers over my breasts. My nipples swell and throb at the touch of his breath. They yearn for him.

I wait to be eaten. My breasts tipped with figs, my belly ripe and yielding as the flesh of a melon, my groin a bowl of sweet honeycomb. I cry out as he sinks into my body. He rocks me slowly, gently. The hardness of him makes me weep with delight. Warmth builds and builds and the waves begin, convulsing around him, deep, deep, within me. I hear my groans, like an animal, but I can't stop. He moves against me again, and I surrender completely, my body pulsing in spasms making me scream.

He finishes with a shout, loud in my ear, and rolls away. I lie still, unable to move, feeling the sweat cool on my body.

I light a cigarette and sit up, wrapping the musky smelling sheets around me. Every cell in my body is thrumming with delight. Edouard smiles at me, his teeth wolfish white in his brown face. He lifts a glass. 'More wine, Freddy?'

'Don't call me that,' I say, my voice sharp. 'No, I don't want wine.' I am already itchy, restlessness rising. Scratching my arms in irritation, I take my cigarette to the balcony, leaning forward to admire the view. I smile as I hear Edouard suck in his breath at the sight of me, glossed by the sun. I am not as young as he thinks I am, but I am still young.

I turn to face him, resting my elbows on the rail. He looks good, drinking his wine, his dark blue eyes meeting mine over the rim of his glass. Edouard is not tall, but his body is well muscled and full of grace. He can lift me above his head with ease.

It wasn't easy getting into this man's bed. That bitch Zita had her claws stuck well into him. It didn't take much to scar that beautiful face, a little herb here, a poisoned ointment there. Using vanity to destroy beauty has a balance that appeals to me. I smile as I remember the skin bubbling under her fingers, her hair, still Rapunzel bright, falling over her face as welts oozed across it, like bursting fruit.

Mmm. I take a deep breath and thunder rolls behind me, though there is not a cloud in the sky. Edouard's face changes as he sees my expression, a stutter of something in his eyes thrills me – maybe he can see the lightning crackling from my fingertips? I want to fuck him right now, when I can see he is struggling to conceal his fear of me. He is already stiffening as I throw my cigarette out of the window and move back to the bed. Pushing him down I straddle him, throwing my head back in triumph as he thrusts up into me.

*

I shake my head as my bones start to splinter and weaken. Someone is thumbing my eye lids open. I use every ounce of my strength to sink back into that long-ago bed of opulence in the South of France, but it's no good.

'Mrs Beaudry. Mrs Beaudry? Come on, dear. Can you open your eyes for me?' An insistent voice, someone pats my hand with sharp taps.

'Leave me alone.'

'Come on now. Let's sit you up. The operation's all done, and you've had plenty of painkillers so you shouldn't be too uncomfortable'

Hands drag me up and pile pillows behind my back. After dreams of being free, my tangled knot of a body feels claustrophobic.

'Wait there, lovey, the Doctor is popping in to see you and then you've got a visitor who has come in for a chat. Isn't that nice?'

Wait there. As if I had any choice. Stupid woman. My eyes are beginning to clear and adjust to the light. I am in a ward with beds on either side, filled with slugs of old people as decrepit as I am. I hear an old man moaning.

'Oh dear. Oh dear,' he cries. Everyone is taking care not to look at him.

The nurse continues to bustle about my bed, fussing and faffing. I growl at her, desperate to flick something nasty her way: an earache, a rot of the gut, a rip of a nail, but I am too weak. My hands are folded, uselessly, on the blanket. The terrible pain that had cradled in the crock of my pelvis has drawn back its claws, but it is waiting to pounce.

A child in a white coat is working his way down the beds. He takes his time with each patient, sitting on their beds, leaning forward and nodding with a serious frown as they speak to him. The nurses, male and female, flutter around him. The ward falls silent, even 'oh dear' man is quiet. We all wait for the visitation and I sigh with impatience. I want to go home.

There is a flicker in the corner of my eye; with difficulty, I turn my head but see nothing. I sniff the air with suspicion – there's something... Charlie? The wizened old crone in the bed opposite starts and gives a hesitant smile. I ignore her; did I say his name out loud? I need to leave this place. I need my books, my music, my things.

Child Doctor is here. He stands by my bed, the nurse mutters in his ear. He looks down, waiting for me to greet him but my dowagers' hump crouches on my back, bending me forward into a crooked twist. I can't turn up my face. He moves to sit on my bed.

I spread out my hands, wincing with the pain, and slice him away. He steps back and draws up a chair. We are now almost nose to nose. I can see freckles, for Christ's sake. How old is he?

'How are you feeling, Frieda?'

'Beaudry,' I mutter, my mouth bone dry, lips sticking to my teeth.

'Pardon?' he leans in so close I can smell mint on his breath.

'It's. Mrs. Beaudry.' My voice is still croaky.

'My apologies. Mrs Beaudry. Now. You've had a nasty fall and you unfortunately fractured your femur. That's a bone close to your hip.'

'I know what a fucking femur is!'

'I'm sorry?' Child Doctor looks startled.

'Nothing, Doctor. Go on.'

'The good news is the operation went well and we have successfully replaced the hip. Given your age we need to monitor you over the next few days, and we will be prescribing antibiotics to prevent infection and of course physiotherapy is essential, you will begin a rehabilitation course tomorrow...'

He drones on. I fade out his earnest ramblings. I can't shake the sense of an energy near me. There's a tang of ozone in the air, it's familiar, and the last time I smelled it was just before I saw Charlie. Is he here? I look round but see nothing.

I tune back into the Doctor's speech as I hear him mention going home.

'When can I go home?' I ask. 'I want to go home.'

'Well, ideally we like to discharge patients within five days, but it depends on your recovery and any infection…'

'Nonsense!' I say. 'I'm perfectly fine. I want to go home now.' I try to swing my legs out of the bed, but an instant, electric shock of pain stops me and a grimace twists my face into a snarl. Child Doctor restrains me with a gentle push of his hand.

'Mrs Beaudry that's not going to happen, I'm afraid. You need to start on your physio programme so we can check your progress before we can let you go. Is there someone at home who can look after you? If not, we will have to discharge you to a care home until you fully recover.' Seeing my look of absolute horror, he adds, 'It won't be for long, just until you're back on your feet. We can't send you home to an empty house, can we?' He laughs until he sees the look on my face and his smile drops as if he's been shot.

I look him dead in the eye and lie without effort. 'Of course, I have someone at home. My niece. She's a nurse, perfectly capable of looking after me.'

Child Doctor gathers up his folder and stands, brushing down his coat as if I have contaminated it. I wish I had; it wasn't through lack of trying. 'That's good, Mrs Beaudry, but you'll still have to stay here for a fair while I'm afraid. I'll make sure to tell the nurses to give you extra special attention and care!' His smile is wide, and I want to punch his teeth to the back of his throat.

As he moves along to the next bed, I lie on the pillows humped under my back. This place drains me, the white walls and cold lights shrivel me up. My arms and legs feel lighter than air - pieces of twisted straw - a gust of wind could blow me away.

I must have slipped into a doze. A jab of pain as I shift wakes me up with a jolt.

'Hello, Frieda, dear.'

Oh Christ. It's Maeve Lockwood with a gentle smile. A small bunch of peonies has appeared by my bed, shoved into a water jug. They are lovely. I close my eyes and breathe in their scent. The curled petals are the delicate pink of the curve of a shell, I draw the colour into me, into my blood. It helps me to take a breath.

'I hope you like the flowers, I know you love them – you had so many in your garden! I got these from Lydia – they're imported can you believe? Goodness knows from where! I have some chocolate too but,' she lowers her voice to a whisper, 'I've hidden them in your cabinet as I am not sure you're allowed them.'

I grunt and uncurl my hand holding it out to Maeve.

'Now? You want one now?'

I roll my eyes.

'Oh, OK.' She rummages around in a large, square, purple box and places something in my hand. I wolf it down. I can't remember the last time I had anything to eat. I hold out my hand again. Maeve gives me another. This time I rest it on my tongue and let it melt. Cheap chocolate but it does the trick.

'Good?' she asks, supressing a smile.

I nod, smacking the last of the chocolate from my lips. 'How did I get here?'

'It was me who found you, actually. Laurie Gray mentioned to Mike you hadn't been into the shop for a few days and he was worried. He sent me up and I found you, halfway down the stairs absolutely out for the count. You must have been there all night! I feel awful none of us found you any earlier. We called the ambulance and here you are! Now, you mustn't worry about a thing. I'm going to pop up to your house with Jean tomorrow and we'll put some food out for the cat and give it a bit of a tidy up…'

Agitation rose in me like smoke, my head began to throb. 'No! No! I don't want anyone going into my house. You stay away. Both of you. Meddling bitches.'

Maeve reels back. I watch her struggling to bring her face under control. 'Now come on, dear, that wasn't very nice, was it? I'll pretend I didn't hear that as I know you're in a lot of pain.' Her tone is stiff and brittle.

'Have you come to see Will as well?' I say, my words as cruel as ice. 'Is he still here?'

Maeve crumples into herself; she looks smaller, and older. Good! I think, with a surge of bitterness. I am punished immediately by an aching throb across my forehead.

'Yes.' She looks down, avoiding my gaze and knotting her hands together to hide the shaking. 'He's still here, they want to keep him in for a little longer.' I see the tears shining in her eyes, but she blinks them away. 'He doesn't want to come home right now, they're admitting him to a clinic, you know, just until they can find the right programme of medication for him.'

She is fiddling and fiddling with the flowers. I can see the dark circles beneath the make-up she has applied; exhaustion pinches her lips, she is drunk with it, her defences are down. My malice triggers another nibble of pain burrowing into my right temple. It's uncomfortable and continues to corkscrew deeper and deeper. Time to be good, I decide with a resentful sigh.

I close my hands over hers to still the nervous movement. I think of the greenness of trees and the blue of the sky, cold, fresh winds and the dampness of rain. All of this I gather up and pour into her, as much as I can. Her eyes flash open and she tries to tug her hands away, but I hold on until the surge of energy fades. I fall back. Maeve almost knocks over her chair as she jumps to her feet, her neck and face flushing a deep red. She has forgotten the last time I did this.

'I… Sorry, Mrs B, er Frieda… I must go. I'll come back tomorrow?'

I chuckle a little as she scampers down the ward, heading for the door. She doesn't know it yet, but she'll be a new woman in the morning.

*

Gradually the ward quietens down and the lights click off, one by one. The nurses want to give me a bed bath, but I refuse, I'm not letting them anywhere near me. I allow one to help me to the lavatory, but insist she waits outside. Oh, the indignity of old age. I can't bear it.

Pills are swallowed, checks are done, and we are left to sleep. The only illumination is the shaded lamp of the nurses' station. I eat more chocolate and hold one of the peonies to the withered skin of my cheek.

'That was a kind thing to do,' a voice whispers in my ear. I have been expecting it; the static buzz has been fading in and out for hours.

'Charlie,' I say. He slumps into Maeve's abandoned chair. I smell smoke.

'You getting soft in your old age, Freddy?'

I shrug. 'She needed it. She was suffering.'

'Oh, and I know how much you hate to see suffering...'

'I thought I told you to sod off.'

'You did.' He arches an eyebrow at my hospital bed. 'That ended well.'

'That wasn't you, that was the damn cat.'

'You were fleeing from me...'

I snort. 'Hardly. I'm too old to flee from anyone.'

'Do you remember when we first met?' Charlie's face is dreamy. 'I can see you now, trotting into the shop, your face all crunched up.' He scowls to demonstrate. his face rubber-like in its ability to mimic, and he captured my sulky, ten-year-old face perfectly. 'Such a greedy girl, things don't change do they, my love?'

He leans forward and wipes the corner of my mouth with his thumb. Every cell of my body leaps towards him, I curse its disloyalty and pull away from him, but Charlie sees and smiles at the effect he is having.

'Why are you here? Bothering me?' I snap with impatience. 'What is it you want?'

'Chocolate was always your favourite, I seem to remember,' Charlie continues, ignoring my interruption. 'Although you don't look as if you are very greedy now.' He gave me a reproving look. 'You're positively skeletal. You'll need to get yourself fattened up; you are going to need your strength.'

'What for?' I ask. 'I'm not doing anything, I'm not going anywhere.'

'You will. You must. But I'm not going to talk about it now. Christ, this place is horrid. Why is it so hot?'

I peer at him. 'How can you feel hot? You're dead.'

Charlie winces. 'Darling, do you have to be so brutal? And keep your voice down, people will think you've gone mad and lock you away and then where would we be?' He lights another cigarette, waving the smoke away as I cough.

'So, tell me, what's it like being dead? Do you sit on a cloud and play on a harp?' I smirk.

'Fucked if I know,' Charlie shrugs. 'I don't remember anything. I'm just... here. Last memory I have is that damned bomb blowing up in my face.'

An involuntary well of tears surprises me. I blink to keep them from falling. All this time has passed and yet my body responds as viscerally as the day when Charlie's younger brother, hair wild and eyes red-rimmed, hammered on our door, sobbing out the dreadful news.

'I remember everything about you, however. My dear, my love.' Tenderly, he takes my old ruin of a hand and holds it to his lips.

I pull it away. 'Oh fuck off, Charlie. My dear, my love. My arsehole. Do you go and visit the deathbeds of all your girls? How many did you manage to screw in your sadly-cut-short-lifetime?'

'A surprising number actually,' Charlie laughs, his beautiful mouth stretched wide so I could see his even, snow-white teeth. He shows not a trace of remorse or shame. 'But it was always you, dear Freddy.'

'It's Frieda.'

'You were special. You had fire in your belly...'

'And stars in my eyes,' I finish for him. 'Yes, I remember. I also remember you said that to Susie Laker; that slut Elsie from Debenhams; and Ivy from next door.'

Charlie laughs again, throwing his head back, and I can see the joy gulping down his throat. My mouth curves up in response, but I drag it back to a pinched pout of disapproval. 'How the hell did you know that?' he continues, wiping his eyes.

'Because they told me, of course! And took great pleasure in doing so, you bastard.'

'Oh dear, oh dear, no wonder you were so cross with me.' His eyes grow serious. 'But I seem to remember they got their comeuppance?' He cocks an eyebrow at me. 'Poor Susie never really recovered, did she? And as for Ivy...' He shakes his head.

'Well I would have done the same to you,' I blurt out, annoyed. 'But you were dead already so...'

'Ah, Freddy, my fiery little witch. Heaven help anyone who crosses you.' He sighs and winks at me, his eyes the colour of autumn leaves.

'I'm not a witch,' I say, irritation making my shoulders tense.

'Anyway, fuck all those other women, they were irrelevant, I was young. Besides, I was led around by my cock from the moment I hit thirteen. You can't blame me.'

I roll my eyes.

'I thought you'd understand. You spent the rest of your life being led around by... well, whatever the female equivalent of cock is... vulva?'

'Clitoris.'

41

'Exactly. I remember you being a bit of a dark horse. Who knew that prim, sulky little Frieda was such a whore underneath? And that was just the start.'

I smile, remembering his touch. The luscious, early days of discovering what my body could do, and feel. The first time he tasted me with his tongue, the shock of discovering the electric fuzz of his hair, animal and pungent beneath the clean, white cotton of his shirts. I shiver. Charlie strokes the inside of my wrist with his long fingers.

The gentleness of his hands reminds me of something else. The love. Oh, the love. I had loved him so much my guts ached with it. A sweet pain melts into me as I remember his kiss, the tenderness of his thumbs stroking my face as his lips touched mine, shy and clumsy.

Ach! This is sentimental bullshit. I have been twenty different people since then. 'That girl died a long time ago,' I say, wrenching back to the present.

Unperturbed, Charlie sits back in his seat and watches me. I shift in vain to ease the ache in my bones.

'Have you everything locked up safe, Freddy my love?' he asks, his voice light as he examines the end of his cigarette.

'Of course, I'm not a fool,' I reply. A shadow moves across his face. 'Everything has been safe for years and years,' I go on, aware of the defensiveness in my voice. 'How do you know about all of these things? Why should you worry about it now?'

Charlie frowns. 'Something's changed,' he says. 'Or something is going to change.'

'I don't understand any of this,' impatience is making me irritated. 'Why are you here? Why now? The dead surround me all the time but they don't look as you do.'

This makes Charlie look smug which is even more infuriating, I mutter a few words, but the shimmering, poison-green traces are lost in the cloud of smoke he breathes towards me. He lifts his eyebrows with a smile. He knows my tricks.

'I don't want to talk to you anymore,' I say, looking away from him. 'I'm tired.'

He gives a nod and shimmers into nothingness. Concentrating hard, I close my eyes and will myself up, up into the roof and beyond. It is a joyful thing to stretch out my crooked limbs, flexing my feet and hands as I rush up towards the sky. I don't bother to look down at the bundle of bones and flesh beneath me.

I see the wood first. A knitted shawl of green and black tossed across the shoulders of the ancient hills. I take a great gulp of breath, my lungs no longer compressed by cages of contorted bone. I want to drink the cool air like water, scented as it is with earth and starlight.

But as I drift close to the house, I falter. Something is wrong. Charlie's words echo in my head. I will myself on, ignoring the whispers of pain beginning to curl up from my bed-ridden body.

A ball of dread is growing in my stomach; it is so terribly black and heavy it slows me down. My hands shake.

The light is gone.

I force myself to move forward, cursing the weakness – my strength is failing. I didn't have long; I would have to return soon. Just a little further. Eldritch lifts her face to the sky, frozen on the grass she screams up at me, her mouth wide and pink against the darkness.

I see now.

The woven threads, the skein of words I had spun, flung, and anchored at every side of the house, are ragged. Great, gaping holes of darkness lie like inky pools where threads have snapped and unravelled.

The shock of it, the sudden, horrified understanding of what this means makes me cover my eyes. I circle my hands until a cloud of water vapour swirls like icy candyfloss, thicker and thicker until I am completely hidden. Only then can I look again.

Who has done this? Who would leave me so exposed? Such danger lurks. The darkness presses on me, rushing into my mouth, my eyes, my ears. The pull of my aching body is too much. I feel the surge, the tug backwards. I try to make fists of my hands, but the strength is gone.

A great groan of pain tears from my throat. The nurses are huddled around me, whispering to each other. As I open my eyes, one nods at the other who injects me with a liquid which bubbles around my veins with the ice of Styx water. Charlie is behind them. He watches me still.

I try to speak. My mouth is dry, so they tip liquid into my mouth; it tastes warm and brackish. 'I need to see Maeve,' I whisper urgently.

'It's OK, love,' replies one shadowed figure. 'You go to sleep now, everything is OK.'

'I have to see Maeve. Please.' In my head I am shouting but I sound like a bird.

'Quiet now.'

The pain in my body is cruel after its brief respite. I keep seeing the fragile, shimmering canopy of protection over my house torn and ragged. What demons would come? And they would come, as soon as they caught the scent of torn hangings.

I want to roar with rage at the horror of it. I am a paper doll, pressed flat against white sheets. Helpless. Useless. The vile stink of pity hangs in the air and I want to spit at it. I try to move but every shift brings pain so powerful my head reels and I sob. I rail and twist and struggle, but a second needle comes, and that is the end of it.

# CHAPTER 4: ANGIE

I dreamed about him again. All that dieting made staying asleep impossible. My stomach felt like it was trying to eat itself. I supposed it was better than the sloshing of acid that I had grown used to, burping up my throat with a swell of bile, but it didn't half keep me awake, all that fasting. I'd have preferred the indigestion, I thought. I would wake up with a jolt, as if someone had shouted my name, but all would be quiet.

Then I'd notice how bloody hungry I was, and the glass of fizzy water by my bed didn't cut it. The good thing was, even though I'd only been on it for a week, the diet had definitely started to take effect. You'd think I was made of compacted fat, a tube of lard that was solid all the way through. But as I lay on my back, I could just about feel a slight prominence of hardness. Maybe a hipbone? I thought and would prod myself until bruises formed.

I didn't want to remember my dreams. Staring into the darkness, I would think of anything else. Work, Andy, what I'd watched on the Telly. They were frustrating dreams, filled with half-understood, mysterious conversations; my brain trying to make sense of Andy's fragmented snores, assuming someone was whispering something important in my ear.

The results were scraps of words, incoherent speeches. My Dad's voice, intent, urgent. Trying to say something and his frustration was so painfully evident I'd be wrenched from sleep gasping, my cheeks wet.

Thank God those dreams seemed ridiculous once the sun came up. Forgotten immediately. The regular routine of my days was safe, ordered; nothing unexpected happened. I clung to normality like a drowning woman grabs a plank of wood in a stormy sea.

Work kept me going. I was a cleaner at the local school. The school Vik, Maggie, Sharon, and I went to and hated. It made me laugh to think of us at sixteen. We couldn't bloody wait to see the back of the place, and yet here we all were, over thirty years later, scrubbing at the bogs where we used to gossip and smoke forbidden fags.

The day before the first weigh in I gave Vicky a lift and, as always, she took the mick out of me as I pulled my bucket of cleaning stuff from the boot of my car. I was a bit precious about my cleaning bucket. I know. Sounds ridiculous, but the stuff the school provided was really manky. Cheap, bulk-bought products that ruined your skin, not to mention the cloths that disintegrated under your hands. No. I liked my microfibers and looked after them well.

Mum's recipes for floor and window cleaners using things like lavender, vinegar, bicarb and lemon juice worked brilliantly. I'd also discovered hacks on Pinterest and my cleaning arsenal was my pride and joy. There was nothing in that school I couldn't leave looking gleamingly clean, beautiful, and smelling gorgeous.

I wouldn't let anyone else use my stuff – thieving witches – I knew once they'd had a go at my glass spray made with vinegar, water, and (the extra special secret ingredient) a few drops of lemon oil, I'd never get it back.

'You're such a loser,' said Vicky, bumping against me in affection as we walked up the steps to the main entrance of Garth High – famous for being a failing school for decades.

It was bitterly cold. Everywhere you looked it was grey. Grey sky, grey concrete, grey buildings. I felt sorry for the poor kids who had to study all that rubbish here. Saying that, at least they got to leave eventually. I'd be here until the day I retired. That thought brought me up short.

Christ. Was that it? Fifteen or so more years cleaning this place and then that's done? Then what? I swallowed down a little gush of panic. What would I do? Sit in the flat with Andy until one of us died? I stopped as a wave of dizziness made me falter and my heart gave a funny little flutter in my chest.

No. Don't be stupid. I thought. Something will come up. You've got ages. Maybe Andy and I would go travelling? See the world beyond Spain – the only country I'd ever visited outside England. Try some pizza in Italy perhaps.

Somehow, this often-repeated mantra of reassurance had become less effective as I barrelled towards my fiftieth birthday.

'Come on you lot – stop gassing and get on with your work!' A voice floated down the steps. Gary. Ah Gary. He certainly lifted your spirits on a grey day. I didn't know why I liked him so much. I'd known him for years. He'd been in the year above me at school, and had gone off to the Army for twenty years – we'd never saw hide nor hair of him in that time – until, like a jack in a box, he'd popped out of nowhere, managing the cleaning staff at the school.

His once coppery-bright ginger hair had softened to a sandy, greyish bristle that he kept close clipped. I liked the way he looked, although he wasn't really anything special. A bit chubby, but it didn't show on his face, which had broad, high cheekbones narrowing to a nice sharp jaw. It was an open face, a kind one. He looked a miserable git most of the time but every now and then - about twice a year we used to grumble - he'd grin and dazzle us dumb.

He treated us with an affable, teasing banter but if we slacked off, came in late, or spent too long chatting, he'd come down on us like a ton of bricks.

'All right, Angie?' he said with one of his rare smiles as I walked past him. 'Boys' bogs today, I'm afraid. Watch out, someone's been crapping on the seats again.' I smiled back feeling a bit shy, I always did a bit around him – silly really.

'Great. Thanks, Gary.'

As we clattered down the corridor, Vicky gave me a nudge. 'You know I reckon he fancies you. He always looks pleased to see you.'

A great blush swept my body. I could even feel the blood prickling the roots of my hair. 'Don't be stupid!' I said. Mortified. 'As if he'd fancy a great old lump of lard like me.' Christ! Was I having a hot flush? 'Besides, he's just given me the boys' bogs to do, hasn't he? Not exactly love's young dream. Nah. Kelly's more his style.'

I nodded to where Kelly was wiping the reception counter, phone in one hand, duster in the other. She'd started working at the school a few years ago, moved to the village when her husband got a job nearby; I'd heard that she treated him like muck, and he'd moved back to his mum's house not long after they'd arrived. I didn't like her much, but that could have just been jealousy.

She was only a few years younger than me but looked great. She went to the gym every day, ate like a bird - always refused the biscuit tin when it came around - and liked to show off her slim figure in very tight jeans. Compared to us lardy ladies she looked like a twig.

I couldn't quite work Kelly out. She tended to keep herself to herself. We used to be friendly when she first started, but recently she'd been a bit offish with me. I tugged at my mop of hair, conscious of the contrast between her long blonde locks and my mess of greying frizz. I knew Kelly wore extensions, but they looked real; they must have cost a fortune.

I watched in amusement as Kelly, clocking Gary coming down the corridor, put her phone down and started rubbing at the counter with her duster. She rubbed so hard her bum wiggled into a blur of movement. Vicky and I couldn't tear our eyes from it, and I noticed even Gary had slowed down and was looking a bit shell-shocked before collecting himself and moving on.

Oh, what must it be like to be able to get into a pair of size 10 jeans! I thought. I had to work hard to stop my teeth grinding with jealousy. It was difficult to blame being fat and frazzled on old age, when Little Miss Kelly here was bopping around looking like a - slightly bargain basement - film star and she was only a few years younger than me.

I tried to remember the last time I had worn size 10 jeans. I knew I had once, they were Calvin Klein, black, I used to look like the dog's nuts in them. They were still in my cupboard as I couldn't bear to throw them away. I did a quick calculation – the last time I wore them was on holiday with Andy, just before I got pregnant.

I could feel the familiar shard of pain nudging at my ribs, ready to slide in and take my breath away, but I wouldn't let it. Not here. Not at work.

The bogs were as disgusting as usual but shone by the time I finished. As always, I felt a little naughty as I closed the door on the fresh smell of bleach. We weren't supposed to use bleach, it was my little rebellion. God. How sad was I that I took pride in such an insignificant show of defiance? I thought of Kelly again, with her bold confidence. I had to work hard to keep my smile going.

'Smiler'. That's what Dad had always called me. 'That smile's going to break hearts,' I remember an old woman saying when I was tiny, gripping my mum's hand. We weren't really a family for crying on people's shoulders. I'd learned to get on with things. Even when we lost Mum, Dad kept on going, cracking jokes – telling stories. He'd had everyone in stitches. I would smile watching his red, shiny face split open into a grin. His shirt would be all crumpled, and he'd be slopping his beer about in the glass, regaling his audience with anecdotes, mostly self-deprecating ones.

Packing up my bucket, I remembered Dad in the pub describing how he'd bricked himself inside a garden wall he'd been building, and had to wait for hours, crying out plaintively, until someone came and hoicked him out. His old mate Dave had laughed so hard we thought he was going to have a heart attack. I gave a bit of a snort at the memory but had to grab a wad of bog roll to wipe away the tears.

The little blond boy was standing by his window as I left, making me stiffen. I kept my head down as I passed, ignoring him as he nudged the dark girl next to him. My footsteps quickened and I cannoned into Vicky coming the other way. The ensuing clatter and squawks of outrage shattered the kids back into invisibility, and the rope around my chest loosened again.

At tea-break, I sat with my back to the window. It was one of those days, and I knew the desperate woman would be roaming the garden. I couldn't cope with seeing her face today. Vicky and I talked about how well our diets were going until the others told us to shut up. I had an extra lump of sugar to make up for refusing a bit of Sharon's chocolate birthday cake and ignored the whispering voice at the window.

It was only when I got home and managed to get past the end of the village without seeing Dad, that I found myself able to breathe a sigh of relief. The old boy crooning to his dog outside the entrance to the estate didn't bother me; he didn't carry any malignity on his shoulders.

The flat was cold when I got in and I rushed around turning up the heat, closing the curtains, and lighting the side lamps. Andy had promised to come back early and I was looking forward to spending some time together. After six days of dieting I was hoping I'd be able to get into my lovely, bright pink jumper that Andy had once said suited me. I changed my mind when I saw it still clung like a wet sail wrapped around a bulky sack of potatoes. I tore it off and settled for a big nightshirt (that could pass for a normal shirt in the evening) with a pair of leggings.

'I feel like I haven't seen you for ages,' I said to Andy as we sat down at the table. I had persuaded him to have tea with me by promising a super-duper healthy meal. It was the day before weigh in so I was on tight rations. I surveyed the bowl of salad, lettuce slightly browning at the edges, and unappetising chicken which I'd put onto skewers and grilled in the oven.

Afters was a bowl of strawberries and I was planning to add quite a lot of cream. I was looking forward to them, my days had been a featureless blur of quinoa and crisp breads and the thought of some sweetness, even if only from a slightly wizened winter strawberry, made my mouth water.

'Eh, Andy?' I repeated, as he hadn't responded. He looked up from his phone.

'What did you say?' he said.

'I said I feel like I haven't seen you for ages,'

'Been busy, haven't I?' he replied at last, finishing a text and slipping his phone back in his pocket. I watched him as I dished the food up. He looked good. I had to admit it. All the exercise and healthy eating had brought a glow to his face, and cycling outside had given him a bit of a tan... unless...

'Have you been using my fake tan?' I cried with a hoot of amusement.

He blushed. 'Don't be stupid, Ange, as if I'd use any of that crap.'

'Well it certainly looks like it.' He was starting to get pissed off so I didn't push it. He'd done something to his hair as well. He'd always had lovely hair, gorgeous and thick. From the front it still looked OK, but a thinning patch at the back had grown and gradually spread until you couldn't miss it. He'd sprayed on some kind of coloured powder, I noticed.

I felt a bit of a pang as I realised he, too, was conscious of his looks going. He glanced over at me and I smiled reflexively, but he didn't notice, he was miles away.

We'd had our ups and downs, Andy and I, like anyone would over that many years, blimey – almost a lifetime - but we were pretty strong as a couple. Losing Jonathan had created a great big crack in our marriage, but over the years we had papered it over a hundred times, and now you could barely see it. There had been moments when I didn't think we'd get through, to be honest. Andy went a bit wild, started gambling, drank too much.

I swallowed as I remembered well-meaning friends warning me Andy was spending too much time chatting up a tart called Jenny in our local, but I ignored it. I couldn't really blame him, could I? All I could do was cry. Lie in bed and cry. For months.

I turned my face to the wall, as they say. He told me once he didn't know what to say to me, so he went out. Pretended as if nothing had happened. Silly. The whole village knew what had happened, but they let him carry on, drinking himself into a daze before stumbling home to his struck-dumb wife. Poor sod.

But you get over it. It's not like we had a choice. We just... carried on. And one day I got out of bed and got a job working at the school. Before Jonathan, I used to work at the big hotel in town. Oh, I loved it there. I worked my way up from a part-time chambermaid in the holidays to getting regular slots as the receptionist. I had my eye on the manager's job. It made me laugh to think of how ambitious I used to be.

Having worked there for so long I had great mates; we were a brilliant team. I got a good deal for our wedding reception and it was one of the best days of my life – all my family and friends around me, wishing me well. Andy tried to persuade me to go back there when I got better, but I just couldn't face it.

I couldn't bring myself to walk through those doors and see them look at me, trying to mask the pity in their eyes. No. I couldn't. Even my boss Lynn came to see me – gave me the old claptrap about how talented I was, and how much they were missing me. But I shook my head. Not for me. I told her. Not anymore.

I watched Andy forking through a pile of lettuce, reminding me of Ermintrude. I was more used to seeing him neck back pints of beer and huge burgers. His rounded cheeks had flattened so that his cheekbones poked out sharp on his face. It made him look grimmer. I felt a little jolt as I stared. I didn't recognise him; my Andy- jolly and indulgent - seemed to have disappeared. A little shiver of unease crawled up my neck and I shook it off impatiently. Stop being stupid, woman, I thought - it's Andy for Christ's sake, you've known him since you were eleven.

I crunched through the salad noisily to cover the silence. We never used to have silences hanging between us. Where has my sudden awkwardness come from? Before this fitness craze, we spent a lot of time together, mostly eating, or out socialising. We'd have friends round, or host a barbecue – go out for Sunday lunch. But since he's had to get his steps in, or do his 10 miles, or get a bike ride done, he never seemed to be at home.

'Andy, love,' I said, my voice sounded embarrassingly loud in the silence.

'Mmm?'

'Why don't we book ourselves a nice weekend away – a dirty weekend? We haven't done that in ages.' I didn't mention how we'd dried up on the sex front too. He was always too tired, or would stay up late watching stupid fitness videos, no matter how long I tried to stay awake, I was always asleep by the time he came to bed. As we looked at each other across the table, I couldn't believe how out of place I felt. What was the matter with me?

He finished chewing. 'Yeah. Sounds great.'

'Well that sounded enthusiastic!' I laughed.

He shrugged and got up to take his plate into the kitchen.

'I'm a bit busy over the next few weeks. Got a job on at the big estate,' he called over his shoulder. 'It's a bit of a trek so Pete said I could stay with him before the work starts.'

'What? So I'll just sit here on my Tod all week, then?'

He came back in. I tried to read his face, but he wouldn't meet my eye. 'Yeah, sorry, love, but it saves me getting up at the crack of dawn.'

I followed him into the front room. 'Ah Andy I was just saying I never see you and now you'll be away all week!'

He was on the floor doing those sit-ups where you twist from side to side. He always did this now; straight after every meal he'd do some push ups or jog on the spot, like a man showering after illicit sex. It made me feel uncomfortable for reasons I couldn't put into words.

'Andy?'

'Oh stop WHINING, Angie!' he shouted, his face red with exertion and exercise. 'I've told Pete I'm coming. End of.'

Well that shut me up. Andy didn't often yell at me, but when he did, there was no point in arguing. I gave him the silent treatment as punishment, not that he seemed to notice – he spent the rest of the evening playing on his phone while I huffed on the settee. He left early the following morning and I tried not to mind that he didn't say goodbye.

*

The night after weigh in I returned to the empty flat triumphant because I'd managed to lose ten pounds. Ten pounds! OK, so taking off my coat and wearing flimsy shoes had helped, but still – ten pounds! Nearly a stone. Vik and I had run past the takeaway on the way home but I hadn't gone mad – just some noodles and lemon chicken.

I wanted to text Andy straight away to celebrate my fat loss news, but I was still cross with him so resolved to give it another day or two. He hadn't texted me either; I imagined he was rushed off his feet. Within ten minutes of getting home, I was comfortably full, feet up on the settee, remote control in hand. There were some benefits to Andy being away I thought.

Although, I had to admit, when the flat was empty it was more difficult to ignore the wizened Indian lady who poked about in the shadows outside the door most evenings. I could hear her shuffling but turning up the volume helped until she went away.

A rerun of *Charlie's Angels* came on. Despite my unease about Andy, it made me smile. Dad and I used to love that show. My mates used to come round and we'd all watch it together. My eyes were drawn to an old Polaroid photo I kept in a frame on the shelf next to the TV. Jayne, Susi and I grinned out across the decades. God I used to hate my big ears and goofy teeth but looking at my thirteen-year-old self, all I could see was pure, undiluted joy and excitement for the future. I tried to remember when exactly the photo had been taken.

I hadn't paid attention to it for years so took it down to have a proper look. It was so washed out now I struggled to make out the background but looking at Jayne and Susi's dear, familiar faces my memory began to paint in the colours and sounds that had faded over the years.

Cathton Bay. Early 80s. Lionel Ritchie, 'Dancing on the Ceiling'. The sun bouncing sparkles on the sea as we lay and giggled about boys whilst eating ice cream. Jayne was always a bit of a tart and we would explode with laughter as she sashayed up and down the sand enjoying the attention her voluptuous figure inspired.

Goodness, we used to get into so much trouble, I thought with a funny kind of yearning. We had my Dad pulling his hair out. He was the one we would call when things got bad. Susi's Dad was a police officer and Jayne's a vicar. Dad, coping with bringing up a girl on his own, was less judgemental, less likely to freak out if we called him from outside a nightclub having got a bit too drunk with no money left to get home.

We even had to call him from a police station once! I remembered with a laugh. Jayne was an absolute minx and had talked us into stuffing some things from Boots into our bags, but we all got stopped by the guard as we tried to leave. Poor Dad, he was raging when he arrived but had agreed when Jayne and Susi begged him not to tell their parents. He had promised, but only on the condition we never did it again. And we never did.

I put the photo back on its shelf, straightening it with care. A lump had risen to my throat. Not just for my dear old Dad, but for the girl I was then. God, I couldn't wait to grow up. The world was going to be my bloody oyster, just like my Dad promised. Jayne and Susi would be my partners-in-crime forever and we would lead full, exciting lives until we settled down to marriage and babies. 'But not before 30!' we would swear.

Jayne and Susi never liked Andy. They couldn't understand why I was so intent on marrying him when I was only just into my 20s. I didn't have the words to explain the thrall in which he had me held. I was bound to him with a passion I had never experienced before. The sex drove everything out of my head: Ambition, Friends, Family, Work... It all fell away. It was the worst thing I ever did in my life. Because while I was screwing Andy whenever I could, I didn't see my Dad's health was failing. By the time I realised, it was too late.

I rubbed away tears and sniffed. Jayne had gone off to university. Susi had surprised us all by setting up and running, with great success, a make-up line aimed at Asian women. As a Pakistani teenager in the middle of nowhere, Susi would moan all the time about being unable to find a foundation that matched her skin. I had been speechless with admiration when her company, *Brown Babe*, took off.

I shuddered to think what they would say if they saw me now, huddled in a crappy little flat working at my old school for God's sake. I was the only one who stayed in the village. Even my break for freedom working briefly at the hotel was in a town only fifteen miles away from where I was born.

I had firmly stuck my finger on pause, while they fast-forwarded into happy, busy, challenging lives. I was connected to them through Facebook, but we rarely made contact. I resolved to send them a message one day. Maybe when I had lost a bit of weight. They would be horrified if they saw me now, I thought as I unfolded the old blanket hanging on the settee and wrapped it around my shoulders. In fact, I would be surprised if they even recognised me.

*

Sunday morning, I woke up freezing. The weather had taken a nasty turn and the drizzling rains of autumn had frozen into ice. Despite not having to listen to Andy's constant snoring, I couldn't sleep. My heart kept racing and I had strange, anxious dreams. I couldn't bear the thought of sitting in the flat any longer. I wrapped a long scarf around my neck and pulled on two pairs of leggings with my biggest fleece.

The cold outside made me wheeze, but its freshness blew away some of the fug thudding around my head. I ignored the lads mucking about in the car park and walked past them into the village. I didn't see any of the ones but kept my eyes on the ground past the church just in case.

As I walked from the estate into the village, I left behind the concrete-cancer greys and washed-out blues of the 1970s flats and came into the village proper. The houses stretched, elegant and serious down either side of the street. The doors and window frames were all immaculate. No peeling paint, no graffiti – it was like I'd gone on holiday to a different country.

Everywhere was quiet, I hadn't realised how early it was. I was just about to turn around and go back when I heard a door slam and a figure appeared a little ahead of me trying to control a big, fluffy white dog who leaped and tugged at its lead.

It was Doctor Lockwood. His grey hair whipped about in the wind and when he saw me he smiled and lifted a hand.

'Angie?' he said, marching towards me with the dog bounding ahead. 'You're up and about early.'

I smiled.

'I'd be glad of the company if you fancy joining Dolly and me on a stroll?'

He tightened Dolly's lead as we walked past the church towards a broad, grassy track that led past the playground to the orchards behind the village. I noticed he slowed to match his pace with mine. It was nice.

To begin with he didn't say much, just talked about how cold it was and how he needed to decide what to get Maeve for Christmas. He opened the gate into the orchard and I went through, panting with the effort. I couldn't remember the last time I had walked this far.

Kindly, the Doc took his time closing the gate, and spent a good five minutes fiddling with Dolly's collar to give me a chance to catch my breath. Great gusts of icy smoke billowed from my mouth like ghostly balloons. Doc unclipped the lead and Dolly shot off, galloping like a horse into the orchard, zooming in and out of the trees with dizzying speed.

For a second she looked back, black eyes dancing with joy, tongue lolling from her mouth, before she whipped around and shot off again. Doc and I smiled in response to the dog's obvious delight at being out and about on this frosty morning.

'Sweet day, so cool, co calm, so bright,' Doc said, making me jump.

'Sorry?'

'Ha! Ignore me, just wittering on as Maeve would say, what a view, though, eh?'

We had followed Dolly to the edge of the orchard and the fields flowed up to the hill that stretched its arm around our village. Now most of the leaves had fallen we could see the big house frowning across at us.

'Lovely,' I said.

'The house?' the Doc said in surprise, 'I always thought it was a bit forbidding.'

'No, what you said - about it being a cold day.'

'Ah yes! Dear, holy Mr Herbert. Days like these always remind me of that poem.'

'You're right about the house, though,' I said squinting up at it, the sun was low in the sky and slanting its light right into my eyes. 'It's big and posh and all that, but Andy said he always found it a bit creepy.'

'Yes, it does seem a waste old Mrs B rattling around in there on her own. It really is quite marvellous how she manages to live independently at her age.'

'How old is she?'

'She must be at least a hundred, but as sharp as ever. I've known her all my life, she and my father were good friends. I don't visit her as often as I would like, but she's not one to relish company.'

I thought of that lighted window that drew me so the night of the first diet class. 'She must get lonely up there, poor old thing,' I said.

The Doc laughed. 'Oh no, she's not one to get lonely.' He paused. 'There's something compelling about her actually,' he gazed up at the sky, his face thoughtful. 'Your mind plays tricks on you when you talk to her. And she can be very fierce.'

There was a pause; I shivered a bit. Now we had stopped the cold was creeping under my clothes. The Doc looked over at me and cleared his throat. 'Look, Angie, tell me if I'm speaking out of turn… but… you don't look very well. A bit nervy, and I don't like how out of breath you were coming up here. Maeve told me you've had a great first week, but I hope you're not starving yourself? Maybe you should come in for some blood tests? I'd like to have a look at your sugar levels.'

I nodded, interrupting him. I didn't want him to keep talking. I pasted on my best 'smiler' smile. 'I'm fine Doc. Don't you worry about me. I don't think it's going to do me any harm to cut back a little.' I gestured at my belly and thick thighs.

'I hear Andy is away at the moment. How are you coping on your own?' His voice is kind and his eyes so gentle my eyes began to water, and my smile started to wobble.

'Ah it's OK,' I rubbed away a tear. 'I quite enjoyed my own space for a bit, but it's been over a week now and I'm missing him quite a lot. He hasn't phoned, just the odd text…' And that was it. Poor Doc. To my absolute horror the strange ball of sadness within me doubled in size and pushed upwards; my chest gave a great heave and I burst into tears. I was mortified to see drops of snot and spit fly across and suspend themselves from the Doc's expensive looking scarf. Once I started, I couldn't stop.

Bless him; he didn't quite know what to do. I expected him to whip out a crisp white handkerchief like in the movies, but he didn't - he patted me on the shoulder. I had to wipe my grotty nose and eyes on my sleeve.

Once I started to calm down a little, he touched my elbow and we continued walking at a snail's pace, following Dolly who had continued zooming backwards and forwards. Staring straight ahead, his eyes on Dolly, the Doc chatted lightly about puppy training until I'd got past the gulping hiccupping stage.

He glanced over at me and smiled. 'I think you'd better tell me all about it,' he said.

Like a sodden load of laundry being tugged from a washing machine, it all tumbled out. How I thought Andy and I were drifting apart. How he'd found a purpose when I increasingly felt I was losing mine. 'It's funny - with him being away, it made me realise that even when he's there he's not, if you know what I mean.'

When I finally ground to a halt, the Doc gave a whistle to call Dolly back and led me to a nearby bench that leaned crookedly against a stone wall. He sat me down, hitched up his trousers and squeezed in next to me. To my surprise, he took out a flattened packet of Marlboro and lit up. He smiled at my shocked face. When he spoke, his voice was thoughtful.

'Not much I can say I'm afraid, my dear. A marriage is a covered dish, so they say. Only you can know what's happening. You must talk to Andy. Have an honest conversation with him. Tell him how you feel. The two of you have gone through a lot over the years,' he reached over and patted my hand. 'I think sitting down and having a good talk through will help tremendously.'

The Doc's words circled round my head for days afterwards. I was filled with an odd sort of excitement. Maybe things could change, I thought. If we could just sit down and talk, maybe we could find our way back to the people we were.

All week I kept pulling out my phone and staring at his number, wanting to call him. I rehearsed what I would say, what words to use to get past the stranger Andy had become, to the jolly bloke I fell in love with a lifetime ago.

I'd stare at his photo and then bottle it. Better in person, I thought to myself. I knew the job was ending soon; Vicky's brother-in-law was a sparky working on the site and had mentioned they were doing the last touches before packing up. He'd told Vik all the lads were going to the pub on Friday night to celebrate finishing.

Learning this filled me with energy. I'd now lost a stone and was starting to feel much better. I could finally get into the pink jumper Andy liked and thought I looked pretty good. I decided to go along to the pub over the other side of town to surprise him.

I'd pull out all the stops, slap on a full face of make-up, get my hair done. My heart thudded with fizzing, nervous energy. I felt like I was preparing for our first date again! I hadn't heard anything beyond a few texts so he didn't know how I'd been getting on with my diet. He'll be so pleased with me! I thought, clutching myself with hope.

I couldn't wait until the Friday. It had now been nearly three weeks since I'd last seen him; I'd managed to knock off another few pounds and was almost a stone and a half lighter than the last time we'd seen each other. The thought of Friday night kept me strictly on my diet, and I'd even managed to push myself out on a couple of walks, joining the Doc and Dolly when I got the chance.

I had to park my car halfway down the street as the yard in front of the pub was crammed full. Flipping down the visor, I gazed at myself in the lit-up mirror. My face felt tight and shiny with its unfamiliar, glossy mask of make-up. I'd gone to the Bobbi Brown cosmetics bar in town and let the girls there work their magic. I worried I looked ridiculous, but Maggie, Sharon and Vicky had fallen over themselves to reassure me. 'I'd do you!' Vik had exclaimed with a roar, making us all fall about in giggles.

Sitting in a freezing cold car, all on my own, I felt less sure. My lips looked awfully bright. I found a balled-up tissue and blotted the colour down a bit before checking my teeth for any smears. I loved my eyelashes. I'd never worn false ones before and was stunned by how different they made me look. I had to give them a bit of a tug to check they really were properly stuck on.

Taking a deep breath, I forced myself to get out of the car and made my way to the pub, which shone like a warm lantern at the end of the dark road.

Cursing Sharon for making me wear high heels, I wobbled my way along the road nearly turning my ankle on a rut of mud. I was trying to hold my coat shut (the buttons had all pinged off) keep my handbag closed – the clasp was prone to breaking open - and stop my scarf from whipping away in the freezing wind, so didn't notice the couple leaning against the wall of the pub until I was a few yards away.

They were kissing passionately. Against the inky darkness of the night they stood out in high definition, lit as they were by the pub's bright, white, security lamp. I felt like someone at a play, sitting in the soft darkness of the auditorium watching, spell-bound, as the lovers discovered each other in bright technicolour.

The lamp went out with a snap and I nearly fell as my eyes adjusted to the shadows. The pin sharp image of the couple kissing was burned onto my retinas. Ooh the lucky things, I thought. That's what I wanted. All that… passion! I couldn't even remember the last time Andy and I had kissed – not like that anyway, as if you want to devour each other, slip into each other's skin.

I felt quite dreamy as I picked my way forward, picturing Andy's hands roaming all over me, both of us lost in a proper snog. At my next step, the security light flashed back on, bathing the scene again in its white light.

I was aware of two things. Firstly, the swell of noise from the pub. I could hear thumping music and lots of men shouting and laughing. Secondly, the young couple had stopped kissing and had turned to make their way back into the pub. They were not as young as I had first thought.

My body recognised them before my brain did.

Something slammed into my stomach so hard I was amazed to be still standing. An ice-cold wrecking ball had swung into my body, almost knocking me off my feet. Shock pulled out my breath, leaving my mouth gaping.

Kelly from work. Kelly from work, my brain was saying but I couldn't make sense of it. She was laughing, a lovely, liquid bubble of a laugh, her head thrown back, blonde hair bouncing past her shoulders. She looked about seventeen.

Her man, whose face I had glimpsed for a tiny second, had bent to kiss her again and I watched as Kelly's hands, with their familiar turquoise nails slid up his shoulders and tangled in his hair. Her slender body leaped and pushed against his. It was raw and painfully sexy. Painful, because I knew. I knew the shape of that head, the familiar move as he curved his hand down Kelly's back and into her jeans.

Familiar because he'd done it to me. Hundreds of times. Thousands of times, over the years.

Andy.

Andy and Kelly. Kelly and Andy.

I stood still in the darkness as they finally stopped kissing. Corkscrews of agony twisted down into my stomach; I watched them shiver in the cold and retreat into the warmth of the pub.

Immediately the spotlight blacked out again and I found I couldn't move. Every time I blinked, the image of my Andy passionately kissing another woman flashed in front of my eyes. I rubbed them until my lids screamed with the pain of it, but it wouldn't go away.

Pathetic. How pathetic. What I fool I was. I felt screamingly self-conscious about my ridiculous, over made-up face. I felt fat, old, and grotesque in contrast to Kelly's fresh, glowing beauty. It was that which made me gasp with pain, allowing the tears to finally choke out of me. What had struck me when I first saw the couple was how right they looked together, slim and fit, neither of them looking their age.

And there I was. A pathetic, over-painted clown wearing a vast jumper in the hope it would disguise I was stones overweight. I didn't want anyone to see me. I needed to leave. Thank God nobody had noticed me in the darkness. My breath was coming in gasps now, a wail was building, a lament – ugly and brutal – was ripping at my throat.

Panic rose as I kept stumbling and falling, jolting the bones in my arms and wincing as my teeth clashed together. I tore off my stupid high-heeled shoes and threw them away as hard as I could. I slipped into a slick of mud, ruining my clothes and banging my hip so hard it made me cry out. Sobbing with relief, I finally reached the car. It smelled of perfume and hope. My heart broke.

# CHAPTER 5: FRIEDA REMEMBERS

I awake to the nurses whispering at the end of the ward.

'I'm afraid she's dreadfully agitated, Mrs Lockwood. Sorry to have to drag you up here but she just won't calm down. We can't be expected to...'

Stupid, idle bitches, I think. My hands are plucking at the sheets and I am painfully aware they see a simple, fretful old crone who has got herself into a tizzy about something trivial. I clench my hands into fists.

Christ, if only they knew what was coming. What might be in store for me. Finally, finally, Maeve breaks free from the twittering group of idiots and makes her way towards me. Her face is strained, but there is more colour in her cheeks. My touch the day before has energised her, I can see the fizzle of freshness, and sky, and cool rain on her skin.

'Frieda, dear, what on earth is the matter? The nurses have been dreadfully worried about you. They absolutely insisted I come over to see you this morning. I am afraid this is most inconvenient but they wouldn't take no for an answer...' It is interesting to see Maeve looking so cross. I like it. She's usually such a mouse.

'What have you done to my house?' I say, furious.

Maeve looks startled. 'Why, Frieda, nothing! I told you we were going to pop over there. Don't worry about Eldritch – she's fine. I got Jean to leave her some food. Goodness it's a mess in there, Frieda. It doesn't look as if you've cleaned it in months. It will need a proper going over before you go home…'

'It's not about the cat, you silly cow,' I explode, interrupting her wittering drivel. 'Listen. You must have moved something, changed something. Tell me.'

Maeve is flustered. 'No, no,' she stammers. 'I don't know what you're talking about. Really, I… well I don't think you should be talking to me like this… after all we've done for you, you…'

I cut her off, struggling to stay calm. 'Maeve, please, think. Carefully. There must be something you moved or changed. Something in the garden?'

Maeve shakes her head. 'No, no – I can't think…' I see something click into place. 'Oh hang on. Jean did notice those terribly sweet figurines getting all choked by weeds at the gate. We thought you might have dropped them. They looked awfully valuable so I told Jean to take them indoors. They're perfectly safe in the front hall.'

'No, no,' I moan. Christ! Stupid, interfering… I am so enraged I can't speak.

Maeve looks defensive, 'I'm not going to say sorry, Frieda. I said to Jean you must have dropped them, and we both agreed they shouldn't be out in the rain. Such delicate carvings! You must know that's real gold at the bottom, and the jade already looks like it was getting damaged.'

I try to shake off the ringing in my head. A clanging bell of warning is deafening. Maeve is looking self-righteous and defensive. I am about to scream at the idiotic cow when I stop. A buzz of static signals Charlie's presence. He is reminding me I need to be careful. I am in the unfortunate position of having to rely on Maeve. There is nobody else, and I am too weak to do anything myself.

I force a smile. 'I'm sorry, Maeve. You're right and of course, you haven't done anything wrong. But I like those statues to be outside. That's where they belong. It's important to me. Could you put them back where they were? I know I'm just a silly old woman…' I ignore Charlie who I can sense smirking beside me. 'This must sound ridiculous…'

Maeve's face softens immediately. 'No, No, *I'm* sorry, Frieda,' she says. 'I know how hard it is for you being here with people fiddling with your things. I'll put them back for you.'

'Thank you,' I say, a gasp of relief escaping, and I feel my body unclench a little. 'And you'll do it soon?' I cast her a look, gathering every inch of my will and drilling it into her. I'm not sure it works.

She nod, stands, and begins to gather her things. Maeve is always weighed down: Coat, umbrella, hat, bag, things are always spilling from her, leaving a trail of detritus willing people scurry to retrieve and return. 'I must go. I've got masses to do.'

She hurries off. I slump back against the pillows, exhausted.

'Do you think she'll do it?' Charlie whispers in my ear.

'I hope so,' I sigh. 'There's nothing I can do.' A thought strikes me. 'Can you go?' I turn to look at him, brightening.

He shakes his head, 'I don't seem to be able to move very far from you.' I shut my eyes. 'But maybe not all is lost. He'd have to be looking at the right place at the right time. Isn't that why you chose to live in the middle of nowhere? Somewhere he'd never think to look?'

'Yes I know,' I say. 'I just don't want to take any chances.'

Charlie vanishes as Mrs Fraser, the grubby looking dinner lady, clatters her trolley towards my bed. The stink of steaming cabbage and pinkish stew makes my stomach turn. With my last little drop of energy, I rub my fingers together, and watch the curtains swish shut, obscuring her fat, startled face.

*

The days in the hospital are endless. The bleached, antiseptic air seeps into my body, thins my blood and robs my hands of spells. I long to go outside, to leap up and leave but my pelvis screams in pain when I move so I remain, marooned, trapped by the sterile sheets of my bed. I sense Charlie's presence near me when night is at its darkest, but he doesn't speak.

It is difficult to sleep. The exercises they make me do are painful. I have no control over anyone or anything. It is the closest I have come to wanting to die.

I try to console myself this is nothing compared to my time in the woods and the trials I suffered there; but then I was young and strong, pain was easier to bear.

Here, I am a poor old woman. Visitors pass, their eyes gliding over me. Just another wreck of a body, washed up on the shores of ill health and old age. I find it infuriating. I battle against being diminished by their pitying gaze. I want to ball up the pins and needles pricking my hands and throw them into their smug, young faces.

Dear God the dreariness of this. Maeve has promised to bring me books, but I am unhappy with the thought of her stepping into my house, seeing my things vulnerable without me there to protect them.

I have managed to avoid hospitals all my life. This enforced stillness is triggering memories in a way over which I have no control. My memory used to work like a box of jewels. I could select any of them to find each contained a delightful affair, or a magical journey across unknown mountains, or maybe just a night drinking with friends as war rumbled on the horizon.

I could select a gem and disappear into it – lost to the world surrounding me. Every colour, every taste, every texture as real to me as it was then. What use to me are televisions or electric devices? Even the cinema didn't come close to these glinting jewels of memory I held within me.

But now I have no choice. I can't escape this bleakness by diving into a memory of dancing with Pascal, or buying dresses in Paris. Memories are being forced into my head. Ones I thought had vanished over the years. I don't like them. I don't want to remember. But it seems that's not how things work now.

My mother is very close. Since that moment I saw her face, when the pain was at its worst, I keep thinking of her. It comes at such strange moments, I might be woodenly jerking my leg back and forth with a physio nurse, or washing my hands at the sink when something comes and pulls me away, back into my past.

The nurses wheel me to a window for a change of scene while my bed is remade. The sky is grey, I feel cold despite the Sahara desert levels of warmth in the ward. I am waiting to be wheeled back when my head begins to spin. A faintness flickers dark across my eyes and with a dizzy swoop I am somewhere else.

*

I see my mother, her face tight with exhaustion, hair awry, mouth open. She is framed by an open window, through which I have just climbed. I am 16, and my skirts are wet and hang heavy. I want to be alone so I can relive my evening with Charlie.

'Where have you been, you wicked girl?' she cries. I can see her hands are itching to slap me. 'It's three in the morning! I've been worried sick. Be thankful I haven't told your father as I didn't want to wake him, but never fear, he shall hear of this.'

She is hissing at me in whispers so not to wake my sister who is asleep, dead to the world. I look round the tiny, cramped bedroom with its faded curtains and ugly prints depicting the sea, an attempt to distract from the lack of any kind of view from these poor little rooms.

Being in this stuffy room with my mother's fury makes me long to rewind time and go back to my evening with Charlie. We had walked on the beach for hours, our footprints leaving hollows in the sand that sucked at our feet. The sea a sheet of metal, hammered flat by the shining power of the moon; a silver road, clear and firm - Charlie and I could run away over the horizon, together forever.

'Stop mooning, you look addled in the head,' my mother says crossly, she is stripping my wet skirts from me, tutting at the dampness and pointing out the stained hems. 'What have you been up to? I don't know what to do with you, really I don't. I've never known such a wayward child.'

I smile at her. I can do nothing else, my happiness bubbles up in me like lemonade fizz. She is exclaiming as she finds great rips in my petticoats. I know what I can do. I grab hold of her.

'Ma. Ma! Sit down, let me rub your head, you look tired.'

My mother stills as I rest my hand on hers, I give her a gentle push so she sits on the bed and I take my time to unbraid her hair. It is plaited so tight to her head it pulls at the skin of her temples. My fingers are cool against the heat of her forehead and I close my eyes. I pull away her tiredness and smooth her white skin. She sighs.

I love this. I love how my powers are strengthening day by day. Thanks to Lilith, I am learning all the time. Quick as a fish darting through a clear stream, my brain leaps on and absorbs every new lesson. Every trick, every spell is greeted with excitement. I gorge on this new knowledge and delight in trying out what I have learned whenever I can. I concentrate hard and focus on my mother.

'You won't get around me like that, my girl,' she grumbles, but her breathing is slowing. 'I know you've been hanging around with that scoundrel Charlie. Your father doesn't like him.'

'Shhh, Ma, don't worry about that now.' My voice is soft and I concentrate on unravelling the knots in her shoulders, my fingers tingling with warmth. She gives a great yawn.

'I'm so tired.'

I encourage her to lie down on my bed and pull the counterpane over her. She starts to snore. The rest of the night I spend gazing out of the window, reliving every moment with Charlie until the sun rises.

\*

A crash of a tray startles me and I blink to see grey clouds scudding overhead through the hospital window. I am disorientated; I don't know how much time has passed. The ward is less real to me than that shabby room where my mother lies sleeping. I can remember my father's fury at my midnight adventure, but I can't remember his face. I can see a cap hanging by a door and shiny patches on an old, brown armchair. His face has gone.

'Mrs Beaudry? Mrs Beaudry!' I am shaken away from my memories.

A nurse walks me back to my bed. She takes my pulse and I am repelled by the hot dampness of her hand.

'I want to go home,' I said. 'When can I go home?' Petulance laces my voice.

'You know what the Doctor said, Mrs Beaudry. We have to wait and see how your new hip is getting on. You'll have to do some more of those exercises, and we can't let you go back to an empty house, can we?'

'My niece...'

'Well you were a bit naughty there, weren't you Mrs Beaudry? Your visitor told us you didn't actually have a niece staying with you. So Doctor Padgham has got us ringing around some nice care homes so we can get you out of the hospital and back on your feet before you go home for good.'

Her cheeriness, fake as plastic flowers, grates on my ears and I wave her away. 'I hate it here, Charlie,' I whisper. My ears strain to hear his voice but there is nothing.

It's been days since Maeve visited. I worry I have upset her and she won't be able to help me. Finally, she arrives as visiting hours start. I am still confined to my bed. My muscles ache from the punishing physiotherapy sessions, overseen by that bitch Lasonja. No matter how hard I try she is impervious to my little tricks.

Maeve waves at me across the room, holding up three books. I am happy to see them, but I need more from her than something to read.

She bustles over and drags a chair from next to the dozing crone who occupies the bed across from me.

'Mrs B!' she gushes, 'you *are* looking better. I've brought you something to read, it must get so boring in here, poor you. I spoke to the nurse before I came in and they seem hopeful you can be discharged soon. They've found the *sweetest* place for you to stay until you are properly up and about, and then you can get back to where you belong. Terrorising us all in the village!'

'Maeve,' I say, struggling to hide my desperation. 'I can't go into a home. I'll die. I need to go back to Pagan's Reach. Can you help?'

I hate this. I hate having to ask her, but what choice do I have?

Maeve looks thoughtful. She's no fool, despite her gush and babble.

'I'd have you with me but Will's being discharged soon and I need to…'

I shake my head, firm. 'I can't stay anywhere else; I need to be in my own home. With my things. Did you put them back? The statues? Are they in the right place?' Maeve avoids my eye and doesn't answer. I knew the cow would forget. I just prayed Charlie was right and the village was hidden enough to avoid discovery.

'But you're simply not strong enough to go home yet, Frieda!' she exclaims. 'I know it's awful for you here, truly I do, but they simply won't discharge you to an empty house. Especially such a big house with all those stairs.'

My mouth tugs downwards with grief, my hands shake with it and I can feel my eyes filling. It has the desired effect. Maeve looks mortified. She squeezes my fingers with one hand, brushing away her sympathy tears with the other. God she's wet, I think, but it is mean spirited of me and my head aches in reproach.

'I'll think of something,' she says, resolute. 'I'll need to get Michael to bring in some papers for you to sign so we can hire someone who can come in to look after you. I assume that won't be a problem?'

'I don't want some stranger coming in,' I say in alarm.

'OK,' she nods. 'I'll see what I can do. But you can afford it? To pay for some care?' I am amused to see her blushing with the embarrassment of asking me about money.

I wave my hand. 'Yes, yes, of course. There is money.'

'Right, I'd better get on then,' she stands, running her fingers under her eye to remove the mascara that has leaked there. 'I'll be back soon.'

I nod and put out my hand. She reaches for it but I pull it away and tut. 'The books?'

'Sorry?' Maeve is puzzled. She was expecting me to gush with gratitude and thanks, I realise.

'The books. Don't forget to leave the books.'

'Oh! Yes! Sorry,' she hands them over and I examine them with relish. She is still standing next to the bed so I look up at her. 'See you tomorrow then,' I say.

*

The boredom is going to kill me. Everything is always the same. The nurses follow their routines like mice in a maze. I watch the same visitors come and go, swarming around their loved ones with cards, and words of sympathy. I wish I had the strength to work some mischief here. I imagine knocking the trays from an orderly's hand. Or shrivelling the skin of the senior nurse who bullies the new ones, making them rattle around in a constant state of nervous panic.

Sister Trotter is a monster. Her voice is filled to the brim with exasperated irritation; she greets every question with a roll of the eyes. The young ones gulp with fear when they have to disturb her as she sits, fat as a toad, behind her desk. She has a sulky face reddened by too many late-night bottles of wine. I can see in her eyes the long nights she spends at home on her own. But here in the hospital she is an emperor, and I don't miss the spark of energy when she berates an underling for a foolish mistake. Her lips drool with the pleasure of making them cower.

I have nothing with me. No potion, no ointment, not even the energy to harm this bitch, this cow who wields her power with a bulldog arrogance. I could cast boils, or sickness – make snakes, visible only to her, slither from her mouth when she speaks. But I have to make do with just watching. I may not be at my best, but my gaze is a powerful one.

*

It was Lilith who taught me the power of eyes. I used to love going to her house in the woods. A little Red Riding Hood, I would pick my way through the brambles and thorns to find her, always in her garden. She was six feet tall with thick, silver hair that fell to her waist. She would knot it into a braid and secure it with a handful of pins; I was fascinated by the gleaming coils. Her eyes were black, and she could make them huge and deep. I would read stories of dangers and delights in those deep pupils – my mother would have been horrified if she'd known what I saw.

Lilith was my grandmother and on my twelfth birthday she decided I was ready.

'I will show her how to use the herbs and roots,' she told my mother. 'So the old ways don't die out altogether.' But that was only part of her teaching. She would hold me in front of her looking glass, and whisper in my ear. The words would make me shiver, some were blessings, some curses. As she spoke, her eyes would lock on mine and my lips would tremble as the hissed phrases wrote themselves in shimmers of green or gold on my skin, leaving silvery traces.

She would slip into my pockets golden rings, or a handful of walnuts with instructions on how to use them. As I got older she would let me read her books and examine her treasures. Some were centuries old, passed down through generations of tall, silver haired women; others were strange, foreign things Lilith had collected on her travels. She would fill my head with deserts and mountains, exotic cities and voyages across the sea, another kind of magic making my safe, village existence seem unbearable.

The noises of the hospital ward fade away as I close my eyes and imagine walking through the door of Lilith's long destroyed home. I see shelves stretching from the front to the back of the house. I could pick up any pot or jar and know what I will find there. I can run my fingers over the tinderbox, the cork-stopped bottles, the bunches of drying herbs and flowers. Everything is still as familiar to me as my own face. Many of Lilith's objects now line my shelves.

Once, one of Lilith's gifts saved my life. I take a deep breath and let the memory pull me under. Venice. Just after the war ended. I am wandering the narrow streets in a tightly fitted crimson dress. I am pleased with myself – I admire my reflection in windows and shop fronts, conscious of the flaming looks from the young men who lounge in squares.

But then the adventure darkens. Two men follow me. Their steps at first lazy, but becoming more urgent. Another appears from a side alley; yet another stands in my way so I have to squeeze past him with a muttered, 'Scusi.'

'Prego!' he calls, then he too begins to follow.

Fear is sparking bolts of electricity to every nerve ending. I don't know where I am going, the street is narrowing and I hear the menacing slap of water to my right. I jerk left, then left again. Light has drained away and I am running now, blocking my ears to the cat calls behind me. The men's shouts grow louder as darkness falls.

The strange game of follow-the-leader ends when I reach a canal with a small, stone bridge. Two men stand at its foot, arms crossed and smiling at me. Behind me a gathering of hoots and whistles. I am cornered. One shadowy figure reaches and touches my shoulder and I whirl and spit at him. He rears back, but another steps forward and pulls at the skirt of my dress.

Fear threatens to drown me. I think of Lilith. Her calm, grave face and dark eyes give me courage. I feel in my pockets. There. Two chestnuts, their surface smooth and hard under my hands. I hold them tight and lift my arms above my head. The men pause, watching me. I throw back my head and crack the chestnuts open.

Rivulets of darkness flood down my wrists and elbows like blood. Rats. Streams of rats. They grow bigger as they drop to the ground and swarm towards the men who scream and try to knock them off. The rats use their claws to cling on and continue to climb, glinting eyes intent on the flesh of the men's faces.

The men turn and run, I hear their screams. Soon the square is empty. I brush the fragments of cracked shells from my hands and make my way home.

\*

'You look cheerful!' the old crone across the way sings out at me, dragging me back to the present. 'First time I've seen you properly smile, I reckon.'

'Yes,' I say. 'Happy memories.'

'Ah, yes, all we have left at this age. What you in for then if you don't mind me asking?'

'Hip,' I reply shortly. I don't want to talk.

'Me too!' she replies. She hasn't a tooth in her head.

'Oh dear, oh dear.' The old man continues his nightly lament.

The crone nods her head in his direction. 'He got 'is cock out earlier. When you were asleep.' She sniffs and works her empty mouth. 'Not that you missed much.' She lifts her hand and raises her little finger.

I give a snort of laughter.

'The nurses had terrible trouble wiv 'im. He wouldn't put his clothes back on. And he's a big tall fella. They had to give him an injection in the end.'

I crane my head to get a better look at this reprobate. A mournful, unshaven face gazes back at me. 'Oh dear,' he says again.

Aware the senior nurse is waddling to her desk at the end of the ward I make an effort to catch the old man's eye. His gaze snags on mine and I lick my lips. Feeling a thrill of wickedness, I allow my eyes to grow lustrous. I haven't the power for anything particularly useful, but I try my best. He is looking at me in bewilderment so I smile and lick my lips again, my tongue slow.

A spark of interest appears in his eyes. 'Oh dear, oh dear, oh dear,' he says. I nod and smile. He begins to sit up. His hands disappears beneath the sheet that covers his long ridge of a body.

'Uh oh, he's off again,' the crone says with a cackle. I am starting to like her.

The old man's arms and legs appear like tentacles as he wrestles with the sheets and blankets to free himself. I am delighted to see he has managed to wriggle out of his hospital pyjamas and is baring his hairy backside to the senior nurse who looks as if she will explode with outrage.

'Mr Sanderson!' she bellows down the ward. 'Get back into bed this instant!'

'Oh dear,' he replies. He is out of his bed now, his eyes locked on mine. His manhood wobbles between his thighs, an unsavoury looking muddle of flesh, like a child's balloon animal, nestling in a thick bush of grey hair.

Senior Nurse is on the phone shouting. The crone is waving her arms and yelling encouragement. 'Go on! Start running!'

The old man grips the rail at the end of the bed. A grin is spreading across his face. 'Oh dear, oh dear.' He takes a step towards me.

Everyone jumps as the double doors crash open. Two security guards run in. The Senior Nurse grabs the old man's arm and he swings round. He begins to rub his groin against her leg with enthusiasm. I am laughing so hard my stomach is aching. The crone opposite continues to goad him on with whoops and whistles.

The security guards pull the old man away from the nurse and grab two pillows to protect the old boy's modesty. The ward is in uproar.

'Be *quiet*, Mrs Shearer,' Senior Nurse scolds the crone, who sticks up her middle fingers. I chuckle.

The struggles continue, but eventually the guards calm everything down and they bundle the old man, still with his pillow loincloth, out of the ward. I hear his cries, 'oh dear, oh dear,' gradually fade into the distance.

# CHAPTER 6: ANGIE

Well, the diet went out the window that weekend. As soon as I stumbled back into the flat, gasping with pain, I ordered a vast Chinese takeaway. Without hesitation, I worked my way through the lot, alternating swallows with swigs of a nasty red wine I'd found at the back of the cupboard.

When I'd finished, I searched the kitchen for more food: Bowls of cereal, slice upon slice of buttered toast with jam, bags of crisps, bars of chocolate. Whenever I saw Andy and Kelly in my mind's eye, I would push more food down until I couldn't see them anymore.

I did everything I could to stop myself thinking. Alcohol helped. Sunday morning I opened a bottle of gin and sipped at it like medicine until I passed out around lunchtime. I was woken up, bleary-eyed, by my phone vibrating next to my head.

Andy.

An explosion of fury crackled through my chest, coupled with a wash of nausea. Ignoring the call, I raced to the kitchen sink and threw up. Only when I'd washed my face and rinsed my mouth out did I find the courage to go and look at my phone. I had fourteen missed calls from the fucker.

He'd left a voicemail. I was tempted to throw my phone out through the bloody window, but curiosity got the better of me and I held the phone to my ear. Hearing his voice was so agonising I couldn't bear it.

'Angie. Er… it's me,' the recording began. 'I've been trying to get hold of you all day, where are you?' Irritation was creeping into his voice and there was a pause. I pictured him trying to calm down before he carried on. 'Um… so… Vik mentioned you were going to come over to The Bell on Friday night and Steve thought he saw your car. The thing is… the thing is I think you might have seen something and I need to explain what's going on. I'm sorry Angie. I should have sorted this ages ago.' There was a big, gusty sigh. 'Look. We need to talk. Can we meet tomorrow? I'm still at… er… Pete's tonight. Can you come to the Beacon when you finish work? We can talk then…' I pressed the phone to my ear as it fell silent – had he hung up? Then I heard him breathe. He cleared his throat. 'I'm sorry, Angie.'

'Should have sorted this?' I said out loud to myself, breaking the dusty silence of the flat. 'Fucking sorted this?' As if I was a difficult customer moaning about a dodgy bog installation, I thought, fuming.

I needed fresh air. My skin crawled and I couldn't sit still. I was livid; I rolled the word around on my tongue, relishing the hard smoothness of it. Yes. Livid. Worms of outrage squirmed in my belly sending shock waves down to my fingers and toes. Jumping to my feet, I paced backwards and forwards. Sentences formed in my head. 'How can you treat me like this? Do all the years we've been together mean nothing to you?' I imagined spitting in his face. 'If it wasn't for me and my Dad you'd be nothing, you piece of shit!'

The flat wasn't big enough to contain my rage. I headed out, smashing the front door back on its hinges, not caring when it smacked against the wall. I walked straight through the muttering Indian woman and a clammy shockwave undulated through me. She straightened and looked at me with sharp dark eyes. I saw her mouth open as she tried to speak.

'And you can just FUCK OFF!' I roared, my voice rising to a shout. Her face brightened and her lips moved. She began to follow me, beckoning with her twiggy brown arms. Gold threads on her sari glittered. With a thud of foreboding, I saw a young man appear and slide into the shadows behind her, his head hung at a strange angle. I shook my head to dislodge the rising whispers.

Fuck!

They always went mad if I acknowledged them.

'I can't deal with this right now!' I warned. I needed to get away. 'No, no, no,' I said. 'Not now.' I turned and cannoned down the stairs, holding onto the rail for dear life. I burst out into the car park and bent double in a desperate attempt to get my breath back. I'd forgotten my coat so within seconds I was frozen.

It was only when I had gone through every possible thing that Andy could say to me, and how I would respond (with great dignity and calm, no begging. No way) that I wore myself out enough to retreat to the flat. Quite a crowd of ones had gathered as I climbed the stairs, but I kept my eyes lowered and made for the door without looking at them and eventually they started to disperse.

It took the rest of the gin to ease me to sleep. My dreams were fractured, fragmented - Andy and Kelly kissed and smiled and broke apart to laugh at me, their mouths wet and wide. My dad, frowning as he tried to speak. Faces of the ones pulling at my clothes, mouthing their messages.

When I woke up, I felt like I'd been wrestling a bear. Every muscle ached and my joints were so stiff I struggled to walk. I washed my face but didn't bother brushing my teeth. I stared at my bleak, wiped-out reflection and stuck out my tongue. It was covered in a revolting yellow sludge. I was grotesque. I watched myself shrug. Who gives a shit?

It took me half an hour to decide what to wear. What does one wear to meet a cheating arsehole of a husband? I wondered. I noted with a kind of weary surprise I was still wearing what I'd wore to the pub on Friday, now stained with grease and food spills. Listlessly, I pulled on my big jeans and jumper, noting - without caring - that they smelled unwashed.

My long, restless night had dampened the fire of my rage, leaving me exhausted and low. To fan the flames I forced myself to picture Andy and Kelly writhing around each other like snakes. I clenched my fists. Right. I thought. I'm ready.

*

The Beacon was a café near the school. We often used to meet there for lunch as it was so central and easy to park. I didn't bother going to work. For the first time in thirty years, I just didn't turn up. I couldn't muster the energy to make a call and the thought of phoning Sharon or Vicky and explaining what had happened made me feel sick.

It was raining when I got out of the car. I could see the big window of the café across the road but there was no sign of Andy. The horror of what was happening kept hitting me. It all seemed so unreal. I remembered bouncing out of the car on Friday night, eager to rekindle the fire of romance with my husband. It made me wince to think of my hopeful face, all dolled up to the nines thinking I was the bee's knees, walking towards the scene that would blow my life apart.

I licked my lips. I was conscious of a stale smell wafting up from my body. I couldn't care less. In fact, I wanted Andy to see what he'd done to me. What he'd reduced me to. What could I do? Slap on a load of make up and put on a fancy dress? How could I compete with Kelly?

As I learned on Friday, it didn't matter how much care I took with my hair, how well I applied make-up, how nicely I dressed – nothing could disguise the fact that I was nearly 50, and stones overweight. You've only yourself to blame, a little voice whispered.

My mind played the movie of the pair of them curled around each other on a loop. It made me want to claw off my skin. Bastard! Slut! Fuckers! I welcomed the flare of anger - it warmed me. What the fuck did they think they were doing? What had I done to be screwed over like this? We were best friends. Partners. Grief pulled at my chest but I shoved it away, I refused to be sad - anger felt much better. I thought of Kelly simpering about at work, smiling at me over tea whilst screwing my husband behind my back.

There. That's better, I thought as rage bubbled.

Andy was sitting at the back. I faltered. The shape of his head was so familiar. My Andy. In the minute or two it took me to cross over to his table, memories of our life together clicked through my head like an out of control slideshow.

The speech I had planned was waiting to be delivered. It took me quite a while to squeeze myself around the table to sit but eventually I flopped down, wedging into a plastic chair and looked up to face Andy. All my carefully rehearsed words flew out of the window.

'So you've been fucking Kelly you cheating bastard.' I said, my voice clear and sharp, causing everyone in the café to turn towards us.

'Keep your voice down, Angie! Christ!' Andy whispered, leaning across the table as if he wanted to hold me down. I pulled my hands away.

'Well? Haven't you? I know what I saw, you piece of shit.' Andy sat back and looked discomfited. He rubbed his nose. He always did that when he'd been caught out, I thought. The surreal craziness of the situation struck me again and I swallowed hard, gripping onto my righteous anger with both hands.

'Look, Angie, I'm sorry OK? Me and Kelly...' Her name in his mouth made me feel sick. A roaring in my ears drowned out what he was saying. '...for months now, she's been on at me to tell you, and I should have told you, but...'

A teenage girl in a beehive was rapping soundlessly on the counter to get my attention but I ignored her, refusing to catch her eye. She was staring at me and I noticed her clothes were stained; I turned my head away from her. Not now. Not now. I thought. Andy continued to speak but his voice kept echoing in and out. The girl was more real to me than Andy. Tempted though I was to zone out, I focused back on him, trying to concentrate on the excuses and justifications drivelling from his mouth.

'I'm hungry,' I interrupted him. I waved at the waitress and ordered a large hot dog with extra chips and a side of onion rings. 'On you,' I said. Andy's face clouded with disapproval when I put in my order, but seeing the look in my eyes, he quickly rearranged his features into a mask of benign concern. I wanted to punch him.

I could see he was impatient to continue with his own rehearsed speech, but I wouldn't let him. We sat in silence until the food arrived. I started to eat and every time he tried to speak, I lifted a finger to shut him up. Finally, I wiped my mouth free of ketchup and sat back in my seat, swigging the last of my diet coke. I forced out a burp, enjoying the look of disgust on Andy's face.

'OK. I said. Off you go. Tell me.' I gritted my teeth to hide the pain.

Andy put down his mug of tea and reached to run his hands through his hair until he remembered it was sprayed to hide the bald patch, so he stopped and fiddled with a pack of sweetener instead. He flicked it between his fingers making an irritating snapping sound. He cleared his throat. I could see he didn't know where to start.

'How long. Andy. Let's start with that. How long?' I said.

'On and off... a year? Two years?'

My mouth fell open in shock. 'Two years?? Are you joking?' My voice was rising again. 'Two years! Really?'

We stared at each other and I gulped with panic; no, he wasn't joking. Stupid question. I searched his face but I couldn't see my Andy there anymore. The great balloon of anger that had carried me through popped and shrivelled into shreds of torn rubber. This was serious. Not a crazy fling we could work through, coming out stronger on the other side, which was what I realised I was expecting.

Taking a deep breath and swallowing my pride, I reached across for his hand. It felt so familiar in mine. 'Andy, listen to me. I know we've lost our way a bit but... we've been married nearly thirty years.' My voice began to break. A lump had formed in my throat.

He didn't answer.

'Andy?'

He let out a gusty sigh. His body looked tense and I could see he longed to be anywhere but here, and my heart gave another thud of panic.

'Angie…' he made a great effort to make his voice gentle and finally met my eyes. 'I'm going to move in with her. You and me… I'm sorry… It's over, Angie.'

I gave a great, involuntary, gasping sob. 'No. Andy. Please.' I gripped his hand again, desperate to remind him of our past. What we'd been through together. An icy wedge of fear settled in my stomach as his hand slithered away.

'You can't do this to me, Andy. Not after all this time. It's not right. You can't leave me alone like this. What am I going to do?' My skin prickled into goose bumps and I shivered with cold. I hated the whine in my voice, the desperation of it, but I couldn't seem to be able to control myself.

Andy stood up. I was trapped in my plastic chair, which was an even tighter fit after the enormous meal I'd eaten.

'Andy, please!' I said again. 'What would your mum say, eh? Don't do this.' For a second I saw him falter. His mother had loved me; she thought I was great for Andy. She became a bit of a replacement mum and I missed her every day since she passed.

It was below the belt but I didn't care. I would have said anything to stop him walking away. He sat back down and my heart jerked with hope but then I saw the look on his face and his expression was so shattered I was terrified; in that split second I knew what he was going to say. I even lifted my hands as if to shield myself from the blow.

'Kelly's pregnant.'

The blood drained from my face. I had never understood that expression, but I did then. The noise of the café faded and all I could hear was a high-pitched whine. My heart thudded. Stopped. Thudded again. I couldn't breathe. My hands were freezing. I couldn't breathe! I tried to suck in air but something was sitting on my chest. A pulse boomed in my ears. Was I having a heart attack?

Andy was tapping my arm, 'Angie. Angie! Christ! Here, have some water.' He signalled the guy behind the counter who brought over a glass. Andy held it to my mouth. The touch of the cool water against my lips brought me round. I drew a ragged breath, and then another. My pulse slowed.

'Kelly's pregnant?'

He couldn't look at me. The bastard.

'I'm sorry.'

'Yeah. You said.'

The silence that fell between us slowly filled with an unspoken conversation. He knew. He knew what damage, what hurt, those words would cause.

The trouble is. I knew he was sorry. I could see it on his face. No wonder he couldn't wait to get away. Who wanted to hang around once you'd ripped at an old wound until it bled? Wouldn't anyone want to escape, leaving the victim gasping like a hooked fish?

He'd flicked the sweetener wrapper so much the paper wore through and the powder spilled onto the table. His voice was soft as he spoke.

'You know I've always wanted kids. And when we found out you couldn't, well I gave up on the idea, but it never stopped me wanting them. And now I've got this chance… I didn't mean it to happen, but now it has…' He opened his hands.

The shock and hurt bubbling inside me wove together to form a vile, bile-filled ball of hatred. My face twisted with the force of it. 'You're over fucking fifty,' I sneered, 'you're an old man. His mates will think you're his granddad. You know she probably put a pin in the condom.' The words spat out of me. 'She's just trying to trap you, you stupid bastard.'

'I'm going to be a Dad,' he said. 'I can't wait.'

I couldn't speak. I forced myself out of my seat, wrenching my hip. My breathing was funny. I had forgotten how to breathe in and out, so as I left the café customers turned to see what was making that odd choking noise.

I wanted to walk straight off a bridge, or into a river. I wanted to do anything that would stop the pain. People looked at me strangely as I walked by and I realised I was moaning under my breath, 'no, no, no…'

*

The happiest Andy and I had ever been was the summer Jonathan was born. I was huge as a whale and suffered dreadfully in the hot weather.

The only comfort I could find was lying in a gigantic paddling pool slap bang in the middle of the shared garden. I was so itchy and hot I didn't care. Neighbours would walk past and ask if I was having a water birth, ha ha, but their comments bounced off my fat, brown, beaming body.

Andy had spent weeks painting the back room sunshine yellow. He'd even gone so far as to sketch little pictures from Winnie the Pooh, the daft sod. We didn't know what we were having, so thought yellow would be perfect.

Those were balmy, dreamy days, I thought as I walked into the rain and wind, my feet blurring and the air burning in my lungs. The faster I walked, the faster the memories came.

We'd sit in front of the TV and I'd balance a plate of food on my belly; we'd laugh seeing it bounce around as the baby kicked. The due date came and went and the long summer days rolled on, as hot as Spain - we'd agree with each other.

I didn't deserve to be this happy, I kept thinking. Andy was attentive and loving, excited about the baby. Something has to go wrong, I would say, nobody stays this happy for long. Everyone would reassure me. The midwife, the Doctor, all my friends - some new mothers themselves. Everything's going to be fine! They'd say.

I was young, married to the man I loved, and I couldn't wait to meet the little one. August had just begun when I started to get impatient. I was two weeks past my due date and could barely move. I'd given up on stairs and waddled everywhere. Everything was ready.

'Hurry up, baby!' I used to whisper to my swollen bump in the night as, unable to sleep, I lay smiling in the dark. I was so excited about this big change in our lives I wasn't even scared of the birth any more.

'I'm not feeling much movement,' I said to the midwife as she finished our weekly check-up.

'Oooh it's getting a bit crowded in there now,' she replied. 'You're what, two weeks overdue now?'

I nodded. 'Yes two weeks over today.'

'Nothing to worry about, baby's grown nicely and is running out of space. You often notice baby moving less at this stage. Let's book you in for Saturday morning to keep an eye on you both. Hopefully everything will kick off soon!'

She waved me away with a smile but she hadn't stopped the growing curdle of unease which now constantly thrummed beneath the surface.

It was a sunny Friday morning when I shook Andy awake.

'Andy, I'm really worried, I don't think I've noticed the baby move since about 8 o'clock last night.'

'Ah, babe, don't worry. Didn't the midwife say they slowed down a bit at this stage?' He threw a sleepy arm across me and patted my bump. 'I'm sure it's fine.'

Anxiety drove me out of bed and I started throwing on my clothes. 'No, Andy. There's something wrong, I just know it. I'm going to call the midwife.'

Andy was pulling on his trousers when I came back in. 'She said to come in now,' I said, numb. I knew a catastrophe was coming.

We arrived at the birthing unit; I was sick and clammy with anxiety. Something was wrong. Andy tried to tell me everything would be OK, but I knew with a heart-pounding certainty he was lying.

The midwife held the monitor to my belly and, for the first time since I got pregnant, she couldn't find the heartbeat. The baby had died. She didn't say so, but I knew. She tried to blame the equipment but wouldn't look at me. She told us to go to hospital to get scanned.

The journey passed in a blur. It took us ages to find the right place to go - eventually we were met by a midwife. She unsuccessfully tried to find a heartbeat and called for the sonographer who searched for what felt like hours before shaking his head. Nothing.

I asked her to leave us alone. Andy put his arms around me, and we wept.

It was late Friday night. I was in a state of shock but I was calm, and Andy never stopped holding my hand. The hardest thing I have ever had to do was to phone my Dad. 'Dad,' I said. 'I'm so sorry. The baby died.' He cried out, and his wail of despair haunts me still. He told me later I sounded as if I was drowning.

We talked and I told him I'd call back. His sadness was terrible. It was then I started to go into labour. I pleaded for a Caesarean but was persuaded that delivering the baby naturally would be the best thing to do. When I argued they told me that it could put future pregnancies at risk; I gave in and agreed.

The medical staff, professional and expressionless, started to administer drugs to speed up the process. I phoned my Dad back - it was about 2 in the morning now - he asked if he could come over: he couldn't bear sitting at home.

The next two days passed in a blur. I was given an epidural that meant I had to lie down, which I hated. The baby had swung round against my back causing a crippling ache. I wish they would have let me go on all fours or at least stand up, I'm sure it would have helped. Dad arrived and couldn't stop crying. I longed and longed for my Mum.

It took me ages to fully dilate. Saturday evening came around and I was ready to push. In the position I was in, along with the epidural, I had no idea how to push properly. The midwife helped but it wasn't easy. Later, I was absolutely astonished to discover I was pushing for five hours. I thought it was no longer than ten minutes.

By Sunday morning, worries were raised about my blood pressure. I was exhausted and longed to go home. Afterwards, Andy told me he couldn't help thinking if he could just take me home everything would be OK. Finally, the staff said they were going to try forceps and if that didn't work, I would have to have a section. I was ready for anything by that point and in pain.

After an episiotomy and forceps, Jonathan was finally born at 6am, Sunday 9th August. The relief was incredible. The baby was taken away to be washed and looked after but I didn't really notice, I was dazed and exhausted. The pain of labour had ended straight away though I then had to suffer the agony of having the placenta scraped out, which was indescribable.

'Did you know what you were having?' the midwife asked.

I hadn't even thought about the sex of the baby. She looked at us with huge sympathy. 'You had a little boy,' she said. I can still hear the sound of Andy's sobs. I held his hand as tight as I could.

I asked Dad to go and see Jonathan; I didn't know whether I wanted to see him. I asked him to see if he was OK to look at, because I didn't want to be frightened of him. He returned to tell me he was beautiful.

They took us into a double private room away from all the other new mothers with healthy, live babies. Whenever I heard a new-born crying it was a knife in my side. They brought Jonathan to us. When the midwife put him in my arms, bundled in a blue blanket with a little hat on, we saw his face and dark lips, blue because of the lack of oxygen; we saw the scrapes on his cheeks from the forceps and Andy said 'Oh, our poor little boy' and I saw how beautiful he was. I held him and cried.

He weighed just under 9 pounds and was two feet long. As I wept, his body jiggled horribly, like a doll, and I felt afresh the tragedy of his death. Andy held him and then they put him in a crib by the bed. We fell asleep wrapped tight around each other.

Through the funeral, through the post-mortem - we discovered there was no obvious reason for Jonathan's death, like many stillbirths - I was buoyed by a wave of determined optimism: I would get through this. Have another baby. All Would Be Fine.

The second worst day in my life was when the consultant sat me down, perched awkwardly on the edge of his desk, and told me that I would never be able to have children.

'I'm sorry, Angela,' he had said. 'There was a great deal of damage caused during your son's delivery and your cervix was compromised. I am afraid you will never be able to carry a baby to term.'

*

The screaming roar of the train jolted me back to the present. I was drenched. I'd been oblivious to the rain, and water ran down my face, my lungs were raw. I had managed to walk all the way across town and had stopped only when I bumped against the wall of the bridge looking down over the station. I could see the tracks snaking back and forth.

I was doubled over with the pain. Passers-by looked at me in disgust and crossed the road. All I could see was Jonathan's face. Usually, I couldn't recall what he looked like, but that day it was as if I'd only just put him down in his chilled cot. I remembered with a cruel clarity the wounds on his face and the terrible mixture of love, pity and shameful revulsion I had felt.

And now Andy would be holding a child, but it would be pink and bonny, not blue and scarred.

The despair was inescapable. I gripped the edges of the wall. What was the point? What was I going to do? Go back to work until I retired? Stay inside, watching TV until I ate myself to death? I imagined seeing Andy and Kelly walking past with their baby and the thought made me cry out loud.

There was a flicker at the corner of my eye. With a crushing weariness, I turned to see the ones, just two or three, but more were coming. They were gathering behind me. Were they going to help me or push me? I wondered.

The tracks gleamed in a sudden shaft of sunlight. A path curved deliciously in front of me. A train was gathering pace as it left the station, it roared towards me.

With mild surprise I realised I was standing on the wall. The wind buffeted me a bit but I stayed steady. Whispers hissed behind me. Oh those urgent whispers, I thought absently, well, now I never will find out what they are saying.

The glitter and shine of the rails blinded me. It made me sway. For a second I paused. Was this the right thing? Think about the poor train driver! I heard someone say, it sounded like my mother.

Then I remembered Jonathan. And Andy leaving. And my crap job. And my empty flat. And my loneliness. And I closed my eyes.

# CHAPTER 7: FRIEDA SUFFERS

I am waiting impatiently for my discharge date when Maeve arrives at the ward. She's wearing a revolting coat the colour of bananas, it is certainly a change from the drab navy and grey she has been wearing. Will must be on the mend.

'Morning, Frieda!' she says, whipping out the dying flowers from my bedside vase and refilling it with fresh ones, red roses this time. I savour their crimson-velvet sizzle on my tongue, a delectable change from the dead-white sterility of the hospital ward. Maeve is bouncing with energy.

She sits at my side, her skin luminous with the shine of the righteous do-gooder. 'I've been worrying about you so much over the past few days. Since our chat, Mike and I have hardly spoken about anything else! We were thinking of putting up an ad in Laurie's shop, or even the local paper and then I find the solution right on my doorstep. Remember Andy Cartwright from the village? I think he's done some work for you.'

'Yes I know him.' I say, struggling to sit up, my back stiffer than ever and my hip still sore. 'He's a louse. An untrustworthy, shifty little man. I only use him because he's the only plumber in the village.'

Maeve's cheeks flush. 'Well, yes, I agree with you actually. It's a pity we all have to rely on him. But I was actually going to talk to you about his wife Angela. The poor thing is in a terrible way.' Her voice lowers and she looks around to see if anyone is listening. 'Andy has got some woman pregnant and has left Angie. After thirty years! She's devastated. In fact,' she drops her voice so low I have to lean forward uncomfortably to hear. I have no interest in the goings-on of some plumber's wife. 'I think she's gone a bit mad. She's been terribly depressed. We've had to watch her all the time as she keeps trying to…' here Maeve's voice drops altogether and she mouths, 'take her own life'. I roll my eyes.

'That's all very interesting, Maeve,' I say, sarcasm sliding into my words. 'But what has she got to do with anything?'

'The thing is, Frieda dear, she's been living with us for a while now and she's much better. She's actually a sweet old thing, and, well, she needs a fresh start…'

I laugh until a cough rattles in my chest, 'got sick of her, have you? You and Mike?'

'That's not fair, Frieda,' Maeve's cheeks are pink. 'She's a kind woman who's been through a lot these past months. We've worked hard to help get back to normal, and Mike says she needs to move on. We thought she could come and live with you. She could act as a bit of a housekeeper and nurse until you're back to your old self.'

'Over my dead body,' is my immediate and instinctive reaction. 'I barely know this woman and you're proposing moving her in? Into *my* house?'

There is a long pause. My words hang in the air between us.

'Right. Fine,' Maeve says, standing up with an abrupt rush of movement. 'I'll go and organise the Care Home for you then, shall I?' She is quivering with fury. The mouse who roared, I thought.

'You really can be terribly ungrateful you know, Frieda. I hate to say it, but it's true. Mike and I have a lot on our plate at the moment, and we've been thinking and thinking of how to help you and Angie, and you just throw it back in our face. We're very fond of you, as you know, and we owe you a great deal, but I cannot see what else we can do if you refuse to meet us half way.' Her voice is high and two bright spots of colour spring to her cheeks.

With a sigh, I put out my hand to still her. 'Stop, Maeve. I shouldn't have said that.' Sensing Charlie's encouragement, I swallow my pride. 'Thank you. I'm sure this Angela woman will be fine. I just want to get back home, and if this is the only way, then so be it.' I am conscious of how ungracious I sound so I try a smile. It's not easy.

Maeve is mollified. 'I understand, dear. I tell you what, I'll go and chat to Angie and get her to come up here and meet you. How about that?'

I shrug.

'She's a very calm and capable woman, you know. Sally says she's the best cleaner she's ever had. And reliable.' She looks at me to try and judge my response but I keep my face neutral.

Her eyes light up, pleased to be solving the problems I have created for her. My guts knot with sickness at the thought of someone in my house, poking through my things. I can barely countenance it, but what choice do I have? Any longer in this damned place and I'll be jumping out of the window.

*

I have to wait another interminable week before Maeve returns. I have only had the strength to return to the house once, and it is still the same. The tears and ripped thread continue to allow the dark to seep through. It breaks my heart and fury fills me anew. How hard can it be to put the statues back?

Charlie is getting increasingly bored. I am surprised it has taken him this long to grow tired of my problems. He can't go far, however, so he spends his time drifting around the ward, reading books over people's shoulders and spooking the nurses by walking through them.

He is a great comfort. Though I would never tell him so. Sometimes we talk about the past for hours as the old folk sleep in their beds, but he still won't tell me why he is really here and why he, of all my ghosts, is the one to be called back.

I am entertaining myself by watching Sister Trotter working through paperwork at her desk. She sighs, flipping back and forth through piles of paper, making an effort to seem terribly important. Every time she puts down her pen, I flick my fingers to make it roll to the edge of the desk and fall off. Childish but satisfying.

Too fat to bend over, every time she loses one she gives a big huff and pulls another from a box in her top drawer. Eventually she runs out and slams her files shut, biros littering the floor. A new, young nurse approaches the desk; she can't be much more than 20. She's a good-looking girl, but the closer she gets to Nurse Trotter, the more her face becomes a mask of nerves.

'Yes?' Nurse Trotter makes it clear she is being interrupted in the middle of doing something very urgent and of great consequence.

'I'm sorry to bother you, Nurse Trotter, but...'

'What is it?'

'Nurse Percival told me to ask you if you knew where the latest shift schedules were?'

'As I have said a number of times before, and in an email to the entire department, they can be found online, in the first folder, marked shift schedules.' She gives an exaggerated sigh. 'The man's an idiot. How many times do I have to tell these people?' she says, appealing to an invisible audience.

Not sure who Trotter is talking to, the young girl gives a nervous glance around the ward. 'Er... Yes, Nurse,'

'Right. Is that all?' Nurse Trotter gazes up, her eyebrows raised. She couldn't make it more clear how insignificant she found this interruption.

'Yes. That's all.' I could see the young girl gathering up courage. 'The thing is...'

Nurse Trotter rolls her eyes. She makes a point of placing a finger to mark her place in a file before looking back up, eyebrows raised. 'The thing is what?'

'Well... sorry, Nurse Trotter, but Nurse Percival said he's looked online, using the link you used in your email and he still can't find them.' She speaks in a rush, gaze firmly on the ceiling.

With a gusty sigh, Nurse Trotter squeezes herself from her chair and lumbers over to the computer behind her. Frowning, she clicks at the keyboard.

'Well they were there this morning. Some idiot who doesn't know what he's doing has obviously moved them.'

Nurse Trotter makes no attempt to hide the contempt in her voice. The whole ward can hear and see the effect her words are having on the poor nurse, who looks mortified. Trotter clicks impatiently with her mouse. 'Here they are. God knows how they ended up there. Pen!'

Without taking her eyes from the screen, she holds out her hand and clicks her fingers. The young nurse desperately searches the desk. 'For God's sake, girl. Get me a pen - if it's not too much trouble?' The girl, finding no pen, drops to her knees and scrabbles beneath the chair to retrieve a biro. She reappears, red-faced and flustered and places the pen in Trotter's outstretched palm; her hands are shaking.

How I long to turn that pen into a poisonous snake with jewelled skin, and fangs that glint like diamonds in the light. I try my best. I ball up my hands and whisper urgent words, gathering up all the energy I can find in this dry, over-heated air.

I manage to send a few little red zigzags of fire, but they sizzle unnoticed on Trotter's uniform and drop to the floor. Ach, I hate this place with every cell of my being, I think. I want to scream aloud. I want to go home.

*

Days pass. I wait and worry about the house and what lies hidden within. I can't shake off a sense of dread. The minutes stretch like elastic and I strain my ears to hear the hourly pips on the almost-too-quiet-to-hear local radio they play all the time. Charlie and I are waiting, but he won't tell me for what – I'm not sure he knows.

I sink into my memories again, my only escape from this antiseptic nightmare populated by bullies, the sick, and the dying. Despite the tiresome exercises, my muscles continue to wither; I can tell Charlie worries I am not strong enough for what he knows is coming.

'You can't do this alone,' he keeps complaining. 'There isn't much time. We need to get you out of here and then you must find someone so you can pass all of this on.' He reaches to touch my necklace; I brush away his hand.

'I don't like being around people, it's bad enough I can't go home without a keeper being employed – as if I were a child,' I say, smoothing the gold, heavy and cool around my throat. 'And besides, I'd be a terrible teacher.'

Lilith had endless patience; something I never learned.

*

'Slowly, Frieda, slowly…' Her words drift across the years to me now as clear as the day she spoke them. As a child I thought her voice beautiful, compared to the coarse accents of my family, the lilt of the East sounded wonderfully exotic.

The sun is hot on my back as I bend over the mortar trying not to sneeze as the musky, earth smell of the dried leaves I am crushing is released into the air. Lilith is with her bees. She has hives dotted all over the garden behind her cottage in the woods, their legs sunk deep into the long grass.

I have grown used to the constant buzzing. I put down the pestle and watch in amazement as Lilith walks from hive to hive. The bees circle her, spinning in and out of the long bolts of her hair but she is unaffected, seeming not to notice as they dance around. The heat and the monotonous drone is making me sleepy. Lilith dips her hands into the hives and pulls up racks of waxy honeycomb. Golden drops swell and fall, coating the grass with sticky streaks.

'Keep going, Frieda. You haven't finished,' she nods at my pestle. I sigh and carry on grinding the leaves, pushing my sweat soaked hair away from my forehead.

I am bored. I want to do the exciting things Lilith has started to teach me. The whispered words that stir up the forest. With a jolt of remembered excitement, I picture those days in early spring when we wandered the woods and Lilith showed me how to touch the green sizzle of the leaves. I shiver as I remember the power I felt pricking my skin and sparking from my fingers.

Grinding herbs and watching Lilith wend her way around the buzzing hives, lazy and languorous, was too dull for my blood.

Finally, the herbs are crushed to a powder and Lilith returns. In her long, white hands are two small bowls. In one lies a thick, amber pool of honey warmed by the sun. It moves like a golden oil and smells delicious. My fingers dart out to scoop a mouthful, but a hiss from Lilith stops me.

Lumpen chunks of squashed honeycomb fill the other bowl. They have been squeezed by the press until the last drops of honey and nectar have been removed, and now lie twisted and misshapen. Lilith places both bowls on the table, close to my powdered herbs.

'Bees have their own magic,' she says. 'Their honey can be used to help wounds and heal burns. It can stop sickness and soothe a cough. It's been used for thousands of years and there are jars of honey found from Ancient Egypt that could still be eaten. Taste. This is honey from bees who have feasted on clover.'

The sweetness is intoxicating.

'We can also use it to mix with herbs to make a paste and that's what we're doing with your sage. I need it for Mrs Fidler, her arthritis is very bad.'

Lilith turns to the wax and picks it up, pressing it between her fingers. 'This can be used to make sweet-smelling candles. If you rub it onto leather it will shield it from water.' She holds a piece to my nose. 'You can make scent, and balm for your lips and dry skin, and it can be safely eaten so it is very good to mix with herbs and flowers as a healing ointment.'

Lilith's voice murmurs on and twines with the buzzing of the bees, I feel my eyes droop. The heat, the sounds, and the sweetness of the honey is overpowering. It is as I have been drugged.

A loud crash startles me so violently my hands jerk and I knock the bowl of honey to the floor. I moan as the honey splatters over the grass and sinks into the ground.

'What the hell are you doing filling her head with stuff and nonsense?' It is my father; his face is red with fury. I can smell the stink of beer on him. He is an incongruous sight in the clearing with the trees soaring above him. His coat looks too small and his shirt is twisted, the collar sticking up at an odd angle. The meat of his belly pushes forward, straining the buttons.

His stink, his redness, his bulk is a shocking contrast to the cool, slender length of Lilith with her coils of silver hair and faded cotton frock.

He pushes his face right into hers. 'What have I told you about taking her here with you? She's a child. She should be home with her mother, not meddling with this unholy trash.'

At this, he sweeps his hand along the table sending everything flying. Lilith's tiny bottles of ointment and medicine fall and are smashed by the mortar falling on top of them. The noise makes me scream and I cover my ears. Lilith is holding up her hand, but he ignores her and I see him reach for her hair.

'You bully!' I scream. 'Leave her alone!'

Flames of rage are scorching through my brain. I look around desperately for something to throw at him, to get him away from Lilith. She flashes me a warning over his shoulder but I shake my head.

'No, no, you must leave,' I keep saying.

'You were told I didn't want my daughter having any part of this!' He is roaring in Lilith's face, spittle sprays from his lips. She does not flinch, but it enrages me.

'Pa! Please! It's not her fault!' I yell with all my thirteen-year-old might. 'I'm the one who stole away to be here, mother doesn't know.' But he doesn't hear me. He winds a length of Lilith's hair around his fist and pulls.

'Please stop!' I am sobbing now as I grab his shoulder. He twitches me off; I am as insignificant as a fly.

As I fall back, I knock against a hive. Maddened, I tear off the top and start screaming words. Lilith's face crumples with shock, but it's too late, the bees are gathering. The buzzing become a roar of noise as they circle faster and faster. I can't see him. The air is black.

Father's arms begin to windmill as the stinging begins. I swing down my arms and the cloud thickens. I am urging them on until Lilith stumbles forward and catches at my hand.

'You'll kill him,' she gasps.

'Yes!' I reply. I raise my arms again.

'No. Frieda. Stop.' She imprisons my hands. Her strength is phenomenal.

She begins to chant and I am outraged when the cobweb of gold ripples from her, dispersing the bees until I can see Father. He has crossed his arms over his face. I see with satisfaction great welts are swelling all over his body.

Father roars like a bull and charges past us, eyes swollen shut. He crashes through the wood and is gone.

\*

I awake with a gasp. Drenched with sweat, my hands are shaking and I am disorientated. The white walls distort and loom over me until I blink them still. Taking a deep breath to steady myself, I allow the memory of Lilith and the wood to fade. Still, it is the hospital ward that feels unreal and the product of a dream.

More unwanted memories! Before I couldn't remember my father's face, and now I can see him whenever I close my eyes. I want to shake my hands to clear the echoes of violence and chaos. It was that moment Lilith realised how dangerous I was, I think with a smile.

'How lovely to see you smiling, Frieda!' a familiar voice exclaims. It is Maeve. A crackle of static announces Charlie's arrival. I don't turn to look, but it reassures me to know he is there.

Today Maeve wears a long dress in a vivid apple green. It looks faintly ridiculous. She is followed by the stoutest woman I have ever seen in my life. She is so strikingly fat I see the heads of the bed-ridden patients snap right to follow her with their eyes, like girls in a chorus line. This must be Angela. She is not only fat, she is tall, and has to lean back to counter-balance the great weight of her tummy, which lifts up and down as she walks.

Her thighs are so big they force her to waddle, and I can see the sweat on her forehead and the sound of her heavy breathing from here. Good God. How is she even going to fit through the door?

'Here we are!' Maeve sings. 'Angie, this is Mrs B, I don't think you've met but she knows your Andy.' She blushes at her tactlessness. 'Hmm, yes, well, never mind about him.' She turns to Angela and brings her closer to the bed. 'As you can see Mrs B is in a bit of a pickle and will need lots of looking after. And there's plenty of room in her house for you, Angie, so good all round.'

Angela's head is down. A trail of angry pimples shade her left cheek. She has no make-up on and her skin is pasty, shadowed grey with ill health. Her hair is short, dark, and threaded with grey. It looks like she has been running her fingers through it as it sticks up in tufts at the back. Her features are small and squashed in the big, round, loaf of her face.

I watch her as Maeve witters on. Angela stands with an unnatural stillness. She is entirely passive, like a giant statue. I am drawn to her calm; it is striking in contrast to Maeve's buzzing, almost frantic energy. I am curious enough to move my fingers, flicking a little dart of a spark. I watch her jump and she looks up.

Her eyes immediately flick to my left and her face blanches with shock. She takes a step back and looks as if she will fall. What on earth...?

A bolt of energy electrifies me.

'You can see him can't you?' Craning my neck to check for Charlie I see he is as surprised as I am. 'Who are you?' I ask in wonder.

Maeve continues chatting away, oblivious to the current sparking between me and this giantess of a woman. The only person I knew who could see the dead as I can was Lilith. I can sense Charlie's excitement and I flick him away, impatiently, as I sense he is leaning down to whisper in my ear. Angela and I stare at each other and I scan her again to look for any signs of anything special. There is nothing. She is a lump, a washed-out, washed-up grotesque. But she can see Charlie, I know she can.

This electrifying discovery almost makes me forget to ask Maeve about the statues. I am struck dumb when Maeve confesses she has not returned them. I have to cling to the hope the house is safe, tucked as it is before an ancient wood. Some protection is still there, I comfort myself.

Maeve is still talking. I am tired and want them to go. 'So I suggest, when you're discharged, Angie comes with you in the ambulance and helps you settle back in. Where do you want her to bunk, Frieda?'

'She's not having any of the main bedrooms,' I snap. 'There's too many valuables in there and she might be as light-fingered as her husband.' Maeve flinches and sends Angela an apologetic look, but she remains impassive, as if she hadn't heard. 'She can have the housekeeper's rooms at the back of the house on the ground floor. There's a separate kitchen and lavatory so she can keep out of my way, except when I need her.'

'Well that's settled then!' Maeve claps her hands together. 'I'll chat to the Doctor and get everything organised.'

She gives me a kiss and I smell talcum powder on her skin. She leaves, and Angela follows, shuffling after her, a gigantic golem in squashed down plimsolls and faded leggings.

# CHAPTER 8: ANGIE

It was a miserable day when we pulled up outside the old building I had known all my life, but only just discovered was called Pagan's Reach. It was enormous, foreboding in the rain, and sinister with its grey walls and huge windows, black with dirt. I stood, passive, as Maeve bustled around me.

I wanted to help her, as she yanked suitcases and bags out of the car, but couldn't muster up the energy. My arms and legs were leaden, the brain fog weighed heavy.

'Come on then! Let's get inside,' Maeve twittered. 'You'll catch your death.' She took my arm and led me to the front door. The wind gusted, a sudden bellowing rush, strong enough to make us stagger.

Maeve went to unlock the front door. Another breeze pulled at her clothes as she looked for the key. I tilted my face and felt the cold energy pummelling my skin; I pictured my body being picked up and spun by its force – a little, useless figure twirled and chased by the wind until it disappeared into the wild grey clouds, as choppy as a stormy sea.

The wide, shallow steps leading to the front door were stained and pitted, the windows filthy and the garden badly overgrown. It must have been magnificent once, I thought. Maeve was dwarfed by the front door that was twice her height. She was muttering under her breath, no matter how hard she tried to push it open, it wouldn't budge.

'We'll have to go around the back,' she shouted, the wind snatching at her words. I could hear a great thrashing in the woods as the trees snapped and bent. Leaving the suitcases by the door, we had to kick our way through the undergrowth choking the path along the side of the house.

The views were stunning, I could see right past the village across the valley to the town beyond. Banks of nettles clawed at my legs. My old leggings were no protection. A gate led to the back of the house but bindweed had wound it shut. Maeve made an undignified attempt to clamber over before giving up and opening it with a shove.

It was quieter around the back of the house. Maeve was sorting through a huge bunch of keys, which clinked and echoed in the sudden silence. The back of the house was less stately than the front. It looked older, more secretive, and its black windows were focused on the woods that stretched way up to the top of the hill.

'Here we go,' Maeve said at last as the door swung inwards. 'Angie, dear, I'll go back and get the bags. You go on through.'

I had the strangest feeling as I entered the large kitchen. It was as if I had interrupted an invisible crowd of people; as I came in, their whispered conversations fell suddenly silent.

'Hello?' I called, suddenly nervous. I pulled the door shut. It was a nice room, though bare, cold, and very dirty. Large grey flagstones needed a good wash, and in the middle of the floor stood a wooden table, empty except for an open, half-drunk bottle of wine and a broken glass, pieces of which had been placed in a wrap of kitchen roll on the side.

At one end of the kitchen was one of those big, posh ovens like Maeve had, but this one was black as paint and looked hundreds of years old. At the other was a fireplace set in a chimneybreast large enough to stand up in. A wooden chair, just like my Nan's, stretched its arms towards the empty grate as if desperate for warmth.

What I thought was a black cushion on the chair, turned out to be a cat; I jumped as it hissed and spat at me, fur on end, before shooting past out of the window over the sink. A gust of air signalled Maeve's return, and this time guilt prodded me into stepping forward and taking one of the (lighter) suitcases from her. They were mine, after all.

'This way,' Maeve said, leaving the kitchen and barrelling down a dark corridor. She moved so quickly I had to pant to keep up. I couldn't shake off the feeling we were moving through hidden presences who stepped aside silently as we walked.

I was grateful for the skin-numbing blankness Doc's tablets had given me. They had stopped me seeing the ones, but I was aware they still stood, waiting, at the edge of my consciousness.

*

It was Doc whose hands pulled me back as I stood, shivering, on the railway wall staring at the tracks below. He had swung me to the safety of the pavement without effort – he was a hell of a lot stronger than he looks, I remember thinking. He didn't ask me what I was doing.

'You're freezing, Angie,' he had said, touching my hands and face with his big, warm hands. 'Now you come back with me and I'll get Maeve to get the kettle on. I've just got back from London – always such a chore. The train was packed...' He continued chattering, carrying me along on a tidal wave of talk, until we arrived at his house, where we were greeted by a joyous, spinning and leaping Dolly clattering around in the front hall.

I had never heard the Doc talk so much; I realise now he wasn't giving me a chance to protest, or explain or, God forbid, get back up on that wall. I didn't mind. I just felt empty by that point. I don't remember much of what happened.

With a kindness I still find astonishing, the Doc and his wife took me in. I allowed them to tuck me away at the top of their tall house, sheltering under the sloping eaves for weeks. Since Andy's words had broken my world in two, I hadn't been back to the flat.

The Doc had gone over to collect some of my things, taking the time to see Andy to piece together what had happened. I didn't find this out until much later. They'd allowed me to hide untroubled and undisturbed, the only thing the Doc insisted on was that I took the pills he'd prescribed, and that I accompanied him once a day on a walk with Dolly.

The thought of leaving the house in daylight filled me with horror, so we would walk out into the cold night, not speaking, following a circuit of the village every evening without fail.

Even now, I'm not sure how long I spent at the Doc's. I might as well have been in a coma. The only thing I was able to do was eat and sleep. Tragedy didn't make me skinny, it made me even fatter. Maeve would make me puritan meals of chicken and salad, fish and vegetables, but she couldn't stop me slipping downstairs in the night and eating slice after slice of bread, hands greasy with butter.

One night, when I couldn't see but could feel the ones pressing against the kitchen window, I picked up a knife and dreamily sliced it through the pudge of flesh where my hand met my wrist. The gloss of berry-red blood welling up was shockingly thrilling, so I did it to the other arm as well - then laid them on the clean kitchen table and watched as the shiny puddles pooled together.

Dolly's barking shattered the stillness, and the alarmed Doc and Maeve spilled down the stairs bringing jagged spikes of energy into the room. As I was carried out, I watched the trail of red, splashing like paint, on Maeve's immaculate hall tiles.

Despite Maeve's pleading, I refused to talk to anyone and the hospital eventually let me leave with doses of alprazolam, which knocked me for six. The bliss of retreating into hours and hours of sleep was so lovely I protested when the Doc began to limit my use of them. He put me back on Sertraline once he started to see signs of slow recovery.

'You can't just sleep your life away, Angie my dear,' he said, holding my hands between his. 'I want you to come back to the real world, harsh as that sounds.' He smiled at me but his face was weary. For a second, I felt something other than the familiar turgid drag of self-pity. He and Maeve had treated me far better than I deserved.

It wasn't a life-changing turning point, but it marked the beginning of one. They watched me until they saw I was washing and getting myself dressed, even bothering to help with the housework. Only then did they make their proposal, the one that changed my life.

\*

We were in the kitchen, my favourite part of the house. It was warm and clean, smelling of coffee, newly washed laundry and beeswax. I still had moments when I shivered, my temperature dropped and my hands and feet would numb. Doc said it was a side effect of the meds. Maeve's big, poppy-red oven radiated a cheerful heat and I sat quietly, allowing the warmth to seep through, warming my blood. I watched Maeve as she moved around. Doc was at work and she seemed nervous. Despite myself, I felt a prick of curiosity. I must be feeling better, I thought.

Eventually, Maeve placed a cup of tea on the table, along with a huge slice of chocolate cake. Hunger pains stabbed. As always, I was ravenous. I picked up the cake and felt the gooey give under my fingers. It was gorgeous. I chased it with a mouthful of tea so hot it burned my mouth. Maeve cut herself a slice before sitting down opposite me, not drinking her tea, just turning the mug round and around until I lay my hand on it to stop her.

'Angie, Michael and I have been talking and we think it's time to talk to you about a proposal we have.'

I looked at her, my eyes dull.

'The thing is…' she said. 'We don't think it's doing you much good hiding away here and, to be honest, we've had some problems with Will. We need to be able to focus on him for a while.'

I felt a bolt of panic. 'You're throwing me out?' I blurted, horrified.

'No, no! Don't be silly,' Maeve replied, patting my hand. I slumped back and took another mouthful of cake. 'We're not throwing you out, but we do think you should start trying to be a bit more independent. The meds you're on seem to be helping, and I know Michael has already suggested reducing your dose still further…'

'I haven't anywhere to go,' I interrupted. I was trying to think. A warning bell was going off in my brain. The thought of leaving the Doc's house was terrifying. My head felt thick and sticky, I needed to find the right words to stop what I knew was about to happen.

Maeve cut another slice of cake, pushed it across to me, before refilling my cup. 'Angie, we have a proposition for you. Do you know Mrs Beaudry?'

Her question was so out of context I struggled to make sense of it.

'The old woman who lives in that big house? What has she got to do with anything?'

'Well, I'm sorry to say she's had a terrible fall and broken her hip. She's been in the hospital for weeks and absolutely desperate to get home. These old dears don't like change, and I worry she's wasting away up there. They want to put her into a care home until she's back on her feet but she's refusing. Trouble is, they won't let her home unless there is someone to look after her.' She tapped her fingers on the edge of her cup.

'Hasn't she gone bit barmy?' I said, trying to remember stories I'd heard.

'She's a bit eccentric, certainly,' Maeve said with a smile. 'Until this fall knocked the stuffing out of her she was fit and well, looked after herself without any problems. But she's now in the difficult position of having to give in and admit she can't carry on by herself.'

'Andy used to do work up there,' I said his name without thinking and it triggered a rush of nausea. I swallowed and kept talking. 'He said she was as rich as Croesus.'

Maeve inclined her head. 'Yes, she is very wealthy and the house is amazing, but terribly run down now, I'm afraid.' She met my eyes, her tone serious. 'That's why I thought of you – you nursed your Dad at the end, didn't you? And I know from Sally you're an outstanding cleaner.'

Sally was a local woman I'd worked for in the past. She was a snobby cow and I'd stopped working for her when I couldn't bring myself to muck out her teenagers' disgusting rooms any more.

As usual, the mention of Dad brought a lump to my throat. I took another sip of tea, trying to work out what Maeve was planning. 'You want me to go and clean for her?'

'Well, a bit more than that, actually. She needs a live-in housekeeper, someone to cook and clean, as well as keeping an eye on her, take her to the lav and so on. Someone needs to make sure she is keeping up with her physio.'

'And you think I can do it?'

'You'd get paid, of course,' Maeve went on. 'Mike and I have managed to persuade Frieda this is the only option, and she absolutely refuses to countenance hiring a professional nurse, Lord knows why, she has pots of money. It would have to be a live-in job, though, and Mike and I will pop in and out to make sure all is well.'

I stared at her, my mind churning. I could barely think straight. I struggled to work out what this meant. The thought of going back to live in my old flat was intolerable, it made my skin crawl. But I knew it was fantasy to think I could just keep living at the Doc's, keeping the door shut on the outside world.

My brain was full of sludge. I couldn't imagine being able to do anything besides sit at this table holding a mug of tea. The thought of taking action - contacting the council, finding somewhere new to leave, explaining what had happened - was as beyond me as running five marathons, or becoming Prime Minister.

The silence stretched between us. Maeve looked uncertain and embarrassed. I thought through what she had said. What choice did I have?

'OK,' I said.

*

That's how I found myself following Maeve down a dark corridor with everything I owned in a couple of suitcases and bags. Lethargy robbed me of any ability to act except doing as I was told. A fat, fifty-year old waste of space, relying on the kindness of other people who had their own problems.

Looking back, I can recognise there was a tiny, fragile little flame of curiosity and excitement, walking into that big old place I would learn to call home. I'd moved straight from my Dad's house to living with Andy, and there was Maeve, showing me a little apartment at the back of the ground floor that was to be mine for the foreseeable future.

'Well! Here we are.' Maeve crossed the rooms and opened the ragged and faded floor-length curtains with a flourish. Ground to ceiling French doors looked over the garden running down the side of the house. We stood for a moment, admiring the view of lawns undulating away from us before dipping down into the valley. Despite the grey drizzle of the day and the length of the grass, the sense of space and sky was breath-taking.

'It's not much, I'm afraid,' said Maeve, looking around the dusty room. 'I can't believe how filthy the place has got. I knew we should have insisted on hiring a cleaner for Frieda – but she wouldn't have it.' She turned to me, her face worried. 'The whole place will need a good scrub from top to bottom before she comes back from hospital,' she said. 'She's ever so precious about anyone touching her things. Please be careful with them - don't move them or put them away will you?'

I nodded. For the first time in months, I could feel something stirring. I pictured the floors wiped so the tiles shone, the glass polished to let in all that lovely light. I'd need a good hoover, I thought.

'There's a little kitchen through here and on the other side quite a nice big bathroom.' Maeve pushed open a door swollen with damp and I saw an old-fashioned toilet with the cistern above it, a chain dangling down. I couldn't help a smile when I saw a huge, claw footed bath. The enamel was stained, but it looked big enough to swim in.

'There's clean bed linen in here,' Maeve went on, opening a cupboard. 'No duvets though, Frieda loathed them, so just sheets and blankets.' She checked her watch. 'I must dash. So, I've ordered a delivery for first thing tomorrow morning - lots of food and a mountain of cleaning stuff, it should keep you going for a while.' There was a pause and she watched me, her forehead creased, as I thumped down on the bed, the sag in the mattress pulling me sideways.

'Are you OK, Angie?' she said crossing the room to sit by me. 'I'm sure this is all terribly overwhelming, and I know none of this is ideal...'

Her voice trailed away and I saw the lines of concern on her face. My icy heart softened.

'You've been very kind, Maeve. I can't thank you and the Doc enough. You saved my life.'

Maeve gave an embarrassed 'tsk' and shook her head. 'Don't be silly, Angie, anyone would have done the same.'

I shook my head. 'No. They wouldn't. And I'm grateful to you. I'll be fine here, honestly.'

'And you promise you won't… you won't do anything, well, silly?'

I smiled. 'No. I promise. I've got the old lady to look after haven't I? And besides,' I patted my pocket. 'I've got the Doc's pills. They've helped. I'm getting through this.'

'Oh I nearly forgot!' Maeve said, jumping to her feet. 'I've got your phone! Here.' She passed it over.

'So we can stay in touch,' she said. 'Don't worry; I've blocked that… shit so he can't contact you'. She blushed at the swear word, which made me smile. 'Will you come back to Weight Watchers do you think? Vicky's been worried about you.'

'God no. Not yet, Maeve. I will though. One day, I promise.'

She trotted off and I listened to her footsteps clicking away until the house fell silent. Despite my sense of being watched, I didn't feel frightened. I took my time exploring my new rooms. They weren't nearly as dirty as the rest of the house, but it was still very dusty and I could see the huge rug was faded from where the sun must have lain over the years. I'd never seen such high ceilings; it made the room feel huge. I was glad I didn't have to pay for heating.

The smell of dust hung in my nostrils. It was starting to coat my tongue and teeth so, despite the weather, I opened all the windows and the doors leading out to the garden, allowing the cold air to gust into the room. It didn't take long to wipe away the dirt.

With satisfaction I used an old T-Shirt of Andy's; his beloved Chelsea top. I enjoyed getting it covered in black streaks.

I found an ancient mop in a cupboard and tackled the dusty floorboards, but it disintegrated, so I made do with sweeping as much as I could. With no dustpan, I brushed everything into a corner and left it, vowing to tackle it in the morning. With the windows wide open it was freezing, so, drawing upon memories from childhood, I made a fire. I couldn't remember the last time I had enjoyed a real log fire. It's friendly, flickering light turned the living room into a warm haven.

It took about ten minutes to transfer the rest of my things into the cupboard and drawers. When I had made the bed and shaken out the rug, the place looked much better. I was gasping for a cup of tea and was resigning myself to a glass of water until I went into the kitchen and discovered Maeve had left milk, tea bags, coffee, sugar, some eggs and, best of all, two large slices of her chocolate cake. The oven was a death trap of a camping stove; I couldn't see myself doing any cooking in this kitchen.

Washing my hands free of the dust, I made a pot of tea and brought it back into my living room. There was a table big enough to seat four, upon which was heaped a pile of 80s novels. I could see the gilt of their covers through the dust. Jackie Collins, Jilly Cooper, Shirley Conran and Judith Krantz. They must have been left by the previous housekeeper. Blimey, I thought. How long had it been since anyone lived here?

I sipped my tea and looked around, feeling a glimmer of satisfaction. Although we had sworn we would, I had never lived in a London flat with Jayne and Susi. I had never danced from club to club in Ibiza. I had never owned my own place; I had never lived on my own. Despite everything, I couldn't help thinking how nice this was. The merry fire crackled away, the tea was hot, and the cake was delicious. It shook me to realise how long it was since I had felt such stillness and peace.

Even when I thought things were fine between Andy and me, there was always a sense of worry. Worry that we were drifting apart, that my life wasn't going anywhere. Sadness at what we had lost and could never recover.

It was strange and lovely to be able to sit, knowing nobody could bother me, in my own place, staring into a fire and eating cake. I decided I would be brave and cut my sertraline dose again. The Doc had tried to get me to do it ages ago, but the thought of losing its numbing crutch was frightening. But perhaps this new home was the right place to try.

\*

I woke up freezing cold, with a thudding head. Ice had fingered its way across the windows and frost lay on the grass. The fire had long gone out and the grate sat black and empty. I was still in my clothes and the warmest thing I had was my dressing gown, which I wrapped around me as I shivered my way to the toilet and back. There were no radiators so my options were electrocuting myself with a heater that looked a hundred years old, or lighting another fire.

My stomach growled with hunger. Maeve's cake had all gone. Searching through my suitcase I found a pack of crisps – mostly crushed – and a bar of chocolate, which I ate in seconds. Dry-mouthed, I ran the tap, filling and re-filling my glass before the water ran clear. I started to fantasise about food: Hot, buttered toast; Cottage pie, with cheese melting on top; Eggs and bacon, with sausages and hash browns.

I wondered if the old lady had anything in her kitchen and felt my way back down the dark corridor to find it. I really had to work out where the bulbs were, or at least clean the windows to let some light in, I thought.

The kitchen was no use. There was nothing but a stale crust of bread and a tin of black tea. God knows what the old woman had been living on. I thought I'd struck lucky when I opened the huge, walk in pantry, but the chemical stink was overwhelming. A mix of plasters and bandages, old flowers and strong spices. Rows of odd-looking bottles and jars were neatly lined up, but none of them contained food. Well, nothing I was going to risk eating.

I jumped as someone banged on the back door. An irritated looking delivery guy was standing there, his arms filled with bags.

'I've been knocking at the front door for twenty minutes,' he snapped, pushing past me and dumping the bags on the table.

'Oh. Sorry. I didn't know what time you were coming and I think the front door is blocked,' I said, embarrassed to be in my dressing gown.

He grunted and disappeared out the door, bringing in more bags and cursing as the nettles grabbed at his legs.

There was enough food to last me weeks, but I couldn't face putting it away into filthy cupboards and a stinking fridge. Separating out all the cleaning stuff Maeve had bought, I snapped on some rubber gloves and got to work. Thankfully, I'd found an immersion heater in the pantry cupboard so I had hot water.

I promised myself a ham roll with mayonnaise and a couple of bags of crisps for lunch when I had finished. Mindful of Maeve's warning about moving the old woman's things, I took care to put everything back in its place once I had wiped it clean, and blasted the mould away with a spray of bleach.

I had just finished gorging on bread and ham, sitting in a spotless kitchen when Maeve blew in with a blast of cold wind. Her expression brightened as she looked around the kitchen.

'Goodness you have done well!' she said. 'You've transformed the place, Angie. I'm so pleased. Has the food arrived?' Maeve marched about opening and closing cupboards. She was smiling broadly despite the rain, which had soaked her clothes and hair.

She inspected the fridge. 'Good. Lots of fruit and veg. You'll need to make sure Mrs B eats as healthily as possible. I think she's been living on toast and wine. I've set up an account for you at Laurie Gray's shop. She'll just send the bill to Michael every month.'

'Why are you helping her out so much?' I asked, something I had wondered about since I arrived. 'Why not just let her go into a home? Best place for her, it doesn't look like she was coping.' I broke the last bit of baguette in half and started to chew.

Maeve got a cloth and wiped away the crumbs I had dropped on the table. I found her energy, flapping like a trapped bird, exhausting. 'Oh we couldn't do that,' Maeve plopped into the chair opposite me and started twisting lengths of hair around her finger, pulling on it before letting it free. 'Frieda's lived here for years. She once did us a tremendous favour, something it would be impossible to ever pay back.' She peeled a bit of crust from the bread and popped it in her mouth.

'You'd better go and get dressed,' she said, eyeing my dressing gown.

'Why?' I said in alarm.

'I'm taking you up to the hospital to meet Frieda. They are hoping to let her come home once you've got the place ready – it shouldn't take more than a couple of days?' She lifted her eyebrows at me and I gave a reluctant nod. 'Just do her bedroom, that little yellow sitting room at the top of the stairs and the main hall for now,' Maeve continued. 'You've done a lovely job on the kitchen already and you've only just got here!' Her voice was encouraging but I dreaded the thought of leaving the house.

Maeve wasn't taking no for an answer. Apparently, Mrs B wouldn't agree to anything until she had met me. 'It's not like she's got any choice, though is it?' I protested. 'I thought it was either me or a care home?'

'You'll find with Frieda it's better to let her think she's getting her way,' Maeve responded. 'Now come on, Angie, I've got the class tonight and I don't want to be late.'

Of course, it had to be the same place where my dad had died. The doors of St Hillier's clacked back with a familiar sound and I recognised the smell - antiseptic and over-cooked food - though it had been years since I'd been there.

Since bringing the dose of my meds down I was more clear-headed, my wits and vision were sharper and I was careful not to look left or right, as I knew ones would be lingering in the hope I'd see them. You always got loads in hospitals; it's why I avoided them.

Mrs B was right at the back of the ward in a bed shielded from the other patients by a half wall. 'They had to move her as she wound up the other patients,' Maeve whispered from the side of her mouth. 'Frieda, my dear! How lovely to see you. Look I've bought you some flowers.'

As Maeve gushed, I took a step back in shock. A tiny form lay twisted on the bed. The hands resting on the blanket were coppery-curled twigs, and her body hardly lifted the covers. In contrast, her head was huge and mostly bald, just a few scraps of white curls dotted over the pink stretch of scalp.

She looked filthy, with grime caked along her hairline. She still had her teeth, but her eyes were sunken hollows in her face, the cheekbones jutting out sharp and bony. Mrs B was painfully thin and it was easy to see the skull gaping beneath the skin.

But that wasn't what made my skin cool and the breath stop in my throat. It was the man standing next to the bed. Tall, young, and slender, his blond hair hung over his forehead and he never took his eyes from Mrs. B's face. He was wearing a beautifully cut suit and a cigarette smoked between his fingers. Unlike the other ones, I could see through him to the window behind. I stepped back behind Maeve.

My movement alerted the old woman and her eyes flared. Green and bright as chips of ice they pinned me in place. She lifted a trembling twig of an arm, signalling Maeve to stop talking. I stared back at her, forcing myself to ignore the young man with the shining blond hair.

'You can see him can't you?' she snapped. Her eyes were sharp with curiosity and her voice was imperious, belying her physical frailty.

'Sorry, dear, what did you say?' Maeve was puzzled looking back and forth between the two of us. The old woman didn't reply but kept her gaze fixed on mine. I felt a strange surge of energy. I had to blink to break the connection. 'Who are you?' she said.

'Frieda, dear, this is Angie. Andy's wife?' Maeve shot me an uncomfortable look at having to mention his name. She had adopted a slightly patronising tone, voice louder than usual, to address the old woman. 'She's the one who is going to be looking after you. She's getting your house all nice for you when get discharged.'

The old woman didn't reply. She looked thoughtful; I noticed her sharp eyes darting up and down, taking me in. I was conscious of my belly pressing against the waistband of my trousers, the thickness of my arms and legs, my heavy jowls and frizzy hair. None of it went unnoticed. If I hadn't been cushioned by my Sertraline cloud, I would have felt more angry at this animated bag of twigs having the cheek to look me up and down in disapproval.

There was nothing personal on her locker. It was empty except for a glass and Maeve's flowers. She wore a hospital gown that billowed. Her skin was translucent; it sagged and swung gently like silk scarves hanging from a branch. I could trace her veins as they twisted and turned along her limbs and up to her throat. Now. That was interesting, she was wearing an unusual necklace, rounded lozenges of thick gold, which hung heavy round her neck. They were engraved but I couldn't see with what. It looked very expensive. How did she get so rich? Where was her family? I couldn't wait to explore the house to find some answers.

Conscious I was studying her as carefully as she had studied me, I lowered my eyes, snapping the connection between us. I couldn't resist glancing at the man. He was still there, calm and still, watching Mrs B as she lay back on the pillows.

A clearly mystified Maeve stepped up to break the tension. 'Well!' she said brightly. 'If you're happy, Frieda, dear, we'll get the house ship-shape and then come and collect you.'

'Did you move back the statues?' the old woman asked, her voice abrupt.

Maeve gave a start. 'Oh, blow, sorry Frieda I didn't. I meant to say to Angie but forgot, I…' she stopped as Mrs B grabbed her arm.

'You must find them and put them back where they were.' I was intrigued to see a look of blind fear cross the old woman's face. 'You must! It's very important, Maeve. Please. Make sure it's done.' She fell back, exhausted, what little colour was in her face drained away, leaving it yellow and bruised. Her eyes closed.

We waited a few moments but the old woman didn't stir. 'She often does this,' Maeve whispered. 'Wears herself out, poor dear. We'd better go.'

She sighed with relief as we left the hospital. 'I'm glad that's all organised properly now,' she said. 'Once you give me the go ahead that the house is ready, I'll get her discharged and organise bringing her back.'

'OK,' I said, my mind was whirring.

'What did she mean, Angie?'

'What?' I replied.

'When she said you can see him too?'

'I've no idea,' I said.

# CHAPTER 9: FRIEDA WATCHES

*The Soul selects her own Society —*
*Then — shuts the Door —*

Why in God's name did I agree to let that appalling woman come and live in my house? I twitch with irritation as I listen to Angela clumping about. The bones of the place groan under her colossal weight. I am a crab whose shell has been prised away exposing the raw, pink skin underneath. For the first time in my life, I am depending on the kindness of strangers and my skin crawls with the horror of it.

And she's such a misshapen, lump of a creature. Her ugliness is infecting the air. I wince at the crashes and bangs which accompany her seemingly endless cleaning. The deep pleasure of being back in my own bed is spoiled by constant reminders of this woman's presence. We have hardly spoken since I returned. She brings me food in silence and backs out, keeping her head so low the fat of her neck flowers out like a cushion.

I don't say anything, but I know she keeps her eyes down so she can't see Charlie. It's the only thing about her I find interesting but I'm too sapped of energy to think about it. I need to get outside. The window is thrown wide open. I insist on it, despite the cold. It means I can breathe in the fresh air, fill my boots with it. I delight in watching ice form on the edges of the glass. Beyond, I see the shimmer of my canopy, now restored. I feel safe again, but a thread of unease tugs at my skin. Is it enough? Was it mended too late? Has he found me?

It worries Charlie too, I can tell. But he won't speak of it. He toys with the trinkets in my room, smiling as he finds a photograph faded almost into nothingness. It is tucked behind a clutter of frames on a shelf. A young soldier and a foolish girl with ribbons in her hair.

'It means nothing,' I snap. 'I'd forgotten it was there.'

'I'm touched,' he says. 'You kept it all this time.'

I snort and settle myself further into my familiar sheets, heaped with sweet-smelling blankets. 'How long do you think you're going to be here?'

He shrugs. 'I don't know.' There is a pause and Charlie slots the photograph back where it was. I blink, and for a second he's not there – the room is empty. My heart lurches, then he flickers back into place.

'So where is it? Is it well hidden?' he asks, as if nothing has happened.

'Never you mind,' I say with a sniff.

'Is it safe?'

'Of course it is.' A headache is throbbing and my hip is sore.

Charlie gives a shiver, he is uneasy. Being back in my house seems to have unsettled him; he keeps looking out of the open window.

'It's late,' he says.

'Yes.'

There is a soft knock at the door. It opens and Angela squeezes through holding so many roses she has to use both hands. Their beauty makes me gasp. I look to Charlie, but he has gone.

'Doc's wife brought these,' she says.

'The vase is on that table – at the end of the bed,' I tell her.

She finds the vase and drops roses into it, one by one, until it is full. She looks around and spots two more on the shelf by the window. She clunks them under the tap in my sink. They too are filled until the room is heady with the roses' rich, velvety scent. Angela curses. A thorn rips her hand and blood runs down her wrist, startling against the blue-white of her skin.

She relaxes when she realises Charlie isn't here. Her eyes are free to dart around the room. I see her gaze catch on various things: a painting of a child, a prayer rug, my jewellery box. She sees me watching and blushes.

'Would you like something to eat?'

'I'm not hungry.'

'Tea then?'

I nod and reach for a rose, peeling a petal from the bloom and letting it rest in my hand. It is so fresh it stays in its lovely curve, a teardrop of blood soaked into a thick, supple satin. I rub it between my fingers, enjoying the smooth resilience. Already, I can feel the power sliding into my veins with a flame as strong as alcohol. My hand reaches for the gold at my throat and I let it rest, warm and heavy.

Angela's tea is good – hot and sweet. I sip it, enjoying every mouthful. The heat sends warming fingers down inside, easing away the pain in my hip like a poultice. Angela sits by me patiently, her hands folded in her lap. As she takes the empty cup, I resist the urge to take her hand to examine the palm, to look for the mark Lilith had taught me to find. No. Not in this grotesque, this blank blob of a human being with her grey skin and bitten nails.

A silence stretches and I'm aware of the words bubbling up Angela's throat. 'It's beautiful. Your house,' she says, the words bursting from her. 'So many things from all around the world. I've never seen anything like it. You must have so many stories.' Her face is transformed; her eyes are jade green and clear as glass.

'Yes.' I say.

'I grew up in the village,' she goes on as if now the words have been released she can't stop them. 'I used to look up at this house and wonder what it was like, and now I'm here! I can't get my head around it really. Andy used to...' she stops. 'Well he used to say it was an unusual house but I never thought...' Her voice disappears as she catches the expression on my face.

Her voice is grating on every one of my nerves. The girlish, gushing quality of it is at odds with the oppressive meatiness of her presence.

'You can go now,' I wave my hand. 'I'm tired.'

Of course.' Angela heaves her bulk from the stool and pulls at the cloth that has gathered up the crack of her tremendous backside. 'Are you sure I can't get you anything to eat?'

I don't reply.

Light vanishes from the room as her body wedges in the doorway, blocking everything from view. She closes the door gently and I sigh with relief, rubbing my aching forehead. Eldritch leaps up and curls on my bed, her fur cooled by the night.

*

I am wrenched awake by a crash as the window slams shut and bangs open again. It is very cold. I lie still for a moment, breathing deeply as the roses around me exhale. I feel so much stronger, can I risk getting out of bed to close the windows? I brush Eldritch aside and she jumps to the floor, landing without a sound before giving a yowling yawn of protest. I search for my cane. I have them dotted all over the house for bad days. I can't see well in the dark and tut as my groping hand finds nothing.

I brace myself, hand steady on the side table and swing my legs round. Ah, there it is. The shape of the cane feels smooth, the ivory bone handle a familiar fit in my hand. I lean and push myself forward. My old bed is high off the ground and I am standing without too much difficulty.

It is such a pleasure to be upright without a nagging physio urging me to lift my legs, or bend my knees. The gnarl and whorls of the old oak boards are firm under my faltering feet. The wood grounds me, and my back straightens. The window rattles again. Leaning heavily on my cane I take tiny steps, one, two, three – nearly there.

A surge of triumph as I bump against the sill. I am shaking with the unfamiliar exertion, and grip the edge of the window, letting the icy breeze of the darkness cool my skin. It makes me shiver; I enjoy the sensation, so clean and sharp after the muzziness of weeks in a hospital bed.

Pagans' Reach was built high on the surrounding hills and from my window the whole of Witchford is spread before me. An old village, it lies calm, silvered by the moonlight. The ancient church sits right at the centre, surrounded by a motley collection of houses huddling up against its sleeping flanks. This view had not changed for two hundred years, except for the ugly council flats, which stand shamefaced to the right of the town.

I watch the sky, the movement of the stars makes me dizzy. Something about the taste of the midnight air, the arching sky and the feel of the sill pressing against my hip ignites a pyre of memories. Here, back in my home at last, I rummage through them like an expensive box of chocolates. This time, no vengeful spirit forces me to think of terrible things. No. Not now. Now I want to remember drinking champagne on a hot night in Singapore, rain drenching my hair so it hung down my back in sheets of ebony silk, like the princess in the old fairy tale.

I remember Italy, in the middle of the war. I stayed with a group of mad poets. I watch myself through the years, slamming a window shut as a storm thunders against it. Smiling, I recall the wind rattling at the glass like a demon wanting to break in, the sky tearing itself apart as lightening ripped through it…

So many fragments, slivers of coloured scenes, they are pinprick bright and scatter around me like showers of glittering confetti.

Eldritch drags me from my reverie with a screech as she shoots past and out of the window. I realise with a start I am freezing cold. I must have stood at this window for an hour, lost in my memories. My hands are shaking and I can hardly close the latch.

I creep back to my bed taking great care not to fall; my body would shatter like glass. The sheets are icy. I lie still. It's no good; sleep is elusive. I have to open and close three of my drawers before I find what I am looking for. The little jar hides at the back. I pull it out, and its weight in my hand is soothing.

There's not much left. The ointment is yellow and pungent but still good. I dab a touch of it onto my tongue, careful to wipe my hands. My eyes roll into the back of my head as the Mandragora pulls me, feet first, under the black waves of dreamless sleep.

\*

It takes a week. A week of Angela's meals on trays and Maeve's regular delivery of flowers to get me strong enough to leave my bedroom and go downstairs. With Angela's arm around me, cursing my shaking legs, I stand in the doorway and breathe deeply.

Oh, the smells of home. My books, my paintings. They are clustering around me in welcome. Eldritch darts forward, a streak of furry black on the floor. Angie grunts and pushes her aside with her foot.

'You should get rid of that cat,' she mutters.

I am feeling sick and weak; I haven't stood for any length of time for what felt like months. I summon up enough strength to shake my head. 'No. Leave her.' I pause as my head is reeling. Angela looks concerned and tries to steer me back to my room but I stand firm. 'I'm fine,' I say. I can't see Charlie, but I can hear the buzz of his presence in the corners.

The house feels different, but I am concentrating so hard on getting down the stairs I can't pinpoint what. Lighter maybe?

Angela has to carry me the last few yards into the kitchen. I am humiliated. She tips me into my usual chair and I clutch tight hold of the edge of the table until I recover myself. I watch her as she moves around the kitchen. Rage crawls through me. I loathe having someone in my kitchen, using my things. The wood beneath my fingertips chars. I could just lift the heat and cast flames across the room, I think.

But then my hands shake, and lances of pain twist into my skull and I am knocked sideways by pain and exhaustion. The headaches are getting worse and worse, and take longer to fade.

Angela, oblivious, carries on buttering bread that she places in front of me. 'You need to eat. You look very pale,' she frowns. 'I think maybe you should stay in your room for a bit longer.'

'Stop fussing.' With a great effort, I smile. 'Something smells nice!' At last, I feel the pain in my head start to ebb away. The bread is nutty and warm. I find I am ravenous. 'Did you make this? It's excellent,' I say in surprise.

Angela gives a shy smile and turns back to the oven. I smell the richness of butter and eggs and my mouth waters. With neat movements, she slides a fluffy omelette, dotted with green and red peppers onto a plate and hands it to me.

It is delicious. She must have used six eggs and half a pack of butter but I can't remember the last time I ate something so satisfying.

While I finish the omelette, Angela sits on the stool across from me with a sigh, and constructs an enormous sandwich made with fried bread, bacon, and three eggs. She refills her cup with steaming hot tea and spoons in sugar. She is absorbed in her task, giving herself up completely to the taste of her food.

'You're a very good cook,' I say.

She finishes her mouthful and wipes her lips clean with the cuff of her sleeve. 'I enjoy my food, as you can probably tell,' she replies, with a wry glance down at the gross swelling of her belly. She takes another huge mouthful of her sandwich and chews methodically. A strange, almost comfortable silence falls between us.

It is a cold, crisp day and the sun illuminates the kitchen, bringing the table into sharp focus. Everything shines, the usual clutter has disappeared, and there is a merry fire blazing in the grate, warming the flagstones. Eldritch is stretched before it, a black, plush-velvet fur cushion, purring contentedly.

'I told you not to touch my things,' I say crossly. 'Where have you put them?'

'I've only cleaned up a bit, the place was filthy,' Angela replies, an apologetic note in her voice. She scrapes her plate and runs hot water into the sink. 'I just put some stuff away in the cupboard and drawers; I needed to give the counters a proper scrub. It's not your fault, Mrs Beaudry, I know you haven't been well and you probably didn't realise how bad it was getting. My Nan went the same way. Do you want any more tea or shall I chuck what's in the pot?'

I hold out my cup and she tops it up; I am dazed by her stream of inane chatter. I don't recognise the teapot, its big and brown with a round belly. Angela opens the back door, letting in a blast of cold air, and shakes the tea leaves into the flowerbed.

'Why do I only ever see you in the same clothes?' I say, indicating her tired blue shirt and leggings. Her feet are bare and look blue with the cold. They are also rather grubby and the toe nails are yellowing. 'Is it a uniform?'

Angela snorts and starts washing up the plates and cups. 'Course not. I just haven't got much else.'

I watch her as she stands at the sink. Her hair is coarse and looks like it has been washed with soap. Everything about her looks cheap, her clothes, her lack of make-up, the homemade hairstyle. Her roots are an inch long and glint silver. Lines are worn into her face. She is a woman who has been ground down by life; it is only the stones of fat giving her any presence.

She turns round, drying her hands. 'Do you want me to take you back up to bed?'

I shake my head. 'No. I'm feeling better today and want to sit and read. Take me to the yellow sitting room.'

I stand up, leaning against the table, Angela reaches over and pulls my arms. I push her away in irritation and reach for my cane. 'I can manage.'

'No, you'll fall.' Angela helps me around the table. 'Take my arm.'

I make my way to the door and survey the long corridor leading to the sitting room. The floorboards gleam in the sunlight. I can smell beeswax and polish. 'What have you done?' I ask.

'What I've been paid to do. Cleaned up your house.'

'Well make sure you don't move anything.' I take a step into the corridor. 'You've polished the floor so much I'm going to slip,' I snap.

'Well you'd better let me help you then.' She hooks her arm around my waist and steadies me as my foot skids and I lurch to the side.

'See?' I say.

'OK, Mrs Beaudry. You've made your point.' She helps me into the sitting room, and lowers me into a little, embroidered armchair.

I sit back with a thump, 'no need to be so rough, and why's it so bright in here?'

Angela lifts my feet onto a little stool. 'Because I've cleaned the windows.' She stretches her back, I am dwarfed as she looms over me. 'I'll make a fire, it's freezing in here. I've never known a place not to have central heating.'

'It's bad for you. Dries you up.'

She grunts drops to her knees and starts to clean out the fireplace. It is irritating beyond belief. I find her bulk repulsive. I lift a finger and Angela jumps, slapping at her neck.

'Ow!' she says.

'What is it?'

'Something stung me.' She carries on rootling away in the grate and I supress a smile. That'll teach her. A spasm across my temple is a warning and I drop my hand.

'There. Done.' Angela sits back on her heels and we both stare at the fire as it crackles away. She hauls herself to her feet and dusts off her hands. 'Right. I'd better get on. Give me a shout if you need anything. I've got stuff to do.'

'What have you done with my book? It was just here. I told you not to touch my things.'

'Do you mean this one?' Angela reaches to the shelf and passes it to me, squinting sideways to read the spine. '*Perfume.* What's that about then?'

I snatch it from her hand. 'So you can read then?' I stroke the cover of the book. 'This is a story about a man who creates perfumes so wonderful they drive the world mad. It was written by a German.'

'Oh yeah,' Angela wipes the sweat from her forehead, leaving a streak of ash on her face. 'I think I remember the film.'

'Good God, woman, don't talk to me about films. Read the damn book.' I shove it at her. 'Pass me those poems instead.' I tug at her shirt and click my fingers. 'There. Behind you. Quickly!'

Angela passes it to me and gives me a level look. 'I've got work to do.' She tucks *Perfume* under her arm and marches from the room.

I smile. My poems await and I nestle deep in the cushions and start to read.

'She's perfect, you know,' Charlie's voice is a static crackle in my ear.

'I wish you'd stop popping out of nowhere without warning,' I say, my hand on my racing heart. 'And who's perfect?'

Charlie roams around my sitting room before stretching himself out on a small blue sofa. I am about to scold him for putting his shoes on the cushion before remembering he is a ghost. He pulls aside the curtain and glances up at the blue sky. 'What a gorgeous day.'

'Charlie?'

'That woman, of course – what's her name…'

'Angela?' I give a cackle of laughter. 'That great lump? She doesn't even read!'

'All the more reason. And she's here living with you. Couldn't be better.' He stretches his hands towards the fire.

'Can you feel the heat?' I ask, curious. He shakes his head.

'No, but it's very pretty.' He looks over at me. 'So. Angela?'

'Don't be ridiculous,' I pick up my book.

'Why not?'

'Mainly because I am too tired. I wish everyone would just leave me alone!' A lance of pain slides behind my eyes and I gasp with the sharpness of it.

Charlie notices and looks smug. 'That's why.'

'I don't know what you're talking about.'

'Yes you do,' his voice is triumphant. 'I didn't realise things had got this bad. You need to do something soon otherwise that's just going to get worse.'

'Stuff and nonsense. I'm probably just dehydrated, that always gives me a headache'

Charlie laughs.

'Well, as a great man once said, *If goodness lead him not, yet weariness /May toss him to my breast.* But in your case instead of weariness, it's pain. I can't imagine goodness leading you anywhere'

'This has nothing to do with God,' I exclaim. 'And when did you start reading poetry?'

Charlie taps the side of his nose and grins, his smugness is infuriating.

'Face it, Frieda, you can't run away for ever. You have to do something with what you have. You could transform this woman.'

'All she wants is bacon sandwiches and cream cakes,' I say. 'She's a lump.'

'Well going by that logic…' Charlie has magicked a cigarette in an elegant holder out of the air. He takes a puff and breathes smoke out of his nose in a steady stream. 'You're just an old woman.' He looks me up and down. 'A very, very old woman.'

I harrumph. 'You know as well as anyone I am not all I seem.'

'My point exactly,' he sits up and swings his legs round. 'And neither is she. You know she can see me.'

I shrug and focus on my book, trying to ignore him.

'She's special, Freddy. You need someone like her.'

This is so ridiculous I laugh out loud.

'I'm serious. You're going to need help.' His face is grave. 'You haven't much time, you'll need to teach her, so she can be here. When he comes.'

'If he comes.'

'No, Freddy,' Charlie's voice is resolute. 'When he comes.'

*

Now I am up and about I can check for myself the house is safe. My treasures are secure and hidden in darkness. But I can't shake off Charlie's words. I remember them whenever Angela enters the room, whenever I see her eyes slide past Charlie. I've noticed she won't go into the little study next to the library; I know why. I know what she sees in there.

I argue with myself. She's too old. Too anaesthetised by the bulk of fat and food in which she swaddles herself. She should have done something with the power she has by now, and she has power. I see it in the way she cooks – she is a natural – her food is ambrosial. Her homemade oils and lotions make my old house shine with glossy newness. Maybe. Maybe, I think. She could learn.

But then I see her, shovelling bags of crisps into her mouth and wiping the grease on her trousers, her eyes empty, and I think no. There's nothing.

Weeks have passed and all seems well, but I cannot escape the sense of danger in the air. I smell it in the mornings, a tang of wood smoke and gunpowder drifts into the house when I open the window. I try to ignore it.

We are in a routine that suits us both. Angela helps me dress in the morning, feeds me, exercises me like an old horse, then leaves me to read as she cleans. I keep asking to go outside. 'Not yet,' she says. 'You're not strong enough.'

The physiotherapist arrives at the house and mutters with Angela for a good twenty minutes before bursting into my sitting room. She looks like someone has wrapped her round and around with a bright pink band-aid. The lurid shine of it hurts my eyes. She makes me stand, and sit, and walk about, before finally declares herself satisfied.

'You've done very well, Mrs Beaudry,' she says in a loud voice. Her eyelashes are a mystifyingly thick strip of black – like the ends of a paintbrush. Charlie, unseen, gazes at her in astonishment as she bounces around the room. It is exhausting to look at her. I am grateful when she leaves.

I feel like a child on Christmas morning the day Angela opens my wardrobe and pulls out a black skirt and a soft, peacock-blue jersey I've had for longer than she's been alive. The clothes feel like armour after weeks in flimsy nightgowns. I am much happier with my drooping skin and rack of bones buttoned away behind sturdy fabric.

As Angela helps me down the stairs, I am struck afresh by the changes. Everything looks brighter, the colours more rich. The air is different. I run my hand along the bannister and it comes away dust free. It is as if I have been wearing smeared glasses for years and someone has come and taken them away.

'You'd better not have been going through my drawers and moving my things,' I warn Angela.

'I've finished all but the library and the top rooms. It's looking better isn't it?' She is proud of her handiwork.

'It was fine before,' I say, cross; but there is something freeing about the lightness of the place after so many years surrounded by swathes of dust I had learned to not see.

We pass by the open door of the main sitting room. I pause to check all is well and nothing is missing. The large, ebony cabinet I had installed many years ago dominates the room and the glass, usually so cloudy you can't see what's on the shelves, is crystal clear and my treasures are arranged in neat rows.

'What is all that stuff?' Angela says, wiping the sweat from her forehead and the back of her neck. She points to a Chagall-blue glass bowl. Rolling together inside are two walnuts, a hazelnut and three withered chestnuts. My gold combs lie next to it, glinting in the light, along with ten little glass bottles stoppered with corks, dark brown with age. The cabinet is filled with bits and pieces, all of which trigger a wash of memories.

'Never you mind. They're mine and not to be touched.'

'Will you tell me what they are and where you got them, one day?'

I am going to snap back a firm no, but the look on her face makes me pause. 'Perhaps,' I say, and with that she has to be satisfied.

My step quickens as I point out to Angela the path across the garden leading to the woods. It isn't raining but there is a dampness in the air that is sweet lichor on my skin. We enter the shelter of the trees arching above us. The ground is layered with a mulch of leaves and dead bracken. I stop. Angela is wrong-footed as I pull on her arm.

'Just wait, Angela. Take it all in.'

So we stand, listening. The birds of the wood recover from the interruption of our footsteps and I hear a robin's song, pure, liquid, and clear as spring water, soaring and swooping nearby. I plant my feet, deep as roots into the earth and unfold, stretching upwards – a delicious elongation of tendons, sinews and muscles. My hands uncurl, my fingers tingle and I breathe in the cool air.

'Blimey! Look at you! You're nearly as tall as I am!' Angela's voice is bright with surprise. She takes away her arm and looks at me in astonishment as I uncrook my back.

I study her. Her pallid flesh, the circles under her eyes and the sores around her lips. The fat bulging at the seams of her skin. 'It's the woods,' I say. 'Try it.' My voice has dropped to a persuasive whisper and I see her eyes widen; she thinks I'm mad, I realise with a chuckle. I move my hand, like a magician. 'Breathe it in. Go on. It'll do you good.'

A frown creases her face but she stills and I see her nostrils move as she takes a deep breath.

'Good,' I nod in encouragement. 'Deeper. You never breathe deeply enough. Close your eyes.'

Angela cocks a suspicious eyebrow at me but obliges, taking in a slow, steady breath, filling her lungs.

'Let it out slowly and take another,' I say. I watch her face and notice with interest an almost immediate shift. Her cheeks are pinkening, her skin seems to clear. Interesting. She is able to absorb some of the energy here.

'I feel like I'm in a yoga class,' she bursts out, 'and I'm a bit dizzy – I'm hyperventilating.' But her eyes glow a richer green, and I can see the change in her.

I nod with satisfaction and take her arm, but this time I am strong enough to tug her along a little, down the hill and towards the village.

'Are you sure you're OK going this far?' frets Angela. 'It's quite a walk back up that hill.'

'I'm fine,' I say, wanting her to be quiet. My heart is thumping. There's a figure in the woods. It is flitting in and out behind the trees. I sense, not danger, but something dark, something fierce and it is crashing towards us. Angela hears it too; her eyes are scanning the damp, twisted black trunks of the trees. Her hand tightens on my arm.

# CHAPTER 10: ANGIE

It took a while to adjust to the old woman living in the house after having the place to myself for so long. God she was a miserable cow; I knew she had been very ill but Christ, Pagan's Reach looked completely different. I'd sweated blood transforming it and I don't think she even noticed – she certainly didn't ever thank me.

The front hall was my highest achievement; it absolutely gleamed. When I'd first arrived, the floor had been carpeted with dust, and it was only once I had scrubbed and mopped it for hours I discovered the black and white chessboard tiles stretching from one side to the other – big as a skating rink. I had polished them until they shone.

I discovered that if spiders' webs are left untouched for long enough they form huge scarves of revolting, dusty fibres, knotted with decaying insects. They drooped, six foot long in every corner of the ceilings, on all three floors. I'd nearly killed myself getting rid of them, I could taste the dust at the back of my throat for days. Urgh. Just thinking about it makes me feel sick.

The huge windows behind the great staircase were so dirty I could pry off flakes of grime with my fingernail. Layers had formed over so many years the filth was inches thick. Buckets and buckets of hot, soapy water turned black and had to be refilled before I could step back and admire the results. Probably for the first time in thirty years, the winter sun could surge into the hall, picking out every dust-free tile in sharp relief.

The glass was strange, I was used to bog-standard double-glazing but this felt alive. It was thicker at the bottom than the top, and had a sort of solid, water-like quality. I expected to see bubbles, and fish, frozen in the glass as I soaked and scrubbed away at the giant panes.

It made me fanciful, I imagined a stream, diverted by some wizard and frozen to form a window so Mrs. B could look out at her woods.

The kitchen was spotless, the counters scrubbed and oiled so the grain glowed. My rooms, of course, were immaculate, and I'd thumped decades of dust out of the curtains and rugs in Mrs B's bedroom.

Before the old woman returned, the Doc's wife had come to visit and in a whirl of energy stripped the house of everything that could be washed. She returned with bundles and bundles of ironed bed linen, which she stored in the airing cupboard.

As always, she had bought cake. After I'd toured her around the finished parts of the house we sat down to tea and a large slice each.

'You really have worked wonders, Angie dear,' she said, picking off a crumb of chocolate icing. 'I'm sure Mrs B will be delighted.' She paused. 'I hope you haven't thrown anything of hers away? She does get… well she gets quite upset at the thought of anyone touching her things…'

'Only what was rotten, covered in mould, rats' droppings or fallen completely apart,' I replied, adding another spoon of sugar to my tea. Maeve never put enough in.

'Oh I'm sure that's fine then,' she went on but a worried frown remained. She gave a little shudder of revulsion. 'I must say, Angie, you are being absolutely marvellous. It can't be much fun for you.'

I shrugged. 'I like cleaning. It's a beautiful house. It takes my mind off things.'

'Good. Good.'

'I tell you what I do need, though…'

Maeve leaned forward her face bright with eagerness. 'Of course – anything, Angie.'

'I really need a hoover – the dust is awful. And there's only so much I can get rid of by banging rugs against the wall, especially with this constant rain.'

Maeve promised to sort one out and, good as her word, the next morning a battered pink fiat 500 with eyelashes on the headlights swung down the drive. Sharon. I'd forgotten she was mates with Maeve's cleaner Jean.

My heart started to race when I saw her climb out, pulling a hoover from the front seat. She gave a big grin as she walked towards me, a little Jenny Wren with goofy front teeth. I realised it was months since I'd last seen her and the others. They'd kept calling and texting but I had ignored them until eventually they stopped trying.

'What are you doing here?' I called from the top step, I was pleased to see her but dreaded having to talk about Andy and Kelly.

'Doc's wife sent me over with this,' she held up the hoover. 'Jean told her I was selling one on Ebay so she bought it and asked me to bring it up. I do love a Henry Hoover. As I always say, he's the only man who's never let me down.' She roared with laughter as she panted up the steps. 'Cor! Look at this place! You've fallen on your feet haven't you, girl? I've got to get back but I've time for a quick cup of tea...'

She was dying to come in and have a good poke around

'Come on then,' I said and led her through to the kitchen.

'Blimey, it's a dump in here innit?' she said, wrinkling her nose as we walked through the back of the house. 'Urgh look at those cobwebs, it's disgusting. The kitchen looks lovely though – bet you've been working your socks off.'

Over tea and a large slice of Victoria Sponge, Sharon chatted about her Kayleigh expecting again, and Vicky's latest adventures. Eventually she stopped. 'We've all really missed you, you know.'

'Yeah, I know. I'm sorry I haven't been in touch. I've been in a bit of a bad way.'

Sharon's eyes filled, she'd always been a bit of a softy. Impulsively, she leaned over and patted my hand.

'I think it's terrible what that pig of a husband of yours has done.' I flinched. 'We all do, Angie. None of us is speaking wiv 'im. And as for that Kelly...'

I held up my hand, though part of me was longing to hear. 'Please, Sharon, I don't want to know.' I tried to make a joke of it. 'You don't want to set me back do you?' I smiled. 'I just want to forget all about it, you know? Move on.'

Sharon's eyes were wide. 'But you can't stay here for ever can you? Cooped up in this big old place with an horrible old woman. Urgh,' she shuddered. 'You'll have to take her to the toilet, clean her – all that. Rather you than me.'

'I haven't got much choice, and besides, I think I needed a break – sort my head out a bit.'

'Well good luck with it,' Sharon said, and knocked back the last mouthful of tea. 'Say what you like about the Doc's wife, she sure knows how to make cake. Can I take that last bit home?'

'Sure,' I said, and walked her back to the front of the house where her ridiculous car waited. Just before she scrunched off down the drive, she stuck her head out of the window.

'By the way, I almost forgot! Vicky wanted me to pass on a message. She said get in touch, you daft mare, and Gary at work is pining for you.'

I smiled and rolled my eyes as I waved her off. I supressed the little pop of excitement at the mention of Gary. He had called me a few times, but I'd always sent it straight to voicemail.

As I stood looking down the drive, I was very aware of the house standing vast and empty behind me. My life with Andy, working at the school, laughing with my mates seemed like a hundred years ago. I could see Andy, Kelly, Vicky, Sharon – all of them – as if they were on the other side of a great river. The water between us the time I'd spent off my head at the Doc's house, trying to gather my marbles back together.

I was down to my lowest dose of medication now and my vision was sharp, my hearing clear as a bell. The dragging, smothering sense of nothingness had faded. I didn't feel like I was at the bottom of a hole any more. Trouble was, it meant the ones took a step closer. There were a few in the house, more in the garden.

Strangely, they didn't seem interested in me, they didn't try to get my attention, they seemed... absorbed in themselves. It's difficult to explain. Not as desperate. Out of the corner of my eye I looked every day for my Dad, but hadn't seen him yet. Maybe he didn't stray far from the village. I quashed a pang of guilt. I knew I would have to go and find him, but at that moment my fear was stronger than my guilt.

The weight of the hoover was solid and reassuring in my hands. I couldn't wait to tackle the old woman's bedroom properly. The amount of junk in there was astonishing, but as I worked my way around from corner to corner, using a damp cloth to wipe away the grime, I was amazed at what I found.

When I first dared to go into her room, high ceilinged with tall sash windows looking over the valley, everything was muddled and cloaked with grime. As I wiped, sorted and replaced I found treasure after treasure. It took a day to untangle the knot of books, papers and paintings, which I piled neatly on a beautiful old sort of bureau – I suppose you'd call it. Taller than me, I'd never seen one like it before. It had barley twist legs, and a piece that folded down to form a solid desk. It was lined with green leather and when opened out revealed twenty or so little cubbyholes.

I found a collection of wooden boxes; one was particularly beautiful. It was made of oak inlaid with walnut and I couldn't work out how to open it. It was very dirty, like everything else in that house, and I spent a good twenty minutes cleaning it, patiently rubbing in wax until it shone like candlelight.

As my fingers worked, I could feel different segments, some of which shifted beneath my hand. It was a puzzle box, and you had to follow a complicated set of steps in order to find the key. I knew it was there because I could hear it rattle when I shook the box.

Goodness, it must have taken me the best part of the day to work out the steps. The front panel slid back with a smooth click, and then you could pull out a stem of wood that revealed a button. When you pressed that, a square of the marquetry popped up to reveal another panel, and so on and so on. I found it endlessly fascinating and infuriating in equal measure because although I eventually discovered the little drawer that held a tiny, golden key, I never found a key hole.

Once I had hoovered the room to within an inch of its life, I made up the bed in the crispest and most lavender scented set of bedding. No duvets allowed, and it was cold – so I piled on two or three newly-washed blankets. All I needed to do was make up a fire when the old lady finally arrived. I sat next to the bed and looked around the room with satisfaction. I wish I'd thought to take a photo before I started but couldn't remember where I'd put my phone.

The room smelled fresh and clean, all the woodwork was buttery rich with wax, and the tumble of colour from the books and vivid paintings gave the room a joyful, expectant air. Although it was raining, the view out of the window was stunning, it pulled you forward to admire the great broiling tumble of clouds in the sky.

'Lovely,' I said out loud and pulled the sheets and blankets tight.

My sense of accomplishment had grown daily as I recovered more and more of the house from its descent into decay and dirt. And then Mrs B returned.

She couldn't walk from the ambulance. They'd wrapped a stiff looking red blanket over her nightie and dressing gown. All I could see was her cross little crone-face with puffs of white hair sticking out of the top, like an irritated sausage in a red wool roll. The Doc and his wife were there and they darted into the house with the old woman's suitcase, leaving me to bring her in.

'You all right carrying her?' the ambulance driver said, looking me up and down. 'You'll manage I'm sure, big strapping lass like you.'

I nodded, my face was already dripping as the rain fell in sheets. He opened the back doors and held out his hand.

'Here you go, Mrs Beaudry, home sweet home. Give us your arm.'

I heard a mutter and a sharp exclamation.

'Now come on, you know what the hospital said. You've got to take it easy, love. You can't just bounce out of the back on your own.' He shot me a 'you've got a right one here' look and I sighed.

I peered into the back of the ambulance where the old woman was clutching onto a rail, trying to pull herself up and out. She kept slapping at the man's hands when he tried to help. She looked as fierce as a wild animal, locked in a trap.

Eventually, the ambulanceman and I worked together to hoick her out, taking an arm each. I swung her up into my arms; she weighed as little as a bag of crisps. The driver slammed the doors shut and sped away. I didn't blame him. On that grey, rainy day the house looked like something out of a horror movie.

Without any difficulty, I carried my red-wrapped bony bundle up the steps and through the front door. I kept my eyes on her face; I wanted to see her expression when she took in the changes I had made in the front hall. She didn't even blink. Just carried on looking cross.

Maeve and the Doc stood at the foot of the stairs smiling like a pair of shop dummies. 'Welcome home!' they said together. It was all very uncomfortable. The old woman ignored them and struggled to sit up in my arms as I walked towards the stairs.

'No! There. Over there.' She said, jabbing her fingers to a chest by the front door.

'I need to take you up to bed,' I said, puzzled.

'Not yet. Take me over there.' She started to wriggle, and I had to hold her tight to stop her from falling. 'Open it!'

Maeve ran forward and lifted the lid of the old chest, it creaked so hard I thought it was going to snap. It was filled with musty smelling blankets. 'Get them out, then,' the old woman looked at Maeve. 'That's where you left them isn't it? Though I asked you to put them back.'

The Doc looked bewildered but Maeve flushed and dug her hands into the blankets and withdrew what looked like four, elongated dolls. 'Give them to me,' the old woman snapped.

Maeve handed them over and Mrs Beaudry clutched them to her chest, two in each hand. I looked down but it was too dark in the hall to see what they were.

'Now take me outside,' she said to me. Maeve cast a look at the Doc who rolled his eyes.

'But it's pouring!' I protested. I tried to walk to the stairs but something made me stop. The old woman had shifted her body so that I was forced to turn back to the door. 'OK, OK, I don't know what's going on but you can stop doing that. I'll take you outside.'

We trooped into the garden, me carrying the woman as if she was the Queen of Sheba. She directed me to a spot down the drive by the gate.

'Look for the little post. This goes there.' Her bony hand extended out from the blanket clutching what I could see was a slender jade statue. It was beautiful. I held it up close to try and work out what it was. It looked a little like a girl holding up a bird but it was done in such flowing, exuberant lines it was almost abstract. I'd seen jade before, but nothing like this. It had a translucent quality, holding light inside it; I almost expected it to feel hot. For all its delicacy it was surprisingly heavy. I turned it over and saw the base was a round disc of gold. It must be worth a fortune, I thought.

'Are you sure? We can't leave this out in the rain!'

The old woman's gaze was resolute, so I shrugged, and placed the statue on its little perch, a tiny notch of wood hidden by the twining weeds that could barely be seen until Mrs B pointed it out.

We did this three more times; it took an hour, as we had to wade to each end of the garden. The grass was long and wet so my trousers were absolutely soaked by the time we had finished. The whole event was bizarre.

Finally, once everything had been done to madam's satisfaction we went back into the house. A tension that had been on the old woman's face had dissipated. She looked more peaceful, and happy to be taken to her room and tucked into bed. She fell asleep almost immediately.

I walked the Doc and Maeve to the door.

'What the hell was all that about?' I said as they put on their coats. Pointless, as we were all drenched.

'She can be very… particular about things,' the Doc said. 'I'm sorry she put you to so much trouble. I find it's easier in the end to do as she says, things seem to go badly wrong if you don't.'

'What does that mean?' I said. I was getting cross. This was ridiculous. The woman was clearly barking.

'I just mean she gets upset,' the Doc said reassuringly. 'She gets ideas into her head. Look how calm she was once the things were back in their places.'

'But why? They looked really valuable – and she just leaves them outside.'

'She's sees them as a protection, for herself as well as the village.'

'Protection from what?' I asked, incredulous.

'I don't know,' he shrugged. 'I've never wanted to find out!' he laughed. I couldn't believe he was taking this so lightly.

'I'm beginning to think you're all barmy,' I muttered and the Doc and Maeve smiled.

He took my hands in his. 'The house looked wonderful, Angie. I can't believe how hard you have been working. You look well. I'm so pleased.' He paused and considered me carefully. 'Are you well? How are you feeling?'

'I'm good Doc. Thanks,' my throat closed a bit and I had to swallow. 'I... I can't thank you enough. Both of you. I don't know what I would have done… you've been so kind…'

'Oh stuff and nonsense,' the Doc replied, with typical gruffness. 'Anyone would have done the same. Besides, you've already repaid us tenfold by sorting out this old place.' He looked across the hall and up through the strange windows. 'I had forgotten that picture, it must have been hidden by dust.' His eyes rested on the huge painting that hung above the table to the right of the front door.

It was a rather lovely landscape of a country garden with the most stunning bush of pinky-purple daisies at the centre. I looked at it whenever I walked through the hall. 'I used to love coming here, Will too,' he said. 'It was so sad to see it falling into such disrepair. It was difficult to get her to accept any help.'

'Well. It's been a pleasure,' I replied.

They left in a flurry of goodbyes.

The house felt different. Even though she was asleep upstairs, the old woman's presence had affected us all. It was as if all the rooms stood to attention, waiting for her to come down.

*

The following weeks didn't change my initial impression that the old woman was bonkers. She would talk to herself when I was not in the room and I heard her wandering around the place in the middle of the night. Her blond companion seemed to keep close by her most days, and I took pains never to acknowledge him. Was she talking to him? If he answered, I never heard his reply.

She was an odd little stick. There was something frightening about her despite being tiny and almost bent double with a hump on her back. I was conscious of her beady little eyes on me wherever I was and whatever I was doing.

Still. I loved my little apartment. I knew calling it an apartment was a fancy word for what was only a set of four rooms, but it was twice the size of my old flat, and an awful lot nicer. Over the days since Mrs B had returned, I started looking for things around the house to make it feel more homely. I didn't bother asking her, which was a bit naughty of me I suppose, but she was dead to the world for the first week, I would just bring her food and take it away and that was pretty much it.

Besides, I reassured myself, it wasn't as if I was taking anything valuable. I hadn't even gone into the big library that looked to be filled with all kinds of interesting things. It was also filled with cobwebs, and I was waiting for a day when I had lots of energy to tackle that one. I'd discovered some nice curtains that fitted my French windows beautifully. They weren't new and were stuffed right at the back of Mrs. B's enormous airing cupboard so I didn't think they would be missed.

I'd found three, funny little rugs rolled up in a back room and they looked proper lovely on the wooden floorboards of my bedroom and sitting room. I had to give them a good shake but once the dust had gone, they shone like jewels; I was constantly fascinated by the way they changed colour depending on the direction of the light.

The big iron bed had been made up with white cotton sheets so old and thick they felt like warm satin. I'd spread two soft blankets over the sheets; one crimson wool and the other a quilt made from hundreds of scraps of different cloths. It looked lovely and cheerful.

I didn't have a TV. I hoped to save up a good amount of money as I wasn't spending anything – no rent, and my food was all provided – but I had a way to go yet. Dad's picture was by my bed, and my Polaroid of Susi, Jayne and me was pride of place on the mantelpiece. The kitchen was stocked, my apartment was clean and comfortable, and the faces of my Dad and my old friends smiled out at me. I had all I needed.

Maeve brought nutrition sheets to help me plan the meals I had to make. I still couldn't believe Mrs B was over a hundred years old, it was mind boggling she was still able to walk about, let alone yell at me for taking down her long-overdue-for-a-wash curtains.

At the end of the week I had to take Mrs B back to the hospital for a check-up. Maeve arranged a black cab so the old woman could climb in easily, but she found the walk down the stairs difficult, and I had to force her to take my arm as we crossed the hall. The effort turned her face white with pain and she remained silent for the whole journey. I was worried, I thought she was getting better. But she wasn't there yet.

'You OK, Mrs B?'

'Fine,' she snapped, then seemed to relent. 'I just don't like these places.'

'Me neither,' I replied. 'I haven't been here since my Dad died.'

'John Tully. He was your Dad, wasn't he?'

'You knew him?' I said, astonished.

Mrs B nodded. 'He used to work for me on occasion, before your mother died. He was a good man. He was funny, used to make me laugh.'

'Yes he was' I gulped.

'It was a shame what happened, to your mother, someone should have...' As the taxi lurched to a halt she winced in pain and her lips tightened.

'What do you mean?' I asked, curious. 'Someone should have what?' But Mrs B was silent.

The nurses wheeled her away and I waited in reception. I grabbed a handful of chocolate bars from the shop along with some magazines and settled myself in to wait. With weary resignation, I sensed a dead-eyed woman pacing behind my chair. It was always bad in hospitals. I felt the weight of her stare on the back of my head. The staggered tap of her heels moved back and forth, back and forth.

I read the same page over and over again, not taking anything in. The muscles in my back were rigid. When would this ever end? I thought in despair. I knew if I concentrated, I would be able to make out words, hissed phrases, but they terrified me, these lost ones. Better not to look – better not to listen. It was a relief when I saw Mrs B hobbling down the corridor a harassed looking nurse leading her towards me.

Mrs B was exhausted by her hospital visit and demanded I take her straight to bed. I wanted to ask her more about my mother, but decided to wait until she was feeling a bit better. She could be very forbidding when she wanted to be.

It took a week for Mrs B to recover enough strength to leave her room. I took some tea to her along with some lemon curd sandwiches and chopped banana. She needed feeding up, and I could tell she had a sweet tooth. She was looking better, not quite the death mask she had in hospital, but still ancient.

'You're looking much stronger,' I said. 'We'll have you up and about soon.'

There was something very strange about this old crone. Sometimes when we sat quietly together, not talking, just warming ourselves by the fire, I would look over and instead of the familiar gnarled old lady, I saw - just for a second – a glimpse of a much younger woman. A queen, strong featured, with hanks of thick, black hair hanging down her back and over her face. It was strange and disconcerting. What made it worse was every now and then she would shoot me a look from her glittering eyes, and I could tell she knew what I was seeing.

It was a nightmare to get Mrs B to do the hospital exercises. I had to coax and cajole but gradually I succeeded, and her movements become easier, her muscles stronger. I worked hard to fatten her up. I loved cooking. I'd find more and more ingenious ways to get her to eat vegetables. She was starting to fill out and I heard Maeve had been singing my praises in Gray's. Even sour old Laurie treated me with a bit more respect when I did my weekly shop.

Helping Mrs B with her exercises gave me a bit of a work-out and my body felt tougher; I started to take walks around the garden and a little way into the woods. I was out of breath less often.

It wasn't until we were in the absolute depths of winter that I managed to get the old woman out past the garden and into the woods. She was planning to get as far as the village, but I didn't think we'd make it.

I was wrong, though. There was something about the woods, grim and dark as they were, that woke her. Every other step Mrs B would make me stop and take deep breaths. She seemed electrified by being out there, as if she had plugged herself into the energy of the trees. Her walk was steadier, she looked taller and I saw a flash of that raven-haired woman, marching through the wood, the light glinting on her hair.

I'd stop, resisting the urge to rub my eyes, and then she would be gone, and the white-haired fairy-tale crone was back, hobbling, in her place.

I was wondering how I'd ended up in this wood with this strange old woman, marvelling how much my life had changed when I noticed her falter. 'Are you sure you're OK going this far?' I asked. There was a flicker in the corner of my eye and I looked beyond Mrs B to the trees. Someone was running, crashing about in the rotting bracken.

'Hey!' I shouted. 'Who's there?' I turned to Mrs B 'Wait here.' I said. She was deathly white, her hands shaking.

I pushed through the bracken and piles of leaves to a gap between two trees. My breathing was coming in gasps but I kept my eyes on the flickering figure. I could hear the old woman calling me back but I didn't turn around. I don't know what possessed me, but I had become protective of this woman who had been put in my care.

'Hey!' I shouted again. I squeezed through the gap and paused. I was at the entrance to a little glade, an oblong-shaped clearing framed by walls of trees, which soared up towards the darkening sky. At the far end stood a figure, I could just make out the flash of his white face as he looked back at me. He wore a dark hoodie and tracksuit bottoms. A young lad. For a second I felt a tremor of fear, had I stupidly run after a one? But no. He was here. His eyes were alive.

'What are you doing here? Are you OK?' My fear and anger turned to concern. He looked desperate. He was holding something in his hand, but I couldn't make it out. I went to speak again but he shook his head; he slipped into the shadows and was gone.

When I got back to Mrs B she looked drained.

'It was some kid,' I said to her. 'I've seen him before around the village. I wonder what he was doing in your woods?'

'I thought... I thought it was something else,' she said, her mouth working. I'd seen this woman angry, weak, imperious, demanding, cruel, and hungry – but I'd never seen her look so frightened.

'Come on,' I said, 'let's get you back home. It was just a young lad – nothing to worry about.'

It wasn't until later I wondered why she said 'something' instead of 'someone'.

## CHAPTER 11: FRIEDA AND WILL

I am sorting through my jewellery when Charlie slides into the room with a crackle and a fizz. I am growing tired of his constant presence. We have talked about everything that needs to be discussed – or I have any desire to discuss – so his role now seems to be a silent observer. I find this, along with Angela's constant clattering about, unutterably wearisome.

I focus on my box of treasures. As irritating as living with Angela is, her cleaning has unearthed parts of my life I haven't thought about, let alone touched, in decades. What was buried beneath layers of rubbish is now sorted and cleaned. Angela has arranged everything in serried ranks, and that morning I'd spent a pleasurable hour rearranging everything into groups, running my fingers down the spine of much loved but long-not-thought-about books.

There is not a speck of dust in my room. I have wiped the tops of the mirrors and paintings and my handkerchief remains white. I see the view over the valley without having to open the window; I can't remember the last time the glass was this clean. The woman is overly keen on bleach, though; I make a mental note to tell her not to use it as the scent in the air is an unpleasant reminder of that godforsaken hospital.

Angela has used my good leather liniment I note. My ancient jewellery box, whose surface I remember as faded and cracked, looks like itself again. The rich, calfskin leather is restored to its burgundy beauty. This must have taken hours of careful, patient work – the leather looks as good as the day I first opened the box, eager to explore the hidden drawers and compartments.

'You're wondering if she's stolen anything aren't you?' Charlie says in amusement. His voice is loud in the happy silence of the room. I don't respond, though he is correct. I feel a tremor of anticipated outrage. If she's taken a single thing from here, I think…

The contents explode onto my desk as I open the lid. She hasn't opened it, I realise with relief. Everything is in such a mess and a tangle. A thrill runs through me. I pick up a great hank of pieces that have twisted together. The trembling glitter of diamonds, gold and precious stones makes my eyes shine and my lips draw back in a smile.

Squinting, I begin to unpick the tangle, hooking out stray earrings and bangles. It is an impossible task. I summon a spark to roll up my hands through my fingers into the bundle and the pieces separate, falling obediently onto the table. I paw through them. Each piece holds a memory, and I have to force myself not to linger, they are so vivid as to be overwhelming.

So many of them: Silver bangles from India, tens of them, a shivering tingle of sound as they move over each other; creamy pearls the size of my thumb; heavy gold cuffs; startlingly beautiful rings and earrings and pins in the shape of animals and birds with emeralds and rubies for eyes. Oh, and the diamonds – all sorts of them – some still uncut, some glittering with the fire of a star.

'Just one of those things would be worth more than a month of Angela's wages,' Charlie says.

'She's getting well paid for what she does,' I snap, and turn back to my trinkets. I hold up a long platinum chain, it slithers cool as water in my hands. The aquamarine pendant with its three cushion cut diamonds still shines blue as a swimming pool. 'This I got from Zita.' I say to Charlie. 'An old friend.'

He frowns. 'She paid very dearly for crossing you, didn't she Freddy?'

I tut and throw the pendant back in the box. 'She knew what she was getting herself into,' I say.

Zita was a first class bitch. She danced her way through the dark years after the first war, blonde hair unfashionably long and a great bewitcher of men. She had the most extraordinary eyes, as blue as her aquamarine pendant. Everyone was enthralled by her American glamour, she'd trail through parties spilling jewels, furs, and silken dresses. I hated her.

But, thanks to a little bit of hogweed, Edouard and this beautiful necklace became mine. I slide the ring Ned gave me onto my finger; a cabochon cut emerald in a circlet of tiny rose diamonds. To match my eyes, he had said. I frown as the glossy stone with its deep, verdant depths swings round on my bony finger. With an effort I gather up the folds of youth and wrap them around me until my hands are white and smooth again. I add more jewels and luxuriate in the glow of rubies, sapphires, platinum and gold against my flesh.

I gaze into the mirror and enjoy, just for a moment, my lost beauty. My hair, thick and dark, the loveliness of my collarbones, the plump flower of my lips.

'There was never yet fair woman but she made mouths in a glass,' says Charlie, breaking into my reverie.

'Oh shut up, Charlie,' I reply. My complexion withers and sinks back down onto the bones. The liver spots and stains crawl over my skin, and my body twists into its crooked knot. I put away the jewels, those tributes to my beauty, one by one and snap the box shut.

'So what are you going to do?'

'What am I going to do about what?' I want to drink sweet tea in peace, and listen to the voices from the past that tug at the edge of my consciousness.

'Will, of course, what are you going to do about him?'

'I'm not going to do anything about him,' I say. 'Why should I?'

'You know who it was in the woods, Frieda, you know what he was trying to do.'

'Oh, for God's sake! None of that is my concern. His parents…'

'He meant a great deal to you, once.'

'Pah, only as a child. I find children interesting, adults are a bore.'

'He isn't an adult!' he protests. 'He needs you, Frieda. Why do you think he came to your woods?'

'I don't know and I have no interest in finding out. I'm going to ask Angela to make tea.'

I struggle to get out of my chair.

'You know what he was carrying?'

I ignore him and rest heavy on my cane. 'Shut up, Charlie.'

'If I saw it, I know damned well you did too.'

'I said be quiet!' My voice is as harsh as I can make it but Charlie is resolute, not taking his eyes from mine.

'It was a rope, Freddy…'

'I don't care, it's not my…' I am struck dumb by the sudden, excruciating bolt of pain that slices into my head and twists through to the other side. I rub my hand against the temple but the pain continues. It forces me to slump back into my seat. Eyes tight shut I hold my head in my hands, Charlie watches me, his face without expression.

*

Maeve treats her pregnancy like the second coming of the lord. Many years of trying and many disappointments have marked her face, and his. Miscarriages and failures dog their steps and their lives are ruled by the tragedy of monthly bloods. I watch, and I wait. They are good people. They care about the village.

They come to the house and we walk in the gardens. I send the Doctor back to the house to bring us lemonade for the hot day. While he is gone, I take Maeve with me into the woods, watching the sunlight dapple on her face until her shoulders fall and the tension of her jaw dissolves. She flinches as I lay my hands on her belly but says nothing – her eyes wide in the green-golden gloom of the trees. I have gathered Lady's Mantle and made a tea. I press the packet into her hand, telling her to drink it every morning.

Lockwood comes to thank me the day Maeve passes three months into her new pregnancy.

'Of course, we don't know if she will carry to term...'

'She will,' I say with confidence.

Lockwood shrugs. 'We've tried everything, done so many tests but... She believes it's you,' he says. 'You have done something. She drank your tea religiously, I told her it wouldn't make any difference but she was insistent. It makes one wonder... I've researched into the placebo effect, of course, and it is recognised and evidenced the power it can have, but still..'

I smile.

He leans forward. 'She sees it as a miracle, Mrs Beaudry, and I must say she's very convincing. Whatever happens, you've given us hope. I don't know how I can ever thank you.'

'Call me Frieda,' I say. 'And you don't need to thank me.'

Once she passed three months, Maeve accompanies Doctor Lockwood on his regular visits. He is always nagging me to check my blood pressure, take his pills, I refuse but he still comes to see me every week.

The excitement of impending fatherhood has taken years from Lockwood's face. He smiles more, watches his wife with pride and cautious delight. She glows with it, of course, her purpose in life achieved. The birth is difficult, I hear, but the boy is delivered safely. They bring him to me, I have no interest in the squalling scrap of meat but they huddle around him - a sacred flame, which needs to be constantly tended. I am irritated by this interruption to the conversations I have with Lockwood. Even as we speak, his eyes keep turning to his wife and babe.

They are unable to have any more children. They speak of it with bright voices, counting their blessings for the safe delivery of Will, insisting they are content with their lot but they both carry a new sadness within them. I want to help them again, but

Lockwood insists it would be too dangerous for Maeve, labouring to deliver Will almost killed her.

The years pass, and Will grows into a stout, apple-cheeked six year old with grubby hands and shining eyes. He runs around my garden looking for rabbits. Obsessed with the woods, he darts into them with a crow of delight as soon as our backs are turned, returning with handfuls of blooms he shoves into my and Maeve's hands.

At eight, nine, ten he appears alone, pockets stuffed with green apples to feed the old pony in my bottom meadow. Freed from his parents' gaze, he explores the house, constant questions and exclamations accompanying his thudding footsteps. To my surprise, I find I don't mind.

One day, I crack one of my walnuts for him. Will's eyes are like stars as he plays with the tiny golden top nestling in the shell. He taps it and taps it, chuckling with laughter as it spins and shines, and sings out its music.

More years pass and Will grows tall and skinny as a string bean. He is a Huckleberry Finn with straw-yellow hair hanging in his eyes. Whenever he can, he escapes to my garden and fields, straight after school I see him picking his way through the fruit bushes and disappearing into the woods.

He stops coming at around 16. I tell myself I enjoy the peace and quiet, I pretend I don't look for his gangling form every afternoon. Lockwood and Maeve still come, and they shake their heads over Will's withdrawal from them. The strange clothes he wears, the music to which he listens – they are alien and unfamiliar to this gentle, rather old-fashioned couple.

They are delighted he passes his exams, though Maeve confides she worries he has chosen a university so far away from sleepy old Witchford.

And he is gone. The boy I knew no longer exists, he has grown up and away from us all, I don't think about him. I dismiss the gossip I hear in the shop about Will abruptly leaving college, getting himself into trouble. None of my business, I think. He has chosen his path.

*

As the pain in my head recedes, I open my eyes and scowl at Charlie.

'It's worse every time, isn't it?' he asks. 'He's still that boy, you know. He still needs your help. Besides, you owe his parents.'

'I don't owe them anything,' I reply crossly. 'I wish you'd stop interfering.'

'Suit yourself,' he shrugs.

I don't see him for a few days. Angela decides it is time to walk me to the village. 'You need a good stretch of the legs,' she says.

I make her find my old tweed suit and together we choose a beautiful broach from my jewellery box. I watch her to see how she reacts to the pile of glinting baubles, but her fat face remains impassive. I pin it to my jacket lapel, it takes me a while as my fingers are stiff but I slap away Angela's hands when she tries to help.

'There,' I say, looking in the hall mirror to ensure the broach is straight.

'I've never seen anything like that before,' says Angela. 'What's it supposed to be?'

'It's a sea urchin,' I say, running the tips of my fingers over the pure gold spikes. 'And these are emeralds. A man called David bought it for me, the emeralds for my eyes and the spikes for the pain he said I inflicted on people.'

Angela looks a little disconcerted. She squashes a repulsive hat on her head and winds a scarf around her neck. 'We'd better get going,' she says.

Although the day is drear, my heart is brightened by the very first stirrings of spring I spot in the woods. At the foot of the trees I find snowdrops lifting out of the darkness, I touch them to absorb their delicate prickle of energy.

Angela and I pause and bathe our skin in the sweet, cold air that has the honeyed breath of spring.

We walk in silence down through the woods and to the fields at the bottom of the hill. We pass the playground and into the village. My hips and legs are strong and I have no need of my cane so Angela carries it, casting me worried looks. I could walk forever, I think. My body moves with a suppleness I haven't felt for years.

Villagers nod as we march past. It feels strange to be surrounded by groups of people after so long with just Angela for company.

'I'm trying a new recipe tonight,' Angela says. Her eyes are bright and her cheeks pink with the cold. 'It's a sort of curry, I've asked Laurie to get in some saffron and paprika.'

The words hang in the air, hot with colour. I am transported to the markets of Kerala, great towers of spices heaped around me, drying in the sun. I have to stop, leaning on the church wall, as memories seem to want to gulp me down. The world tilts and I am dizzy. For a second I am there, in the heat, the noise, the roar of India.

'Mrs B! Mrs B! are you OK?' Angela's moon face looms close. I push her away.

'Yes, I'm fine, I just…'

'Come on. Let's go and have a sit down. The Rose is open. I think we may have walked too far.'

I allow her to help me into the nearby pub. I have to shake my head to dislodge the last traces of those memories; I lick my lips and taste turmeric and coriander, cumin and black pepper.

More shaken than I care to admit, I allow Angela to guide me to an armchair by the fire.

The Rose hasn't changed in the slightest. I try to remember the last time I was here. I seem to remember it was at the wake for Elsie Fortescue, my old housekeeper, a woman as ugly as she was stupid. The only change being it doesn't stink of cigarette smoke.

My mouth is dry. I long for wine. 'I'll have a large glass of red, Angela.'

'Why don't I get you a nice cup of tea?' She looks uncomfortable.

'What on earth is the matter?'

'I don't think you should be drinking alcohol.'

'I assure you I am over 18,' I say dryly. 'Go on. I'll wait here while you get your things from the shop and then I'll treat you to lunch.'

Angela gives in with a sigh and squeezes her way to the bar, knocking stools aside as she walks. Good job the place is empty.

It is the best wine I have ever tasted, though I suspect it is because I have drunk nothing alcoholic since the day I fell. Each sip floods me with heat and my lips plump with the power of it. I drain the glass dry and signal to the barman to bring me another.

Angela returns, weighed down with bags she stows under the armchair opposite me. 'What do you want to eat?' she says, passing me the menu card.

'Bread and cheese,' I reply. 'And another glass of that wine.' I push the glass towards her.

She orders and we wait in silence for the food to arrive. I note with amusement Angela is staring straight ahead so as not to see the old man who is leaning on the chair next to her. He is trying to attract her attention, one of his eyes bulges obscenely from its socket.

We are distracted by the barman bringing over our plates. Angela has ordered a huge baguette with a bowl of chips, and a pint of some sugary drink that smells of plastic cherries. She starts wolfing it all down, eating as if she will die if she doesn't consume everything immediately. It is distressing to watch.

She looks over and I pick at my food. The cheese is rubbery, the bread white and flaccid.

'You not going to eat that?' she says, her mouth full.

'I'd rather wait for your curry,' I reply, finishing my wine and waving for another.

Angela grunts and pulls my plate in front of her. She works her way through it all and washes the lot down with the last of her drink. With revulsion, I watch her throat work as she gulps everything down.

The old man with the eye has shifted position, moving to the fireplace, never taking his eyes from Angela. She continues to ignore him.

'You know, they are much easier to handle if you find out what they want,' I say.

Angela's look of utter astonishment is comical. Her mouth falls open and she is frozen with shock. She recovers herself quickly, but I can see she is stunned. She shakes her head.

'I don't know what you're on about,' she says, her face losing all colour. I smell fear rising from her.

'There's nothing to be frightened of,' I tell her. 'Trust me. Watch.'

Her eyes are as round as head lamps as I hook myself out of my chair and move in front of the old man. He smells of damp and loss. The temperature drops as I near him, but I am used to that.

He tears his eyes from Angela and looks at me. I reach up and rest my hand against his face as gently as I can. My palm grows hot against his cold cheek. I lean in and let him whisper in my ear, his breath is urgent. He pours himself into me and I hold him tight, one hand on his side, one still on his face.

I hold him steady and speak my words. Not gold, this time, but pale blue and silvery. They fall onto his skin and his hands like the most delicate of butterflies. Time stands still, the room is frozen, the old man begins to fade. I hold onto him until there is nothing left. It is draining, I don't do it often now, but it always brings with it the power of a good deed, and the aches in my bones lift for a while.

I return to the seat and sit back with a sigh, taking a good gulp of wine. Angela's mouth is still open, she is white with shock, her hands are shaking.

'What did you do? What happened?'

'I let him tell me his story, the one he needed to tell – then he was free.'

'You make it sound simple.'

'It is,' I shrug.

'My Dad…' I look up at the harsh scrape of pain in Angela's voice. 'My Dad has been trying…' Her throat closes and she takes a great sniff. She wipes away tears with the heel of her hand. 'I've always ignored them, those… people, I've seen them all my life, but I could never, not in a million years, do what you just…' She gestures with her hand and a sob ratchets up from her chest. 'I couldn't ever… touch them the way you did.' Her mouth twists in revulsion. 'Some of them are just so… gross. But my Dad, my Dad….'

'He's been trying to connect with you?'

'Yes!' She sounds like a child. With a blink, I can see the little ginger girl with freckles she used to be, not this sad, frumpy middle-aged woman with greying hair. 'But I can't bring myself to go near him and I feel so awful, but I don't know if any of this is even real!' I hand her my napkin as the tears fall.

'Then you're just not ready,' I reassure her. 'You need to practise on others first.'

A laugh bubbles out of her. 'Practice? On the ghosts?'

'They're not ghosts,' I snap in irritation. I am feeling very tired all of a sudden.

'What do you know about all of this, anyway?' Angela says as she starts to pull herself together.

I put my hand on her wrist and feel a fizzle where our skin meets. Angela looks down at her arm in surprise and then looks at me.

I grasp that familiar falling feeling as I focus on the green of her eyes. I look for reflections, for pictures. 'You miss your father. Very much,' I say. 'And you can sing. Oh, and when you were very small you picked up a soldier doll made of wool, and a wasp flew out of it and stung you, here.' I touch her cheekbone, just below her right eye.

Angela reels back. 'How the hell…?'

'I told you, I know things. Come on, we better get back.'

Outside, the clouds have drifted open to reveal a tender blue sky. It is still cold, though, and I hold on to Angela's arm, my legs are tired and my hip is aching.

Across the road, I see a tall woman with a little girl in a bright red coat next to her. She is pulling at her mother's arm and pointing at me. She smiles and waves her doll; it is the girl from the playground. I lay my finger on my lips and she copies me.

'I don't think we should walk back,' Angela is saying. 'You look tired, and you're hunching over again.' She is dithering with indecision and looks at me with unease. I have spooked her, I think with a chuckle. 'Oh it's the Doctor!' she exclaims in relief. 'I bet he can give us a lift.'

Lockwood is a little way down the street chatting with a couple of plump young women. One has a toddler who is holding his mother's hand and leaning horizontally, tired of the grown-up conversation. Angela, who doesn't seem to know if she is coming or going, calls out.

'Doc! Hi, Doc! Do you think you could give us a lift? Mrs B's overdone it a bit, I'm afraid.' I look over, but she avoids my eyes, the shutters have come down.

He helps Angela put her bags in the boot, and we drive out of the village. Angela is silent in the back of the car. Lockwood seems distracted. I am irritated by the knot of guilt and worry which stirs in my stomach and try to push it down, like bile, but it surges up my throat.

'How's Will?' I say, reluctantly. 'I've heard he's dropped out of university? And he's been wandering around the woods.'

I sense Angela's stirring interest but ignore her and focus on Lockwood.

He sighs, and is silent for a few minutes.

'He's not good, Frieda. We are both very worried about him. He did something very silly and had to go to the hospital for a while. He is better back at home, but still very low. We've spoken to some excellent people but… well…' He concentrates on the road ahead. 'Here we are!' he says, turning into the drive, relieved to change the subject.

We climb out. Angela lines the bags on the front step and turns back to the car. 'Doc, I'm sorry to hear about your boy,' she says. 'If there's anything I can do…'

He acknowledges her with a nod. 'That's very kind, Angela, thank you. Frieda, let me know if he bothers you again, he shouldn't be roaming about your woods without asking.'

I wave dismissively, 'It's not a problem,' I reply. 'But I will let you know.'

'Poor bloke,' Angela says as the car disappears. 'I wish I could help. They've been so good to me.' She carries the shopping into the house and I follow her. My bones are sore after the long walk and electric zaps of pain pinch my hip.

I am crossing the hall and am about to mount the stairs when there is a crash. I pause; my heart thumps. I tilt my head but can hear nothing, then, Angela appears at the end of the corridor. She is panting and glances around wildly until she sees me.

'It's the boy!' she gasps, 'the one we saw in the wood! The one you said was the Doc's son. He's standing in the garden, gave me the fright of my life!' She holds her hand out to me. 'Come on! You need to come help him.'

Exhaustion weighs me down, heavy as an anvil. I was looking forward to a quiet moment with my book, followed by Angela's curry, a bath, and an early night. Now the peace of the evening will be shattered by upset and worry and too many conversations. The thought makes my heart sink.

'Oh Christ, just what we need,' I say. 'Call Doctor Lockwood, tell him Will is here and I'm looking after him. He doesn't need to come up to the house; I'll send him back in the morning.'

*

The garden is cold, my breath frosts as I crunch across the grass, it will be dark soon. Will is hunched under a tree, his hood up. He is staring up into the woods. As I near him he turns around. I struggle to keep my face without expression but my body reels with the shock of how much Will has changed.

His face is dead-white, even his lips are colourless. His puffy eyes won't meet mine and since I last saw him he has shrunk to an etiolated pen and ink sketch. He has the body of a lanky 12 year old boy who hasn't grown into himself. His hands and feet look clown-like at the end of his slender limbs; it is a shock when he pushes his hair back, it looks like he's strapped on the mask of an old man. It is an abomination. He is 19.

I take a moment, shutting my eyes for a second. He waits, every fibre of his body vibrates with tension, he is ready to run. I remember with an ache Will standing here ten years ago, fat as butter, his pockets bulging with conkers and his mother's biscuits. This miserable young man is an obscene palimpsest of the boy I remember.

'Hello, Will.' I say. I keep my voice soft and my hands by my side. A kind of demented force spirals from him. He can't sit still, and he picks at his hands, peeling away the skin from around his nails. Blood wells up, a glossy red plush. He wipes it away and continues peeling. I can't help reaching out to stop him. He is sweating despite the cold, he is clammy and his breathing is shallow. He has demons in his black eyes.

'Will you come inside? Have some tea?'

He doesn't move. I take a step closer. He jerks his head up and I stand still. I murmur soothing words, a constant stream of them, until he calms. Swiftly, before he can pull away I reach for his hands and force him to look at me. I have to suppress a shudder. He is in hell.

Nightmares pour from his pupils into mine: I see naked bodies displayed like hanging pieces of meat, hands clap apart and together in a strange dance, whispers and bright flashes are blinding. None of it makes any sense. Twisting shapes, screaming faces, horrors crawling, black-winged insects swarm in his head.

I allow his darkness to spill down my arms and into my body; I hold it, a brimming bowl of black deep in my belly. I see the relief in his face, he is blank-eyed, but it is only temporary.

'Come on, come on, that's right. You come with me, dear.' With gentle words I draw him into the house and lead him to the kitchen. I nod at Angela who rushes to put on the kettle, turning up the Aga so the warmth fills the room. Will collapses onto the chair, an elongated tumble of skin and bones. Despite the heat, he shivers. Angela looks at him with horror.

'Stay with him,' I say, my voice thick and desperate; the darkness is surging and roiling up from my belly. I can feel it coating my throat. Angela moves to me in concern but I hobble past her to the bathroom. Reaching the sink just in time, I lurch towards it vomiting pints of black bile. I heave everything up until the bowl inside me is empty.

# CHAPTER 12: ANGIE

For a couple of days, I was looking after two invalids. The old woman took herself to her bed; once she'd brought the boy in from the garden, she showed no interest in him. The boy, Will was a zombie. I made up a bed for him in the room along from Mrs B but then she called me in and told me off for invading her peace and quiet, so I had to clear out a whole room on the floor above - another filthy space filled with dust.

The boy said nothing as I appeared with hair filled with cobwebs, my clothes powdered with dust. I handed him a clean towel and took him upstairs. It was a pretty little room with green silk wallpaper and scarlet curtains faded to a soft flamingo pink. He walked in ahead of me and curled up on the bed, knees tight to his chest, not answering when I asked him if he needed anything. After a few moments I realised he'd fallen asleep and was dead to the world. It wrung my heart to look at him, scrunched up like a little boy.

Maeve was worried sick when I called. It took all my powers of persuasion to stop them racing up to the house.

'I think he needs a bit of space,' I told her. 'Mrs B knows what to do. I won't take my eyes off him, I promise.' I explained how hard it had been to get him into the house, I told them I suspected he'd bolt if anyone came.

It was an uncomfortable night. I couldn't sleep on the chair I'd drawn up outside Will's room and the old woman's words kept rolling around my head. I still couldn't get over the shock of seeing her walk over to that old one. It made me feel sick to think of her touching him, that dreadful, ruined face.

Only my mother understood when, as a child I would chatter away in an empty room, laughing and talking to people who weren't there. I was never scared of them as my mother showed no fear, she welcomed them silently and they drifted in and out. Dad knew nothing about it; it was mum's and my little secret.

And then she died, and the ones were no longer a smiling, friendly presence. They would surround me, I'd see them drifting across the playground at school, pressing their faces up against the windows of my classroom. Once, when it got too much I screamed and passed out – right in the middle of that cow Mrs West's lesson. It was dismissed as a panic attack, the effects of the loss of my mother. I never told anyone what I could see. The only one who understood was dead.

I'd spent years pretending they weren't there, that I couldn't see them. It was easy to do, as most of them were horrifying. Some were disfigured or injured so just looked awful; the worst were the mad ones. They had a desperation and a sort of despairing rage I couldn't deal with. After a while, I was so expert at ignoring them I could convince myself they weren't there.

I hadn't recognised how much of a burden this 'gift' was, until the ones were banished out of existence by my medication. It was a shame I was so sunken into depression I didn't appreciate how wonderful it was to be left in peace by these strange, lost beings.

I knew the second the meds were no longer messing with my brain because I saw the old boy who sang to his dog. I was leaving the shop and he was walking past the church. I stopped still, trying to work out if anyone else could see him. When the postman walked straight through him I recognised he was a one.

I walked past him quickly and held my breath all the way back to Pagan's Reach, terrified that if I could see the old man, I would be able to see my Dad, and I just couldn't handle it. He continued to haunt my dreams. I hated ignoring him, but the thought of approaching that thing, whatever was left of my Dad, filled me with a dragging, paralysing reluctance.

To be honest I was ashamed. I was sticking my head in the sand and letting my Dad down, my Mum too. She was the bravest person I knew. I couldn't remember much about her, as she died when I was so young, but I knew when she walked she kept her head up and her shoulders squared. Her chin was always tilted as if preparing for battle.

Guilt squirmed in my belly. I didn't know what to do, the old woman made it sound so easy but I couldn't bring myself to take the next step. What did Dad want? What was troubling him so terribly he was still here, trying to talk to me? I was too afraid of the answer, so with a conscious effort, I choked off that questioning voice inside me until I couldn't hear it any more.

I sighed and shifted on the chair, peering in on Will to check he was OK. He hadn't moved. I wondered what had brought him to this state. The Doc and his wife were good people - he was obviously a bright lad, getting into university. But he looked awful, all pale and thin - Mrs B couldn't persuade him to eat, maybe he was anorexic? I'd read in magazines it happened to boys as well as girls.

That reminded me, I had a whole slab of galaxy chocolate in my bag. I tiptoed quickly down to my rooms and, grabbing *Perfume*, I was back at my seat outside the boy's room within minutes. I let a chunk of chocolate melt on my tongue before wiping my fingers and leafing through to where I had left off.

I used to love reading when I was younger and for me nothing could top Jilly Cooper's *Riders*, but I had to admit I'd never read anything like this book. The author was able to pick me up and chuck me into his scenes. Ones that stank and were full of noise. The characters were ugly, strange and awful to each other, but I couldn't put it down. I would read and realise with a shock of surprise that hours had passed.

I thought of Mrs B's old gnarled walnut of a face and her cotton wool puffs of hair. I found it impossible to find a connection between her and this remarkable book. Murders and prostitutes, a man being torn apart because of the way he smelled, I shook my head, all very strange.

Saying that, though, there was definitely something odd about Mrs B. The way she tricked my eyes, for one. When she was cross, I swear she flicked darts at me or something – it could be most unsettling to be around her when she was irritated. And that strange way she changed in the wood!

The sun was just starting to brighten, time to get on with Mrs B's breakfast, I thought. I wasn't really tired, my brain was stuffed full of too many thoughts to sleep, but my body felt stiff and heavy. The boy wasn't showing any signs of stirring, so I left him sleeping and went to get the porridge on.

I couldn't help a smile of pride as I walked down from the third floor. The house smelled of fresh air, polish, flowers, and wood smoke. As the sun got stronger, light flooded in from every window. All the clutter was gone, and the wonderful things the old woman had collected were clean and beautifully displayed. She still hadn't spoken a word of thanks, but it was reward enough to see this gorgeous house preening itself, restored to its former glory.

I positively itched with the urge to start exploring the house properly - now the cleaning was mostly done – there must be secret tunnels and priest holes all over the place, and I couldn't wait to find them. Maybe I'd find hidden old gold coins, or secret papers and maps. I'd read far too many *Famous Five* and *Secret Seven* books in my youth.

I had one last room to do and it was time to tackle it. Mrs B's library ran along the entire front of the house and you could barely open the door it was so full of junk. I couldn't wait to clear it. As I put the kettle on and got the honey from the pantry to pour over the porridge as per madam's desires, I worried whether all this cleaning and absorption in Mrs B's affairs was my way of hiding from my problems. A cold, frightened part of me knew I couldn't bury myself away from life here forever. Mrs B would die and then I would be homeless.

A pang of sadness doubled me over at the thought of leaving the place I thought of as my own. I was a fool. Just because I'd wiped, polished, oiled and cleaned every inch, didn't make it mine. I would have to start thinking about what to do next. At some point I would have to go out into a world which held Andy, Kelly and the baby.

But not yet, I thought, as I grated a little nutmeg into the porridge which bubbled creamy and delicious smelling. I still had rooms to clean, Mrs B still needed looking after -and this strange boy had crashed into our lives and needed help. There was no way I was going to let him take advantage of the old woman. She was rich in a way I didn't think possible, and I knew nothing about Will Lockwood.

He could be on drugs! I thought with a lurch of panic. The house was filled with treasures he could sell down the pub for twenty quid. I remembered a skanky cow, Tanya, a girl I used to work with – we'd see her pinching stuff from the hotel, which she'd swap for a wrap of coke at the Bell and Crown. There was no way I'd let Will do the same at Pagan's Reach. I resolved to keep a close eye on him.

*

I was shocked when I took my tray up to the old woman. It looked like a bomb had hit her room. She looked dreadful, and I worried she was running a temperature. She seemed a bit delirious, and must have been racketing around her room all night to make such a mess.

She looked better after her tea. I cleared up and gave her a sponge bath as she was beginning to pong. She then knocked me for six by talking about Jonathan.

'Maeve told me about the child,' she said after talking about my new clothes. It came completely out of the blue. I don't know how she knew his name, only Andy and I knew what we called him. I know now, of course, but at the time I was stunned. Talking about him made me cry, goodness, I hadn't cried like that for such a long time, but as she talked, it was as if I had lost him that morning.

As I left her room, sobbing, something moved and settled inside me. As if a clog of pain, matted like hair, had dislodged itself. Stupid, but I could have sworn I was breathing differently – like a tight band had been unhitched. I can't remember everything she said, but somehow she had freed me. It was a long time before

I realised it was then I started to forgive Andy, and I no longer thought about his baby without feeling sick.

I knew there was more I had to face up to, only that morning a girl had peered in through the window as I finished making my bread. The blue around her mouth made my skin shiver. I wasn't ready. No. I had work to do, I resolved to face those demons once Will had left, and the house was finished.

It was time to work my magic on the library. Mrs B was up and dressed and seemed happy to read outside Will's room, though she insisted I carry a big, squashy armchair up to the third floor so she would be comfortable. I'd left a pile of sandwiches and a bottle of homemade lemonade next to Will's bed; he was so still I gave him a prod to check he was still alive – to my relief he snorted and rolled over.

The library was the biggest challenge of the house as it was huge and overrun with crap. I filled a bucket with cleaning stuff and rolled up my sleeves. I'd saved the best until last. The library ran all the way along the front left of the house and took up two floors. My heart sank when I opened the double doors. Apart from a quick peek when I first moved in, I'd not ventured any further than the doorway. I'd forgotten how bad it was.

Books were littered everywhere. It was as if Mrs B had dropped them as she read. I could barely get into the room, despite its size. Dark, wooden shelves ran along every inch of wall. Beneath them was scuffed walnut panelling in desperate need of a rub with some polish to bring out the shine. Four enormous sash windows looked out over the garden towards the valley. Each of them had sills deep enough for seats to have been built there.

I'd got someone in to clean the windows and the cold, winter sunshine streamed in. A big improvement, the last time I had looked into the library the windows were so filthy it was as if the curtains had been left forever closed.

I looked around. I couldn't do anything until I'd got the books off the floor. It took me over three hours of methodical work to put every one back on the shelves. To begin with, I'd flick through them, admire the covers – many had beautiful leather covers with gold-edged pages – reading the titles before putting it on the shelf. After about an hour I gave up and just shoved them in willy-nilly. I was a robot, bend, pick up, put on shelf, bend... Over and over again.

My reward was seeing the beautiful room slowly reveal itself. Half way down, opposite the windows stood a fireplace with a mantelpiece taller than my head. Four wide, sturdy leather armchairs were grouped around it with a little, red footstool. As I worked my way down the room I noticed the back wall looked odd. One panel of it didn't have any gaps on its shelves. When I cleared enough to get closer, I realised it was because the books weren't real, just the backs glued on. My heart raced, was this the secret tunnel I was hoping for?

I pressed against the backs of the books until I noticed one stood proud. I gave it a tug and the fake shelves swung back. A childish surge of excitement made my heart race. A door! Behind it was a black spiral staircase. Trembling with curiosity I peered up, but was disappointed to find it just took you up to the second storey of the library. There was no way I could squeeze up there, but I could see a small platform leading to a balcony running all the way round the room, about ten feet up, so a (very thin) person could access the top shelves.

At each end of the library were giant settees with matching buttoned backs. They were piled high with cushions but I had to throw them all away as they had got damp and were ruined with mould.

I stopped for lunch and went to check on Will. He was awake but not talking. He'd drunk the lemonade but refused the sandwiches. He lay on the bed, staring at the ceiling. I burned with curiosity, and longed to sit down and question him; the misery scrawled across his face, contrasting with the boyish tumble of hair and young skin, stopped me, and I left with his untouched plate. Mrs B was grumpy when I brought her soup on a tray.

'What are you looking so cheerful about?' She scowled, looking tired.

'Nothing, Mrs B' I said airily as I knew it would annoy her. 'I'm sorting the library. You'll be able to sit by the fire in there when I'm done.

She looked a bit alarmed. I raised my hand. 'No, I'm not throwing away anything, just some mouldy old cushions. And I'm not going into your drawers neither.' She grunted and dipped her spoon in her soup. Her lips smacked when she tasted the richness of the flavour and the tang of the olive bread I had made. I left her to it - enjoying her soup and reading her poems.

Back in the library, I picked up and shelved the last few books. There were still some that wouldn't fit, so I piled them in neat rows on the table which stood in the middle of the room. The last book had fallen behind the long settee and I had to hook it out with the end of my hoover. It was thick with a purple cover and the pages were yellow. It felt very heavy and when I pulled it out it fell open to reveal a cunning little hole cut into the pages. Another sizzle of excitement.

This was exactly like the Famous Five, I thought – feeling about eight years old. I couldn't see anything at first then saw a gold key wedged into the pocket. I hooked it out and examined it. Too small for a door, too big for a jewellery box. I shoved it into my pocket. I'd show it to Mrs B later.

With the room clear of books I could see the paintings. Hundreds of them were stacked behind chairs and propped against the panelling. One caught my eye. It was unframed, about the size of a sheet of A4. I turned it over and wiped it with the edge of my shirt. A girl laughed out of the canvas.

She was sitting on a bench, a dog on her lap, her skin a clear, luminescent pearl; it glowed against the swirls of green and gold behind her. I loved it. The artist seemed to have just thrown the paint at the canvas but somehow it had settled in bright splashes bringing the scene vividly to life.

I propped it on the mantelpiece and it blazed in the sunlight. I found another different kind of painting. A silver-haired woman on a straight backed chair, half in shadow so you could only see a sliver of her face. She looked about the same age as me. It made me shiver, but it was compelling. That went on the mantelpiece too.

The next three were dull landscapes and I left them leaning inwards against the wall. The fourth made my little gallery because it took my breath away. A view of a town painted in yellow and oranges with the sea and sky shining blue as glass beyond. I could almost smell the heat of the sun. Up it went to join the other two.

I was so absorbed in my task I forgot to stop for a cup of tea, and was surprised to see it was nearly six o'clock. I was boiling hot, sweat had crusted on my skin, and my hair hung in rats' tails; but looking around the room every minute had been worth it. It didn't matter this wasn't my room, that all the things in it belonged to someone else – I was grateful to it, if you can be grateful to a room, because it had given me hours and hours of escape.

Instead of worrying about my Dad and the ones, or what I would do when I would have to leave, or the whole agony of

Andy's desertion and Kelly's pregnancy; all I had to do was methodically work my way from one end to the other and the room would move from chaos to order – dirt and mess were washed away until everything was clear and clean.

Mrs B persuaded Will to come down for some tea. It was an awkward evening. We sat around the kitchen barely talking, eating the curry I'd made the day before. I was pleased with it. The chicken was all the more delicious for another day in its marinade, and it was so tender it fell off the fork. The rice was fluffy and tasty; I'd used bay leaves fresh from the garden, and the cardamom and cumin worked beautifully. I was well chuffed, it tasted better than a takeaway. I'd even made naan bread but managed to burn the edges.

'What do you think, Mrs B?' I said.

'Not enough cumin,' she replied, stuffing her little face with chicken and rice before wiping her plate clean with a torn scrap of naan. She sure could eat when she wanted to.

'Well it's the first time I've made it and I think it's very nice,' I said stoutly. Mrs B stopped chewing for a moment and shot me a glance.

'Come on, Will, at least try it,' I said to the silent boy who were staring into the fire from his end of the table. I'd piled his plate high but he hadn't touched a thing. 'Go on, it's the first curry I've ever made, I'd love to know what you think of it.'

Reluctantly, he selected a cube of chicken and began to chew. I was delighted to see him chewing faster and faster before forking up a great wodge of rice. His cheeks bulged. He must have been starving, I thought.

It surprised me how much I enjoyed watching Mrs B and Will eating my food. I'd lived off sandwiches; I never used a recipe book when I was with Andy. I was always so knackered it was all I could do to chuck some oven chips and a few chicken Kievs from Aldi under the grill. Don't get me wrong, I'd eat anything when we went out, I was quite experimental, but I couldn't be doing with the faff of cooking.

Being with Mrs B had changed me, I realised. I had loved crushing the spices and herbs, releasing their smells and stirring them into a marinade. Thanks to the Doc's wife, I was forced to use a variety of veg and I enjoyed the feeling of plunging my hands into a multi-coloured riot of food.

Will had finished, so I refilled his plate. Mrs B watched him closely.

'Let me get you a beer,' she said.

'I'll get it, Mrs B. Don't get up,' I said. 'Sorry, Will, I didn't know we had any or I would have got you some earlier.'

'I said I'll get it,' the old woman snapped, and she hopped out of her chair and disappeared into the pantry. She was in there so long I followed her in. I found her pouring a foaming stream of liquid into a glass. In the darkness, I saw a little shower of green sparks. Something fell in with a splash. I frowned at her in suspicion at her wide smile, innocent as a child.

'What are you up to?' I said in a whisper so Will couldn't hear.

'Never you mind,' she said and bustled past me, placing the beer in front of the boy.

The curry was hot, and he looked grateful for the chance to cool his mouth. He took a deep draught and I saw his throat bob as he swallowed. Foam coated his top lip and he wiped it away. I passed him the last of the naan bread and he ate it hungrily.

Meanwhile Mrs B had disappeared into the pantry again and returned with an ancient looking bottle of wine, which she poured into two glasses, almost to the brim.

'Here,' she said, plonking one in front of me so hard it sent a shower of blood red drops onto the table. I took a sip, it was gorgeous, thick, rich and highly alcoholic. My head spun at the first drop.

Will finished his beer and the old woman topped him up. Her eyes met mine over his blond head.

He had finished eating and leaned back in his chair, sipping at his beer. The heat of the food and the kitchen had brought a flush to his cheeks. He looked a bit dazed.

'Do you remember coming up here when you were little, Will?' Mrs B asked. She had already knocked back half of her wine and nodded at me to refill it.

Will's eyes widened then focused on Mrs B. He had strange coloured eyes, a kind of bluey-violet, they were very pretty, I thought, feeling a little dreamy myself.

'Yeah,' his voice was rusty and he gave a cough to clear it. 'Yeah I do, I used to love coming here.' Eldritch, who had just streaked in through the window over the sink, jumped onto Will's lap. He stroked her as he gazed out of the window towards the woods.

I jumped when I saw the strange, blond man drift into the room to stand behind Mrs B. His hand was on her shoulder but she didn't respond. She hadn't taken her eyes from Will. When she spoke her voice was soft, coaxing – almost a whisper. I wanted to speak, but found I couldn't break the quiet that had fallen over the room.

'Your mother tells me they gave you pills? Up at the hospital?' I looked over at Will with interest.

He nodded slowly, still looking as if he was caught in a dream.

'Are they helping?'

He was so quiet we had to bend our heads to hear him. 'I think so, a bit, but they make me feel dead.' My skin prickled, I knew exactly what he meant; that's how I used to feel, I wanted to tell him. I opened my mouth to speak, but Mrs B lifted a warning finger and gave a tiny shake of her head. There was a pause.

'What do you mean, dear?' she said.

Will took a shuddering breath. His voice sounded robotic it was so without expression. The words wrenched from him, hesitant, and punasctuated with long pauses. 'I made friends with a bloke when I was in hospital,' he began. 'A bit of an odd ball, but I liked him. He was a bit fucked up – like me.' He smiled, but it had no humour. 'He got discharged a couple of days before I did... yesterday I heard he walked straight under a lorry. He was smashed to pieces and I was so... gutted, but I couldn't cry. These tablets stop me slashing my wrists, but they take everything else away too.' His voice cracked, and my heart broke for him.

'What do you mean, slash your wrists? I heard you took too many pills and that's why they sent you up there. Why did you do that, Will?' Mrs B's voice was level and probing as a barrister. I was open-mouthed at her bluntness but Will sat unperturbed.

'I didn't want to be alive any more,' he said. Pity swelled in my throat. It was unbearable. He was putting into words everything I'd felt, but it was obscene to hear them spoken by someone so young. What the hell had happened to him? Mrs B continued her questioning.

'Why is that, Will? What happened to you?' We waited, our breaths held as Will tried to speak. His mouth moved and I could see the words hanging on his lips, but he stopped. I clenched my fists to stop myself shaking it out of him. 'Is there someone who has done this to you?' The boy looked startled. He looked up, and then out to the windows. He paused, then shook his head.

'Will?' Mrs B's voice was a breath.

The boy shrugged and said nothing, glaring at the table, running his fingers through the crumbs.

'OK, boy,' she said with a sigh. She stood and tapped my hand, jerking her head towards the door. She took my arm. 'Call Lockwood,' she said, her voice low. 'Tell him to come and get his son. There is nothing I can do. He's not going to get better until he talks, and he's not ready. If he won't talk to me, he won't talk to anyone. Tell him to put the boy to bed and I will see him soon. He will be safe tonight, I've made sure of it.' She looked me in the eye. 'Tell him that, yes? I've made sure of it. He will be safe tonight.'

Understanding dawned. 'You *drugged* him, Mrs B?' I was astonished. 'You can't go around drugging people with your pills and potions. God knows what effect it might have on him, especially if he's on anti-depressants. What were you thinking?' My words fell away as I saw the expression on the old woman's face. No longer gnarled and sunken, she had the face of a goddess, implacable and stony. I felt a shiver of fear. 'OK, fine. But I'm telling the Doc you've given him something.'

'You'll do no such thing,' she snapped in reply. 'That won't help at all. Trust me, Angela. I know what I'm doing.'

Doc and Maeve arrived looking as if they'd aged twenty years. Will stood stiff in their arms, but let them lead him to their car, meek as a lamb. Now I knew Mrs B had given him something it was obvious; his pupils were as round, dark and glossy as blackberries.

Maeve sat in the back with Will, her white face strained with fear. The Doc waited on the steps as Mrs B talked to him in an undertone, her words urgent. He nodded and bent down to kiss her on the cheek.

'Thank you, Angie,' he said as he passed me. 'Thank you for looking after him.'

'Of course. I wish we could have done more,' I replied, I felt a bit tearful. 'I hope he's going to be OK,' I said. 'Mrs B said he had to talk about it. Doc, try and get him to tell you. He won't want to, but I think he must.' I gave him a hug and he returned it warmly.

We watched the car drive away; a terrible sense of foreboding weighed heavy in us both.

# CHAPTER 13: FRIEDA REGRETS

Will has brought darkness. The house shifts in pain to accommodate the black emptiness now residing within. He is so closed off I can't reach him. It took all my force and focus to bring him in from the garden. I try to read, but my mind keeps drifting to this open wound of a boy who is infecting everything around him.

I cannot settle. I wander about my room picking up trinkets and baubles and setting them down. An itchy restlessness crawls across my skin, a close harmony to the ever present song of dread, my companion since I had to leave the house because of that damned fall.

He didn't want to live. I pause in my roaming to examine this thought. No, I think carefully, closing my eyes to remember what I'd seen. It's not that he wants to die, he just can't see any other way of being. He is trapped in something intolerable.

I think hard. As we had stood in the garden together I had slipped as far as I could into Will's mind. He'd built a wall so towering and bleak around his inner self I couldn't see into the core, but what I realise now was there was someone else there. A dark energy that obliterated everything; it didn't come from within – it came from outside. I needed to know what or who that was, or Will would be destroyed.

I cannot bear, I simply cannot bear what I'd glimpsed in the boy. His bliss at the thought of ending it all. The knowledge he roamed my woods with a rope in his hand is tearing me apart. It has woken dark memories; they are flying around the room, perching on my shoulders, I can feel their claws digging into my flesh as they flap their black wings around my head.

I hold my hands over my eyes as memories vomit their way to the surface. I am too weak to hold them off: David's body, hanging limp as wet washing, his toes pointed as he circles around; years later, hearing Larry's mother scream with grief as we watch his coffin slide into the ground, his corpse still wearing the silver polish I had painted on his nails.

'Remembering all your lovers?' Charlie asks, making me jump. I can just about make him out as he stands in the shadows of the corner of the room.

'Oh leave me alone, Charlie, please. I'm tired,' I say.

'What's the good of me being here, if not to make you face your demons?' he says. His voice is playful, but his face is grim.

'Not now,' I reach my bed and lean back on the pillow, curling my body, trying to ease the weight on my hip.

'You think saving Will is the answer?' he asks, his tone mocking. 'Suicide is a terrible thing. They must haunt you, those lovers of yours.'

'I was careless then,' I admit. 'A different person. I was young.' Charlie is levering these words from me; a painful prying open of deep incisions, dislodging pebbles of rotted memories.

'You tortured them,'

'Ach,' I wave my hand. 'They weren't children. They made their own decisions.'

'You're a cruel woman, Frieda dear, but those memories are disabling you – I can see it on your face. Don't try to pretend you don't care. Do you think saving this boy will bring you redemption?' His laugh is harsh and full of scorn.

With difficulty, I tear my eyes from his and reach out to scrabble in the bedside drawer.

'No. Not tonight, Freddy.' He steps to the side of my bed and with a quick movement, sends the cabinet skidding across the floor. It crashes over, sending its contents spiralling across the rug. With a cry, I see my little jar bounce across the rug and disappear.

Charlie?' I call, but the room is empty.

This night is long and I am tormented. Demons flit back and forth, swooping behind my eyes and filling my ears with whispers. My hip throbs, and my legs are restless. Will's monster, and the monsters of my past run like an infection in my blood. Acid spills into my throat. I am desperate for my Mandragora. I try to climb out of bed to look for it but am weak as a bird, and I fall back, my body trembling.

It is the longest night of my life and I almost weep with gratitude when Angela appears, carrying a tray steaming with tea, porridge and hot buttered toast in the morning.

'What on earth's happened in here?' she says in amazement, looking at the chaos of my bedroom. Rubbish is scattered all over the floor, bed sheets and blankets hang free exposing the stripes of mattress. My nightdress is wet and stained. 'Have you got a fever?' Angela steps over the fallen cabinet and touches my forehead.

'I'm fine,' I say. 'I just couldn't sleep.'

'I told you to take some painkillers. Yesterday was too much for you. Why won't you take it easy? You're an old woman, remember?' Angela grumbles. I wet my raw throat with hot, sweet tea.

'Will...' I begin.

'Don't you worry about Will,' Angela says, her voice cross. 'He's slept all night and is still dead to the world. You can sit with him today; I'm sorting the library.'

I take a bite of toast and watch as Angela squeezes round the room, restoring order. I know the key to saving Will is unlocking what he is carrying inside. Once I know what happened, I can save him. I have seen off many demons in my time, and I am certain I can do it again.

I feel better after gorging on Angela's thickly buttered toast. The bread is freshly made. She has proved a genius in the kitchen. I wince as she draws the curtains and pushes the windows wide with a crash. It has rained; the gust of air is damp and smells green. I look at her. Thank God, I persuaded Maeve to take Angela up to the big town to buy her some clothes, I told her to spend whatever she needed.

Instead of those revolting leggings and old shirt, Angela is wearing inky-dark denim trousers and a forgivingly loose pink jersey, which brings out the green of her eyes. Despite the ravages of the previous night, I feel a glow of satisfaction. Angela is blooming; I knew she would.

We have fallen into the habit of sitting in the kitchen after supper to talk about books. She is bright, and I am excited to introduce her to new writers. Regular walks have strengthened her body and her fat is hardening into muscle. She accepts my nightly tisane of St John's Wort, though she complains of its bitterness. I tell her it helps with 'women's problems' and she has no reason to doubt me. It is partly true, after all.

'You've lost weight,' I say. 'Got some colour in your cheeks at last.'

Angela blushes. 'We're so out of the way here I can't get takeaways delivered. And I'm probably doing loads more walking than I used to when me and ...' She trails off and shrugs. 'Well, you know, when I was with Andy.'

'He was a shit,' I say.

'He wasn't always!' she protests. 'I wouldn't have married him otherwise.'

'Maeve told me about the child,' I watch Angela's face, the memory still haunts her I see. 'Jonathan?'

She reels in shock. 'How did...?'

Closing my eyes for a moment, I allow sunlight and warmth to fill every cell of my body. I picture my blood running gold with it before touching Angela's arm, tugging her gently onto the chair. It is a good feeling after the terrifying darkness I struggled with the night before. I press light into her as I speak.

'It was a tragedy. It is a tragedy for all women who suffer this, but you have to let it go now. You feel the memory has maimed you, and it has, in a way. But you have to absorb it, allow the scar tissue to harden and let yourself take on this new shape. Pain is what makes us, not happiness. Any fool can be happy. Scar tissue is strong. Don't try to pretend it's not there, because then you are denying you are a mother – and you were a mother; you are a mother.'

Angela's tears are a stream but she doesn't move to wipe them away.

I hold my hand to her cheek. 'You remember being pregnant? Do you remember him alive inside you?'

Angela gives a watery smile. 'Yes, yes of course.'

'And you felt him move? Respond to things?'

She sniffs and nods. 'I remember I was about six months and Andy sneezed, ever so loudly – it always used to wind me up – and I felt the baby jump in surprise. It did make me laugh.'

I smile. 'There. He had a life, a whole nine months with you, together. He knew the sound of your heartbeat and voice, and you knew him. Don't see it as a life cut short, you were blessed for that time, see it as a completion – not a tragic ending.'

Angela's weeping is terrible but redemptive. The damage within her will close, and the scar tissue will pinken and fade.

'Thank you, Mrs B. Nobody has ever... you make it sound...' Her voice is wet with tears and almost incoherent.

I pat her hand. 'And when you're ready, you need to go and find what your father needs from you.'

She nods and rubs her face with the sleeve of her new jersey - getting snot all over it, I note with distaste – then takes my cup and plate and leaves the room.

I sigh, stretch, and relish the pleasure of the last dance of gold sparkling in my blood.

'That was kind of you,' says Charlie.

I let my arms fall. 'Christ, can't you give me any privacy?'

He shakes his head in amusement. 'I'm always here, Freddy, until you don't need me anymore.'

'I don't need you now,' I mutter. 'I'm perfectly capable of looking after myself.'

'I've never seen that side of you,' he says thoughtfully. 'You must be getting soft in your old age.'

'She needed to hear it; she won't be anything until she lets that go.'

'Well let's hope your sentimental little talk has the desired effect,' Charlie says briskly. 'You're going to need her before too long – and not just to keep your house clean and your greedy little body fed.'

I open my mouth to reply, outraged, but he has disappeared.

*

Will returns home and the house sighs with relief. I have to walk it end to end to banish the last shreds of darkness he left behind. After my good deed helping Angela, energy courses through my body. It has helped her too, I can see it in the way she is standing a little straighter. The tightness around her mouth has loosened for the first time since we met.

I spend hours in the newly cleared library. It's like meeting an old friend after years apart. It is my favourite room and I can't understand why I let it get so overrun, I must have closed the doors on it twenty years ago and hadn't thought of it since.

Now I sit in the old armchair I inherited from my mother. Its pair sits across from me and I let the memories swirl. It is strange I am so old and yet my mother feels close to me, closer than she ever had when I was a young woman.

My book of recipes weighs heavy in my hands and I drop it to the floor. I can't find anything stronger than what I already gave Will the night he stayed. Whatever has a hold over him is too powerful. I have some ideas, but it is too early in the year for the flowers I need.

Will is stable. Angela calls Maeve every day and reports there has been no change. He isn't talking but has started taking his pills again. I am driven by a sense of urgency – we don't have much time.

I look into the fire my mind racing. I haven't felt this animated for years. I relish my body's strength after so long ill and bed ridden. It is good to see my arms and face fattening up, like Hansel in his cage. I rub my palms together and watch green sparks dance above the fire.

A week passes as I plot and plan. Angela ask if she can take the morning off to see her friends. She is reluctant to leave me, but I have convinced her I'm fine – even she cannot deny my good health and strength. I am learning the power of good deeds and perform acts of kindness whenever I can. I treated Eldritch to a whole side of salmon and it almost turned my white hair dark.

I must go and see Will, but I have to meet him alone, without the distraction of his parents, or Angela.

*

Angela is dressed to the nines when she wakes me up. 'You look lovely,' I say in surprise.

'No need to sound so astonished,' she replies crossly but I can see she is pleased. She's wearing a wrap dress with thick black tights, and long boots. It's made from a gorgeous soft, jersey fabric splashed with poppies. I am pleased to note she has taken my advice and is wearing a proper brassiere.

'They won't recognise you,' I say. 'You look like a film star from the 50's. Now all we need to do is sort out your dreadful hair.'

This makes her laugh. 'Are you sure you'll be OK on your own? Don't do anything stupid.'

'I'll be fine. I promise to be good. Enjoy showing off your new look.'

The house falls silent and I gather everything I need. The garden is unfurling beautifully in the warmth of the spring sunshine. Drifts of daffodils lie almost hidden in the long grass, yellow as canary diamonds. Charlie falls into step beside me, I am not surprised – he knows I am up to something.

'You're warming to Angela,' he says. 'I can tell. Are you ready to teach her?'

I walk on in silence, 'I don't know. Maybe. I can't think straight at the moment.'

'I'm sorry what I said about you saving Will,' he says.

'Don't be. You were right,' I admit. 'Don't look so damned pleased with yourself, this wasn't down to you. Well not all of it anyway. Those stupid, wasteful deaths have haunted me. Maybe saving this boy will balance the scales a little.'

'I wish I could touch you,' he says.

'Me too.'

We smile at each other then turn to the woods. My heart feels lighter. When I am with Charlie I am a girl again. I walk as easily, am as beautiful and strong as I was the day we first kissed. I have known him from the days before I became the Siren, the Enchantress, the Oracle, the Priestess. Whatever it is I am... From

Circe through Morgan le Fay to Baba Yaga the fire lines run in me. When Will is saved, I will look to find the fire in Angela.

Charlie reads my thoughts. 'You have to try,' he says, his tone urgent. 'You are lost otherwise. Who you are and what you know will all be gone.'

'Yes, as you keep saying,' I reply irritably.

'Freddy I have to warn you.' Charlie says, his voice so sudden and loud in the silence a flock of birds startle and clap their way to the sky in a flutter of wings.

I stop. 'What?'

I glare at him and he looks discomfited, 'It's Marroch…'

As he speaks the name the wood falls quiet as if straining every fibre to hear what will be said next. The air crackles with ice, and the breath is sucked from my chest. I force myself to stand upright.

'I know,' I say reluctantly. 'I've known for a while. I had hoped that I was so well hidden he'd never find me but then I fell… which I blame you for, by the way.'

'He only needed a tiny glimpse it would seem.'

My shoulders droop.

'Don't Freddy,' Charlie leans in close, as close as he can be. 'Don't give up. You have me. You have Angela. If you could just get past that damned pride of yours…'

'I'm not going to think about that now,' I say. 'I still have a little time. Will has to be my priority.'

'Well don't leave it too late.'

As we near the village, Charlie's face is serious. 'Nearly there. Do you know what you are going do?'

'Not yet, but I will.' I notice he is no longer following me. 'Aren't you coming with me?'

He shrugs and lifts his hands, 'I can't.' His skin is green under the canopy of the trees. His golden hair is silvered with damp and falling into his eyes. I shiver a little; his face has the beauty of an angel carved on a tomb. Oh God, I have an ill-divining soul.

A rattle of leaves makes me turn, and when I look back, Charlie has gone.

I pause for a moment, steeling myself, before walking into the village and heading for the Lockwood's house. I check the high street, looking left and right. Angela will be livid if she knew I'd walked to the village on my own.

The house looks empty. The red curtains are shut and nobody answers the bell. I begin to hammer on the door with my stick until it opens. Will holds the door open a crack and looks down on me.

'Oh. It's you. What are you doing here? Mum and Dad are out.'

'I know,' I say. 'It's you I've come to see.' I use my stick to push the door back against him and follow up with my body, marching up the steps with the wind at my heels.

He shrugs and walks back into the house. I follow him down the corridor. Will bypasses the kitchen and continues to the chilly conservatory at the back. I notice his blue trousers hang low on his skinny haunches. It doesn't seem possible but he has lost more weight since I last saw him.

The conservatory is vast, but the rain has started and clouds the glass with a grey mist so you can barely see the garden. Will is in the corner next to an open window through which screeches a vicious wind. He is lighting a cigarette and hunches protectively over the little flame. He puffs a few times, blowing the smoke towards the window.

His skin is sallow, his jaw line rigid and closely follows the line of his skull. Unwashed and gritty, his hair sticks up in clumps. As he lifts his cigarette to his mouth I notice his hands are raw and red. Little sores at the end of his fingers weep. Truculence and aggression are marked heavy on his face, but I am moved by the vulnerability of his hands.

I go to sit by him, and tap a finger on his cigarette packet. He looks at me in surprise and, in an oddly suave movement, lights one for me and passes it over. I relish the burning smoke and hold it deep in my lungs.

We smoke in silence for a few minutes. Every now and then he coughs. It's a painful, croaking bark.

'Have you talked to your parents? I told you how important it was you let them know what was happening.'

He shakes his head, a rapid 'no' and lifts his fingers to his mouth, gnawing on the skin. His knee jitters and he has to hold it to still the tremor.

'Who's doing this to you, Will? Please tell me what has happened to you. I promise I can help you.'

He laughs. 'Not possible,' he says. There is something almost triumphant in him. I can't work it out. Something has changed, there is a hard-edged energy radiating from him, glass-sharp. It's frightening.

'You drugged me,' his voice is accusing.

I look him dead in the eye. 'Yes.'

'Why?'

'Because I needed to get through to you, find out what's going on in your head.'

'What the fuck was it? I was out of it for days,'

'Never you mind,' I say primly and am surprised when he laughs. He is genuinely amused. He falls silent and the view of the cold garden pulls his eyes away from me again.

I lift my hands, focussing on the tar-black, drifting reeds that stream from this broken boy. Curling my fingers, I pull. I try to disperse them a little. I have to close my eyes; it takes effort. They are deeply rooted. Some begin to come free and I rip them out, throwing them onto the floor where they slither away like black snakes. Will straightens, just a little.

He flicks his gaze over to me then turns away again.

'I don't know how you know this. How do you know? What did you see in me that day? It's scary, you're...' He uses his fingers to press away the headache that is building behind his forehead. 'In the garden... You looked into my head and I... I know you saw stuff. You knew about Mark. How could you... how could you know about him?'

Energy zaps electric up the back of my neck. Got him, I thought, but keep my face neutral.

'Tell me about him. This man Mark.' Will is, at last, opening up to me. I know someone is involved but had no idea who. My mind races as I try to work out if there is anyone called Mark in the village. I can't think of anyone. Maybe someone from university?

There is a long silence. I worry I have lost him, and then he speaks.

'He was my best mate,' he blurts finally.

'I know,' I soothe.

'He was so brilliant. He was in the third year so knew everyone and where to go – all of that. I was such a loser I didn't have a clue. Fucking country bumpkin up in the big city. He'd take me out, introduce me to all his friends - he really helped me. He'd lend me money – he was, like, always loaded...' Will stubs his cigarette out as if he wants to destroy it. He immediately lights another. 'The first term at uni was really hard. I didn't know anyone and was getting this weird anxiety. I'd never had anything like it before and didn't know what to do. Mark kind of sought me out, I'd had a kind of panic attack after getting stoned at some crappy freshers' night...

'Mark just sat there and listened to me until I calmed down. I'd talk for hours and hours and he'd just,' Will gives a great gulping sob as if his heart was tearing from his body. 'Be there for me, y'know? Christ, I sound pathetic.' He rubs his big hand roughly across his face, wiping away the wetness and sniffs.

'And then?'

There is a long silence. I am shocked by the white flame that shines from his skin, which is glassy with sweat. I lean forward. Every fibre in me is straining with the effort of willing him to go on. He has to keep talking.

'I told him about this girl, Anya... I was really keen on her. But... she messed me about a bit, and I was like... Well, I was angry. She really hurt me and I didn't know what to do. I didn't handle it very well and she ended up blocking me on everything, wouldn't talk to me...'

He follows his cigarette smoke with his eyes and I see the tears welling. He rubs his nose again. 'Mark thought we should teach her a lesson, show her what she was missing like. He said she'd been well out of order. I thought it sounded like a laugh and, well, serve her right, yeah? She'd been a bitch.'

I nodded with understanding and put my hand on his as it bounced on his knee. My touch seemed to calm him. 'So what happened, dear?'

'Mark arranged to meet up with her at a bar. He'd got chatting with her on Instagram, I'd told him how to find her. He put something in her drink and carried her out to the car park when she passed out. Told everyone she'd had too much. It was rammed in there, nobody thought anything of it. I was watching the whole time from the back. It made me sick seeing her...' His face twitched, making him look grotesque. 'Flirting and that with him. It was like I never existed.'

I wait. He reaches under his chair and retrieves a bottle, half full with some clear alcohol. He unscrews the top and gulps down two or three mouthfuls, wiping his lips with a shaking hand. The bottle is nearly empty.

'He told me to... like, do what I wanted with her... I couldn't believe it, I never thought he'd go that far...he said she'd never know, that she was too out of it. I should take my chance. He was laughing; it made me laugh too... I was off my head, to be honest, didn't really know what I was doing.'

'What did you do?' My voice is calm, I make myself shrink, fade away so he is barely aware of me as he speaks.

He shrugs and gives a bitter laugh. 'I couldn't do it. Didn't have the guts.'

I let loose a breath of relief I didn't realise I was holding.

'So he strips her. Right there in the back of his car. He kind of shows her to me, shows me her body. It made me feel a bit sick but he kept joking about it. And then...' his face convulses with misery.

'What?'

'He starts taking pictures. With his phone. Tells me we can enjoy them later. And all the time she's just lying there...'Another shaky pull on his cigarette.

Pieces are falling into place. I remember what I saw in his eyes and my mind rattles along. 'He's been blackmailing you hasn't he? Were you in the photographs?'

Will nods, all I can see is the top of his head as he has sunken into himself.

'He made me do some poses with her. I had my clothes on so you can tell I hadn't done anything but she was, like, nude and like, a little bit awake but proper drugged, y'know? I thought that would be it. Joke over. I made him drive Anya back to her halls and he dumped her there. Just chucked her coat over and we left. But then he started making me do stuff for him, and told me if I didn't, he'd sent the pictures to everyone, Anya and her family, my family...'

I remember what I'd read in his eyes, I hadn't made sense of it before, but the hurried sense of secrecy and tiny bags being swapped hand to hand was something I now understood. 'Drugs?'

He pauses. I let the silence stretch between us like a long wire, until it snaps. 'Yeah...' his voice creaks with reluctance. 'He told me I just had to use the train to go to different places and drop some stuff off. Just a few times he said, then he'd delete the pics...'

I jump out of my skin as, with a roar, Will hurls the glass bottle through the conservatory windows, shattering them into fragments. A piece strikes my face and blood ripples down my cheek. I am too shocked to move. The silence returns, broken only by the tinkle of glass as it shifts in the breeze.

'I don't know why I'm telling you all of this, Mrs B...' His voice is slurring a little. His head bobs onto his chest and back up again. 'I used to love going to your house, you know. I was really happy there. You were cool.' He blinks at me and lifts a shaking finger. 'You were well weird, though, you did some strange tricks.' He giggles. 'I always thought you were a witch... I used to spy on you sometimes and you could do some cool shit...' He holds his fingers to his mouth and gives a slow wink as he shushes. 'Not that anything matters now. I've been waiting for Mum and Dad to go out, and finally they did.' With a start, I see his pupils are enormous, great black holes trying to swallow me up. I see the whole room reflected in the black depths.

Something isn't right. A flash of alarm hits me. I look around the room and realise what I'd seen. Two empty pill boxes are under the chair and another packet lies on the table by the ashtray. Will is swaying, his eyes are vacant

'Can you tell them how sorry I am?' he says, his tone is urgent but he is almost incoherent. 'I didn't want to do this to them again but I didn't know what else to do. Nothing seemed to be getting any better and I was frightened what he'd make me do next...' His voice trails away and his eyelids begin to flicker.

Never have I cursed more at my stupid, slow old body. Will falls to the floor with a sudden crash, splintering the chair under him. I look around but can't see a phone. I give a cry. I am haunted by David and Larry who seem to stand beside me, their faces pale as death. I hurry into the hall but can't see a phone; my vision is blurred and I keep blinking to clear it. My heart is hammering. I have to go back to Will to search his pockets to see if he has one of those hand held phones people use now.

I find a small, slim, metal and glass tablet just under Will's hip. As I pick it up the screen lights up. It is asking for a number to enter, but I don't know what it is. There is a button at the bottom. I press it again and again until the word 'emergency' runs across the screen. I touch it and the phone begins to ring. As I wait, I hold my hand on Will's chest, willing life into him as I feel his breaths grow shallow.

# CHAPTER 14: ANGIE

I couldn't have asked for a better pick-me-up than meeting the girls in town, wearing my new dress.

'Fuck me, girl, you look stunning!' said Vicky as she twirled me around, making my skirt flare.

'Oh my God Angie, you really do!' said Sharon. 'I can't believe it!'

'It's only a dress,' I laughed, feeling a bit giddy.

'Are we going in or not?' Maggie interrupted, 'I'm starving.'

'Good point, Mags,' I said.

'Not that you don't look lovely Ange, but food is food.'

We went into the café chattering like parrots. It had opened a few weeks ago but was packed full of locals. It was very posh for Witchford; what had been a rather drab tea room was now a funky coffee house with brightly coloured plastic chairs and piles of odd looking bread and muffins.

Giggling like teenagers as Vicky flirted with the barista, we ordered fancy coffees and a plate of cakes. I was delighted to see them; I'd been stuck in that house cleaning for too long, I thought.

'You still going to Weight Watchers, Vik? You look like you've lost a ton of weight,' I said. She stood up and shook her bum at me. 'Two and a half stone, baby!' she crowed. We all cackled.

The food arrived and I begged for the latest gossip. It was a proper girly catch up, I hadn't laughed so much in ages. The spectres of Andy and Kelly hung over the table but we ignored them.

'So living up that old place suits you?' Maggie said.

'Yeah, it does,' I admit. 'I love it up there, it's such a beautiful house.'

Sharon shuddered, 'I think it's well spooky. I'd go off me head stuck on my own up there with no company but an old woman.'

'She nice!' I protested. 'Well actually she isn't, but she is interesting.'

'What do you do up there?' Vicky asked. 'You can't be cleaning all the time, I'd be bored stiff.'

'She gives me books to read and we talk about them. And I've learned how to cook – proper food, bread, curries, all sorts.'

Vicky looks disgusted. 'Reading? What about *Love Island*?'

'Oooh, did you see what Michael and Greg got up to last night?' Mags said, leaning across the table to pinch another breadstick.

'I don't have a telly,' I said, and they looked at me open-mouthed. 'It's nice, actually. I don't really miss it, and I like reading. Mrs B talks to me about books as if I had a brain. Makes a change.'

'You were the teachers' pet at school,' agreed Sharon. 'Your head was always in a book in year 7.'

'Yeah, and then she realised boys existed,' said Vicky with a lascivious wink. We all chuckled.

'Hello, ladies, fancy seeing you here!'

Vicky, Maggie and Sharon exchanged meaningful glances. What was going on? I wondered.

I turned towards the voice. It was Gary from work. The bitches! I thought. Have they set me up? One glance at their faces, tomato red with the effort of not laughing, told me the truth. They must have known he'd be here.

'Angie?' His voice was so surprised I realised at once he had no idea. I was slightly flustered to notice he looked delighted to see me.

'Gary! How nice to see you.' I jumped to my feet, managing to knock over my chair. We bent to pick it up and bumped heads.

'Oh God, sorry,' he said, mortified.

'It's fine! It's fine!' I reassured him, rubbing my head as he'd proper cracked it. He put out his hand and for some reason I thought he was going for a hug so I moved forward, accidently trapping his hand between my arm and my left tit.

At this point Maggie shoved her napkin in her mouth, gazing steadily at the table, her shoulders heaved with hysterics. I didn't dare look at the other two.

Gary extracted his hand, blushing furiously. 'Shall we um…?' he nodded to a little high table with stools at the front of the café. There was no way I was going to perch on one of the bar stools, so we stood awkwardly just in front of them.

'It's good to see you, Angie,' he said at last. 'It's been months. I tried calling…'

'Yeah, I know, sorry I didn't ring you back. I was all over the place.'

'I wanted to talk to you. I felt terrible about…'

'Firing me?' I asked.

He laughed. 'Er yeah, it's a bit awkward isn't it? Anyway. I felt a bit shit about having to leave a message but I called loads of times and you didn't answer. The bosses were doing my nut in so I had to… it's a shame… you were a great cleaner. I just, er wanted to say that really.' Oh, he was adorable. His jeans were tight and faded, and I liked his dark blue jumper, it suited him.

'Thanks, Gary,' I was touched. 'You don't have anything to apologise for – what else could you do? I should have sent you a message at least, sorry, that was crap of me.'

We looked at each other, he's got lovely sparkly eyes, I thought.

'I like your dress,' he said. 'Never seen you all gussied up.'

'Thanks. I like your jumper.' What the hell was I on about? Luckily, he laughed.

'So, you all right? You've found something else, Vicky said?'

'Yes, that's right. I'm working for a woman in the village, caring for her like.'

He rubbed the back of his head. 'Ange, er, I'm sorry about what happened to you. The girls haven't stopped talking about it. I can't believe what Andy's done, what a wanker, he's a fool to pass you up.'

'Blimey, Gary! Careful - You'll turn my head carrying on like that!' Christ, now I was blushing.

'It's true,' Gary looked embarrassed but was steadfast. 'You're a good person and you deserve better.'

'Well thanks. That's really nice of you.'

'Well, I better let you get back to that lot.' He gestured to Maggie, Vik and Sharon who were watching us with the same attention they afforded the latest episode of *EastEnders*. They averted their eyes hastily when they saw us looking at them.

My stomach fizzed with champagne bubbles and my head spun. I cleared my throat. My lips were so dry I could them smacking over my teeth. 'Gary... I don't suppose...' I kept my eyes on his hands. They were brown and freckly and strong. 'I don't suppose you fancy going out for a drink or something?' The words tumbled out in a rush. I daren't look up, but when I did, he was smiling.

'I thought you'd never ask,' he said.

'Really?' I said, I couldn't stop the grin spreading across my face.

'I'll give you a ring, shall I?'

'Yes, that would be brilliant,' I said, and made a mental note to find and charge my bloody phone as soon as I got home.

Before I could say any more, he put his hand on my arm and bent down to brush a quick kiss on my cheek. Then he was gone, the café door slamming shut.

I spun back to the girls a beam splitting my face.

Vik stood up as I got close, a naughty grin on her face. 'He asked you out, didn't he? I *knew* it! I knew he fancied you!'

'Actually… I asked him!' I said. God! I felt like a fourteen-year-old. The girls screeched and hugged me. They were so delighted and happy I forgot about everything except deciding with the girls what I was going to wear.

*

Vicky grabbed hold of my arm the minute we left out of the café. 'Come on, Angie. I've got a surprise for you,' she said, waving goodbye to the others.

'Vik I can't! I've got to get back to Mrs B.'

'We'll only be an hour or two, this can't wait.'

She marched me down the street; I could barely keep up. Goodness, losing weight had made Vicky twice as fast, I thought. Funny thing, as we walked past the Chinese, I took my usual deep breath, but something had changed. All I could smell was burnt oil and cheap meat – it turned my stomach, when it used to make me salivate.

'Here we are!' Vicky said. We were standing in front of the posh hairdressers at the end of the village. 'He owes me a favour', she said darkly, before shoving me in through the elegant maroon doors. 'Paulo!' she shouted at the desk. I stood back as she engaged in a muttered argument with the receptionist, who called over a stocky bald bloke who quailed when he saw Vicky. She took him aside and issued a stream of instructions. He looked over at me and nodded.

Within minutes, I was wrapped in a gown and ushered towards the sinks.

Two hours later, I was admiring myself in every window. I couldn't believe it. I looked bloody gorgeous. Vicky kept cackling and coughing on her berry-mint flavoured vape. 'I told you,' she said smugly. 'He's a genius that Paulo – I knew copper would look great on you.'

After exclaiming at the state of my hair, Paulo ordered a deep conditioning treatment and when that was done, cut off inches and inches. I was horrified, watching great chunks fall on the floor. But when he finished the blow dry, I saw how clever he had been.

He'd taken all the weight from the back and chopped into the hair to create a long, side-parted fringe, which fell over my forehead. Then, long layers that swung forward. Paulo called it a lob, slimming my face and curling just under my jaw.

But the absolute best thing was the colour. It was a sophisticated version of my old redhead days, a swirl of coppers and bronzes. I kept shaking my head to see my hair swing from side to side, looking ten times thicker. Mind you, it cost three hundred quid – most of what I'd saved so far living with Mrs B - and I knew I'd never be able to blow dry it the way he did - but in my new dress and boots, fantastic hair and a date with Gary coming up, I had never felt so happy.

I couldn't wait to get home to show Mrs B. I walked back through the village and that's when it happened. There was that old boy. The one with the dog.

*

I didn't stop to think. I marched over before I could change my mind. The closer I got, the more scared I felt, but I clung onto that bubble of happiness I'd been riding and kept on going. As I approached, I remembered what Mrs B had done in the pub. It was important to keep calm, I thought.

He smelled bad. It was a mix of cold air and stagnant water and I had to do some rapid mouth breathing. I couldn't bring myself to look at his face, so I took hold of his hand. It was icy cold. He made a strange sound and I looked up. His face was so close to mine, I wanted to rear back but held my nerve. His mouth was moving, so I bent closer to hear him

At first, all I could hear was a distant sort of whistling. A dusty, dry sound – no words. I rubbed his hand to warm it. He continued to speak.

He didn't speak in words, but I understood him. He told me terrible things, but also that he had loved his life. He was so desperate to talk the stories were a constant stream. I had to concentrate hard to remember what he said. There was so much to hold onto I started to panic. He gripped my hand so tight I couldn't pull away.

'No, no, please stop. I can't hear any more. I'm sorry. Please,' I gibbered. He stopped. I waited but there was no more. I looked up into his face. It was so old and sad, his expression so kind, I couldn't resist putting my hand on his cheek. He bent his head and leaned into my hand. I felt a soft pressure followed by a sort of *give...* and he was gone.

I gasped in surprise. It was as if a jet of air had blown through me, taking my breath with it. My hands were shaking. I looked around. No. He was definitely gone. I felt strange and peaceful; the old man's stories settled into me, soft as ash.

I looked down at a yap. The dog. The fricking dog! A brown mongrel terrier looked up at me, tongue out and panting. I'd assumed it would disappear along with the old man, but here it was, clearly alive. I sighed and bent down to give it a pat. Luckily, I had a scarf folded in my bag. I threaded it through the dog's collar.

My mind was mess. I was so proud of myself for approaching a one, but the experience had been frightening and exhausting. Would I have to go through that with everyone I met? Ridiculously, I was also still really pleased with my hair, and kept running my hands through it – marvelling at its smoothness and shine.

*

As I reached the church, I thought about stopping at the Doc's house to see how Will was getting on. Just as I got there, the door flew back with a crash and the old woman appeared, nearly toppling onto the step. What the hell was she doing here? I thought. I was bewildered; I had so much to tell her and then there she was, like a jack in the box.

'Mrs B!' I called, and grabbed her arm, supporting her to a chair inside before running back to slam the door closed. 'Are you all right? What's happened?' The old man's dog trotted past, trailing the scarf behind it, and curled up on a settee in the hall.

Mrs B rested her crooked back against the side of the armchair and closed her eyes. I could see tears at the ends of her lashes. I had never seen her show such weakness. Dropping to my knees beside her, I rubbed warmth back into her frozen hands.

'What's happened?' I said again.

'It's Will,' she said, her voice wavering and thin. Nothing like the strident, clipped tones of speech I was used to. 'He's taken another overdose.' A tear ran free and slipped down her cheek.

'Oh my God,' I said. 'Is he OK?'

'I don't know. He swallowed whole packs of those damned pills.'

'You were with him? Wait... I thought you were at home... Did you call an ambulance?'

'Yes of course,' she snapped. 'Do you think I'm a fool? I couldn't work out how to use the stupid phone thing and all the while,' she started to cry. 'All the while I could feel his heartbeat slowing...'

'Do his Mum and Dad know?' I asked. God, how awful, I thought. Maeve and the Doc must be in bits.

She nodded. 'They're with him now.'

The phone rang, making us start. I didn't even know there was a phone there. Its harsh, old-fashioned jangle echoed around the hall. I leaped to my feet.

'No,' Mrs B said, her hand on my arm. 'Let me get it.' I helped her out of her seat, and she stepped wearily towards the clanging bell.

'Hello? Maeve? Oh, Michael it's you. How is he?' She screwed up her face and pressed the phone close to her ear so she could hear. There was a long pause and I felt my nerves stretch to breaking point with the tension.

'Oh, thank God,' she said, and relief sagged through both of us. 'That is good news. And he's talking? Good. Good.' She continued to listen.

It was agony hearing these broken fragments of conversation. I shifted from foot to foot with the tension of it. At last, she finished the call and slumped onto the seat next to the telephone table.

'We need to get you back home,' I said. 'I'm going to call a taxi.'

Mrs B was beginning to recover her strength; she sat up as straight as she could and pinned me with the sharpness of her gaze. 'I'm going to need your help, Angela. That poor boy finally explained what's been going on. Will you help me?'

I was gobsmacked. 'Yes of course, Mrs B. Anything. I'll do anything I can.'

'Good,' she sighed. 'Come on.' She stopped and looked at me properly for the first time. 'What on earth have you done to your hair?' she said, before looking around and blinking. 'And where did you find that dog?'

\*

So much had happened it felt like a year since I left Pagan's Reach, chuffed with my dress and ready to meet the girls. Mrs B and I headed for the kitchen. In silence we worked through a pot of tea, I put down some mince for the dog. Eldritch was unimpressed and shot out of the door the minute she caught sight of him. I cut some cake we had left in the pantry, but neither of us felt like eating.

I could see the old woman was thinking hard. She tapped her fingers on the table in a relentless rhythm. That, and the sound of the dog's nails clattering on the tiles, was doing my head in.

'So, what's going on?' I said, pushing away my empty mug and thinking about what to make for tea. It was getting late.

All thoughts of food were forgotten as Mrs B began to speak. She told me everything Will had revealed before he'd collapsed.

'Oh my God. I don't know what to say,' I breathed at last. 'How awful. Christ! No wonder he wanted to end it all.'

Mrs B flinched. 'We need to find this man Mark and destroy all his pictures, then he has nothing with which to threaten the boy.'

'Mrs B we have to go to the police!' I exclaimed. 'I can't see what we can do on our own.'

'Absolutely not,' she replied, smacking her fist on the table. 'If we involve them it will all come out and that will destroy Will. He's far too fragile to cope with a court case – surely you can see that?'

Reluctantly, I agreed. I didn't have any choice, to be honest, Mrs B was pretty formidable. 'All right. So, what do you propose we do?'

With an air of ceremony, she rummaged around in her pocket and extracted an iPhone, which she placed on the table between us.

'This is Will's phone,' she said with reverence. I imagined she wasn't very used to smart phones; she was staring as if it was some instrument from the future. 'Mark's name will be on there. Can you have a look?'

I reached for the phone. It was locked with a PIN code. I sighed. 'It's locked,' I said.

'Locked? How can you lock a phone?' said Mrs B, bewildered.

I held up the locked screen. 'You have to tap in a passcode. It's usually 4 or 6 numbers.'

'Damn,' she said, her shoulders slumped.

'Well, hang on, we can have a go. Some people can be really stupid with their passcodes. Only thing is we have a limited number of tries before the phone shuts down on us and is locked forever.'

'We'd better think very carefully, then,'

'Right, OK. Let's try the obvious ones.' 1234 doesn't work and neither does 0000. I try 2580 and then 1379. Nothing. We are running out of goes. 'Argh this is so frustrating. If only we had his thumb!' I said crossly.

'His thumb?' Mrs B's eyebrows shot up.

'Yeah, look, see that round button? On these new phones you can use that to scan your fingerprint and then the phone opens.'

'Extraordinary. Unfortunately, that option is not available to us at the moment, Angela.'

'Yes I know, I just thought you'd be interes… Never mind. Can you think of any numbers that would be important to him?'

'No, not at all. I can't think of anything. I don't know him at all, not recently anyway.'

'Do you know his birthday?'

'Of course I know that!' she's about to speak then closes her mouth. She is trying to work it out. 'I think he was born just as Autumn was beginning. It was definitely October…'

I squirmed with impatience. 'What day?'

She paused and tapped her lips with her fingers. 'It was the sixth,' she said at last.

0610 I type. A chime sounded. 'We're in!' I said.

*

Mrs B leaned forward her eyes bright with excitement. 'What are you doing now?' she said. She squinted at the screen, but I knew she couldn't see a thing.

'I'm just looking at his contacts to see if I can find this Mark.' I typed the name into the search bar, but nothing came up. I try scrolling through but there are thousands of contacts. 'How the hell does a 19-year-old boy know so many people?' I sighed. 'I can't see anyone called Mark.'

'Maybe he wrote him down under another name?' Mrs B suggested.

'If he has then we're buggered,' I replied. 'Didn't you say he was on Instagram?'

'Whatever that is.'

I found Will's Instagram app and started flicking through the people he followed. Again, there were too many to count. I sat back and sighed. I didn't know how to narrow down the search. He had Snapchat and Houseparty as well, but I had no idea how to use them.

I clicked on the Instagram 'home' button and scrolled through the hundreds of photographs that appeared as the app refreshed.

'Any idea what he's like? The man we are looking for?' I asked Mrs. B. She frowned.

'He said he was third year so probably around 21. Look for someone surrounded by younger woman, probably at a nightclub or something. Anything that links with drugs.'

I looked at her, shocked, then carried on scrolling. 'God, there are hundreds of posts here, how do they keep up with all of this?... Hang on... Bingo!'

It was strange the certainty I had when I zoomed in on the post. The minute I saw his face I knew it was him. He looked ordinary enough, just a young man – hair a little too long, unshaven - but not a full beard – dark eyes… but there was something about him, a kind of cruelty around the mouth. He was grinning into the camera, holding his arms out in the classic selfie pose. Surrounding him was a pack of pouting girls; they looked very young. They certainly weren't wearing much.

'Are you sure it's him?'

'Yeah, I don't know why but I'm getting a bad feeling about this one. It looks like he and Will follow each other. Let me look at his other posts.'

I clicked onto his profile. 'His username is marktm7,' I said. I was working through his pictures one after the other.

'What are you doing?'

'Looking for any pictures of Will on his feed.'

'His what? None of this is making any sense. Angela, please explain.'

I opened my mouth and closed it again. 'It doesn't matter Mrs B it's all a bit complicated. Basically, this guy has a sort of photo album that anyone who follows him can look at and interact with. When they interact, you can then follow to see what all the others are up to, if they have their profiles public, of course.' I trailed away, Mrs B was glazing over and looking increasingly irritated. 'Hang on, I'll just tell you what I find.'

'marktm7' had so many posts my head was hurting; it took a huge effort to concentrate on each one. Apart from the odd artfully posed picture with his shirt off, Mark seemed to enjoy presenting himself in the heart of party groups.

It's like time travel going through his posts. They stretch back years, and he clearly posts at least once a day. In reverse I noticed girls appeared, smiling and laughing, taking centre stage with Mark, before being edged out to the outside circle of the group and disappearing. All sorts of girls, tall, short, skinny, voluptuous, dark and blonde, black, white and Asian... the only thing they had in common was their youth, their beauty, and the looks of appalled horror creeping onto their faces before they disappeared.

Mrs B had got to her feet and extracted an ancient set of glasses – the ones you perch on the end of your nose – from a kitchen drawer and stood behind me staring down at the phone.

'There! Look! There he is.' Her finger tapped the screen.

'No! God don't!' I said. 'You've just liked it!'

Quickly, I tapped the red heart back to blank. Crap. I hoped he wouldn't notice.

'What do you mean I've liked it?' Mrs B was as outraged as she was confused. 'Why would I like it? Horrid, vain little man.'

I selected the photo and zoomed in. It's definitely Will. He's turning away from Mark so we could only see his profile and a blur of blond hair. I saw with a shock of unease Mark's hold on Will's wrist is so tight the skin is pressed white. The contrast between the tension of his grip and the relaxed smile on his face was chilling.

'Well we've found him,' I said. 'Look at this – pretty conclusive.'

'Can you find out more about him? Where he is?'

'I can have a look on the internet. Hey where are you going?'

'To get my things of course! We need to leave tonight.'

*

It was only by sticking my heels in and threatening to call the Doc that I managed to persuade the old woman we couldn't leave that night. There were all sorts of things we needed to organise, I told her pointing at the dog.

'At some point you are going to have to tell me where you got that dog from,' Mrs B said.

I spent most of the night on the internet. Will's phone was on some kind of unlimited data programme and I'd been able to dig around for hours.

God, I loved playing detective. It was astonishing how much you could find out about someone just by going online. Especially young people, who uploaded every moment of their lives online. I stumbled across the most explicit blogs; one girl, who followed Mark, had shared photos of bruises on her thighs - 'look at these bite marks!' she had captioned the image, alongside a crying laughing emoji. I thought I was open-minded, but I found this shocking.

I fell down a rabbit hole, finding out everything I could about Mark Lowell. I scrolled through hundreds of posts featuring Mark on holiday, Mark in clubs, Mark at the gym. No pictures of parents or any family. He drove expensive cars and wore designer clothes, he made no secret he was rich, he flaunted the fact.

Mrs B had mentioned drugs – I found it sickening to see these photos of luxury and indulgence as I suspected the lifestyle was funded by his willingness to intimidate, corrupt and exploit vulnerable kids like Will.

I read news articles about criminals adapting as cities became saturated with dealers. How they were using young people to travel out of cities to sell their drugs in county towns previously immune from the charms of the big smoke. Kids, young women, and – this made my skin prickle with dread – increasingly, students who were used to sailing past the police - class A drugs in their pockets - using their white, middle-class privilege as a cloak of invisibility. God, the Doc would go mad if he ever found out Will was caught up in this.

The note pad beside me filled as the hours passed. The kitchen grew cold, but I was too engrossed to get up and relight the fire. I discovered what clubs Mark went to and when, what TV he watched, what food he ate when he had a hangover. What designers he liked and how often he went to the gym. He had a nasty sense of humour. His twitter feed was linked to his Instagram. I'd heard of twitter and how awful it could be, but nothing prepared me for the vileness of what I found there.

Mark joked about rape in the same way people used to joke about their mothers-in-law. He'd left a trail of comments detailing the fuckability of various female celebrities. He made my skin crawl, what a foul man, I thought, as I read through comment after comment.

I had no idea what Mrs B had planned. We needed to retrieve the photos Mark was blackmailing Will with, but I couldn't see how. At least I knew where he lived and what sort of things he did. The rest was up to the old woman.

*

Thanks to Mrs B's incessant nagging and despite my exhaustion, we left early. It took ages to get the car started as it had languished down the road from my old flat for the past few months. I had to prise the door open as everything had got so rusty and Mrs B was in a right old state by the time I parked up outside the house.

We were halfway down the motorway. It was a beautiful day and I was dreaming a bit about Gary and a bit about how much I was looking forward to the hot sunshine of summer when I suddenly sort of came to.

What the hell was I doing? I looked across at Mrs B. She was leaning forwards, peering through the windscreen as if trying to make the car go faster. I couldn't help but admire her smart, berry-red wool suit. Her bony hands grasped a big black handbag.

I shook my head. How had I ended up in my car driving to London with a mad old woman? Of course I was worried about Will, and this Mark sounded like a complete tosser, but what on earth did I think I could do about it? What was the plan when we got there?

I couldn't believe we had got this far without even discussing it. Once I'd left the dog with Vicky, checked where I thought Mark lived, and filled the car with petrol, I'd just got in and started driving. I remembered Will's dazed expression when the old woman sent him home.

Outrage bubbled up and my knuckles turned white as my hands tightened around the wheel.

'Mrs B have you *drugged* me!?' I exclaimed.

'Don't be ridiculous, dear,' she replied, not taking her eyes from the road.

'Don't you 'dear' me,' I replied hotly. 'How else have you managed to get me on this lunatic journey?'

'We need to help Will,' she said.

I threw my hands up in the air. 'This is ridiculous!' I said. 'I told you we should have gone to the police. They would have sorted it out.'

She gave me a mutinous look.

'Don't look at me like that,' I went on. 'I want to help Will just as much as you do, but this really isn't the way to go about it. I mean what were you expecting?' My voice was getting shrill. 'That we'd go up to him and say, "Oh, hello, Mark, you've been blackmailing a friend of ours. Would you mind handing over all the photos you have of him with a drugged, naked girl? Thanks ever so!?"'

I checked the mirrors clicked on the indicator. 'I'm turning around and taking you home. I don't know how you tricked me into this…'

And that's when it happened. Mrs. B leant over and placed her hand on my forearm.

Heat radiated out from her fingers, I tried to pull away but couldn't. Then, I felt bloody marvellous. Of course, we can do this! I thought. I wasn't surprised to look over and see a beautiful woman next to me. She was Boudicca, Joan of Arc, Amelia Earhart. Together we could do anything. I straightened my shoulders and stuck out my jaw. I moved up a gear and pulled out into the fast lane – London 63 miles.

'I've found out Mark's in his last year of his Politics degree,' I said. I had to shout over the roar of the engine. Mrs B nodded, the swing of hair, black as a crow's wing, fell across her face. 'The trouble is he'll have stored everything on the cloud.' The woman looked puzzled. 'It's like an invisible cupboard online,' I went on. 'Everyone nowadays keeps everything there. It means that if you lose your phone or your computer, nothing gets lost. You can bet that's what he's done with Will's pictures. I don't know how we can get to Mark's cloud, though It will be protected by his password.'

'I thought you could use fingerprints as well?' The woman said.

'Actually, you're right,' I said. 'Some apps you have on your phone people set up their fingerprint. Then they don't have to keep entering their password.'

'So, all we need is Mark's phone and finger?'

'Yes,' I replied.

'Good,' she said.

# CHAPTER 15: FRIEDA HUNTS

Sitting on the floor, feeling Will's life draining away as fast as water, knowing there is absolutely nothing I could do about it, is one of the worst moments of my life. I lie on the floor using all my strength to speed the ambulance to Will.

I hate the thought of handing him over to machines, but it is his only chance. The pill packets are clutched in my hand; I have to give them to the people when they arrive, so they know what to do.

Misery smothers the few flickers of strength I have. I pour the dregs into Will. I sob to see him fade. I can't save him. I can't save him. In my long life I have destroyed or lost many; but I have also saved. I remember babies I have rubbed into life, sickness I have banished, cancers I have burned away.

But this boy. I can't help. I don't understand his world. It is beyond me. Everything in me rails against this, but it is true. Not only that, but I am weak. Yes. It is true. The headaches are crippling. They've sapped my strength over time, and good deeds no longer replenish my stores.

What will I do when Marroch returns? And he will return; I can feel it in the marrow of my bones. Hiding is no longer possible. He is close - I can smell him, prowling around the village. There is not much time.

I want to howl with the frustration of it all. I have never felt this hopeless, this fearful. It is disabling. When I first faced Marroch I was young and strong, yet he still almost destroyed me. I shiver to remember his face.

The sirens wail in the distance, Will's breaths are so shallow I worry he's gone. I whisper words of encouragement, but they are so faint they shiver into nothingness; desolation has robbed me of my powers.

All is chaos and noise. Urgency explodes around me, at the core of it Will lies blue-faced and still. The uniformed men and women lift him up and out of the house. They speak to me, but I don't understand their words. Then they are gone, and the room falls silent. I want to crawl into the woods and cover myself with leaves and let my body rot.

I picture Michael and Maeve's faces hearing what Will has done and I weep until exhaustion hammers me flat, my heart flutters, and I allow the darkness to tug me into oblivion.

Waking, what feels like hours later, my mouth is dry, and my head is dull. Somehow, I am wedged into a space by the hall table, slumped against the wall. I am not used to the way my body takes over and shuts everything down. It has been happening more and more often since my stay in the hospital.

I look around for my bag. It has fallen from the table and some scent and my compact have rolled across the floor. Wearily, I gather them up and pack them away. Wedged in there is a novel I had stuffed away, planning to give it to Angela when I next saw her.

Angela. Charlie's words. The taste of her cooking. The way she has transformed my house. Her green, green eyes. My mind jumps from one stepping stone to another. I imagine facing Marroch, but with Angela's bulk by my side.

She is the answer. As Charlie has said since he first appeared. I have resisted the idea until now, but my failure to help Will has broken my defences. I have no choice.

Angela has changed since she arrived at Pagan's Reach, but I'm not sure how willing, or able, she is to help. She would consider every obstacle, rather than solutions. I have some tricks that will help with that, I think, rubbing my hands together and watching the sparks flash.

She can help me save Will, and then I will teach her to help me destroy Marroch.

*

The city stinks. Streets heave with people – ants spilling from a dunghill. The noise is intolerable. Cars, lorries, buses roar past; my brain screams. The buildings are filthy and scrawled with crude symbols. The air is tainted with poison; I can taste it coating my teeth and lips: Petrol, burning fat, melting rubber. A neon fizzle of electric power buzzes heavily around us. How can people live here? I think.

I yearn for a sliver of green to draw upon, the tender furl of a leaf, or even a pad of cool grass. There is nothing. There is no *give* in anything - everything is hard, glittering and sharp. Straight edges box in stagnant pools of air. There is nothing but concrete and glass, metal, tarmac, and brick. It is suffocating.

Angela slams and locks the car door. She is defiant, but fear makes her hands shake. She is as uncomfortable here as I am.

She is doing well, I think. I nearly lost her as we drove into London, but I got her back with some persuasion.

I have some Mandragora on me, just in case, and my jewelled combs; I hope it doesn't come to that.

'So, what now?' Angela calls above the boom of traffic.

'Are we close?'

She nods over to a grey building behind me. 'He's in one of them flats, he uses that posh gym on the ground floor. According to his Instagram, he goes in there every day.'

My mind is working double time. We can't stay away from Pagan's Reach for long, and if I stay in this bowl of polluted air beyond a few hours it will kill me.

'I just need to get close to him,' I say. 'How much do you think he weighs?'

'Mark? I've no idea – he's slim but muscly – 12 stone maybe? Why?'

'Could you carry him? If you had to?' I say, 'Can we get to his flat by lift?'

Angela's eyes widen. 'What on earth are you planning?' she says, marching around the car to me. 'This all sounds bloody complicated, and dangerous. We could get into a lot of trouble.' The green in her eyes is fading; she is starting to dither, clutching her car keys like an old woman. She is itching to bundle me back into the car.

'You have to trust me, Angela,' I say, and let my fingers brush her arm. The effect is immediate.

She sighs. 'Look there's a café over there. Let's go and get a cup of tea and work out what we are going to do.'

I feel better after a pot of tea and collect my bearings. The café is hellishly noisy with hard floors and high ceilings, the purpose of which seems to be to amplify any clatter as much as possible. The waitress is tall and slender with strange pouting lips and those thick, fringe-like black lashes, which looked so odd on my physiotherapist.

She is rude and dismissive, and I happily flick a shower of yellow sparks over her face as she leans in to collect the empty pot. Tomorrow she will be blotting the pus from painful boils.

'What are you doing?' Angela says suspiciously. She has Will's phone out on the table and is tapping away at the screen.

I ignore her, rubbing away a mild headache. 'Do you know where he is?' I say, leaning forward and trying to see.

'As far as I can tell, Mark's gone to the gym around this time for the last few weeks. He should be there now.' Angela squints out of the window. 'You can just see it over the road.'

I look, but all I see is a great sheet of black glass reflecting the bustle of the street.

'So, what are we going to do?' she says, looking across at me. Her eyes glow deep and green. Something has changed in her. Not just her hair, but her skin, her muscle tone – she is stronger, more relaxed, happier. Her mind is muddled – that's my fault – but there is also a strong sense of purpose. She is as determined to save Will as I am. This is encouraging, as there are dangers ahead.

I make a decision. 'We meet him, we get him back to his flat and then we get rid of everything we can to do with Will.'

'You make it sound easy,' Angela laughs. 'Come on, let's get this over with.'

The block where Mark lives is expensive. It is an oasis of calm after the chaos and roar of the road. A waterfall burbles opposite the bank of lifts. It is stained with chemicals, but the sound of the water is cool and restorative. Huge, dark green plants line the walls, planted into bronze pots, the floor is a gleaming teak. A constant stream of people walk in and out.

'How the hell can he afford to live here?' hisses Angela. 'Mind you, it's lovely inside but when you walk out of the door it's a dump.' She is discomfited, I see. Everyone here carries the sheen of money, but many are too thin and haunted looking, with hands that twist together and twitch compulsively. The women are a strange race with their grey skin hidden beneath brown paint, heavy make-up and identical, arched eyebrows..

I am amused by the contrast between these glamorous, pouting creatures and our homespun presence. Under the glittering spotlights, Angela's hair looks more brassy than copper, and my skin turns translucent.

'Not one of them has seen us,' Angela marvels. 'Have you turned us invisible or something?'

It's true, their eyes skim past us.

'They think we're the cleaners,' she goes on. She is still anxious. There is a battle struggling within her but, for the moment, my influence is winning. I will need to watch her as her energy is jittering in spikes.

Then her face changes. 'That's him!'

A tall man strides across the lobby. His dark hair falls in his eyes and he is wearing blue shorts and a tight dark top. The material is wet with sweat. As we watch, he rubs the back of his neck with a towel. He has an interesting face, narrow and dark with eyes hidden under low brows.

'Are you sure…?' I say, and then stop because I can smell him. Unmistakable. The feral stink of a wolf. My hairs stand on end and I step back behind a pillar.

'Damn,' I say.

'What is it?'

'I'm going to have to change my plan, I can't just go up to him.'

'Why not?'

'He'll see through me. He's a wolf.'

'A what?' Angela's face falls, she thinks I have gone mad.

'It doesn't matter, just trust me. Damn, I should have realised…'

What?' Angela is getting angry. 'What on earth are you on about?'

I touch her hand to reassure her as I think. We watch as Mark eschews the lifts and heads for a double door that must lead to the stairs. His calf muscles bulge.

'Wait over there,' I say pointing to a square of sofas next to the main entrance. 'Go on!' I urge as she looks defiant. I move to the middle of the lobby and put on my best bewildered face. A small group of people emerge from the lift and I scan them. There. That one, I think.

I approach a young woman who looks barely out of her teens. She has thick hair the colour of wheat; it is improbably long and reaches her elbows. Close up, her face is fair and lightly freckled, her eyes wide and trusting.

I catch her arm as she goes by, 'Excuse me, dear,'

She stops, phone in hand, and looks down. She towers above me in her heeled boots. I press my fingers against her skin, and she looks puzzled. I catch and hold her clear gaze, as blue as catmint flowers. I search her mind quickly and am satisfied - she knows Mark, but not well.

'Can I help you?' she says.

'I hope so, dearie,' I quaver. 'I'm here to visit Markie, my great grandson, but I've come all this way and I'm such a fool, I've lost the piece of paper with his address on. I simply don't know what to do – it's been such a tiring journey. I've come all the way from Edinburgh, and I can't remember what flat he's in. I know it's this block as I remember the name - Mermaid Square House – such a funny name! But now I'm here and I don't know what to do next.'

'Can't you call him?' The girl is dazed, and blinks.

'Oooh don't be silly, a woman of my age with a little phone like that?' I laugh and notice she smiles in response. Good. She is suggestible.

'What's his name?'

'Mark Lowell,' I reply. 'He's a lovely handsome young man, probably not much older than you? Quite tall?'

A look flashes across her face – too fast for me to read.

'Uh… yeah… I know Mark,' she says looking over at her friends who are waiting for her by the door looking impatient. 'I don't know though… He might not like me telling people where he lives.'

'Oh goodness, what do you think an old woman like me could do?' I say with a wide smile. 'I would love to surprise him; I missed his birthday as I was on a cruise with my friends Vi and

Edna. We had such a lovely time, I told them, Marky will be so disappointed...'

Her eyes are glazing over and she is desperate to leave. A man shouts across the lobby and she startles.

'It's flat 7 on the fourth floor,' she says in a rush. 'Please can you not tell him I told you? I'm...' There is another shout and she trots off, throwing a nervous glance over her shoulder.

I wait until she has gone and then signal Angela. 'Fourth floor!' I whisper.

*

'You ready?' I ask, my finger poised over the button. She flashes me a nervous smile and shrugs.

'We've come this far...' she replies.

We are silent as the lift glides up to the fourth floor. As we come out onto a long corridor decorated entirely in beige, I pull Angela to one side and keep my voice low.

'Angela, this is it. We must get this right first time. It will have to be you as he will be suspicious of me.'

'OK,' she replies. 'What do you want me to do?'

I eye her up. 'You've got a good few stone on him, so use that. As he opens the door, push him back into his flat. I'll deal with him then.'

I hustle her down the corridor before she changes her mind. Luckily, number 7 is right at the end, with no doors nearby. I hide behind Angela's width. We pause for a second, exchange a glance, and she raises her hand.

I'm not sure what happens next. I hear the door open and a tremendous roar. Angela rockets forward and there is a thump. The man we saw earlier is on the floor, groaning. He is in a white dressing gown and his hair is wet.

'What the fuck are you doing?' he shouts. 'Who are you?' He is wild and disorientated. He tries to sit up, but Angela kneels and pulls him back down by the hood of his gown.

Angela looks over at me, she is scared. She won't be able to hold him down for long; his body is hard with muscle. I move towards the two of them, pulling a jar from my bag. I just need to get a few drops in him.

He is writhing about and spitting curses. Somehow he has cut his head, and the blood drops red on the white towelling of his robe.

'Hold his head,' I tell Angela.

She does as I say, but her face is strained with panic.

I manage to flick the drops into his eyes. Mark swears again and blinks. It takes a few seconds, long enough for me to worry it hasn't worked, then he stops struggling and his head falls onto his chest.

'Christ,' says Angela, jumping to her feet and pacing around the room. She wipes her forehead; she is dripping with sweat. 'What have you done to him?'

I am stiff and it takes me a while to clamber to my feet. I stretch my back and look around the room. I am dazzled. Everything is white; it's like being inside a shoebox. There are no books, and the furniture couldn't be more minimal.

'Is he dead?' Angela is verging on hysteria. 'What did you do? And why did you spray it in his eyes? Urgh God, the poor bloke.'

'Angela, do I really need to remind you that this man drugged a young girl and sexually assaulted her? He betrayed Will's trust, forcing him to do terrible things using the most filthy of crimes – blackmail.' I look around the room. 'I can assure you Will and that poor girl were certainly not his only victims. Just look at this place. How do you think he affords it?'

Angela gives a tight nod and begins to search. 'We need to find his phone,' she says. 'Or a laptop, I'll try his bedroom.' She skirts around Mark, who lies still as a stone, and follows a curving wall towards the bedroom.

Although Mark is unconscious, his shadow is heavy at the centre of this strange, white room. I am tempted to call Angela to come and search his pockets but then steel my nerve. He's not going to wake up anytime soon, I tell myself, scornful of the fear that is making my hands quiver.

Every young person I see has their phone permanently in their hands. They walk from place to place with their heads bent over their electric screens. The chances are Mark has his phone on him. I get down on the floor next to him and slide my hand into a pocket. Empty. I have to crawl around painfully to reach the other one.

My heart beats fast and hard as I touch the slim, metal edge of the phone in Mark's pocket. I am just pinching the edges between my fingers when there is an explosion of movement. Mark scissor kicks his legs and catches my hand, twisting the wrist so hard I scream in agony.

There is a whirl of movement. A blur of iron-hard tanned brown limbs, and a thrash of white cotton. As easily as flipping a card, Mark has tossed me onto my front, his knee slamming into my side. I gasp as my breath is driven from my body

'Who the fuck are you?' Mark hisses in my ear. He rotates my wrist another turn and I scream again. I can't catch my breath, he has all his weight on me – I fear my bones will splinter. The strange white room goes dark, and a fleeting sadness that I wasn't able to save Will is my last thought before I close my eyes.

*

'No!' Angela's shriek is loud enough to shatter glass. There is an indescribable crashing sound and I groan with relief as Mark's body rolls away from me. 'Are you OK? Oh my God! I thought he'd killed you!'

Angela drags me to my feet. We both stare at his body. She holds her weapon high in the air but he doesn't stir. I bend to check on him. He is breathing, but deeply unconscious. I can't understand why my drops didn't keep him under for longer. I give him one more to give us some time. My wrist is ballooning so I pull my sleeve down to cover it; I don't want Angela to fuss.

'What did you do?' I ask, rubbing my wrist and struggling to get my breath back.

'I whacked him with this,' she says holding up a thin square box. 'It's his lap top.'

She catches my eye and we giggle.

'Well, we're not going to get anything from this now,' Angela says, examining the laptop. It has a head-shaped dent in the broken cover and its wires hang like entrails. She gives another hysterical snort. 'Is he OK?'

I nod, 'for the time being. Nothing worse than a bad case of concussion that will hopefully put him out of action for a few months.'

Angela's voice grows serious. 'I think you'd better come and have a look in the bedroom.'

She helps me down the corridor. I am surprised at how small it is compared to the rest of the flat. The atmosphere is choking, thick and dark, belying the continuing white theme. There is nothing but a great, white, square of a bed in the room. It is neatly made with white linen. Otherwise, the room is empty.

Angela slides open a wall that conceals floor to ceiling shelves. A large, sophisticated looking safe is at the centre, and one shelf is lined with neatly stacked note books. She picks up one of them and shows it to me. 'They are all full of deals, I think. Lots of money going in and out.'

I nod. My wrist is burning with pain and my body is sore with bruises. 'What's that?'

Clear plastic packets are scattered on the shelves. Angela holds a selection up for me to see. 'Lots of different pills, coke, some brown stuff,' she says.

'Why has he got it all on display like this? Surely this is illegal?'

'I think this is usually locked up. The door was ajar when I came in so I could slide it open, look.' She pointed to a cigarette packet sized panel on the wall. 'When this door is shut I don't think you'd know it was here, and you'd need the code to unlock it.'

'Good. Leave it open,' I say. 'I know where his phone is, come on.'

I stand by the window looking out over the polluted city as Angela studies Mark's phone.

'Oh fuck,' she says. I turn, knocking my wrist against a rail and the pain makes me faint. My heart is flapping around in my chest, missing beats then thudding loudly in my ears.

'What is it?'

'It's one of them new iPhones,' she says. 'It doesn't use a thumb print, it recognises your face.'

I am in too much pain to take in how astonishing this is. 'Can't you just hold it up in front of him?'

'No,' Angela shakes her head. 'I've tried that, it won't work with his eyes shut. Wait! Is that an iPad?' She scrambles over to the kitchen table where what looks like a giant phone rests. 'Brilliant!' she exclaims. 'This will work with a fingerprint.'

Her face screwed up in distaste, she picks up Mark's hand and presses his thumb to the tablet. I see her sag with relief. 'It worked.'

We sit at the table. I can't see the screen, so study Angela's face. It shifts from concentration to triumph. 'What is it?'

'He's got all his passwords saved so I can open everything. I can get onto his Cloud. Oh My God.'

'What?'

'These pictures,' her fingers dance as she scrolls through picture after picture. She looks like she is about to be sick. 'Oh, Mrs B they're disgusting.'

'Let me see.'

Wordlessly she passes me the metal screen. She's right. Every possible sexual deviancy is here. Angela shows me how to swipe through each image. There are hundreds but it doesn't take long to find the pictures of Will and Anya.

They are just as bad as he'd described, but he was not the only one to find himself ensnared in this bastard's machinations. Many of the photographs feature blank-eyed pin-prick pupiled young people of both sexes. Some are naked and brutally exposed, some are taking drugs, but the worst are at the end. Angela shows me, her face grave.

'There's a folder, kept separate from the others,' she says.

I let out a gust of air. Children. Some no more than five. Their faces plead at me from the screen as they are pawed by pink-faced, fleshy men with bulging stomachs. I force myself to look at them, swiping through each one carefully, though my stomach heaves in protest. Angela is shaking and turns to retch into the sink.

I study the backgrounds of these vile pictures. Many feature Mark's flat but it varies. Most look like private houses. I am clenching my jaw, terrified I am going to see Will, but he's not there. Thank God. 'He's not there, Angela,' I say. 'Will's not there.'

She sags back into a chair with relief. 'Who are those blokes? Sick paedos. They should be strung up. What? What is it?'

I can't take my eyes from the screen. A busy room, taken at a strange angle so it is difficult to make out. A circle of men and one woman, three children trying their best to be invisible. It is sickening, but that is not what has caught my eye. I can see a man's profile. Surely not, it can't be… I blink. My body is telling me what my head is refusing to believe. It's him. I can even make out the thin line of the scar, less livid now, curling down the side of his neck.

'Mrs B?'

'It's nothing,' I say gathering my thoughts, 'The main thing is to get rid of all of these. Can you do that?'

Angela nods and takes back the screen. I see her work methodically until all the photographs have gone. 'What about the folder?'

'All of it,' I say. 'There's enough filth in this place for the police to be getting on with. The important thing is there is nothing linking us to Will. If you destroy all of the photographs he won't know who we were protecting. Rest assured Mark will be looking for who did this to him, and his reach will be far, even if he's in prison.'

Angela gave a shiver and stood up. 'All done. We better go. Have you got a handkerchief or something? We should get rid of any fingerprints, just in case. I'm going to destroy his phone and iPad. Hopefully he'll get banged up before he gets a chance to try and retrieve anything.'

Back down in the lobby, Angela heads to a payphone to call the police, making sure she uses one shielded from the cameras in the ceiling. I had no idea they were there.

Ten minutes later she scurries over, keeping her head low and the hood of her coat pulled up. She is glowing with exhilaration.

'I did it!' she exclaims. 'I told them I lived in the flat next door and that I'd heard a big fight going on. They should be here soon and hopefully they'll find everything and we'll never have to worry about that shit again.'

\*

I can't wait to get home to bind my wrist, take something for the pain and sleep for a week. But first, I have to see Will. I don't care how late it is, I make Angela drive to the hospital.

'You wait here.' I say. She frowns as I stagger a little getting out of the car.

'Mrs B I don't like this, you're all shook up and that bastard gave you a right going over. Please let me take you to see the Doc.'

'I'm fine,' I say crossly. 'I won't be long.'

It feels like one in the morning so I am shocked to see it has only just gone seven. The journey home from London passed in a haze as I had slept through most of it. Poor Angela, I think as I head towards Will's ward, she has been brilliant, and probably saved my life.

Will has a bed tucked at the back of the ward. On the drive back, Angela called Lockwood who assured us Will had pulled through and was waiting for an assessment before being released from hospital.

The room is dark and quiet. Will lies staring at the ceiling and doesn't move as I get close. I sit on the chair beside his bed, wincing as I knock my side, which is screamingly tender. The skin will be black with bruises in the morning.

'It's over, Will,' I say and pass him his phone.

He turns his head towards me; his eyes are dead.

I lean forward and whisper in his ear. 'I promise you, Will, they've gone. All the pictures? We found them, and Angela erased every one. There were all sorts of bad things in his flat. The police are there now.'

'The police?' his voice is high with alarm.

'Don't worry, we didn't call them until after everything was destroyed. They'll find the drugs and money though. Plenty to lock him up for a long time.'

Will's eyes snap into focus and he struggles to sit up. He is still thin, bordering on skeletal, but seeing a flower of happiness and relief begin to blossom makes my heart sing.

'Is this true? You found Mark?'

'Yes we did,' I say proudly. 'Angela and I used your phone to track him down, and we paid him a visit.'

He is incredulous; I want to sing with joy when I see the last of the slimy black reeds begin to shrivel and drop away. The knots in him are loosening. Light begins to steal into his skin and his eyes

'Keep an eye on your phone,' I say. 'I think your friend Mark will be in the headlines pretty soon.'

Will smiles weakly. I'm not sure it has quite sunk in.

'You're free of him Will.' I take his hand and, with a deep breath, roll my memory of the day into his skin. Mark's white flat; crashing him to the floor; searching for the photos before Mark woke up and attacked me; the secrets of the sliding door; and, finally, destroying the phone and calling the police. I force into him the fear and the pain, the horror of what we saw until he is convinced.

'Oh, Mrs B' he says with a shaky breath. He squeezes my hand. 'You saved my life. Twice. I don't know how I can repay…' he breaks down. 'I've been so scared. I hated myself for what I did to Anya and then everything got so out of hand. I was dreading telling Mum and Dad…' He leans back on the pillows. 'And they've gone? The pictures?'

'Yes. I promise.'

My heart is light as I go to find Angela. She is leaning on the reception desk, yawning widely. She grins when she sees me and bustles to my side.

'Well thank goodness that's all over with,' she says. 'Do you think that's the end of it? He won't come to find us?'

I remember the way the skin on Mark's neck burned red as I dropped the last of my hemlock onto him.

'No. Trust me. We're safe,' I say.

'Good. Bloody hell, Mrs B. What have you done to your arm?'

She draws back my sleeve to see my wrist bulging red and black.

'It's nothing, stop clucking around like a mother hen.'

'You're coming with me,' Angela says in a voice that brooks no argument. 'At least we're already at the hospital.'

# CHAPTER 16: ANGIE

I must have been manic with exhilaration for weeks after our trip to London. Every time I thought of the police bursting into that weird flat and finding all that horror, enough to ensure Mark Lowell ended up in prison for a very long time, I wanted to punch the air. We had been such warriors. I'd lie in bed and remember smashing his head using his expensive MacBook Pro and it would set me up for the day.

Having seen those disgusting photos of the kiddies, I didn't feel a trace of guilt. For the rest of my life I would be haunted by those images. I'd read about celebrities being caught with child porn on their computers and, of course, I would be disgusted. But seeing the abuse in front of me, kids being groped and brutally explored by men my age and older… it was incomprehensible.

I hadn't told the old woman that I had emailed some of the clearer shots from the secret folder straight over to the police, using Mark's email, before deleting them. There was no way those perverts would get away with it. I looked forward to seeing those faces again, in the news, when the arrests began.

I remembered the whole crazy adventure in fragments. It was a mystery how we got there and back as I couldn't remember the drive. Bits were very sharp. The photographs, Mark lying on the floor in his white room, wearing a white dressing gown spattered with blood... Everything else was muddled.

The reason for my exhilaration was not that the two of us had destroyed a villain like a pair of super heroes, but that we had saved Will.

The change in him was immediate and gratifying. He was a different boy. Within weeks he had put weight on and could come and visit. We'd embarrass him by cooing over how handsome he looked. I would stuff him full of as much food as I could, and sometimes he would stay and talk until it was dark.

The guilt and fear had left their mark on him. Of course they had. But Will had all the resilience of youth, and some days you couldn't see the darkness in him at all. Mrs B was as happy as I had ever seen her; but the day had taken its toll and she was frail for a good while afterwards.

That brute had broken her wrist. I only realised after we went to see Will at the hospital. She tried to cover it up, but the swelling was so bad it couldn't be missed. A spiral fracture. Just what she needed. The hospital worried about her age, and demanded she stay overnight, but she refused, and forced me to take her home.

When we got back, I bounced around the house bubbling with energy and excitement. I'd be washing the floors planning what villain we should take on next. There were plenty of them about, after all. But Mrs B retreated to her room and slept. I worried about her, she was so grey and faded.

Of course, we hadn't told anyone what had happened and how Mrs B was injured, but I longed to call the Doc to come and check her over. She was getting forgetful, and would repeat herself, or not remember what we had talked about the night before. I dismissed my worries, she'd had a stressful time and was in pain, but resolved to chat to the Doc about it as some point.

Although she utterly denied it, the dog helped get Mrs B up and about. I'd decided to call him Trevor as he looked like a terrier. He was a happy little thing. Goodness knows how old he was, but he certainly took to the old woman.

Much to her irritation, he would sit on his haunches for hours, gazing at her with his bright brown eyes. If she shooed him away, he moved exactly three feet, curling into a little comma, twitching his eyebrow with excitement if he sensed she was going to move. If she did, he'd spring onto his paws, mouth open and tongue lolling in a broad smile.

'Oh, get on with you,' she'd growl, and he'd yap in reply. I noticed every now and then, when she was particularly engrossed in a book, her arm would drop to rest on Trevor's head, and he would huff a contented sigh and fall asleep.

Gradually, Mrs B recovered enough to allow Trevor to accompany us on our walks. May was turning into June and I realised with a shock how long it was since Andy had left me. Every now and then we'd have glorious days that spoke of summer, and Mrs B and I would walk into the woods and across the valley watching the trees greening, appreciating a world warming and unfurling.

These days did more to get Mrs B on the road to recovery than any medicine. I could see her revelling in the freshness, the greenness of being outside. Often, we had to stop so she could pick some flowers, or comb through leaves to refill her mysterious stocks of teas and potions. It wasn't long before I could see again the dark-haired woman who lay beneath Mrs B's skin.

The arrival of early summer transformed the house. The warmth of the sun eased its old bones, making its colours glow. When it was too hot, the cool tiles of the hall floor were delicious under my bare feet, and the great windows embraced the transfiguring qualities of the light. Now the sun was higher in the sky, it no longer slanted into the house in its nit-picking way, highlighting any speck of dust like an overzealous housekeeper. No, once spring drifted into summer, the light was in no hurry. It welled across the floor in long, lazy stripes of thick honey.

Instead of wood smoke, the air smelled of freshly washed laundry, and keeping the windows open meant ripples of warm, sweet-scented breezes threaded their way around the house. It was so lovely not to be cold all the time. I had to save up to buy new summer clothes. I found some cheap cotton dresses in town and was delighted to find I'd gone down a size.

I'd only ever known the house in the winter, and it was a revelation when the days grew longer, and the garden stirred into life. Flowers burst from the ground, zipping up above the grass and shaking out their dresses in every colour of the rainbow. Mrs B demanded I visit them all, and each flower prompted a story about an old lover, or a trip to somewhere gorgeously exotic. Shanghai, Persia, Delhi, Australia, Boston, Paris, Berlin... Some of the names were familiar, others I'd never heard of, but they breathed glamour.

'The furthest I've ever been is Malaga,' I would say to her. 'The places you talk about, they sound like something from a fairy tale, or a posh fashion magazine. You make me want to go out and explore the world.'

'And so you should,' she said. 'I'll go with you.'

I was getting my hands dirty in the garden. I couldn't bear the house, now so clean and light, being surrounded by tangles of weeds and long grass. It was like setting a beautiful opal into a plastic ring from a Christmas cracker. It took me two weeks to discover a stone terrace flared out from the steps up to the front door. It was so choked with weeds and rubbish I had no idea it was there.

Once cleared, it was a lovely space and I dragged out a table and chairs so Mrs B, Trevor, and I could sit there for lunch on warm days. I had time on my hands as, apart from cooking for the old woman and keeping on top of the house, I didn't have much to do. Mrs. B got into the habit of passing me a book every few days and happy hours passed discussing our thoughts. Some I loved, some I hated. I couldn't bear *The Bonfire of the Vanities*, or *American Psycho*, but adored *White Teeth* and *Great Expectations*.

We argued for hours, as our tastes were different. Mrs B never let me get away with lazy thinking. She attacked me like a teacher, firing questions, refusing to accept my first answer. I loved it. I even wondered if I should do a night course or something.

Approaching the less scary ones in the village, on Mrs B's advice, had given me confidence. By the time summer proper had started, I had listened to three of them. A girl who whispered of love, and how it had driven her mad. A man around my age who lamented his children had grown away before he found the time to know them. And an old Indian woman, the one who would wait outside my flat.

I'd seen her as I was driving out of the village into town. She had haunted me for so long, it was time to approach her. I pulled the car over and sat on a wall, waiting for her to come near. She was scary, but I let her fill my head with heat and dust, and the burn of strong spices. She wanted her son but couldn't find him. She told me everything about him and when she had finished, I passed the words back to her in the form of a child, and she smiled as she faded away.

For the first time I found myself looking for Dad. I felt I'd be able to cope. I wasn't so frightened, but he was never in the village and I didn't know where else to look. It troubled me more than I liked to admit. I would wake in the middle of the night and torment myself with the thought he had given up on me. I had left it too late.

Otherwise, it was one of the happiest times of my life. Saving Will had proved to me I could be strong, that I could help get rid of demons. Mrs B began to treat me, if not as an equal, at least a tolerable companion – and I was happy with that. I loved living in Pagan's Reach.

Every day I found some new secret: A hidden cupboard I'd never noticed, filled with a complete dinner set painted most delicately with butterflies; In the garden I found a carved stone statue of a girl crying into her hands hiding beneath a willow whose leaves stretched to the ground; I closed a door and discovered a tiny painting, the size of my hand, hanging behind it – a portrait of a serious looking man in a loose white shirt, flames burning behind him… So many unexpected things. The house was beginning to trust me, happy to reveal some of her hidden treasures.

And Gary. After my trip to London, still wild and wired, I phoned him. By the time the Oriental Poppies were blooming, we had been on three dates. One didn't count, as it involved Gary helping me lug tons of gravel to spread onto the driveway, but the other two had been wonderful.

I was so nervous calling him I thought I was going to be sick. Mrs B knew something was up and kept shooting me curious glances as I jittered about the place. Finally, I settled the old woman in her room and retreated to mine. I'd smuggled an ice-cold white wine from the kitchen. Not that Mrs B would have minded, but I knew if she saw me with the bottle she would pepper me with questions until I gave in and told her everything.

I filled a glass to the brim and admired the lemony gold colour of the wine before knocking the whole lot back in two gulps. Then, before I could change my mind, I called him.

Even now so many years later, it makes my toes curl to remember the awkwardness of that conversation. I despaired. The ease with which we had bantered back and forth in the past seemed to have deserted us. I asked him to meet me at the Rose as I knew it would be fairly quiet, and there was no way I was going to meet him without getting a bit pissed.

I trotted into the village on foot as Mrs B would have noticed if I'd taken the car. I'd told no one I was meeting him. I knew Vicky and Mags were away, I just prayed that the Doc and his wife, or Sharon, didn't decide to pop down to the local that evening.

*

He was already there when I arrived. He hadn't seen me, so I took a second to have a bit of a gawk. He'd dressed up, bless him, and instead of the usual jeans and jumper combo, he was wearing a white shirt and soft, dark brown corduroy trousers which clung beautifully to his strong thighs. He'd even had a haircut, and the back of his neck looked pink. I was debating whether to nip to the bar to get a large gin and tonic before he saw me, when he turned and waved.

I flushed beet red and waved back. He motioned me over to the seat next to him and I took off my coat – trying and failing to stop myself from using it to disguise the push of my belly – and sat down.

'Hi Gary. Thanks for coming out. You look nice.' I said in a rush. He smiled and pecked me on the cheek. He smelt gorgeous.

'What would you like?'

'Sorry?'

'To drink?'

'Oh! Sorry! Um, a gin and tonic? Thanks. Large! Please.'

He returned with the drinks and two bags of crisps wedged under his arm. Normally I'd be salivating at the sight, but that night I had no interest in them, and happily watched Gary munch through the lot.

After a few awkward pauses we relaxed and chatted about work. He made me laugh, and when I told him some tales about Mrs B. I was astonished to see how he responded. When I described how she'd hidden down a corridor to jump out and catch me in the forbidden act of using bleach, he was in stitches.

I loved his laugh. it was slightly reluctant, as if I was tugging it from him. It would start as a deep bark and then a glorious chuckle. I tried my best to make him laugh again.

Andy never found me funny, I thought as I stood at the bar to order more drinks. He'd smile at my jokes, but I never got a proper belly laugh from him. I wondered for the millionth time why I had stayed for so long.

Two hours later, Gary and I were on our fourth round, giggling hysterically, trying to outdo each other with funny stories. I was tipsy, but in a good way. I couldn't stop smiling.

I looked down at the table and smiled goofily at our hands, which were very close to touching. Gary took a last gulp of his lager and slammed the glass down with a bang.

'Did I ever tell you, Angie Cartwright...'

'Angie Tully now, Gary.'

He didn't miss a beat, 'Did I ever tell you, Angie Tully, that I am a very well-known and proficient reader of palms?' His careful pronunciation of the 'p's told me he was as drunk as I was.

I smiled. 'No, Gary, you haven't.'

He picked up my left hand and his touch sent a throb of pleasure through me, all the way from my fingers down to my toes, cramped as they were in my best black boots. I was shocked by the warmth of his skin on mine. I realised, with a pang, that I couldn't remember the last time I had been touched like that. My body sighed like a frozen plant plunged into warm water.

'You see now this...' Gary's big thumb traced across my palm sending shivers up my arm. 'Is your lifeline.'

'Is it long?' I croaked. My body was all over the place. A long-forgotten engine, deep, deep inside me, cranked into life. Sparks and smoke crackling away; every bit of me on high alert.

He cocked an eyebrow at my response, and I almost spat out the rest of my drink. I slapped his arm.

'My lifeline, you git!' I exclaimed.

He continued to trace the line, up and down before stretching across from side to side. I couldn't take my eyes from his fingers. My hand looked tiny in his. 'It's telling me you will have a long life.' He said at last. His voice was a little husky too. 'Look, it stretches all the way around.' Gary turned my hand and allowed his thumb to circle around the back until he was stroking my wrist. 'You've got lovely skin,' he said.

I swallowed. I didn't know what to say. I only knew I wanted him to keep touching me. I couldn't stop looking at his mouth. He had good, firm lips and when he smiled, his teeth were crooked and white. I knew he was looking at me, but I couldn't lift my eyes from his mouth. He had me mesmerised.

He moved to take both my hands in his. They were dry and warm. He tugged them, pulling me forward. My mouth was inches from his. Startled, I looked up, he was gazing at me steadily, his hazel eyes smiling, and then, with exquisite slowness, he closed them and bent his head. His lips met mine in the sweetest, softest touch.

I groaned. He slid his hand up my throat and into my hair, cradling my head as he kissed me on and on. I was torn between thinking I was going to faint or burst into flames.

'Come on, you lovebirds!' a raucous voice wrenched us apart – it was the landlord. 'Have you two gone deaf or summat? Time, gentlemen please! I've rung the bell twice.'

Gary leapt to his feet but kept a firm grasp of my hand. 'Sorry, mate. Lost track of time. We'll be off.'

He pulled me out of the pub, and we walked sedately for a few yards before he turned to look at me and suddenly, we were kissing again. My heart hammered in my ears; I'd never felt anything so gorgeous.

'God, you're lovely,' he whispered in my ear. His hands slid round my waist and curved over my backside. He gave a moan.

Oh, how I had missed the pleasure of snogging! He walked me all the way back to Pagan's Reach, stopping every few minutes to kiss me until my face was raw with stubble burn. 'You make me feel like a teenager,' I told him.

'Good,' he replied.

He left me at the front door; we had arranged to meet the following week for dinner. I had to clench everything to stop myself from asking him to come and stay the night. God! I'd turned into a right old slag.

I danced my way into bed but couldn't sleep. I lay there grinning, replaying every single moment until I fell asleep as the sun rose. It meant I was good for nothing all day and Mrs B was most irritated with me.

*

I spent the following weeks in a dreamy haze, Gary never far from my thoughts. We'd met a second time for dinner and found we were, again, falling over ourselves to find out as much as we could about each other.

Not having children had stagnated me into a kind of limbo. I had done so little with my life since getting married I was defining myself by the madcap adventures of my teenage years. It would have been too dreary to talk about my failed marriage, too dark to explore how Andy and I splintered and shattered following the loss of our son, and how the grief of that and Andy's affair had nearly killed me.

I realised with a shock that thirty years of my life had passed in a blur. The only times I found interesting enough to chat about were the years when I was young, and the past months at Pagan's Reach with Mrs B. No wonder I only felt twenty years old. The realisation made me sick - what a waste, I thought.

Gary had a grown-up son and daughter and had been tugged by them into a future I would never know. A future filled with graduations, weddings, even grandchildren one day. I felt naïve and unformed, stuck in the village where I was born, while Gary talked about the deserts of Iraq and the dangers he had faced there.

But still, part of me revelled in the feeling of a new start, of my life beginning again. Living with an ancient old woman made me feel young, and I was beginning to believe I was the woman Gary seemed to see.

Then the cold winds came. The sun disappeared and Gary called to tell me the holiday he'd booked months ago was non-refundable and he would be going away for three weeks.

'I'm sorry, love,' he said, 'It's not great timing, I was looking forward to spending the summer with you but it's a lot of money to lose and, well, I'd promised the lads I'd go – Danny's still a bit cut up about his divorce and Bob's just lost his mum...'

'Of course you should go, Gary!' I exclaimed, making sure I pasted on a grin, so my voice sounded happy and relaxed. 'Don't worry. It sounds like they need you and it's kind of you to go and cheer them up. Where are you going again? Off for sun, sand and sangria?'

He laughed. 'I bloody wish!' he said. 'No, Danny's got a mate with a place just outside Keswick in Cumbria. Not much sun but I'm sure there will be plenty of whisky and ale.'

'I'll miss you,' I said into the phone.

'Yeah, me too. I'll try and call when I can.'

\*

The weather reflected my mood. It poured with rain for a solid three days the week Gary left. Mrs B was fretful and crotchety; obsessed with her little garden statues, she checked them twice every day. She constantly worked at the heavy gold necklace around her neck, smoothing her fingers over the pieces with an obsessive, repetitive movement. All the high spirits of the trip to London had drained away.

I couldn't work out why I felt so uncomfortable. The house had a shuttered, withdrawn feel as if it was hiding from the dense clouds that pressed heavy on the shoulders of the wooded hills behind us. The temperature climbed and climbed but the weather showed no sign of breaking. Thunder bugs crawled over my skin, irritating, tiny black dots - and wasps kept looping in through the windows, drunk with the heat. It was dreadfully humid, and I could only bear to wear the lightest of cotton dresses but sweat still slid down my neck. My lovely new haircut spiralled into frizzy curls.

The birds who normally chattered and called to each other throughout the day were silent, the emptiness of the woods stretched eerie and hollow. It made my ears hurt as they strained to make out a sound.

I couldn't shake off the feeling the house was waiting. I kept catching Mrs B looking out of the window as if looking for someone. She wasn't eating much, and I found her quick irritation contagious. The heat sapped away everything. All we could do was snipe at each other and slump exhausted in the back dining room. It was the coolest room in the house with the big wooden shutters locked shut, but with the windows open in a vain attempt to catch any breeze. I didn't particularly like the blood red walls, dark ebony floorboards and low ceiling, but at least it was clean and the thick stone walls gave it a chilly, subterranean feel.

The tension was broken temporarily by Maeve calling to warn us of some break-ins that had happened in the village.

'I've never known it this bad, Angie, do make sure you lock everything up tight, will you? Mrs B's got so many lovely things up there and I'd hate for anything to happen – the two of you all alone. Mike said he was chatting to Donny whose brother works for the police. Apparently, there's a nasty gang prowling about. They even broke into the fire station and stole the cutting equipment – you know, the big machines they use to break people free from crashed cars? Isn't that awful? I hope they jolly well get caught in a car and find nobody can free them and then see how they feel.

'I know I shouldn't say it, Angie, but it's true. It's wicked what they've been doing. Even breaking into poor old Mr Burgess' shed and stealing his expensive tools. It doesn't bear thinking about. We've never had this sort of thing happening in the village as you well know Angie...'

I tuned out as she chattered on. I watched Mrs B standing in the corridor outside the dining room, peering out of the window up at the woods behind us. I didn't like the look on her face. I saw her hands creep unconsciously to her throat to stroke the gold that gleamed dull in the strange, grey light.

'Come on, Mrs B let's get you into the dining room, it's like an oven out here.'

I guided her to the little settee at the back of the red room and refilled her water glass.

'Was that Maeve on the phone? What did she want?' Mrs B said after trying and failing to read her book. It was too gloomy to see, and she was too vain to ask for a light.

'Oh nothing, really. Just worrying about some gang prowling around, breaking into houses.'

The old woman's response was immediate. 'What gang? What did she say? Exactly.'

I looked up in surprise. 'It's just some group of scumbos chancing their arm with loads of people on holiday,' I said. 'Don't worry about it, Mrs B.'

But she wouldn't let up. 'What were they looking for?' she kept asking. 'What had they taken?'

I told her about the cutting equipment, and Mr Burgess's tools, and her face went dead white. She stood up and started muttering to herself, pacing back and forth and twisting her hands together in agitation. A weird, flickering light danced from her and I saw her young, blond companion come out of the shadows to stand close.

It took a lot of persuasion to get her up to bed. She insisted I check the locks over and over again. The heat still climbed higher and higher – I could barely breathe and longed for a good storm to clear the air.

At last she was settled, and I took my third shower of the day. The house was quiet, and I decided to put on a load of washing before bed. It showed how tense I was feeling that when I heard a great crash at the back door, followed by a volley of yaps from Trevor, I nearly jumped out of my skin. I dropped the dirty laundry on the floor and put my hand to my chest to still my heart, which was hammering away nineteen-to-the-dozen.

Berating myself for being such a bloody silly cow, I hastened for the kitchen. A gust of wind must have blown the back door sopen, I thought; the storm must have arrived at last.

I was cursing myself for leaving the towels on the line as the rain would be thrashing down any minute, when my heart stopped to hear a heart-wrenching yapping scream, and Trevor slid out of the kitchen and smashed into the wall.

'Trevor!' I shouted and ran to him. I stopped when a man who was standing, silent and still in the kitchen, stepped forward.

*

'Who the hell are you? Get out of this house.' I said, as calmly as I could manage, holding Trevor in my arms and desperately trying to make out a heartbeat.

The man was so big he looked bloated. He wore a black and white tracksuit that clung to his bulk. Greasy, matted hair was tied back in a knot and an ugly black tattoo swarmed up his neck. The air around him vibrated with menace. I backed away.

There was something odd about the way he moved. He had small eyes set close together, like a bull and aggression steamed from him; his hands clenched into fists and he glared at me, his head on one side.

'What do you want?' I said, sounding much braver than I felt.

'You know exactly what we want,' he hissed. 'You've hidden it for so long you thought nobody would ever come.' His voice was weirdly high-pitched; it made my skin crawl. I couldn't identify his accent. 'But now we have, and you can hand it over. you fucking *bitch*!'

I screamed in shock as he roared, his spit settling on my skin – I didn't dare move to wipe it away. I tried to stay calm but could see with an odd sense of disassociation my hands were shaking as if palsied. I couldn't make them stop. Terror loosened my bladder and I struggled to stay in control of myself.

'I'm sorry. I don't know what you're on about. You've come to the wrong place.' As I spoke, I tried to remember where my phone was, and flicked my eyes around the room for any kind of weapon.

He swung round and pulled me into the kitchen and pushed me against the counter.

'My name is Luka,' he said, watching my face closely and seem puzzled I didn't know him. 'You need to show me where it is. Is it here? In the house?'

I considered myself a strong, well-built woman, but in the face of this man's tremendous physical presence and his wild aggression I was powerfully aware of my how weak I was – I had never felt so vulnerable.

I heard the crash before I felt it. He sprung across the room, knocking a chair to the floor, and his hand was tight round my throat; he banged my head again against the wall with a sudden jerk. Pain bloomed behind my eyes. I grabbed for his hand, 'Don't,' was all I could say.

'Listen to me,' he said, his mouth close enough I could smell the stink of his breath. 'I want you to go to wherever you have hidden it and bring it to me. OK?' He slammed my head back again.

I cried out. 'I can't! I don't know what you're talking about! Please...' The pressure of his hand round my neck and the pain in my head was unbearable. I couldn't move; his strength was inhuman.

My mouth gaped open, trying to snatch a pocket of air. I shook my head.

What happened next was such a blur no matter how many times I looked back to try and piece everything together I couldn't. First was a sound, which must have been the kitchen door opening. The man, Luka, and I, locked in a monstrous embrace, turned towards it.

Mrs B was there, her eyes blazing. She said something but I couldn't hear through the roaring in my ears. She lifted her hand, and I don't quite know how the hell this happened... *flung* the man across the room – slamming him into the wall opposite. It was as if a giant had reached into the room and tossed him away from me. I sucked in air with a great gasp.

It wasn't Mrs B standing there anymore. It was the dark-haired woman who stood in the doorway, her arms raised so her clothes rippled around her. Her mouth opened in a shout and flames streamed from her fingertips. Luka's body lifted up in the air and slammed down again, limp as a rag doll.

The air in the room shrieked, making me dizzy. I looked again at the doorway, head throbbing. I caught the woman's eye and she smiled, a smile of power and command and victory. It was terrifying, and the last thing I saw before the darkness swept over my head like a hood, and I was falling, banging my head on the table and crashing into unconsciousness.

# CHAPTER 17: FRIEDA HEALS

*Adder's fork, and blind-worm's sting,*
*Lizard's leg, and owlet's wing,—*
*For a charm of powerful trouble,*
*Like a hell-broth boil and bubble.*

The joy of seeing Will growing fat is delicious, but it is not long before he looks out at the world again and, in time, he leaves. That is how it should be, but I can see how it pains Lockwood and Maeve to see him packed up and waving from the car as he returns to re-take his second year at university.

Lockwood's gratitude is deep but unspoken. He knows I had a hand in Will's dramatic recovery at a time when he was so lost he seemed beyond redemption, but we don't speak of it. The Doctor talks instead of medicines and therapy and I smile and pour him another cup of tea.

Angie has been lolloping about with a silly smile on her face that makes me want to gag. She thinks I have no idea, but I know everything I need to know about her little love affair. She drifts about the house flushed and dreamy as a teenager, a look not so attractive in a stout, 50 year old woman. I much prefer her when she is arguing with me about books; she can be very fierce when she wants to be.

This man is important to her, and I need to know he won't crush her blossoming confidence. I engineer a meeting with him, unbeknownst to Angie, by going to the café where I knew he lunches most days during the summer. She thinks I am in for a check-up with Lockwood, but before she comes to collect me, I slip out and walk down the road.

Gary is not what I expected. Solidly built with hair cropped close to his head, at first glance he seems thuggish. But the minute I enter the café and he walks towards me, I see the warmth glowing from him. It's the heat of towels and sheets that have hung in the summer sun all day; linen to bury your face in to inhale that clean, fresh-air warmth. It is the heat of bonfires on cold Autumn evenings, the comforting burn of a hot mug of tea in cold hands.

'You must be Gary,' I say, stopping him in his tracks and introducing myself. I shake his hand, which is enormous and completely encloses my own.

'And you must be Mrs B,' he says. 'The woman Angie works for.'

'Indeed,' I say. His face, which looks quite grim in repose, transforms when he smiles. It is infectious. He's not a good looking man, but I respond to him, he is powerfully attractive. His eyes are striking, an unusual, clear amber, fringed with thick lashes and framed by crows' feet that lie white against his weathered face.

A spark in his eye stirs a memory of an old lover, the only man I knew with yellow eyes. He was extremely skilled at broute-minou. As we looked at each other I wondered if Gary had the same skill. Judging by the soft fullness of his lips it was a strong possibility. Lucky Angie.

I can find no malice in him. I hold his hand in mine for a moment and concentrate. Gary waits, patient, there is a core of peace at his heart; he happy with who he is. I am satisfied. He will be good for Angie.

'It's good to meet you at last,' I say.

'Yes, for me too. I have heard a lot about you.' He leans over and kisses my cheek and I can feel my pulse thudding as I smell his skin. I enjoy it more than I should.

I don't tell Angie of our brief meeting, and it would seem Gary doesn't mention it to her either.

*

The summer grows hot and then hotter still. With the heat comes a growing unease I can no longer ignore. I can sense him prowling closer and closer, circling the house with his teeth bared. I keep staring out of the window, certain someone is standing and watching, but when I look again there is nobody there.

The heat is enervating; this frightens me. I am not sure I am going to survive this. Charlie has nothing to say, and when he hears of the machinery being stolen he darts me a look full of fear. I check the seals over and over but am never reassured they are safe. I know he is coming.

The day it begins my head throbs with the heat. I know I need to keep checking the wood as it has been sending me urgent, whispered messages for days – but the heat has sapped me of the will; my limbs hang heavy and useless.

In my bed ready to sleep, I make Angie open the windows wide so I can see when the storm begins. I can smell its crackle in the air. We are desperate for the storm, so the rain can come and cool down the days, and I can return to the wood. I begin to doze, Eldritch beside me. I let my mind drift and rise above the house, stretching my gaze left and right, searching for danger. A sudden, dreadful scream snatches me back into my body and I surface with a shudder.

The house is silent for long enough for me to wonder if I had imagined the scream, when a smashing thud shakes the walls of the house. A man's voice tears through the fabric of the building, and my guts turn to ice.

As fast as I can, I skid across the corridor and down the stairs, clinging onto the wall and cursing Angie for polishing the floorboards to such a high, slippery shine. Dreadful thumps are coming from the kitchen. The door is shut and I take a deep breath before forcing it open.

For a few seconds I can't make out what is happening. There is a roaring in my ears. All I can see is black and violent movement. Another crash, and red ink splashes. The shouting is so loud I am disoriented and then the scene snaps into place. A man is smashing Angie against the wall, snarling into her face. Black clouds of rage buffet the air, and the stink of unwashed body and fear is overwhelming.

I watch in horror as he slams Angie's head against the wall for the third time. Her eyes roll back as his hands tighten around her throat. Her lips begin to turn blue.

'Angie!' I scream.

I stand still, bow my head, and pull the energy of the earth up through my legs and into my body. It blazes from my eyes, my hair crackles with it, and my hands grow hot as I lift them above my head. A bright, white wind spins around me and, with a bellow, I gather it, twist it around the heel of my hands, and hurl it at the brute who has invaded my home.

He is ripped away from Angie and disappears.

Then, as if a plug has been pulled, I fall.

If this is how I end up dying, I'm going to be furious.

*

I have to sit for a good hour in the doorway, slumped against the frame, before I find the strength to get to my feet and check on Angie. The bulk of her body is such I can't make out her face, but she hasn't moved since she fell. The man has gone, screaming into the woods where I hope he falls down a ravine and dies. He is not Marroch, I recognise with relief, but he has been sent by him.

Angie is terribly pale, but breathing, and an egg shaped swelling marks where she fell against the table. Deep purple bruises already bloom on her neck like poisonous flowers. They are inky dark and look like stains. They look so vivid and so violent against her white skin I can't bear to look at them.

I swallow hard to stop the curds of bile rising in my throat. I taste the bitterness of guilt and regret on my tongue. This is my fault. This is my fault.

I am weak and my hands shake with a constant tremor, but I find the strength to go into the pantry and get my box. It is high on the shelf and it takes a while to knock it down; it falls heavily into my arms with a thump, knocking painfully against the cast on my wrist. It is years since I opened it. The jars are sealed shut, and I hope the contents retain some of their freshness. I carry it back to the kitchen and rest the box next to Angie, still prone on the floor.

First, calendula. The scent is strong and the rich orange colour of the oil is promising. I pour some into my hands and hold it there, letting it warm before smoothing it over the swelling. I have no ice but running the water until it is cold, will have to do. I soak a tea towel and wring it out, placing it across poor Angie's forehead.

While the cold water soothes the swelling, I empty the last of the dried arnica flowers into my old mortar bowl. I note how age has weakened my wrist; I can hardly hold it and have to drop it to the floor with a clang. The pestle scrapes against the bottom and I inhale the pungent scent as the petals are crushed, making my eyes water.

I add oil from a little glass jar to the crushed petals and mix it into a thin paste, before searching for my tin of beeswax. The lid is stiff and I struggle for a while before I prise it off. The wax is hard and brittle from being stored for so long. I break off a piece and rub it with my fingers.

The sparks flash from my heart, down my arms into my hands. This old, methodical task, one I have repeated for decades since Lilith taught me, is soothing. The wax softens and I roll in in the arnica oil, allowing the warmed wax to absorb the oil until the colour changes and it is as soft as butter. The kitchen is still and warm, the flagstones smooth under me; all I can hear is the gentle sound of Angie breathing.

The arnica salve is ready and I spread it across her throat, covering those vivid bruises with smooth yellow-white ointment. As I work I can feel my fingers start to burn, pulling her blood to the surface so it heals the bruises, carrying away the dark blood and removing the pain.

The echoes of Marroch's message of violence, darkness and chaos has left a vacuum. The first rumblings of the long-awaited storm begin. Placing my fingertips at the back of Angie's head, careful not to disturb the towel on her forehead, I feel around for any more lumps or cuts. She is fine. I wonder whether to use my salt of Hartshorn to bring her round, but decide to let her to wake up naturally.

As I sit next to this brutalised woman, I'm haunted by the steps that led to this moment. There is no denying the simple fact: I am responsible for what has happened to Angie. Every bruise, every cut may as well have been placed there by my hand. I knew danger was coming, that Marroch would find me eventually. I was stupid to think only I would be involved – only I would be hurt. I curse my weakness and my age for gathering Angie up in this terrible, final storm of my life.

Angie's hands are cracked leather. Her nails are bitten so short they are almost invisible. I hold them for a moment, feeling the strength in them. I pause. It is time, I think. Holding my breath, I gently open out her fingers so I can see her palm. There. It's there. The mark of us all is there, clear as day. It makes me want to weep. I should have trusted her months ago.

*

With a snort Angie shifts and her eyes open. She sits up, the towel falling away. I see her sway as the pain in her head registers.

'Steady, Angie,' I say quietly. 'Be careful. I can't lift you up. Can you sit?' She nods and as she clambers into the chair at the end of the table, grunting with the effort, I shuffle about making a Chamomile tisane.

'What happened?' she says at last, watching me boil the kettle. 'One minute that man was choking me, then all of a sudden he was gone.' She pauses. 'And then you were there!' She looks at me, her eyes wide. 'But it wasn't you... it was, like, some kind of witch or something – she kept yelling and he just... disappeared.'

'Ach, you must have been hallucinating,' I respond, pouring the hot water into the pot. 'That brute was squeezing your neck so hard your brain had no oxygen, I'm not surprised your mind started playing tricks on you.'

'But…' she protests. She is struggling to remember what happened, but it makes her head hurt and she holds the towel I have dampened against her forehead again.

'Don't talk now,' I say. 'You're not thinking clearly.' I am feeling dizzy myself, and Angie's face is chalk white.

I am torn. I know I should call Lockwood, Angie has suffered a nasty blow to her head. But then a sly, selfish voice whispers in my ear. 'You'll have to go into a home without Angie here to look after you,' it says. 'They'll take her away and you will have to leave.'

No. I can't let that happen. I am perfectly capable of looking after Angie in my own home. It's not as if I haven't done this before. Lockwood and Maeve are away on holiday soon, leaving in the morning for a week in France. That lovesick calf who never takes his eyes from Angie is also away up north, so we will be undisturbed for a while.

'What happened?' Angie looks completely dazed. 'Who was that man? I've never been so frightened.' I put my hand on her shoulder. She jolts in surprise and after a moment, puts her hand over mine.

'I'll tell you everything in the morning, if you want to hear.'

'Of course I want to hear,' Angie looks puzzled. 'Do you know him then?' Her eyes flash bright green. 'He was looking for something!' she exclaims, remembering, and then blinks three or four times. 'What was he looking for?'

'You're in no state to hear anything now,' I say. 'I need to get you into bed. You'll sleep in the room next to mine as I will have to check on you through the night – you've had a nasty bump to the head. Here,' I hand her the steaming Chamomile. 'It will calm you.'

Angie puts the towel down and takes a sip. She starts and looks around the room, 'Where's Trevor? He kicked him, so hard. He tried to warn me…'

'Calm down, he's fine,' I say nodding to the scrap of fur who is lying next to the fire, muzzle resting on his paws. He has a slight limp but looks fit enough now. He quirks a hairy eyebrow, knowing we are talking about him. Angie smiles weakly. She is still dazed and keeps feeling the marks at her throat with delicate fingers.

'Come on.' I place my hand on her shoulder, encouraging her to stand. The last of my strength is draining away and it seems to take forever to get Angie up the stairs and settled into bed. She falls asleep immediately and I sit beside her to keep watch. Eldritch jumps onto my lap and her warmth is a comfort as I settle in for the night.

*

Two days later Angie's bruises are an ugly green-yellow but what I am most concerned about is her air of defeat. Fear has robbed her of the strength the house and I worked so hard to instil. Her eyes are dull; she is plagued with headaches and dizziness.

I keep her drugged. Sleep is the only thing that will help, so I hide draughts of poppy in her food and keep applying the salves to her bruises. The storms have come and the weather breaks. Outside, the trees thrash themselves against the window and the panes rattle like chattering teeth. The hair on my arms and neck prickle and stir. Something animal in me is aware of danger crawling towards us.

Angie is able to sit up and read in bed. She is keen to come downstairs but I won't let her. She isn't quite ready. Meanwhile, I am unable to sit still. Someone is watching the house and I know who it is. I sketch a golden circle around Angie's room. I whisper as I turn and bend around her, the words spilling from my lips and falling to the ground like leaves, flaring for an instant before disappearing.

When I know she is safe, for the time being, I stand by windows in the darkness and watch. I remember Lilith and fill my pockets: A small knife with a jade handle; my golden comb; a handful of chestnuts and walnuts, a diamond that spins on a silver chain. I carry these treasures with me. I will need them for the battle ahead.

Angie will also need her talismans, I tell Charlie. Not long after the house was breached, I call her to my room. It is good to see a spark has begun to return to her eye. She has convinced herself the man who attacked her was one of the gang about whom Maeve had spoken. She wanted to call the police but I dissuaded her. I will tell her the real story in due course. When she is ready.

But to begin, the first test.

At my dressing table, I wait for her to bring me tea. She sits down and, with some ceremony, I place a box between us.

'What's this?' she says.

'It's for you, a kind of apology.'

'An apology? What do you mean? What for?'

'For the attack, for what happened to you. It was my fault.'

'Don't be ridiculous,' she replies. 'Of course it wasn't your fault – it was just one of those things.'

'Don't argue with me. Just accept it, please.'

I open the box, which is flat and lined with purple velvet. A bangle. It is thin but strong. Hammered out of gold, it shines brightly.

'That's pretty,' Angie says. She can't take her eyes from it.

'It's yours,' I say, and hand it to her. I see the glow of gold light up her eyes as she examines it. I watch her. Excitement sends an electric bolt across my skin when she speaks.

'Oh look! There's writing on the inside. I can't quite…' She turns to the window and tilts the bangle back and forth. 'How funny! It's like the words shift about, I think I can read them, then I can't,' she laughs. 'Must be my eyes going funny.'

'They're spells,' I say softly, my eyes hungry on her face. 'Put it on.'

'Oh don't be silly,' she looks a little taken aback. 'It's far too small for my fat old wrist.'

'Try it.'

She gives a cry of amazement as the bangle slips over her hand and loops around her wrist, swinging smoothly, shining in the light.

'I knew it would fit you,' I said with satisfaction. 'Most people can't see the writing. You must be special.'

She laughs again, spinning the bangle. 'Well it's lovely. Thank you very much.' A thought strikes her. 'What do you mean, spells?'

I pause. The moment has come. I am aware of Charlie's approval as he stands close behind me. I remember how we talked the night before. I told him how wherever I walk Lilith walks by my side. 'Of course,' he had replied. 'You have to pass on the old ways, just like she did. That's why she walks with you, as a reminder.'

I can almost see Lilith's tall, imperious figure now in the shadows of the room. Eldritch senses her, I can tell by the way she cocks her black head and stares. She always ignores Charlie.

'Angie...' I begin. 'I would like to... show you some things. I think you have... a gift. If you are willing, I would like to share with you what I have learned.'

She sits back, looking flummoxed. The bangle slides on her wrist and I see her eyes follow the flash of gold.

I clear my throat, I have never had to have this kind of conversation before and I find it strangely embarrassing to talk about it.

'I want to help show you how to be...' I search for the word. 'Powerful.'

There is a very long pause.

'Powerful?' she clears her throat awkwardly. 'Powerful... like you're powerful?' she says. The air between us sizzles with tension.

I give a reluctant nod. A tremor of something, fear or excitement, tingles the end of her fingers.

Do you mean...' She licks her lips, 'you can teach me... to be...' Now she is the one who searches for words. '...Magic?'

I tut in irritation, I hear Charlie give a snort of laughter.

'What?' Angie says.

'I don't like the word magic.' I say.

'What?'

'Magic.' I shake my head. I hate the word. 'It sounds silly. Like a children's game or a trickster. I prefer… powerful.'

'Was it power that got us up to London to save Will?' she says in a small voice.

'Yes, in part,' I admit. 'But I couldn't have done it without you. To begin with I can't drive, and it was your power that knocked him unconscious with his laptop.'

We share a small smile.

'OK,' she says, but part of her still wonders if I am mad.

'Come with me,' I say, getting to my feet. 'You've always wanted to know about my treasures, so come and see.'

*

Angie gives Trevor a whistle and he jumps up and trots after us, his nails clacking on the floor. I want to stop him, but the familiarity of his presence is a comfort to Angie.

I take her to my ebony cabinet. It is a little dusty with Angie out of action for the past few days and she darts forward to wipe it with her skirt. She falls silent as I unlock the bowed, glass-fronted door and swing it open.

'Pick something,' I say to her, smiling at her awestruck face. She looks like a child in front of a toy shop window. 'Go on.'

I know she is drawn to the blown-glass bird I was given half a century ago. It is exquisite, and the craftsman has layered tissue thin streams of colour across the wings to capture joyful movement even as it stands still.

But Angie hesitates, and passes on, studying every item. Though fascinated, I can still see the threads of doubt weaving through her thoughts. She casts a nervous look back over her shoulder at me. My ghosts and I lean forward, urging her on.

'There,' she finally decides, pointing at the dish of walnuts. I smile.

'Take one out.'

She reaches in her hand, careful not to knock over my precious trinkets, and chooses the darkest walnut.

She holds it tight in her hand as she withdraws, and then opens it to show the nut resting on her palm.

'Crack it,' I say.

'Is that all?' she replies, disappointed.

The walnut is old and dry and splits easily in her palm. I chuckle in delight at her complete astonishment at what she finds within. Yards and yards and yards of gossamer thin embroidered white silk explode out of the shell. A wedding dress.

Angie holds it up, shaking out the folds. It glitters with silver spun net and the skirt is sewn with a thousand seed pearls. It is so beautiful she cannot help holding it up against herself allowing the dress to sway, shining in the light. It is a powerfully feminine gesture.

'It's a real dress,' she says, looking up at me in shock.

'Of course,' I say. 'And if you tried it on you would find it fits perfectly.'

Her eyes and mouth are perfect circles of amazement.

'How is that possible? Is it some kind of special material?' She examines the dress closely, she cannot help running her fingers over the glowing rasp of the silk.

'Do they all have wedding dresses in them?' she asks, nodding at the bowl.

'Oh no,' I say. 'You will find inside those walnuts what it is you need, or I should say, what it is you most desire.'

She blushes a deep, hot red.

'You open one,' she says, excitement shines in her eyes.

I reach for one and crack it in a single movement with my right hand, delivering a shower of plump, green grapes into my left. There are tens of them and they bounce on the floor. I put one in my mouth and let the juicy coolness burst in my mouth.

'But that's not possible!' Angie cries, catching a grape and putting it to her nose to smell it before cautiously biting it in half.

I find I want to keep astonishing her and, feeling like a cheap conjurer, I reach for the glass bird and hold it balanced in my hand in front of her. With a jerk, I throw it into the air.

'No Mrs B!' she cries, and reaches to catch it, then looks up at the ceiling, mouth hanging open as a humming bird swoops and twirls, its turquoise feathers as blue as a summer sky.

I wave my hand and it stills, coalesces and liquefies, before landing in my outstretched hand - glass again.

'Wow!' she says, like a child.

I shrug. 'Old woman's tricks,' I say.

'Well, they're amazing.' She looks around the room. 'So what's this for then, this room?'

'It's my collection. I was taught by a woman named Lilith when I was a child. Many of these things are hers, but over the years I've added my own discoveries.'

'Why aren't these books in the library?'

I walk over to my wall of books, which stretches from the floor into the shadows of the roof. All of them are at least a hand span thick. Some covers are faded cloth with a glimmer of the gilt remaining; others are fine leather, while at the bottom are simple paper note pads. 'They're not very pretty. But these books are among the most precious possessions I own. Look.'

I reach for the most familiar, a tall book with a violet spine. It is so old some of the pages fall away from the cover so they stand proud in clumps. I open it and place it carefully on a pretty little side table. I remember buying it in Vienna in the late 1920's; it stood in the window of a very formal antique shop and I fell in love with it.

As with all these books, it is full of the writing of women, going back centuries. This one, though, is the most special. I lay it open and leaf through the pages to the back; there are still a handful of blank sheets waiting to be filled. I feel Angie's breath on my neck as she leans closer to see.

The paper is brittle and thin. 'This is what I've written,' I tell Angie before leafing back until the ink is faded to brown. The handwriting changes to Lilith's distinctive slanting letters, flowing and loose where mine are cramped. I run my fingers down line after line of observations, vividly drawn sketches of flowers, birds and animals. There are recipes and incantations mixed in with sharp-eyed comments about the local villagers.

'Is it a diary?' Angie asks.

'Some of it could be called a diary,' I reply. 'But it is also where you can find solutions to problems both practical and spiritual.'

We leaf further back and the handwriting changes four, five, six times before fading away almost to nothing. It makes me giddy to think Angie, though she doesn't yet know this, will complete the book and begin a new one that she will pass on to the next woman. My hand on these pages is a link in a chain of women stretching behind and in front forever. No wonder I feel dizzy.

I sit down in the window seat and scan the gardens and woods, the golden threads sway intact, and no eyes are watching. Angie is hunched over the book, marvelling.

'This is incredible!' she exclaims. 'To think of all those women, it must go back to, like, medieval times. Look at this! Love potions, and how to summon a spirit, and then a bitchy comment about the priest.' Angie laughs and keeps skimming through until she is at the front-piece. I watch her face closely as she registers what is drawn there.

'Do you recognise it?' I say, sharply.

'I think I do,' she frowns. 'What is it?'

'All these women have that mark, I have it, look,' I hold up my hand and she stares at my palm. Slowly, reluctantly, she turns her hand over. 'Your mother had it too…' I say, with absolute gentleness.

Shock blanches her face. She closes the book.

'Did you know?' I ask.

She shakes her head and then stops. Tears spring to her eyes. 'Yeah,' she shrugs. 'You know, thinking about it, there *was* something different about her. She could see the ones the same way I could, but we never talked about it.'

'She closed down that part of herself when she married your father,' I explain. 'The old woman who lived here before me hoped to pass on her books to your mother but she refused. She didn't want any part of it. She loved your father very much, and longed for children.' I sighed. 'So when I came, her books came to me instead.'

I can see this is too much for Angie. She doesn't know what to do with what she has learnt.

'Let's just see what you can do, shall we?' I say, excitement rising. Now I am committed to this I am full of energy. All thoughts of the darkness ahead are driven from my head. How powerful is she? I wonder. Will her power outstrip mine?

I start to search the drawers set into the window seat. The red box I am looking for is right at the bottom, wedged behind a boot-cleaning kit and a handful of tarnished silver knives that belonged to my grandmother. I pull out the box and settle back with a satisfied sigh ready to open the lid. I calculate it must be ninety years since Lilith opened it for me. It is a ridiculous amount of time, I think.

The wood is a little stiff but eventually I wrench it open. I need room for this so clear a pile of books from the main table in the window. The silver fragments slither into a pile on the dark wood. Angie, jerked out of her reverie by curiosity comes and watches as I start to piece everything together

I have forgotten the knack and tut with impatience. My knotted old hands are clumsy and I remember with a pang how nimbly I put this together when I was a girl. Time passes in silence as I find the base and then hang the beautifully carved horses with their tossing manes onto their hooks. Finally, I screw on the round top with its enamelled stripes of red and white.

'Oh!' says Angie in delighted surprise. 'It's a carousel! How beautiful.' She stretches out a finger and touches it gently. 'Gosh, they look almost alive, and each one is different. Where does it come from?'

'It was Lilith's,' I reply. 'But I don't know where it came from before then.' I set it on the table and we watch the horses with their tiny movements; they are so delicate the slightest breath of wind makes them rock back and forth.

'Now watch,' I say, and place the toy on the palm of my hand. I close my eyes to concentrate and hear a gasp from Angie as it begins to spin. We watch the smooth movement as the top turns, and as it goes faster and faster a high, silvery tune plays. We smile at each other. Her eyes glow green as emeralds.

'Your turn,' I say and place the carousel on her hand. She studies it. 'What are you doing?'

'Looking for the switch!'

'There is no switch. You use the energy around you. Try.'

Angie holds the toy in her hand and stares at it. Apart from a tiny shiver of movement from the tremble in her hand, nothing happens.

'Close your eyes,' I say quietly. 'Feel your feet on the ground. Try and listen for the buzz of the trees and flowers outside. Imagine there's a green light around you. I want you to try and gather it up and pass it down so your palm grows hot.'

Angie is frowning with concentration but still nothing happens. She sighs with frustration. She keeps trying but still no movement. I lean forward and lightly touch her arm, allowing a green spark to roll down it. She jumps slightly.

'Feel that?' I say in a whisper. She nods. 'That's what I want you to feel for,' I say. 'Try again.'

She closes her eyes. We wait. Her face is tight; concentration clenches at her lips and drags her brow down over her eyes. Achingly slowly, the carousel begins to turn. Almost too slowly to see. Angie's eyes fly open and it stops. 'Almost...' I say.

She closes her eyes again. This time it starts to move almost straight away, it spins faster and faster and the first few notes of the tune begins to play.

'I did it!' Angie says and her face is alight with joy.

# CHAPTER 18: ANGIE

At the time I thought the impact of the attack lingered for so long because of being middle-aged – I wasn't the spring chicken I used to be. I couldn't handle shocks anymore, I thought, and it had been terrifying. Frustratingly, I had nobody to talk about it with as everyone was away.

Apart from a rather brusque WhatsApp to say he had arrived, I'd heard nothing from Gary. He'd warned me the cottage where he and his mates were staying had no signal, but it was still very annoying. Surely he could have travelled into a big town to contact me?

Now I know the extent of Mrs B's meddling. He *had* called, once or twice, when I was flat on my back in bed, but she didn't pass on any of his messages. Her excuse was she wanted me to concentrate on getting better. I understand now she wanted to keep everyone away, worried more people might get hurt; or - what was probably closer to the truth - she didn't want anyone making me go to hospital, with the risk she'd be forced to move into a home.

I couldn't be upset with her. In all the months with Mrs B, I would never have guessed her capable of the tender kindness with which she cared for me. Thanks to her strange smelling creams and ointments, my cuts and bruises disappeared quickly; but it took days before my head stopped aching and the dragging sense of brutal constriction around my throat faded.

The worst thing was the effect on my nerves. I was jumpy as a cat, fearing the animal from the gang would return. I flinched at every noise, and after that dreadful, stormy night my sleep had been haunted by nightmares. I dreamed of my Dad and I knew I must look for him again, and not allow myself to be distracted by the old woman, the house, and my growing dependence on Gary. An endless loop of thoughts played in my head but the combination of exhaustion and anxiety kept me in bed for a while.

And then, of course, I was distracted beyond all imaginings by what Mrs B showed me one night when the house was full of shadows. There were many times when I felt like I was in a dream while I was in that house; that was one of them.

She showed me the secrets of the room with the ebony chest. I chuckle now to remember my astonishment when that dress burst so mysteriously from a  tiny walnut. It was incredible, as light as if woven from beams of moonlight. Now I know it for the trick it was, just as Mrs B had told me, but I still remember my wonder at the time.

That was the night I learned about my mother, and the old woman showed me the mark I carry in my hand. It took a long time to take in the significance of what Mrs B told me. In time, I did get my head around it, and it gave me a sense of place – something I'd never had before – but at that point, I didn't believe it. Even when she showed me how I could spin that toy I wasn't convinced, though it was very odd, and I couldn't explain what had happened.

At first, it was a game. I thought I should indulge the old dear, a thank you for looking after me. But hearing about Mum and the strange things that seemed to be happening to me freaked me out for a while.

But I couldn't deny a small, secret part of myself became obsessed with finding out what I could do. I persuaded Mrs B to let me read one of the books that should have gone to my mother. I couldn't read half of it, not only was much of the ink faded, but the handwriting was ornate and hard to make out. Just as I thought I was getting the hang of it, the writing would change as the book passed into the hands of the next woman.

I couldn't make head nor tail of some of the spells written there, but I found a fantastic recipe for steak and ale pie, which Mrs B and I ate so quickly the heat of the pies made our breath steam like dragons.

What tipped the balance into the madness that followed was the day Mrs B decided it was time she took me into the woods to teach me how to summon.

*

After the big storm that broke the terrible heat of the summer, the sun disappeared off to the South of France, along with the Doc and his wife. It started to rain, a soft drizzle, but before too long great stair rods fell, and parts of the village flooded. It was quite cold too, and the last thing I wanted to do one miserable afternoon was go outside with the old woman.

She'd been twitchy all day, and couldn't settle to anything. I was leafing through what I mentally called my mother's book – though she never received it, or wanted it apparently – while Mrs B sipped tea, never taking her eyes from the kitchen window. It made me nervous, and I kept looking over my shoulder to work out what she was looking at.

'Shut up that book,' she said, making me and the dog jump.

'What?' I asked. I was miles away, caught up in decoding a gruesomely vivid description of a breech birth.

'Enough reading – and I don't say that lightly. We need to be out in the wind and the fresh air.' She creaked to her feet.

'But it's pouring!' I protested. Too late – she was gone. The back door swung back and forth. Trevor shot over to his lead, which was curled on the chair by the fire, and brought it over to me in his mouth. His eyes fixed on my face, tail wagging hopefully and eyebrows raised.

'No, sorry, Trevor. Not now. It's pouring and you'll get soaked.'

I sighed and searched out my old umbrella from the cupboard. Mrs B was already half way up the garden. Opening the door I held Trevor back with my leg, apologising and promising a walk later, before closing it on his furry, disappointed face.

I had to hurry to keep up with Mrs B. The rain didn't bother her as she stumped ahead of me into the woods. Within seconds I was soaked, the wind rendered my umbrella useless so I tossed it into a bush and trudged on.

'Is there any reason why we can't do this inside? In the warm?' I called after her, my words disappearing into the wind.

'No!' She tossed back over her shoulder. 'Maybe one day, but to begin you must be outside, among the trees!'

This was bonkers. Something had been released; energy zapped from her in waves. The weather was terrible. Above us the sky roiled and rolled like a stormy grey sea. The trees were bent double, matching Mrs. B as she headed into the dark green shadows.

'This is mad!' I shouted, but she didn't hear me. I began to worry. Maybe she really was mad? Dementia? And here I was following her when I should probably be calling an ambulance. The wind was so strong I had to push through it, an invisible wall. My hands and face were dripping wet.

It was a relief to get into the calm and shelter of the wood, and I followed Mrs B's disappearing figure, bright in its scarlet coat. I could hear the rain pattering on the canopy. The wind made an eerie, high pitched moan.

I should have been terrified. I was out in the woods on a horrible day, soaking wet, freezing cold, and chasing after a hundred year old woman who had gone bananas.

And yet…

It was thrilling. Absolutely thrilling. Every part of me sang with life. I loved the sound of the wind and the rain, shrieking around us. I loved seeing the exhilaration in Mrs B. Her smile was broad as she recognised what I was feeling. It was as if, in a moment, the wind would pull me from the ground and throw me into the air and I longed for it. Couldn't wait. Pictured flying through clouds and speeding around the earth.

Mrs B had stopped. I had to keep blinking as she flickered between bent-backed old dear and the tall, stern, queen whose hair blew violently around her head. A part of my brain kept insisting, 'This is insane. This isn't real. You're hallucinating.' But another, wilder voice was joyful. 'This is amazing. If this is madness, bring it on!'

'This is where you find the source,' Mrs B said. The wind had died down and I heard her voice, clear across the green space.

'The what?' I said.

'You need to harness... this!' She gestured to the wind, the rain, the dancing trees. My bangle spun on my wrist.

I couldn't help grinning at the glitter in the old woman's eyes. They looked huge and I would feel a shock of static if I touched her.

'You'll need the words,' she said, squinting up at me.

I bent down. 'Sorry?'

'Listen,' she said.

She started to whisper words into my ear. They weren't ones I could remember or write, they were like golden shapes that wiggled and danced into my head, leaving traces of glinting light in the darkening air as she spoke.

'Now you say them. It's a simple one. Try.'

I tried to repeat the phrase she had whispered. She corrected me and I tried again. They echoed in my head like music, and the more I spoke the words, the more they rang in my mouth. Mrs B nodded and smiled in satisfaction.

'Louder,' she said.

So I said them louder. And then louder still. To my amazement, leaves that had lain scattered across the ground, shifting in the wind, started to move. They lifted, as if caught by a breeze, but didn't fall. I kept speaking and they began to whirl like a swarm of bees. They continued to circle, faster and faster - a blur of red, gold, and dark brown. As I spoke, I saw they were clumping together and my brain reeled to see a figure was beginning to form.

It frightened me, and I looked to Mrs B for reassurance. She looked like she had been electrocuted, her little white fluffs of hair stood on end. She was staring at the figure then looked back at me, eyes alight with sparks and fire.

'Go on!'

I turned back to the figure and carried on speaking, I unconsciously lifted my arms and the figure copied me. It was gathering in density as the leaves flew towards it, wrapping themselves into layers.

I stopped speaking. The wind fell silent and an odd stillness made me think for a second I had gone deaf. The leaf figure stood, half turning, arms falling to its side. Everything felt frozen.

'Begone!' said Mrs B with a clap of her hands as loud as a gunshot. Immediately the leaves were just leaves again. They swirled into a puddle before dropping, limp and wet to the ground.

Exhaustion slammed into me like a wrestler, knocking me to the ground. I lay, panting, looking up at the green roof wondering what the fuck just happened.

'You did very well,' said Mrs B with a chuckle, easing herself onto a fallen trunk beside me. She looked delighted with herself. Behind her. Just for a second I saw the face of the slim, blond man staring at Mrs B. Then it was just a knot in a bending silver birch.

'What the... I mean... What did I... What was...?' I said.

She patted my knee. Her whole demeanour was joyful. 'Goodness that was much more fun than I thought it would be. I had forgotten...'

I was lying in a rank, damp, slick of leaves and sat up. My clothes were in a right state, covered in mud and soaked.

'You truly have the gift, my dear! And it's strong. I will enjoy teaching you.' She nodded. 'I've never seen anyone summon so quickly before. I think you may even have been as fast as I was – though I was a lot younger than you when I did it.'

My mind buzzed with questions but my body was limp with tiredness. Mrs B was looking very pleased with herself.

'But what's the point of all of this? What do I do with this?' I indicated the wood's green shadows and layers of leaves.

'Ah yes. Well this is only the start. You have much more to learn yet. And I will need you to learn quickly. We haven't much time…'

I stood up. Did she mean because she was so old? I thought. It seemed rude to ask, so I stayed quiet.

'Now come on, I don't know about you but I am soaked. This is not good for a woman my age. Let's get inside. Come on! What are you waiting for?'

I could barely move; it was as if I'd run a marathon. Anyone watching would have thought I was the old-age pensioner as I limped after Mrs B who had set off at a good trot back through the woods and towards home.

It was bliss to be back in the kitchen in warm, dry clothes. Despite her protestations I had wrangled Mrs B into a hot bath and she sat, pink-cheeked, with her white hair all fluffy in front of the fire. Despite the glowing Aga at one end and the roaring fire at the other, the corners of the kitchen still felt cold, and I urged Mrs B close to the warmth. It was cosy, though, the crackling fire scorching our faces and the windows fastened tight against the wind outside.

I'd made thick, dark, hot chocolate and added milk and sugar until it was creamy and sweet. Its restorative powers were remarkable. Maybe it was the power in me, I thought with a laugh, spilling some tiny sparks into the mix.

*

I couldn't sleep that night. I lay there grinning. I couldn't believe what had happened. I played the scene in the wood over and over. I remembered the incredible green whoosh of energy sparkling through my whole body. I had never felt anything like it. Again and again I pictured the leaf man rising from the ground, mirroring my movements. I wanted to rush out to the woods right then to have another go, even though it had left me ready to pass out with tiredness.

I opened the book again. It was so big it made my wrists hurt to hold it, so I lay it on the bed and hunched over to read. Mrs B had told me to go to the beginning and work forward, she wasn't happy I was dipping backwards and forwards. The first pages were so faded I couldn't make out the words; the handwriting was small and cramped, sloping madly to the right. The paper reminded me of the tracing-paper bog roll we were given at school. There were sketches of leaves and flowers, and tiny drawings of stick figures being thrown into the air; it made my head hurt to look at them.

I was so tired but couldn't stop reading. I spun the golden bangle on my wrist and watched the gold lights dance like little sprites around it. There was a whole section in one of the books about changing your appearance. I had seen Mrs B do that to a certain extent and I resolved to ask her about how to do it. Imagine if I could turn myself into one of those Instagram princesses! I laughed with delight at the thought of meeting Sharon and Vik down the pub with blonde hair down my back, a size 6 figure and a trout pout.

The following morning Mrs B didn't come down for hours. When I'd gone to bed the night before I'd heard her talking, an endless rumbling murmur which echoed down the stairs as I passed; it seemed to happen every night.

The house had a strange feel to it, walking around was lovely; everything was clean and shone brightly but there was an emptiness, a sense of anticipation I couldn't put my finger on. I admired my handiwork but felt restless, itchy. I didn't know what to do with myself. The thought of the strange books lying on my bed scratched away at the back of my mind.

I tapped on Mrs B's door to see if she wanted any breakfast but there was no reply. I peeked in to check she wasn't dead, and was reassured by her whistling snores. The room was freezing, the window left wide open and she was lying in a tangle covered only with a scrap of blanket. I shut the window, noticing the unseasonal frost cloaking the lawn, and covered Mrs B with a thick coverlet and left her sleeping.

In the kitchen I took my time making two rounds of perfect bacon sandwiches. White bread, ketchup, a touch of mustard and proper, crispy bacon in thin strips. My mouth watered. I sat looking out the window and enjoyed a cup of tea so hot it burned my tongue. Eldritch streamed round and around my ankles until I got up to find her some food, while Trevor sat pathetically, dangling his bowl from his mouth so I fed him too. I couldn't manage all of my sandwich, so threw it away.

My bangle spun hot around my wrist as I went back to my room to get the book. It was no good, the impulse to pore over it again was irresistible. Tucking it under my arm, I checked on Mrs B again, made myself another cup of tea and headed for the library. I resolved to look properly at my Mum's book as I had been so weary the night before I hadn't taken much in.

I flicked past the recipes for ointments, potions, and tisanes – a kind of tea, I thought – and looked for the big stuff, ignoring Mrs B's orders to read from front to back, properly. There were drawings of people flying or levitating things but the instructions all looked way too complicated. Finally, I settled on a page illustrated with a reassuringly ordinary looking fireplace.

Whoever had written these pages had spent some time detailing a sequence of hand and finger movements. The last picture showed a fire burning merrily in the carefully drawn grate. Underneath a dark inky scrawl listed three words.

I remembered Mrs. B in the woods whispering into my ears. With a bolt of excitement, I dragged my chair close to the fireplace, grabbing a handful of tinder from the metal bucket in the corner. I studied the pages again, trying to copy the shapes with my right hand. My bangle stirred with the movement. I read the words out loud, feeling self-conscious.

Nothing happened.

I cleared my throat and tried again, experimenting with different pronunciations. All the while I flickered my fingers, just like the picture instructed.

Nothing.

I felt like an idiot. Even though I knew nobody was nearby, my cheeks flushed. What did I expect? That I'd click my fingers and an explosion of flames would light up the fireplace? I looked around the room to double check nobody was watching. The little pile of sticks and twigs in the grate looked at me reproachfully.

I tried once more before giving up and chucking the books onto the settee in a sulk. I could hear Mrs B bashing on her floor, probably wanting her cup of tea.

'I can't believe how late you've slept in!' I exclaimed as I brought a tray up to her room. She was sitting up in bed with the pillows in a pile behind her crooked old back. She was pale but her eyes had their usual sizzle.

'I couldn't sleep,' she said. 'And why haven't you put any sugar in this tea?' she took a sip and grimaced.

'You usually have it black,' I said. 'And I did put sugar in it, two good spoonfuls which is plenty.'

She grunted.

I folded her blanket and a dressing gown, which had fallen to the floor. The room was silent except for the greedy crunch as Mrs B wolfed down her toast. Pretty good going for someone her age.

'I've er… I've been trying one of the things, er, spells, written in those books you gave me.' I had my back to her but could sense her interest. When I turned round she was as alert as a bird, her eyes sparking, head cocked on one side. There were crumbs all over her and a smudge of jam at the side of her mouth.

'Oh yes?' she said, her eyes not leaving mine. A flash of heat swept over my shoulders up my neck. I couldn't shake the worry this was all nonsense; perhaps Mrs B *was* mad, and had somehow bewitched me into believing her – or given me drugs, I thought, remembering Will.

'Yeah, not much good though,' I said ruefully.

'What happened?'

'Nothing. I did everything right and kept checking with the book, but zip. I don't think I have it in me. I'm not like you.' I studied my shoes.

Mrs B put the tray on the side and wiped her mouth. 'What were you trying to do?'

'Light a fire.'

Mrs B nodded towards the bedroom fireplace. 'Show me.'

Her voice brooked no disobedience.

I sighed and walked over to the grate, grunting as I squatted on my heels and put in some scraps and sticks. I pulled myself into the nearby chair, which gripped my hips. There was a pause.

'Go on.'

'It won't work, Mrs B. I'm sorry…'

'Just do it.'

I held out my hand, hearing Mrs B moving to lean over to watch what I did. I spoke the words; they were garbled and twisted in my mouth. I tried again. Nothing. I looked round at Mrs B and she was smiling.

'Nearly!' she whispered, her eyes bright.

I turned back to the grate.

'Flick your fingers a little more quickly,' she urged.

I kept doing it, three, four times and then…

'That's it!' Mrs B exclaimed. 'Did you feel it?'

Yes. Yes. No fire had burst out of me, but I could feel it. A kind of staticky buzz at the end of my fingers, just at the base of my nails. I leaned forward and stretched towards the kindling with my hand and tried again. I whispered the words fiercely to myself and there! A spark!

I jumped back in fright and Mrs B laughed.

I held my fingertips to my cheek but they felt perfectly normal, dry and cool. Steadier this time, I reached out again. I flicked my fingers and a tiny ember began to glow I blew on it and within seconds a yellow flame curled its lazy tongue around a shard of wood. I could feel the warmth on my skin.

I turned to Mrs B and could see my delight reflected in her face.

'I knew you could do it,' she said in satisfaction.

*

A torrent of questions bubbled up. I wanted her to show me everything. What else could I do? Could I heal people now? Be invisible? Could I fly!?

Mrs B shook her head. 'Don't be stupid, girl. You've a way to go yet.' My face fell but she patted my hand. 'It takes time, dear. And you can exhaust yourself if you're not careful. Go walk in the woods and get some energy back. And take this with you! I want to sleep.' She handed me her tray and I positively danced down the stairs.

Leaving the tea things in the kitchen with a clatter, I shot into the library and sat down on the fireside chair. It took a couple of goes, but within a few minutes flames were burning in the grate. I sat back in the chair, a broad smile on my face. My hands were shaking, I noticed, and when I balled them into fists they felt weak, the muscles ached.

As I left the library, I noticed a new photograph was propped on the mantelpiece. Black and white, it pictured a room packed with people. A nightclub. A band played in the background, five men. One was holding a saxophone, another a drum. They were smiling. In front of the stage whirled a group of men and women, the women had bobs cropped to the jaw, some had scarves tied to hold hair off the face. The camera had caught them as they danced, many of the faces were blurred.

I searched for Mrs B. There she was. Dead centre, standing still and staring at the camera; her features were pin sharp. Two men stood either side, arms looped over her shoulders, one looking away his face a smudge of movement, the other whispering into her ear, blond hair falling over his eyes. Mrs B was smiling wickedly.

It was a great photo. It looked pre-war. The more I looked the more details I noticed. To the right at the back two men were kissing passionately. Blimey! I looked more closely, half of the woman in the photo weren't women at all, they were men. They grinned widely, slashes of black marking what must have been very dark red lipstick. I'd definitely have to ask Mrs B about that, I thought as I looked for my coat.

I was all over the place as I walked towards the woods. I couldn't ever remember feeling this way, well not since I had been a kid. I kept playing a sort of movie in my head, lifting the leaves last night, the spark of fire bouncing from my fingertips this morning. Excitement crashed around my stomach making me feel sick. I walked faster and faster, slipping and skidding on the frosty grass until I reached the woods. I stopped, panting a little, and took a great, deep breath of the sharp, sappy smell. I kept moving, more slowly now, letting my shoulders fall and my skin to bathe in the fresh, cool air.

I pictured the battery icon on my phone when it was charging. The pulsing lines that gradually moved across the screen, changing from red to green. Was that what I was doing? Re-charging myself? Remembering the effect being here had on Mrs B. I breathed more deeply, tried to imagine the green energy in the air and pulling it inside so I could feel a buzzing tingle; my legs felt strong and limber.

I walked for miles and miles. Following a big loop around Pagan's Reach, I pushed myself until my heart was thudding and my breath frosted out of me in big gasps. I had to take off my scarf as I was getting hot, despite the dampness of the day. Whenever I saw or heard something I would stop and drink it in, as if I was replenishing my stores from the goodness and life springing up all around. I didn't feel at all hungry.

I pulled out my phone and took a selfie, the wood stretching behind me and the sky above. Adding the caption, 'Out for a walk in the fresh air!' I uploaded it onto Facebook and was gratified that, within a few minutes, likes and thumbs ups began to appear. Mags was one of the first to comment. 'Wow! Good for you. You look fantastic!' she'd written, followed by a stream of heart-eye pictures.

I looked again at my photo. She was right. I did look good. Pretty much as fat as ever, but my eyes glowed green against my pink cheeks and my smile cracked my face open. I'd never managed to copy Paulo's blow dry, but he'd cut my hair so well it still looked pretty good. I looked ten years younger.

I should smile more often, I thought. Maggie's comment had given me confidence, so I used my new selfie to replace my profile picture. It used to be an old photo of me at my wedding. I'd scanned it in when I'd joined Facebook and I'd never bother changing it. Time for a new start I thought.

I'd finally managed to talk to Gary when he called me from the only place he could get a signal. I could hear sheep baaing in the background and he kept getting abruptly cut off but over about twenty minutes we managed to piece together a five minute conversation.

He was horrified to hear about the attack and said he would come home straightaway.

'That's crazy, Gary! I told you I was fine,' I reassured him, though a mean part of me would have loved for him to come back. 'Honestly, don't spoil your holiday. Mrs B and I are tucked up nice and safely – there's nobody about, everyone's off on their holiday.'

'Maybe it'll be you and me next year,' Gary said, making my heart leap. I toyed with the idea of telling him about the lessons the old woman was giving me, especially that incredible afternoon in the woods, but decided not to. I couldn't work out a way of saying it that didn't make me sound insane. I'll show him instead, I thought. The idea of that made me grin.

Mrs B shot me a sour glance as I made lunch. She always knew when I had spoken to Gary, telling me I got a 'calfsick look' on my face.

'When's he back, this young man of yours?' she asked.

'I'd hardly call him a young man,' I laughed. 'And he's not mine. But to answer your question, Mrs B, he will be back in a few weeks.'

I smiled all afternoon as I busied myself with laundry and cleaning. I took great delight in lighting all the fires without having to find the matches. I was getting better and better at it, and was planning to try learning some new words to help me clean the place up. I imagined pointing at things so they jumped into place, looking like Mary Poppins. Whistling 'A Spoonful of Sugar' I was polishing my way down the main staircase when the old woman called me into her yellow sitting room.

It was one of my favourite places in the house - not that I spent much time there - it was where Mrs B went when she wanted to be on her own. She didn't often invite me in. I loved the wallpaper. A golden-yellow background was painted with the most gorgeous long-legged white birds, which I think were herons. They stalked their way around the room, some hiding their faces behind scrawled bushes and trees, some spreading their wings with a silver fish flapping in their beaks. I could sit and look at it all day.

A round oak table sat in the window that was draped with heavy, silk curtains the colour of corn. I wasn't surprised to see a

315

vase stuffed full of a crazy array of flowers from the garden. Mrs B was never far away from flowers, she adored them, and would insist I accompanied her into the garden every other morning to collect armfuls of roses, poppies, peonies… whatever was most beautiful that day.

She sat in the armchair by the fire. It was so huge it almost swallowed her up. She looked a bit formidable, actually, wearing a black suit with a crisp, white blouse. I admired her broach, today it was a leaping gold dolphin with deep blue sapphires for eyes.

'Can you come and sit down, Angie,' she said. 'If you have a moment.'

'Of course, Mrs B.' I said, dropping my polish and cloth by the door and wiping my hands down my jeans. As I came in, she inclined her head towards the settee next to her. Its faded red and gold stripes and luxurious deep seat made me worry I would rip the cloth if I sat back in it, so I perched nervously on the edge.

'I feel like I'm in a job interview!' I said. Everything felt oddly formal. I noticed she was flicking a photograph back and forth on her lap. I felt a spark of interest when I recognised it as the black and white picture I had seen in the library. The one with the kissing men and the wild band.

'Angie…' she finally said and paused. She flicked a glance at her ever-present blond companion, and he nodded. 'Angie, dear, I need your help. I'm sorry not to have longer to train you properly, but I need to tell you about a man named Marroch.'

## CHAPTER 19: FRIEDA AND MARROCH

The house spirals as I go up to bed. There is a frenzied, jittery feel in the air. Everything is unsettled. My mind is muddled; too many thoughts are crashing together. Out in the woods I am invincible, joyful. Seeing Angie summon so effortlessly, speaking my words without hesitation... that has been a shock. A good one, but a shock. Now my years smash over me, a huge tidal wave crashing over rocks, knocking them flying

I am longing for the years of peace and solitude before Charlie and Angie appeared, splintering the anaesthetised simplicity of my life. I am tired, and age pulls viciously at my skin, my bones; my blood thickens and slows in my veins. I have never felt such exhaustion; it feels like death.

Angie's story, Will's story, they hang heavy on me and I am irritated by their weight. The enormity of the task ahead is beyond Angie's comprehension. Beyond Charlie's comprehension. Oh, I could deal with that pervert Mark easily enough, but Marroch - he's a different matter. I touch the weight of gold at my throat; I swallow my fear down, ice water pools in my stomach.

I slam my bedroom door. I don't want to lie on the bed so I sit by the fire, the hard wooden chair pushing me painfully upright. I remember why I had cut myself off in this little village in the middle of nowhere. It was peaceful because everyone left me alone. I could just sit, and remember, and read my books. I sigh to hear the crackle of Charlie appearing behind me.

'And you can fuck off too,' I say. I ache with tiredness.

'How lovely you can be, Freddy darling.' He gives a chuckle. 'Oh come on. You loved every minute with Angie in the woods. I could see you positively fizzing with the joy of showing off.'

I tut. 'It was a stupid indulgence.'

'No. It wasn't,' Charlie replies. He leans against the mantelpiece and looks down at me. I feel a pang of sorrow to see his shape has become more insubstantial, he is beginning to fade. 'It's what you were supposed to do, the fates brought you Angie.'

Irritation made my skin prickle. 'Oh for God's sake stop will you, Charlie? You make it all sound so easy, so straightforward but I don't want to be bothered with all of this.'

I push myself up and walk to the window, keeping my back to Charlie. I don't want to see him. I open the window and see a bright circle around the moon. The garden is silvered with a glowing white mist and my breath ices in front of me. I dream of stretches of white beaches bleached by the sun, and long for the chance to lie, liquid and pliant in hot sand with the sounds of the ocean in my ears.

Charlie comes and stands at my shoulder and we are still for a moment, enjoying the cold and the quiet. He is reading my thoughts.

'I wish I had gone to those places with you,' he says with a sigh. 'The closest I got to abroad was the mud-filled rat holes of France.'

'Hmm.' I have no energy for sympathy for anyone else but myself. I want them all to go away, to leave me alone.

'What is it?' Charlie pulls away from me and sits on my bed. 'You can be a bitch, but this is new. It's almost as if...'

I continue to stare out of the window and wait. He is silent.

'As if what?' I say, crossly.

'As if you're afraid,' he says. A change comes over him as realisation dawns. He comes back to the window and rests on the edge so he is looking at my face. 'Why are you so afraid of him, Freddie? Surely with Angie here to help...'

The mess of anger and fear that has lain in the bottom of my stomach for weeks now lurch and swell up like a ball of vomit. I swallow to try and keep it down but it keeps pushing at my throat. My idiocy in allowing myself to get carried away with Angie has left me exhausted and weak. I can't prevent what is happening. The room begins to turn and I blink to try and keep it still. I can't stand, my legs shake in an epileptic tremor which forces me to my knees and then to the floor. I fall forward onto my hands, the dizziness is uncontrollable. I close my eyes.

Marroch is the reason I never remove my gold necklace. The gold lozenges lie heavy on my collar bone, the comfort of the words burning their shapes into my skin. But it's not enough. He has returned. The closer he gets, the more conscious I am of his dark presence sending tendrils, octopus like, into the air around the village. He is coming for me. A sadness hits as I contemplate my end game. I had enjoyed getting to know Angie. I would have liked more time to see her power become all it could be.

*

I met Marroch when I was brazen with the idiotic confidence of youth. The grief of losing Charlie had compressed my heart, hardening it into iron diamonds. I was drunk on the arrogant belief that Lilith had taught me everything there was to know; I turned my back on my family and went out into the world. With ease I shrugged off any sense of responsibility. At no point did I consider Lilith had taught me so I could eventually take her place when she passed on. Instead, I left my home without a second thought, looking for what the world had to offer.

Oh, there were plenty of men pleased to have me on their arm and, like a dance, I spun from one to the other, each one a stepping stone to a richer partner. None of them touched me, my heart remained frozen, and I glittered, smiled and dazzled until I had everything I wanted.

I was thirty, still twenty years away from the start of the peak of my powers but I didn't realise that then. I was married to a deathly dull man whose name I can't even begin to remember. But he was rich, very rich. We were in Germany, Berlin. I loved the delectable decadence and androgyny of the artists, writers and musicians I found there. I collected them like gorgeous pieces of jewellery and would wear them on my arm as I trailed around the clubs.

As the months passed I ventured further and further into the heart of the Berlin night life. My Artist friends introduced me to their muses, the men and women who entertained and inspired them – and supplied their drugs. My husband was preoccupied with dreary politics; any irritation he felt at his young wife hanging around with degenerates and queers was immediately dissipated by my knowledge of his own secret predilections, which I had learned to indulge without any inconvenience to myself.

Endless evenings entertaining politicians and ambassadors were unendurable but inescapable. It had been made clear to me that if I wasn't prepared to be a charming young foil to my husband's grey-haired gravitas, I would have to return to London. There I would be expected to get on with the serious business of bearing and raising his children, something I refused to countenance.

Late in the night after the horrors of formal dinners and balls I would slip from the house, leaving my husband snoring, fine wines souring to a stink on his breath. I would wear clothes I had never worn before, trousers and tight waistcoats, my hair tied flat to my head. I needed no face paint, a wave of my hand would render my eyes huge and dark, my lips a blood red slash.

Beautiful boys in smoky bars would take me to breath-taking shows which filled me with a wild excitement. I plundered their bodies and found girls with whom I could explore Sapphic delights that for years would haunt my dreams so I would wake breathless, a moan dying on my lips.

Experimentation was all around me, in music, film, the theatre. Drugs were everywhere and I couldn't wait to get my hands on them, voices would whisper, promising my mind would be quicker, faster, more focused. Cocaine made me vicious and cruel; one night it drove me too far, I lost control. The consequences were catastrophic. Maiming rivals, disfiguring enemies, this I took in my stride – but drugs pushed me down a path where every thought I had unravelled wildly, leaving a destruction from which others struggled to recover.

Even now, over seventy years later my heart shrinks at the memory of the damaged people I left in my wake. I never took another drug.

We'd lived there for about a year when I first met Marroch. I had become quite the Patron der Künste, using a great deal of my husband's money to commission paintings and support interesting young playwrights and writers. Of him I saw little. A new political movement was stirring and he very much approved of the men who led it. He would meet with them regularly, representing his country's interests and strengthening ties with England and the new regime. He would talk to me endlessly over breakfast about the new changes, but the droning monotone of his voice would irritate me so powerfully I would rattle my tea cup and clatter my cutlery, anything to drown him out.

I wasn't a fool. I could sense a change coming, like the shifting of the wind. Friends were moving away, clubs were starting to close, but the core of my people were determined not to accept things were no longer the same.

We were at the Kleist Kasino, a tiny place where I played the voyeur, flanked by my beautiful boys – Larry and Felix – who had come to Berlin having been sent down from Cambridge and rejected by their families. We sat together, drinking and watching with amused fascination the assignations which took place in hidden booths.

A menu would be passed around detailing what was on offer, young, white, black, slender, muscular – anything a fairy could ask for. Larry and Felix stayed with me for a while before being drawn in by the temptations on offer, and I would be left alone, smoking my cigarette and enjoying the show.

The night Marroch walked in an electric shiver rippled through me and I remember looking in astonishment as the hairs on my arms stood on end, despite the stifling heat of the dark, rose-tinted rooms. He was standing by the bar, hair unfashionably long and falling into his face so I could only see the white curve of his jaw and his jutting cheekbones. He looked like he was carved out of ivory.

He was holding a drink in one hand while with the other he ran a long finger down the naked torso of the little statues holding up the lamps at the bar. He seemed to be lit from within and drew the eyes of all around him. I didn't like the way he stood, so still, allowing himself to be studied. His face was without expression, immobile as a stone.

People began to approach him; offers to buy drinks, a sly slip of a hand as a menu was tucked into his pocket. His face broke into a smile, altering his demeanour completely. It was broad with strong white teeth, his lips smooth and young, pink with health, almost girlish. He was pulled into groups of chattering young men, more drinks were ordered and passed around. The music was louder, the roar of conversation unusually lively; I was used to hushed murmurs and caresses behind screens, not this ribald jollity.

Marroch, his name was Marroch, the whispers and murmurs swirled along with the smoke in the air. I kept drinking, sitting in the shadows, keeping watch. I saw this strange young man walk away from the crowds to the stinking gents out the back. When he returned he paused in the doorway, scanning the room. I felt my hackles rise. There was something intent and cold about his face. He had caught sight of someone.

I looked across the room. There. A young man with flame red hair was leaning against the wall; he was gazing at Marroch. I had seen him before at the edges of parties and bars, handsome but a bit insipid – Max. His name slotted into my head.

The connection between then thrummed like a wire. Max began to walk forward, his eyes never leaving Marroch's face. He looked terrified but kept moving. My eyes were burning but I dared not blink. When he was close, Marroch reached out his arm and grabbed the back of Max's head. With agonising slowness he twisted his hand into his red hair and turned his face towards him. He smiled, studying Max's mouth and jaw before pulling him into the darkness of the corridor behind him. I shivered despite the boiling, murky heat. The boy's helpless excitement repelled me, Marroch was a snake twining victims to him, dragging them into his lair.

I didn't take my eyes from the doorway. Eventually, Marroch reappeared, wiping something black from his mouth. I stiffened. His gaze tangled with mine like hair on thorns and he smiled. I could see blood on his teeth. He lifted one hand, I saw it gleam white through the gloom.

I gave a gasp as I felt him pull something from me. Violently. It made me fall forward over the table. I held onto my chest and belly to keep whatever he was taking inside but it was no good, I could feel it spilling through my fingers, silk ribbons pulled across the room.

His smile gleamed through the dark. He knew what I was. He was trying to take it from me. I whispered words, urgent and sharp and he let me go. I drained the dregs of my drink so quickly the glass knocked against my teeth. I needed to go. Felix and Larry were long gone, sucked into the crowd. Every face around me was distorted and threatening. I hurried to leave and once outside took gasps of the icy night.

I never saw that boy Max again.

For the next few months my life in the city was accompanied by a tuning fork hum of dread. I knew it was linked to this man, Marroch. The unfamiliar stink of fear was on my clothes, in my hair. It was an infection I treated with clear, antiseptic doses of ice cold vodka, which worked admirably, and if

I drunk enough I was able to carry on as normal, my eyes glittering with alcohol as they restlessly scanned and re-scanned the rooms and clubs.

He was a constant presence at the edges of my life but he never came as close as he had that first night. Rumours circulated, he liked girls, he liked boys, he liked to dress up, there was endless speculation about him. His face began to appear in the sketches and drawings of my friends – often powerfully nude.

But something was wrong, nobody seemed to notice what happened to the boys and girls he would choose. They would glow like firebirds for a few weeks then fade and disappear. I'd ask after them, where's Helena? - what happened to Otto? But my questions would be waved away airily; many people were leaving Berlin for safer shores I would be told.

More strange things started to happen. Violence began to creep down the alleyways sending my friends scuttling into the shadows. Arrests were being made but Marroch was unaffected, his cruel white face glared at me mockingly as I lost my footing, looking for my companions.

I went out at night less often. I would spend hours in my room looking out of my window at the streets at night watching police and men in uniform patrol by. One evening I couldn't settle; I was being watched. I saw a figure, Marroch, I thought with a shiver, but when the shadow moved towards the house I recognised Felix, black-eyed in the moonlight. I hurried down to him.

It was cold. I made tea and brought it to Felix who was shaking, his face drained of colour.

'I need you to help me, Freddy.'

'Anything, darling, you know that.'

'It's Sigi, he's got himself in trouble. He needs to leave Berlin.' Felix's voice was tense as a wire, his tea shook itself down the side of his cup.

'Can't you just take him back to London with you? It would be far safer…' Felix shook his head violently.

'No Freddy, I'm leaving tonight, my father has managed to get me tickets home, he got a tip off that people were looking for me and wanted me home despite…' he gestured to his florid, beautifully cut emerald green coat and the smudges of kohl around his eyes. 'Well despite our previous differences.'

'But why should anyone be after you? Because you're a Jew?' I had heard of attacks on Jewish shops and communities.

Felix broke into a torrent of speech. With mounting horror I discovered he and many of the others had got involved with dangerous politics and were intent on sabotaging rallies and speeches which had been happening increasingly often over the past months.

I had read about it but it hadn't crossed my mind that anyone I knew would have been involved. And now Felix and many of the young men I had grown to love were being hunted as degenerates, prostitutes and criminals.

'What about Larry? I haven't seen him in weeks.' I said, my voice sharp with anxiety.

Felix shrugged. He looked ashamed. 'I don't know. He started hanging around with Marroch.'

My blood froze and I stood up and started to pace. 'There's something wrong with that man,' I said. 'I don't like the way he watches all the time. Do you think Larry went back home?'

'I told him to, the last time I saw him,' Felix replied, lighting a cigarette. 'I warned him that we weren't safe but he just laughed, said Marroch would protect him.'

A heavy weight of doom formed in my stomach. I didn't like this. Darkness was circling around us, I could reach out and touch the greasy tendrils. I couldn't help lifting my arms and flicking my fingers, whipping a skein of golden light around the room. I felt better when the shadows shrank but I knew they would return.

Felix looked at me in astonishment.

'I knew there was something about you...' he said.

I ignored him.

'So, Sigi, what does he need?'

Money, it turned out. It was what all of them needed. For false identification, passes, tickets. Before he left Germany Felix handed me pages of names and addresses hastily scribbled in blunt pencil. For two weeks I searched for them, some had already gone; I hoped back home safe, but too often I would find myself peering into rooms with broken doors hanging like smashed teeth.

I felt as if I was going mad. As I surveyed the empty, poor, little rooms I kept feeling Marroch's presence, I could smell him. Had he been here? These rooms filled with abandoned grease sticks and garish silk dressing gowns. Scarves and hats scattered about in a vain attempt to bring colour and beauty to drab, vermin infested dumps.

For the first time in years I used the words Lilith had taught me to render myself as inconspicuous as possible. In those days I could shift without effort, play with my appearance, sometimes a stout middle-aged woman, often an overlooked crooked old hag, picking her way through the winding streets.

Three, four, five of them I sheltered and passed along. Shivering, skinny, broken men I remembered as gorgeous butterflies, provocative and bold – it broke my heart to see them so changed by fear. Violence and unrest was everywhere, a thread of danger heard in splintering glass, jeering voices and chanting crowds. My husband was unhappy, he wanted to return urgently to London – Berlin was too dangerous.

Finally the train tickets were bought, we were due to return at the end of the month. I was relieved, the terror and dread was exhausting me.

There was one name left on Felix's list – Larry. I had been looking for him for weeks. He wasn't at the address Felix had given and nobody had seen him in months. The house was empty and echoed as I walked through the rooms. It was time to go but I wanted to try one final possibility before I boarded the train home. One of the dancers at The Eldorado whose favours I had enjoyed in the past, told me she had seen Larry at a show the night before. She said he seemed 'drunk, or drugged, dearie.'

'Was he alone?' I asked.

Liza coughed and waved cigarette smoke out of her eyes. The thick kohl she wore had rubbed into the creases around her eyes but her mouth was as luscious and cherry red as I remembered. She shook her head, 'no, and good job too as he could barely stand. Tall man, dark eyes – handsome but...'

'Frightening?' I said, my heart was starting to thump.

Liza frowned. 'Yeah. He was. Gave me the shivers.'

Marroch.

I prepared carefully. I thought about Lilith. I searched gardens for the herbs and plants I needed. I pulled as much strength as I could from bright flowers and the cool green leaves of trees. Spring was just beginning, the riot of colour mocking the drab, frightened little streets that echoed with the march of booted men.

Few people were out as I made my way to the centre of town I passed many, many, smashed windows – some boarded up but many gaped open and shards of glass crunched and splintered under my shoes. I swallowed and slipped my hand into my coat pocket feeling for my gold comb, I drove the prongs into my hand, the pain kept my head clear.

Like an animal, I followed my nose. The potions had made my vision sharp and my skin tingled. Through half closed eyes I searched the streets for his trace. And there he was. Wrapped in a long overcoat that flapped around his knees. His head was down, sheltering from the wind. I passed my hand down through my body, making it sink into the pools of darkness under a railway bridge. He was hurrying, focused on the stones beneath his feet.

I traced the path that was quickly fading behind him as he passed me by on the other side of the road. A thread of energy stretched to a grim apartment block. There.

I swung through heavy doors and climbed the stairs, my senses burning, picking up every whisper, every fragment, and every scent. The door was locked but I pressed my palm firmly against it and heard the locks rotate and click.

And there he was. My darling Larry. His blond hair the only bright thing in the room, but when he looked up at me I gasped in horror. He was skeletal. His lips were blistered and sore; I could barely see his eyes so hollowed as they were with black bruises, livid against the yellowed-whiteness of his skin.

I rushed forward, spells spilling from my lips, my hands stretched out ready to heal -when I stopped. The table was covered with papers and photographs. I recognised a face, then another. I turned them to see more clearly. Helena, Eva, Otto, Frankie… Friends of mine, of ours.

I took a step back in horror. Larry couldn't meet my eyes.

'What is this? Why are these here? What happened…?' Realisation was dawning. I snatched up a piece of paper and read the words typed there. *Prostitution, third sex, theft, sodomy…* 'You… you betrayed them.' My voice was a harsh bark. 'You've been spying… passing things on… you disgusting, little…' I felt a sob rise in my throat. 'Where are they, Larry? All these people? What's happened to them?'

I stared into his eyes, pulling memories from them, hooking them free. The flashes and glimpses assail me with such speed I was dizzy. Bodies curved with muscle writhed together, bites pulled blood from the skin, a mouth whispered words, needles, smoke, the first betrayal, the first reward, more drugs, white rose petals soaked with oblivion. I moved blindly away from him my head reeling. I bumped against a leggy cabinet which crashed to the floor, splitting open. A heavy green box fell from a hidden compartment. I picked it up and shoved it into my coat. Larry hasn't shifted from his chair.

A door closed quietly behind me. I turned to look and screamed, an involuntary rush of noise. I put my hands over my mouth to stifle it.

Marroch smiled. I edged back until my shoulders hit the wall. The hand in my coat pocket balled into a fist around the comb. I gripped it tightly. He was a monster. He had swelled in size since I last saw him; no longer the elegant, elongated youth with the chiselled cheekbones. His face was leathery and coarse. The hair, without brilliantine, frizzed in short, mad curls threaded with grey. His shoulders pressed against the cloth of his shirt. A brown shirt, I suddenly noticed, with a leather strap looped across his chest. A military looking hat was under his arm. Long black boots gleamed.

His nostrils twitched and his smile spread. The muscles in his chest seemed thicker, more powerful. My fear. He could feel it, snuffle it up, absorb it into himself. It made him stronger. As if faced with a dog, I forced it down. I realised my lips were moving when I saw words starting to spill into the air, gold scratches. I cursed how feeble they seemed in the presence of this dark animal.

It was no good. Nothing was working, His shadow grew, a strange, distorted shape that crawled up the wall towards the ceiling. I felt myself cower in response; it made him grow still taller.

'Frieda,' he whispered. 'Why are you here? You were a fool to come. He's lost to you.' He gave a contemptuous nod at Larry.

I turned in desperation to the pale little scrap of bones and skin that still sat at the table. Larry's face was without expression.

'Larry,' I called. 'Larry. Help me. He must be stopped. He must. Look what he's done to you, how he's used you.' There was a sob in my voice. I stretched my hand out towards him, tried to pull up strength from the ground to pour into him but he remained impervious, a wall of blankness.

Wind was rushing in my ears, I faltered, took a step and finally managed to touch Larry's hand. My voice grew louder as I cast my words into the air around him. I saw them land like glow worms on his arms, his shoulders. He began to move, my heart lifted. Together we would be strong enough, I thought in exultation.

At first I couldn't work out what had happened. Larry was looking at me – as still, pale and bony as when I had walked in.

But something was different. The wind was deafening me now, I felt my feet being tugged from the floor. I looked again at Larry. I blinked.

What I thought was a bright red scarf he'd thrown around his neck I now realised was a circlet of thick, crimson blood welling as glossy and rich as bubbling jam before spilling crazily down over his clothes, splashing on the table.

I turned to Marroch in shock. He was standing ten feet away, still smiling, but now he was holding up his hand, his fingertips glowed with blood.

'What have you done?'

Marroch shrugged, 'I don't need him anymore.' His smile dropped and he turned his frowning face, the face of a brute towards me. He lifted his other hand and, with his fingers flattened, gestured towards my throat. Despite being on the other side of the room from him I felt the skin on my neck begin to tug. I imagined it peeling away, revealing the throbbing tendons and red tissue underneath.

I cupped my hand around my neck. I could barely think. I was as wild with fear as an animal. I could see the effect it had on him. I could see him swollen with it, licking it up from the air around me. He took a step forward, then another. The door was behind him, I had nowhere to go. Larry sat like a broken puppet, the slash in the skin beneath his jaw flapping open like a grotesque, fleshy tongue dripping blood.

The comb in my pocket was forgotten. All I could think about was the dreadful, tugging, pressure on my throat. The wind continued to drive all sense from my head until I heard a frenzied tapping. A tree was thrashing itself against the window. *Summon* I shouted. *Summon!*

The window burst open with a deafening crash. A shard of glass with the point of a dagger flew, arrow-straight, past me and split the skin of Marroch's neck. Leaves swirled into the room until I could no longer see him. I kept speaking the words, lifting my hands now. More and more leaves came - clumping together, growing stronger, wrapping themselves around me and pulling me towards the open window. The last thing I heard as I was passed through the broken glass into the arms of the tree was a howling roar of rage.

I bumped down the tree, slithering and landing with a crash at the bottom. I ran. My breath juddered in my chest, I sobbed as I stumbled home. My heart didn't stop racing until we were on the train that evening, fleeing Berlin, heading through the darkness back to England. It was only then, in the velvet cocoon of the carriage did I realise Marroch's treasure box was in my coat pocket

*

I would have laughed at Charlie's face of absolute, appalled horror if I hadn't felt like I had been driven over by a truck. My bedroom is freezing. I don't know how long it has taken me to tell the story, but dawn is already brightening the horizon.

I don't bother to take off my clothes. Wrapping myself in a blanket hanging on the chair I hobble over to the bed and lie on top of the covers. The pillow is a cool blessing against my cheek. I long for mindless sleep and close my eyes. I feel the air shift as Charlie sits next to me. I can sense him, propped up against the headboard.

'Did you ever see him again?' Charlie asks, I notice his hand is shaking as he lights yet another cigarette.

'Not for years,' I replied. 'An old friend told me he ended up in the S.S. I used to look for him in news reports but never saw him. He certainly disappeared after the war, I saw his name mentioned in a list of Nazis war criminals but that was it.'

'So why on earth is he here in the back end of the English countryside?' Charlies asks, exasperated. 'Where's he been all this time?'

'I don't know where he's been but I know why he's here. I have something of his. He's been trying to find me for over fifty years. That monster Mark... Marroch had something to do with him. I don't know why I was surprised to see his paw prints in that flat. Blackmailing, drugs, and the abuse of children would be an amusing distraction for him. He's keeping his powers sharp.'

Charlie's eyes are wide.

'So he's older than you – how is it possible he's still so strong, so powerful?'

'Because he is a wolf,' I say. 'And he draws his energy from fear. He thrives on it. And he can always find people to dominate and terrify.'

'And yours?'

'From the natural world, living things, Gaia, mother earth, whatever you want to call it,' Charlie's face is troubled. He is trying to hide it, but he fears for me, I can tell.

'You don't think you can defeat him do you? Because you couldn't before.'

I shrug. My eyes are closing with exhaustion.

'Maybe you can... maybe with Angie..?' His voice is fading.

'I don't know, Charlie,' I say as I slip into sleep. 'I don't know.'

At last, the longed for oblivion of sleep washes me away,
but the darkness is the darkness of uniforms, and long, black boots.

.

# CHAPTER 20: ANGIE

Mrs B told the story of Marroch in a flat voice, but I was knocked sideways by the drama of it. It's like something out of a film.

'And you think this man you knew from, what, seventy years ago was involved with Mark?' I asked incredulously. She nodded.

'I wasn't sure at the time, but I am certain it was his face I saw in one of the photos. He has barely changed. When the gangs appeared and you got attacked, I knew he had found me. He could smell me the way I could smell him, I suppose.'

I didn't know what to say. There were about a billion questions in my head and I didn't know where to start, so I went for the most obvious one.

'So what is it you took? What is so important he's hunted for you all this time?'

'A good question.' There was a pause.

'Which you aren't going to answer.' I said. 'And where is it?' Another pause. 'You're not going to answer that either are you?'

The horrifying details of her story kept circling around my head. It was so surreal that this Nazi monster was also somehow involved with that sick predator Mark.

'That necklace you always wear,' I said, 'that's got something to do with this guy hasn't it?'

Mrs B automatically reached for her neck and smoothed her fingers over the gold in a familiar gesture. 'Yes,' she said. 'When we returned to London, I was so frightened, so weak from my time in Berlin, I went back to see Lilith. I hadn't visited her in years but she knew I would come. She was very old by then, but was kind and didn't rebuke me for leaving so thoughtlessly. Together, we forged this.' To my astonishment, she unhooked the necklace and passed it to me. I had never seen her take it off.

It was much heavier than I expected. I had never seen anything like it. Each piece was different with an irregular shape, as if the molten metal had been poured and allowed to cool in whatever form it fancied. Strong, gold links chained the pieces together so they hung like a string of islands. It was so cleverly designed and the shape of the pieces were such, it was like holding water in your hand. God knows how much it was worth.

'We fired it from the gold of many magical and precious pieces Lilith had collected over the years.' Mrs B said as I marvelled at its beauty. 'Lilith herself inscribed the spells on the back.'

I turned the necklace over and at once I could see hundreds of words spilling across the lozenges. All criss-crossing over each other. Whenever I tried to read them, they shifted and twisted as if alive. 'Just like the bracelet you gave me,' I said.

'This is more powerful of course, but they serve similar purposes.' She reached for the necklace and refastened it, settling it around her throat.

'Some kind of protection?' I said.

'Yes, but the necklace was worked with words to shield me from Marroch.' We both gave a little shiver at his name; the sound of it had a weight that darkened the room.

'But you think he's found you?' I said. 'Why did it stop protecting you?'

Something tugged at the corners of her mouth, sadness or regret, I couldn't read it. She gave an awkward shrug. 'I was a fool to think it was enough. All those weeks in that damn hospital meant the house was exposed, and going to London was just looking for trouble. Stupid of me. I knew I was taking a risk but it didn't cross my mind he would be linked to Mark.'

'What do you mean? Taking a risk?'

'You must have felt this house is special?' She looked at me with her bright little eyes.

'Yes... I have. Funny you should say that, all the time I've been here I've felt more and more that it's not a house, it's more like a person. Sounds daft now I'm saying it out loud.'

Mrs B leaned forward and gripped my hand for a moment. 'No it's not. You're absolutely right to think that. I'm pleased, not many understand it.'

'So what now?' I said. 'Marroch sounds terrifying. How the hell can we possibly deal with him? He nearly killed you when you last met and, well, not to be rude but...' I waved a hand, taking in the wrinkled, thin-skinned tangled knot of ancient bones sitting before me. 'You're not at your best. To be honest.'

The old woman looked stung, but gave a rueful laugh. 'That's why I need you, Angie. I'm just sorry it's taken me so long to work that out.'

She exchanged a glance with the blond man, who nodded gravely.

'Mrs B who is that man?' I felt slightly awkward asking as he was right there, but hoped he couldn't see me.

'He's an old beau of mine,' she replied. 'And why he, of all of the legion of lovers I've enjoyed is the one who has come to me... well, your guess is as good as mine.'

'Was he your first love?' I asked shyly, struck by the romance of it all.

'Ach,' she replied, 'I can't remember. He died in the war, in France. He led me a merry dance before he left.'

'Really?' I said, intrigued. 'What did he do?' I looked over at him. I usually pretended he wasn't there, but now I wanted to know what made him so special.

He looked more faded than he had when I first saw him at the hospital, a silvery sketch. Handsome, though, with thick blond hair and strikingly dark brown eyes.

'What's his name?' I asked.

'Charlie,' said Mrs B impatiently. 'But enough mooning over the pretty boy...' I saw Charlie smiling.

'Can I talk to him?' I said.

'You can try.'

I opened my mouth to speak but saw, again, he had eyes only for Mrs B. He hadn't registered my presence at all. I didn't go on. It would be like talking to an umbrella stand or something, so I turned back to Mrs B.

'OK, so you can't do this on your own. You need me?'

She nodded.

I gave an impatient sigh. 'But how? I don't see what on earth I can do. You say I have a gift but I've barely learnt to light the odd fire. That's not going to be any good against him, is it? He sounds like some kind of all-powerful wizard!'

'You will have to learn more,' she said, her eyes flaming. 'And you will have to learn very quickly.'

'How much time do we have?'

Mrs B shrugged. 'I don't know. It could be tomorrow morning; it could be in a week's time. All I know is it won't be long.'

I sat up straight to hide the cramp of fear her words have sparked. 'How will it happen?'

'I don't know that either,' she said crossly. 'Our focus needs to be on preparation.' There was a long beat of silence, her voice was gentle but with a thread of steel running through it. 'Do you trust me, Angie? It is important you are completely committed to this. I appreciate this is a great deal to ask of you. You owe me nothing and are under no obligation to stay. I would understand if you wanted to leave.

'I'm an old woman and have lived far, far longer than I should, so dying doesn't hold the same fears for me. You understand this is dangerous? Marroch is a very frightening and ruthless man. Many have tried to defeat him and failed.'

An unexpected lump rose in my throat. Not at the very scary things she was saying, well, not only that, but her words about owing her nothing.

'Mrs B you have no idea how much I owe you,' my voice cracked as I spoke. 'The Doc and Maeve as well, of course, they got me out of the dark hole I found myself in, but you have given me back my life.' My eyes welled with tears and I blinked hard to hold them back. 'In fact, no, that's not true. You've given me a new life. A life I could never have dreamed of. I've loved being here. I love this house. My time here has been the happiest of my life.' I swallowed.

Working hard to find the right words, I went on. 'It's as if I spent thirty years wrapped in damp, grey clouds, thinking that was it, that's what life was, and being here has pulled them away so I can see the sky. Because of you, I can make sparks fly from my fingers and summon men made out of leaves. I don't know quite what to do with them,' I couldn't help a sort of laughing sob. 'But I am going to learn. You've made me braver than I could ever have imagined. Whatever dangers you are facing, I want to be there with you. I'd do anything for you, Mrs B. I've lived more of a life here than I did the whole time I was married to Andy. I'll never be able to make it up to you.'

I ran out of words and sniffed wetly. Mrs B's eyes were suspiciously bright, but her only response was a sharp nod. 'So you're going to stay,' she said, and we both laughed.

*

We began the next day.

'What you must understand, Angie,' said Mrs B as we walked briskly across the garden and into the wood. 'Is Marroch draws his power from fear. Trevor!' She made me jump roaring at the dog. 'Stop rolling in that, you disgusting animal.' Trevor froze mid roll, his shoulder wedged into an ominous looking slick of black mud. With a guilty start he shot over to us, we could smell him ten feet before he arrived.

'Yes, you said. Why is that important?'

'It means that without fear he weakens. He cannot replenish from the air around him like you and I can. But if he gets a sniff that you are frightened, it can make him double in size.'

'Christ that's horrifying,' I said. 'You make him sound like a dog – don't let them smell your fear.'

'That's exactly what he is, well – a wolf anyhow.'

'You said Mark was a wolf,' I said, remembering.

'Indeed I did,' Mrs B nodded.

'Well we handled him OK, didn't we?' I said cheerfully.

'I suppose so,' her step slowed slightly. 'But this is a wolf who has trained and learned and honed his skills over seventy years or more. Mark was barely in his twenties. I don't know how old Marroch was when I met him. But the reason this is important is we have to work on controlling our fear, well stopping him being able to sense our fear.'

'And how do we do that?' I asked.

'With courage of course!' she said, as if I was an idiot.

'Of course,' I said and looked over to see her bounding up a low, grassy bank, her skinny witch legs scrabbling against the brown earth. She was heading for a green bush decorated with small, star-shaped blue flowers. 'What are you doing?' I said.

'Borage!' she said, in triumph. 'I've been looking for this everywhere. I thought there was some in the garden but couldn't find it. You and Gary probably ripped it out thinking it was a weed.'

'No we didn't!' I said, outraged. 'I've never seen flowers like that and I wouldn't have pulled anything up without checking with you.'

'Humph,' she replied, intent on picking the leaves and flowers. 'It doesn't matter now I've found this. The Romans used to add this to their wine before battle.' She held up a clutch of the flowers such a bright blue it looked like she was holding a handful of fairy lights.

Back home Mrs B took me into the library and made me push back all the tables and chairs so we had plenty of space.

'We can't hope to successfully attack Marroch. He will always be ten times stronger than we are. To begin with, we will have to concentrate on protection,'

'You mean like a force field?' Mrs B looked puzzled so I explained what I meant.

'Yes, exactly,' she nodded. 'You must learn to create a shield around you. It will stop the smell of your fear leaking towards him and offer some defence against anything he might throw at you.'

The details of her awful tale flashed past my eyes. 'What the hell do I do if he does that horrible finger slashing throat thing?' I said nervously. 'That sounded hideous.'

'Well I ran away,' said Mrs B simply. 'But unfortunately we won't have that option.'

I leaned against the windowsill and automatically scanned the garden for intruders. Christ I was getting as bad as the old woman.

'Mrs B is this all worth it?' I asked impulsively.

'What do you mean?' she stopped walking up and down and looked at me.

'Can't you just give it back to him? Whatever it was you took? From what you say he's not the sort to stop at anything, is it worth putting ourselves in danger?'

'Trust me. It's better I have it,' she replied.

'But why?' I persisted. 'This whole thing seems so scary and crazy, that bloke who attacked me wasn't mucking about.' I shivered at the memory of his hands around my throat, choking the breath out of me. 'And you think he was just like, a minion of Marroch's? God, it doesn't bear thinking about.'

'It took me many years to understand fully what it can do, how powerful it is,' Mrs B went on. 'It is something Marroch wants very, very badly. If he finds it, there would be a catastrophe.'

'So why not just destroy it?'

This gave her pause.

'Oh, Angie, if you knew how long I agonised over whether I should just throw the damn thing into the sea!' she exclaimed. 'But it seemed an obscenity to destroy something so incredibly special.' Her face sagged with a flicker of defeat. 'I recognise my decision was due to my arrogance, plain and simple. In my hubris, I decided I was its best guardian. I would keep it safe. And now, thanks to that decision, it could end up back in his hands anyway.' She shivered. 'God knows what he will do with its power.'

I had to march up and down the room to work off some of my frustration. Curiosity was burning me up. What the hell was it?

I thought. What could it do? Did it hold the secret of eternal life? The power to destroy the world? Mrs B watched me in silence.

'You just have to trust me, Angie,' she said, seeing me tear myself apart with indecision.

'Would the house be different if you weren't hiding it here?' I asked, turning to face her.

She looked at me for a long moment before nodding. 'Yes it would. Very different. But that's only part of its power. It affects any close environment in many different ways. But now shush. That's all I can tell you, it won't do you any good knowing any more.'

'OK,' I said. It's not like I had anywhere else to go, but more importantly, I did trust her. Besides, maybe this was all in her head and Marroch died years ago gibbering away in an German old folks' home.

'So!' she said, straightening and clapping her hands. 'Let's work on your forced field.'

'Force field,' I said.

*

We worked for hours, well into the night. The pink of the sun was just starting to warm the valley when I finally managed to hold up the shield for longer than three seconds.

'This is hopeless!' I burst out, slumping defiantly into the big armchair by the fireplace. I was starving hungry and so exhausted I could barely lift my arms.

'You're not doing it properly, that's why,' Mrs B snapped. She was white with tiredness, looking as bad as I felt. She hobbled over to one of the windows and with a grunt, heaved it open. It rattled up, letting a great gust of air rush into the room. 'Come stand here,' she commanded impatiently. 'I want you to look out and breathe in the air. Try to tap into the experience of the living things you see out there. Pull the energy into you. I'm going to make some tea.'

I sighed. I just wanted to go to bed, and though the air blowing in was refreshing, it wasn't long until I felt cold. The windowsill was deep enough for me to step up and curl into its corner. Slightly perilously, I sat with my back leaning against the frame and looked out, past the garden, towards the village and the valley beyond.

It was beautiful. There was no denying it. In fact, from where I was sitting it was difficult to make out anything from the 21$^{st}$ century. The fields banked and sloped, hiding the roads, and if I didn't look at the council flats, the view can't have changed much for hundreds of years. It was going to be a lovely day. The chill in the morning air marked the beginning of the end of summer, but the soft pinks and clear blues of the sky promised a warm, sunny day.

I let my eyes wander. I could just make out Garth High School, and tracked my journey back from work to the flat and then on to where Mum and Dad lived in the heart of the village. There was the Doc's house, and further back, almost on the horizon, the train station where everything had very nearly ended.

I could see the patch of green behind the church where we had buried Jonathan, near my mother, and later, my Dad. Somewhere out there Andy lay in bed next to Kelly – probably with a baby sleeping close by. The thought made me pause. I registered a pang, but it passed within seconds, and I let it go with a light heart. I even found I could wish them well.

I stared and stared at the sweep of the wood; I tracked the birds wheeling and dancing in the sky and followed them as they plunged down towards the patchwork quilt of the fields. Tap into the experience of the living things, Mrs B had said. Resisting the idea this was all hogwash, I softened my gaze until everything blurred. I let the greens, pinks, blues and browns swarm together and concentrated on letting my mind reach out to them.

It was the strangest feeling. Slowly, slowly, I became conscious of the sense of the livingness of the living things. A sort of extended web of humming electricity but not like the sort you found buzzing in houses or along telegraph wires. It was warmer than that, rounder, and softer. I breathed in, slow and deep. Tried to pull the warmth and fizz deep into my skin.

Gradually, it began to work. Properly work. Not just the superficial boost I had felt in the woods. It reminded me of the time when, feeling desiccated with dehydration on a hot day, I had gulped back pints of water and felt my cells plumping with the cool liquid. Within minutes, all traces of exhaustion had vanished. By the time Mrs B returned with the tea, I was bouncing with energy, ready to try again.

'OK, Mrs B, I think I've got the hang of it, I'm going to try again,' I said, jumping down from the window.

'Imagine it as a shield,' she urged. 'You need to picture it so strongly in your head it appears in front of you. Don't rush the words.'

So that's what I did. I didn't need to check with Mrs B as the words had been said so many times they were engraved in my head. I remembered the colours outside and imagined I was hooking into them, like a generator. I recited the words, it no longer surprised me to see them appear as glints of light, like dust motes lit by the sun. I concentrated hard and stretched them, wide as I could – like cheese on a pizza – I thought.

'Good,' Mrs B breathed, putting down her tea. 'Now make it stronger.'

It was beautiful. I criss-crossed the layers of gold over and over until I was inside a finely wrought cage. I could see it so clearly it was a shock when my outstretched hand pushed through it as if it was smoke. 'Oh,' I said in surprise.

'Of course you can't touch it!' Mrs B tutted. 'It's not a physical thing, but it will work, trust me. Watch.'

She stood in front of me and lifted her fists. She opened her hands and two black balls of greasy looking smoke hurled towards me. I flinched involuntarily, but I needn't have worried. The balls hit the golden fretwork I had created and sizzled into nothing.

'There,' said Mrs B with deep satisfaction.

'Woo hoo!' I yelled.

'Now comes the hard bit,' she said, and passed me my tea.

'That wasn't the hard bit?' I said.

'Now you need to learn to attack.'

*

By the time three days of this had passed, I was confident I could take on anyone. I read and re-read my mother's book, and combed through some of the ones Lilith had passed on to the old woman. Every morning I would go into the wood and experiment. Summoning, protection, attacking – I tried them all. I was getting better all the time but was still very conscious I was scratching the surface.

'You're still not ready,' Mrs B would fret. 'You've done very well, Angie dear, but you are learning things that take years and years to master. We can't rely on you to handle it all on your own.'

'Well I'm trying my best,' I said. 'What more can I do? And don't suggest any more of those disgusting teas. Let's stick to builders', if you don't mind.'

We were in the kitchen and had just finished a very nice Spanish Omelette I'd made with the eggs from the wild chooks who roamed Mrs B's back garden. The pan was crusted with the dried remains reminding me to ask the old woman about any cleaning spells she might know. Or failing that, get a dishwasher fitted.

'I think I'm going to have to give you some things, just in case,' she said, looking thoughtful.

'Ooh like what?' I said and dried my hands. 'A wand?'

The look on Mrs B's face was priceless. 'No, not a wand,' she rolled her eyes. 'Come.'

I followed her into the room with the ebony cabinet and the shelves lined with treasures.

'I am reluctant to give these to you, Angie. It is very, very important you only use them at the right time. You will know it when it comes.'

With great solemnity, Mrs B opened the cabinet and selected three things. A walnut, a small cork-stopped brown bottle, and a gold comb, the size of my palm. It was heavy and the top swirled with deeply carved letters - the prongs were sharp teeth. I shook the bottle and held it up to the light. 'There's nothing in here!' I said. 'And I can't imagine any situation where I'm going to need another silk dress.'

'It is only a dress when you need it to be a dress,' Mrs B said impatiently. 'Do you listen to anything I have told you, foolish girl? This, and this,' she went on, pointing at the walnut and bottle. 'Use these to help if you feel you are losing. Only use this,' she pointed to the golden comb. 'If you know you have lost.' She put her hand on my arm. 'Do you understand me? Only if you know you have lost. This is very powerful; I was given three of them by a strange Russian witch with iron teeth. I only have two left.'

'What happened to the third?' I asked.

'I used it to get out of a sticky situation but it was unwise. The village suffered terribly.'

'What happened to the village?'

'It fell into the sea.'

'Oh right,' I said.

'Keep them close to you,' she advised. 'We may need them soon.'

*

Although both of us, and the house, felt rigid with anticipation, when the men came it was still a shock. We had waited for so long I had to remind myself what it was we were waiting for.

As the days passed I almost forgot why Mrs B was teaching me with such urgency, I just enjoyed the lessons. I sent flirtatious texts to Gary and spent more time clearing the garden. Enjoyable, absorbing activities that were present and real – not like Mrs B's fairy tales of monsters and dragons.

The days were long and a week seemed to take a month to pass. I wonder now whether the old woman had done something to slow down time. To begin with, I carried the three things Mrs B had given to me all the time, but after a while I lined them up on my bedside locker and forgot all about them.

It is impossible for the mind and body to balance on the knife edge of terror and fear for very long. Even my daily lessons of attack and defence became routine. Mrs B never relaxed, though. Her features grew sharp as she lost her appetite, and I saw her light on well into the night as she tried to distract herself by reading, Charlie always at her side.

It was Friday night and I had gone to bed early, cross with the old woman for refusing to eat a scrap of the most delectable roast chicken I had made for tea.

'I'm not hungry, Angie,' she said, pushing away her plate and filling her wine glass. She crumbled the last of the star blue flowers into it and offered me a tired toast before swigging it back.

'You should eat,' I said and crashed about, clearing up the plates. I scraped the chicken into the dog's bowl and muttered what a waste of food it was. 'I'm going to bed,' I said at last, resentful. I had been on my feet for hours, cooked a meal and cleared it up while Mrs B day-dreamed, and sunk a bottle of wine at the table. 'Are you OK getting to bed on your own?'

She nodded. 'Take the dog with you,' she called after me, leaning back in her chair. 'He keeps gnawing at his nails and I can't stand the noise.'

Trevor shot her an injured look as I whistled for him to follow me. I let him out for a quick pee and saw the moon was broad and full with a black circle of cloud threatening to engulf it. Unease shivered down my spine and, suddenly conscious of the darkness pressing against the house, I called the dog in, my voice sharp and urgent. He skipped back, tail up, and I felt reassured, but still took care to double-check the doors were locked before I turned out the lights.

*

The men came at the darkest hour of the night. All was silent, but something had woken me; my heart hammered in my ears. I was disorientated and had no idea where I was or what was happening. My mouth was dry and I couldn't find the switch to turn the light on. Eventually I sat up and used my phone to light the room.

My whole body gave a shiver as the light picked out Trevor standing at the door. It would have been less frightening if he'd been going mad barking. But the way he was standing made my hair rise. He was stock still in front of my bedroom door. His head was cocked on one side, ears pricked, and his tail – normally wagging so joyfully – was rammed between his back legs. Every bit of him was focused on what was on the other side of that door.

'What is it, boy?' I whispered.

He looked back at the sound of my voice, but immediately turned to the door again. He raised his paw to scratch it, then let it fall, as if afraid of being heard.

With a strange, deep, icy, clarity it hit me - this was it. Someone was in the house. In silence I pulled on the jeans and jumper I'd left on the chair by the bed. My breath was shallow and fast and I had to force myself to think carefully, not to rush into anything. My absolute number one priority was to get to Mrs B.

I padded over to the door in my thick socks and ever so gently pressed my ear against the door. I couldn't hear anything but there was a change in the energy of the house, a kind of tightening. Trevor pushed against my leg, pulling at the cloth of my jeans before trotting back to the bed. I cursed at my stupidity, and sped as quickly and quietly as I could back across the room. I shoved the walnut and little bottle deep into my left front pocket and made sure the comb was secure in the other.

I looked at my phone – should I call the police? But then what would I say? The house was strangely quiet and felt a bit tense? No, I'd go and have a look and wait and see. I pushed it into my back pocket and opened the door a crack. I slipped through and shut it, locking Trevor safe in my room.

I waited in the corridor as all I could hear was my heartbeat. I slowed my breathing and listened, my ears straining to pick up any sound. Nothing. I took a breath, crept to the end of the corridor and looked across the hall. I could just make out the black and white floor in the gleam of moonlight, but otherwise was all in shadows. Something was wrong. I kept scanning left and right. All was quiet and peaceful, but I couldn't shake off the feeling that the house was, rather urgently, trying to tell me something.

There. Across from me I could see the painting of the garden with pink daisies. Shockingly, it swung drunkenly – wrenched from its hooks. The crooked, leering angle of the frame was eerily out of place. It made me take a soundless step back. The house had warned me. Someone was here. I peered again into the darkness at the edges of the hall.

I nearly screamed out loud when one of the shadows silently detached itself from the gloom and stood in the hall, looking up at the staircase.

I stuffed my fists into my mouth. My heart crashed against my rib cage and sweat began to pour down the back of my neck. I didn't dare move in case he turned and saw me. Was this Marroch? It couldn't be, he looked too young. My eyes ached with the effort of making out his face.

Another shadow appeared and stood to the right of the other, shorter and more stocky than his companion. I rubbed away the sweat stinging my eyes. A hot stink of fear rose from me, goatish and salty, I could almost see it stain the air. Fuck!

In my panic, I forgot the words Mrs B had spent so many patient hours teaching me. I closed my eyes and forced myself to remember the shape of them. Eventually I was able to whisper enough to spin a gossamer-thin skein of gold. It shimmered around me, and though nothing like as strong as the spells I cast earlier, it was enough to reassure me I could take a shaky breath.

What were they doing? I thought. How can I get a warning to Mrs B? There was no way I could get to her room without going up the staircase. I took another look. The two men were still standing there, craning their necks upwards.

Wringing my hands, I felt like sobbing with despair. Sooner or later they were going to see me and there was no way I could handle two of them. Just as the thought crossed my mind a third man emerged from across the hall and crossed to the bottom of the stairs. It was weird I couldn't hear a sound. I had to rub my fingers in my ears to check I hadn't got deaf.

The two men had been waiting for the third because the moment he appeared, the others began to make their way up the stairs. They didn't speak, they hardly acknowledged each other, the only signal I saw was when the third man gestured for one of the men to wait in the hall.

They crept up the stairs with agonising slowness. My thoughts rattled, bouncing from one side the other, I didn't know what to do. The second the two men were out of sight I crept forwards a few paces, the golden mist swayed with me but it looked awfully thin.

The shadowy man's back was to me, his hair was cropped short and I could see the bulge of his neck coming out of his black collar. He had his hands crossed in front of him like a bouncer.

I clenched my fists and tried to gather up the black smoke Mrs B had taught me to bring someone down. It was hopeless. A few trails drifted across the room but disappeared yards before it got close to him. Urgency screamed in my ears, I willed myself not to think about those two men stealing towards Mrs B as she slept.

Panic was jumbling my senses into a flapping mess. I'd been standing here for what felt like an hour, I knew I could be discovered any second. All he had to do was turn his head an inch and he would see me.

In desperation I reached into my pocket and pulled out the first thing my fingers touched. The little stoppered bottle. I had no idea what to do with it. The glass was cold and hard under my hand and in the dark I saw an oily liquid with a glittery sheen move softly inside. I knew it was pretty old so didn't fancy drinking it. I was in an agony of indecision.

I pulled the cork with a wet pop and flung a stream of the liquid towards the silent figure, scattering droplets across the floor. For a moment, nothing happened. I was just thinking what the hell I was going to do next, when the droplets began to spread.

Like great puddles of the blackest oil they grew wider and wider; in amazement I realised they weren't puddles, they were holes. One drop, the one that had fallen right next to the man, slid closer and closer until it gaped, black as a skull's mouth behind him. It trembled, the edges elongating silently. I held my breath. An inch more, just an inch more...

Bang! He was gone. Just like that. I almost laughed out loud as he just dropped out of sight into the darkness. Hysteria rose and I swallowed to keep myself under control. The liquid holes closed and the floor resumed its smooth, black and white solidity.

With tiny steps I tiptoed over to where the man was standing. I bent down and ran my hand over the smooth tiles – it was as if nothing had happened. Standing, I looked up the stairs, all was silent.

Gripping hold of the bannister, I went up the stairs, grateful for the thick socks that kept my steps silent. At the top, I had to turn right for Mrs B's room but I couldn't see the men and I didn't want them to find me.

I felt stronger now I had got rid of the first man without effort. Maybe the next would be as easy, as long as I kept quiet and got to them before they got to me.

It was black as pitch on the first floor. I still couldn't hear a sound. I slunk to the wall and pressed myself against it. My eyes were adjusting to the dark, but I could still see very little. Moving an inch at a time I moved along, grateful for the cool press of the plaster against my back. The house was shielding me, wrapping its shadows into a thick cloak to hide me from view.

I was nearing the old woman's door. It was closed and no light marked the frame. I was about to take another step when a crippling tug on my arm sent fireworks of pain bursting across the back of my eyes.

One of the men was behind me. He wrenched my wrist painfully up between my shoulders. I couldn't help crying out in pain and he clamped his hand over my mouth. I struggled and kicked, my shoulder on the verge of popping out of its socket. I'd never felt such agony. He was so tall he lifted me without effort and I turned my head away from him in fright as he hissed in my ear.

'Shut your mouth, you fat cow.' He gave another pull on my arm. 'Who are you anyway? And where's the old witch?'

## CHAPTER 21: FRIEDA FIGHTS

*Ring the alarum-bell!—Blow, wind! Come, wrack!*
*At least we'll die with harness on our back.*

Teaching Angie the old ways is more absorbing than I would want to admit. But the house knows as well as I that something is coming. Something that will be the end of me. I know what Marroch wants, and I have hidden it away as safely as I can; I whisper words of protection as I circle the house. The weight of the gold around my neck is never more welcome.

At night, the sense of dread is overwhelming. A dark presence creeps its threads along the hairs of my arms. The mornings are better, as the sun spills warm through the window melting the darkness. For now.

Angie's progress is astonishing. She's a natural, able to master some of the words within days – something I have never seen before. I can see she thinks she is failing, I hear her cry out with frustration as she practises in the woods. She doesn't understand what she is achieving. I wonder whether I should begin to show her how to make ointments and medicines from the herbs and flowers, but then decide it is better to work on protection and attack first. I'll teach her medicines when this is all done, I think, and my heart sinks at the realisation that there may be no 'after.'

I walk round the house touching the paintings, the furniture, the walls. Looking out over my valley every tree, every field and house and road is as familiar to me as the back of my gnarled hand.

I thought my life was over when I came to Pagan's Reach. Too many years had been spent running. I carried Marroch's jade and gold box wherever I went, finding new places to hide, enjoying the riches, power and the influence it carried. I would congratulate myself for not unleashing everything of what it was capable. For not being tempted to open the cask. With typical arrogance I assumed I was the best safe-keeper. That it also gave me huge advantages and a life anyone would envy was irrelevant, as far as I was concerned.

Of course, now I can see the mistakes I made. The life I led after the war was feverish, hedonistic, indulgent, always searching for the next experience. I had journeyed the world with the wolf on my tail, never looking back.

Until I had to stop. A few near misses frightened me enough to make the decision to hide away. I lived in the house passed to me by the old woman who so longed to pass it to Angie's mother. My world, which had included the rivers of India, the mountains of Abyssinia and the fizzing streets of New York and Paris, dwindled to the mile or two of my stretch of valley and woods. The village of Witchford and my house on the hill replaced the sophistication of Shanghai and the dark cocktails of New Orleans.

I sigh, all that remains of that woman is a handful of paintings and three cupboards somewhere in the house filled to bursting with rails and rails of beautiful gowns and furs. It amuses me to think of what the Frieda of those days would think to see me now, old and tired and, possibly even worse, friends with a fat cleaner.

She would have been stunned, unable to believe I find satisfaction in the beauty of my house, the pleasures of my garden, and the reward of passing on the ways of the old ones. She would be screaming at me to run, having smelt the approaching wolf: Gathering up her jewellery and dresses, looking for the next lover, the next delight.

It strikes me, with a small but powerful shock, that there is nothing of that woman left in me. Except, perhaps, for a love of beautiful jewellery. I don't want to run any more. I don't want to waste energy pulling the cloak of youth over me to go dancing into the night. I want to sit and watch my roses grow, and teach Angie all my skills so she can go out into the world to discover everything that it has to offer.

I chuckle at the look of contemptuous horror my younger self would be casting if she could read my mind. I wander through my library running my hands along the books, remembering the stories held within them. I pull odd ones out as I go along, thinking Angie would enjoy them, then have to put them down as I remember there is no more time.

I realise I am saying goodbye. To the house, to my garden, to the valley. Charlie knows this and walks with me.

'Will I be with you?' I ask him. 'At the end?'

'Oh, Freddy, darling, I wish I could tell you what is going to happen. I wish I knew we would spend an eternity together, but I have no idea.'

'Humph, I'm not sure about an eternity,' I say. I lean against the window and look up at the sky. 'I always thought I'll just go spiralling up there, dissolved into a million pieces. Join the clouds and stars and just whizz around.'

'Sounds perfect,' Charlie says. 'But enough of this. It's not like you to be so maudlin.'

'He's coming for me, Charlie. I've run far enough and long enough and I'm tired. I can't win this fight.'

'Yes you can, Freddy!' he exclaims. 'You can see as well as I can how extraordinary Angie's powers are. Between the two of you…'

A car door slams beneath us and we look down to see Angie, back from a trip to the village shop, bounding across the drive and up the steps. She stops to moon over her phone and then looks up to enjoy the soft sunshine on her face. She glows. I wouldn't have recognised her as the swollen golem I had met in the hospital. The air around her is bright and sparking with energy.

'Look at her, Freddy. You can do this. I'm certain of it.'

'Blow, wind. Come, wrack.' I say, but a stone of fear sinks heavy in my stomach.

'That's my girl,' he whispers.

\*

I am surprised the resigned calm with which I greet the moment when the men finally steal into my house, breaking through the defences and prising open my doors. I'm wrenched from the deepest of dreams by Eldritch jumping onto the bed, her back arched and teeth bared. I cannot hear a sound, but I know they are there, I can sense the shadows creeping closer.

I sit up and place my hand on the walnut panelling behind the head of my bed. I concentrate hard, sending my thoughts down through my fingertips, deep into the wood and along the walls of the house. The house tells me of the men at the doors, the silent tools they use to splinter the locks.

I think hard. Not wolves, but they are hard, ruthless, professional men. Nothing like the drunken fool, sent on a reconnaissance, who attacked Angie and failed – sending us a valuable warning. These men won't be so easy to handle.

I wonder why Marroch isn't here. I hope it's because he thinks I am old and frail. There is no way the man who attacked Angie would have been in any fit state to report what he had seen here; Marroch must think I am alone, and that his men would be able to overwhelm me in minutes.

Closing my eyes, I try to picture Angie and where she is, but can't find her. Perhaps she is still sleeping. I daren't think of the hidden box, just sending my thoughts in that direction will alert Marroch if he is nearby.

I am running out of time. The steps are almost completely noiseless but I can sense the give of floorboards and a shift in the atmosphere outside my door. Quickly I stand, pleased I'd had the forethought to sleep in my clothes, so I wasn't waiting in my nightgown, vulnerable and cold. I need to give myself a breathing space. With steady hands I run my fingers along the stone of the mantelpiece until I feel the graze of the metal stud, rusty and rough with age.

As the left panel of the fireplace swings open I think how much Angie would love this and vow to show it to her one day. There isn't much room, only a hollowed out depression, but enough for me to tuck into, closing the wall behind me. There is a slot underneath the overhang of the mantel just broad enough to peer through and keep an eye on most of my bedroom.

At first nothing happens, then I take a sharp breath as a firefly flicker of light scans across the room. It pauses on my bed and I curse myself for leaving the sheets thrown back. The light darts around some more before a tall shadow of a man follows the torch towards my bed. It is difficult to see, my view is made up of sharp light and murky shadows, but as my eyes accustom themselves I see him place his hand on the bed.

Immediately he looks up and around. My bed is warm, he knows I must be close. In two steps he is over at the window and he tears back the curtains – looking left and right. I hold my breath and examine him closely. He is strong. I can see the ruthlessness in him, he carries the mark of murders on his hands. Though tall and thin his tight jersey shows strong, sinewy muscles. I would have no hope against him, he would snap me like a twig.

There is another presence at the door. I see him signal to whomever waits outside. The shadow moves silently away and the tall man resumes his exploration of my bedroom.

I gasp as he begins to search. Careless now of making a noise, he pulls out drawers, tossing the contents onto the floor. I hear the crash of my collection of boxes as he examines each one, prises them apart, before throwing them behind him, one after the other. I wince as they splinter and crack into firewood. My fists clench with fury.

Now he is at my jewellery box and I see him open it up and pause. He digs through it with his meaty hands. With a grunt he picks up a piece or two and examines them, shoving the most precious in his back pocket. I am so furious at this invasion of my most private and precious space red sparks are gathering and burning at the ends of my fingers.

With practiced efficiency, he sorts through my books. He pulls them from the shelves, ruffles through the pages and drops them where he stands. As more fall he moves along, treading the precious volumes into the ground with his muddy black boots. I can barely see through the black mist of anger that threatens to blind me. I want to scream out loud when he skids on my precious first edition of *Captain Corelli's Mandolin*, ripping the pages from the spine.

No. This is enough. I begin to whisper some of the darkest, most dangerous words I know. They glisten like frost and crackle from my lips. My fury ices them into silent lightning that freezes into the air, sending threads through the gaps in my priest hole. With my eyes pressed flat against the gap I continue to speak, watching the threads twist and knot together, making their way over to the plundering figure who is now smashing into the panels of wood on the wall.

I move my fingers, weaving the threads tighter and tighter into a glittering black web of ice. They move through the air closer and closer, sliding up his clothes and gliding over his shoulders.

I see him straighten, look around and pull at his collar. His face blanches and he shivers; his breath clouds in front of him despite the warmth of the autumnal evening. His breathing is growing more and more shallow. My lips curve into a smile as he collapses to the floor.

As quickly as I can I unlock the stone panel and step out, stretching to ease the ache in my back from being cramped in the hole. I pause to listen if anyone else is near and, reassured, stumble over the pile of my precious, ruined things to reach him. I pull hard at the knotted block of ice in his mouth, tearing at the threads until the matted lump falls free.

363

He begins to breathe, but is deeply unconscious. I grab the jewels stuffed into his pockets and place them on the shelf above him. Thankfully, he has passed out right by an alcove I had set into the window seat, and I manage to lift the door and roll him into it – turning the catch with a snap. He won't be able to open it from the inside, and even if he screams at the top of his voice nobody will be able to work out where the sound comes from.

I pant with effort. I have to sit on the floor to catch my breath. It is alarming how weak I feel. Despite the sense of pressing urgency and worry about Angie, I open the window to replenish my energy levels. It takes a long time to recover, longer than it should. The damp freshness takes forever to seep into my skin, hardly reaching the marrow of my bones.

At last I feel strong enough to get to my feet and stand by the door. I am just about to open it when Angie gives a bloodcurdling scream.

I resist the urge to bolt out there. Instead, I press my ear against the door. I can make out a deep voice muttering, and Angie's gasps of pain. Footsteps thud towards me and I slip behind the door just before it slams open. I look through the crack above the hinge to see Angie, face almost blue with pain, held brutally upright by a thickset man dressed in black. He has doubled her arm up behind her back and is pressing on it cruelly, an inch more and it will break.

I stare at her, willing her to look at me. It works. She darts her eyes in my direction and I gaze back at her steadily – trying to force some strength into her. She blinks in acknowledgment, but her face is rigid with fear and panic.

I can't do anything when he has her so tightly in her grip. He sticks his big head through the door and scans the room.

'They're not here,' he grunts. 'Come on. Downstairs,'

He drags her back and Angie whimpers in pain.

'Shut up,' he says, manhandling her in front of him down the corridor. As he clatters down the stairs I slip out of the door and follow, keeping my feet light.

'Johnson! Pearce! Where the hell are you?' he shouts, and the silence of the house takes a step forward. He pushes Angie into the library and from the crashes I can tell he is searching the place as brutally as his companion had searched my bedroom.

I need to get him away from Angie. I'm not sure I am strong enough to manage him on my own, my heart is beating a strange, jerky tattoo and I am dizzy. If I can just give Angie some space I know she will be able to deal with him.

At the bottom of the stairs I slip into the shadows and listen hard. I can't sense anyone else in the house. It is just us three left. I move to the library door using the bangs and smashes to cover the sound of my steps.

The door is open and I am appalled by the devastation he has managed to wreak in a few minutes. He is working his way from one end to the other. His left hand is gripping Angie's arm so tightly I can see the flesh swelling and darkening. She is weeping with pain. With his right he is searching every inch of the library.

The man is huge. Completely bald, his head, neck and shoulders are shaped from a single block of muscled flesh. He handles Angie as easily as if she were a child. His energy is dark and sharp, thoroughly focused on his task. He, too, has the stain of blood on his hands.

I step into the room and stand still. 'Stop,' I say.

He pauses and looks over at me. A grin spreads across his face; it is a cold as steel.

'There you are,' he says. With a shockingly sudden gesture he lifts the book he is holding and smashes it against the side of Angie's head. She drops like a stone.

'No!' I scream. 'Leave her alone!'

He is in front of me in a bound. 'We've been looking for you,' he snarls. 'My mate says you've got something very valuable – said he'd pay most handsomely for it.'

'I can match anything he's offered you,' I say.

'I'm sure you can, darlin', but I'm not interested in bargaining. Just take me to it and I'll leave you alone. Can't say fairer than that.' His tone is light, almost bantering, but it is belied by the empty, shark-eyed, blankness of his gaze.

Behind him Angie begins to stir. If I can just give her some time…

'We'll need the key,' I am defiant, desperate for him to believe me.

'I don't need a key,' he says, lips as close to mine as a lover's; it makes me want to vomit. He holds up his fist.

'If you smash it open you'll destroy it. Your friend won't be pleased if you damage anything.'

He looks at me, not taking his eyes from mine. 'If you're lyin'..' he says.

'I'm not.'

'So where's the key?'

'It's in here, hidden in a book We'd have been able to find it much more quickly if you hadn't just thrown everything all over the place.'

He holds up his fist again, but I have convinced him.

'Look for a big book with a purple cover. It should be over in the corner by the fireplace somewhere, as long as you didn't throw it too far.'

I didn't dare look at Angie, but I knew she was gathering herself together. With the man's back to me I start to whisper some words but they stutter and die. To my dismay, my hands are shaking and useless. Come on Angie, I think in desperation.

'It's not *here!*' the man yells. His temper is rising, a black smoke of rage steams from him. He is nervous, too, as he doesn't know where his companions are. He is throwing books left and right. One flies through the window with a great smash.

'We need that key,' I call over to him, keeping my voice as steady as I can while inching over to Angie. She is getting to her feet, holding her head and wheezing with pain. Her arm is hanging limply, but I don't think it's broken.

'You're lying!' the man suddenly roars, spinning round and advancing towards me. 'There's no fucking book there, you'd have me searching for years there's so many. Take me to it now.'

I glance at Angie. To my horror she is standing white-faced and terrified. Her eyes are darting from left to right and she steps back.

'Angie!' I say sharply.

She looks over at me but it's no use. I have lost her. Fear has swallowed her up; her body shakes with it. The man takes another step, hampered by the tumbling piles of books.

I grasp Angie's hand and face him. He is a thug, I tell myself. Nothing to be scared of. I tighten my grip and whisper to Angie, she straightens her shoulders a little and squeezes my hand to show she is there for me, but I am not convinced – there is a sliver of terror in her, like a spike of ice. It runs through from top to toe and weakens her, a crack in glass. I can sense her splintering.

She needs to stand up to this man. She needs to use what I have taught her, to see the power she holds within herself. Not just to save me, I think as my strength drains away, but to understand what she can do, what she is capable of. I try to communicate this to her through my hand but she seems very far away.

He is stumbling forward, closer and closer. Angie's hand vibrates in mine. I hold up my arm and spread my fingers, I cast words loudly, they whizz and weave together, a golden net that hangs, glittering. The mesh holds him for a moment and he gazes at it in wonder lifting his hand to touch it.

'Angie, listen to me,' I whisper urgently. 'It's time. Use what you have learned,' I feel breathless and have to stop to pull air into my lungs. 'Use it, Angie, you can do it.'

She steadies herself. Her lips shape words, and tiny, golden sparks fall from her lips. The air begins to move.

It is too late. With a sudden, dizzying rush he is upon us, knocking us flying to the floor. A stabbing pain in my chest tears my breath, and I lie helpless for a few moments. The man has fallen on Angie like an animal. I see his arm raise and hear a muffled cry as his blow lands on her side.

'Angie!' I yell as loudly as I can but my voice is a croak. She doesn't move.

With every ounce of strength I have left I pull myself up, hugging the wall as my legs are trembling. I don't have the energy to create the words I need so I search my pockets. Thank God, thank God. The Russian's comb.

I pull it out and hold it to the light where it glitters, the teeth grinning. I hold it high in the air and throw it to the floor.

There is a convulsive movement, like an animal shaking water from itself. The comb lengthens, elongating into a muscular snake the width of my thigh. It begins to twine around the man as he beats Angie. First his arm and then down and round his chest, his neck, his face. I see the golden skin flex as it tightens around him. His arms drop away from Angie, his face is turning blue and I hear the death rattle.

'Angie! Angie!' I shout. A tempest roars in my ears. I bend down and try to tug her up but it's impossible. She is dazed. I keep pulling; the muscles in my chest tear and I sob with relief when I see her eyes snap open like a doll.

'Mrs B?'

She scrambles to her feet and looks down at the intruder who lies prostrate before her. 'What happened? Is that a snake? Is he dead?'

I feel strange. Light-headed, oddly weak.

'Mrs B. Mrs B! Are you OK? Oh God! What happened?'

I try to explain, but my voice slurs. Angie reaches over to hold me up. 'I think I need to…' I try to unfold myself - to uncrook my back which aches as if my bones are melting - to stand.

'Frieda!' I hear a voice call but I don't know who; I look around but there is only darkness. My hands search for something solid but I am flailing. Not now, not now, I think. I have so much to do, Angie still needs me and Marroch will be coming for us. I struggle to stay on my feet, but there is a great pulse of pain in my chest and I fall, I can't breathe.

*

I come round to the crackle of radios and blue lights flashing in through the windows. I am lying on the sofa and Angie is beside me, holding my hand. I try to speak but my lips are dry, she holds a glass to my mouth and I gulp down the water.

'Oh Mrs B I feel terrible, this is all my fault. I tried to stop him but I got so scared I forgot everything.' Her face is wet with tears.

'What... who?' I point towards the lights.

'It's the police,' she says. 'I called them straight away. An ambulance will be here soon. They told me to make sure you didn't move.'

'Police? Ambulance?' I am horrified.

'They've found all the men who broke in,' she went on, not hearing me. 'The one in here looks like he had a heart attack, the other two have been arrested. The police said they were well-known criminals. They think they're part of a group who have been robbing big houses, looking for antiques and paintings – that kind of thing.'

'Angie,' I say, struggling to sit up, trying to shake off the dizziness. 'You know that's not true. You know who they were – what they were looking for.'

Angie wouldn't meet my eyes. 'I'm not sure...' she says, faltering. 'I got such a bang to the head I can't really remember what happened. My arm's killing me, that bastard nearly broke it.'

'Angie, you know this isn't over. This is only the start. Marroch will be here, and soon. His men have failed, he will come next.'

'Maybe we should just leave?' she says, still not looking at me. 'Tonight was so scary, and you nearly died thanks to me falling apart. I couldn't do it, Mrs B. I'm sorry. But when it came to it, I had nothing.'

I grip hold of her hand. 'Angie, you were dreadfully frightened, in pain and he hit you. Of course you struggled. But I promise you, you will learn how to manage your fear. Please. We can't leave. I can't keep running. Please trust me.'

Black dots swarm, I have to keep blinking to clear them. Angie squeezes my hand before gently removing it, turning to speak to a policeman who is standing in the doorway. They talk for a long time. I fall back on the sofa exhausted. I wave away the paramedics when they arrive, refusing to leave the house. 'I just need to sleep,' I keep saying to them.

They exchange glances with Angie over my head. I am infuriated by the way they are treating me like a child. 'If I am going to die I want to die at home,' I say as clearly and forcefully as I can manage.

Eventually the house is silent. Wherever I look I see the effects of the men's rampaging presence. Everywhere is a mess and Angie takes me to Will's old room to sleep as mine is ruined.

'They think I should leave Pagan's Reach don't they?' I say as she folds the sheets and blankets around me.

'Let's not talk about it now.'

'Angie, if they make me leave this house I will die. If I'm going to die anyway, I want to die here.'

'But I don't want you to die!' she bursts out, tears now streaming down her cheeks. 'This is all my fault, in fact I just made everything worse.' She flaps her hands in distress. 'Those... bastards! Breaking in like that and ripping the house apart. Just taking what they wanted and smashing all our things up.'

'But we did stop them Angie. You must have stopped one of the men all by yourself?'

A shy smile crosses her face. 'Yeah I did. I couldn't make strong enough spells, but I used the little bottle. It was amazing, the drops turned into holes and he just fell down them!' She gave a slightly hysterical laugh. 'The police found him in the cellar – he must have just fallen through. I still can't believe it.'

'Well done, you,' I say warmly.

'But that last man…' she goes on with a shiver. 'He was a monster, I felt like he could snap me in two.'

'But he didn't, did he? He's dead.'

'Heart attack they said. But it was you, wasn't it? You created some kind of snake. I must have been dreaming, everything went a bit wobbly after he knocked me out.'

'I used the second comb.'

We sit in silence.

'I thought you'd died,' Angie says at last.

'No. Still here,' I smile, giving her a pat.

'You think Marroch is going to come?'

'I'm more certain than I've ever been.'

'Soon?'

'Very soon. He will know how weak I am…' I struggle to stop my eyes from closing.

'OK that's enough.' Angie rubs my shoulders and moves to the door. 'You need to sleep. Don't talk any more, Mrs B.'

With profound relief I let my eyes close, and Charlie is next to me, his hand on mine. His sorrow is almost too much to bear. I try to hold his dear face in my mind for as long as possible, but fall asleep just as Charlie fades, and a vision of Marroch appears, smiling, teeth red with blood.

# CHAPTER 22: ANGIE

Closing the door to Mrs B's room I rubbed my face, hard. I was poisoned with guilt. Thanks to me and my disgusting cowardice a woman was dying, battered and bruised, fighting a man I should have dealt with. For the hundredth time I re-lived that moment when the animal had flown at us, felt again the liquid terror that splashed through me, turning my legs to jelly.

Why didn't I use what I had learned? Why didn't I stop him? I had the words at my fingertips, I could see them forming; they would have knocked him for six but when he loomed close, and I felt the meaty stink of his breath on my face, my body just collapsed.

I'd let Mrs B down. She had been so patient with me, so gentle helping me recover after that first attack. A sob caught at the lump in my throat. My hands were covered in bits of tissue. I had rubbed them to shreds soaking up the tears and snot streaming down my face. My lips were swollen and my eyes red raw. I barely noticed the pain, I was heavy with shame, numb with it.

It was all my fault. I had behaved like a child, a scared little brat hiding behind my mother's skirts. And now the old woman lay sick in bed looking worse than the day I first met her. Why didn't I do something? I thought, playing and re-playing an endless repeat of that awful night. I watched myself, mouthing like a goldfish as the man advanced. I could feel my heart breaking. I hated myself.

I made a pot of tea but the thought of swallowing anything made me want to retch. I sat gazing into space, occasionally walking in tight circles around the landing when the agitation got too much.

A heart attack, the paramedics had said. She should have been taken straight to hospital but she'd refused and they couldn't force her. I couldn't believe it. I argued with them, but they said they had to agree with Mrs B's wishes.

They warned me that although this 'event', as they called it, was relatively minor, there was a very high chance it would happen again, and the next time would probably kill her. A great lump rose in my throat at the thought of this happening, but I couldn't bring myself to move her away from her beloved home. Mrs B had agreed to an injection, and promised to take the medication they left, but I could see the paramedics thought it was hopeless.

Every inch of my body ached. My arm burned as if someone had slid a hot knife into my shoulder socket. Mostly, though, I was knocked sideways by exhaustion. The police had insisted on me recounting over and over again what had happened that night, and I was to go into the station at some point to submit a formal witness statement. I just wanted to sleep.

Suddenly I was conscious of a faint yapping. Trevor! Oh God, I'd forgotten all about him. I stumbled along to my room and opened the door. He shot out and ran through the house to the hall and then on to the kitchen. He seemed oblivious to the war zone that had appeared while he was shut up. I let him out, and when he came back I picked him up, reassured by his furry, warm, solidity.

I needed to sleep, but didn't want to be at the other end of the house from Mrs B. Instead, Trevor and I set up camp close to where she slept. Wrapped in a pile of blankets, I fell asleep to dream of monsters ripping apart the house with bloody jaws.

\*

When I woke it was gone four o' clock and my phone had about a million messages and missed calls. The whole village had heard about the 'Home Invasion,' as it was all over the news. I switched it off. Mrs B would not be happy to have her business made so public, and the worst thing was the mention of the owner 'collapsing with a suspected heart attack'. If Marroch didn't know Mrs B was weak, he did now.

The only person I called back was the Doc. He was mortified not to be there and suggested he fly back.

'Please don't worry, Doc,' I said. 'There's nothing you can do. She's as pig-headed as always, wants to die here if she is going to die. I just feel terrible I couldn't do more.'

'Don't be silly, you've done wonders for her, Angie, really you have,' he replied. 'You've given her a whole new lease of life. But she's old, far older than many of us could ever hope to be. She can't live forever. Take comfort from the fact you've brought friendship and care into her life. She won't admit it, but she has been a very lonely woman for many years. Seeing her sparring with you, a glint in her eye, has been wonderful. You should be proud of that.'

It was as if he was running a knife into my heart. Swallowing down my tears I looked out of the window. I couldn't bear to hear him being so lovely about me after what I'd done. I hadn't been a good friend to her. She'd faced danger to protect me, as I was too gutless to protect myself. Despite her age and frailty she had stepped up, damaging her heart in the process.

The good news was Gary wouldn't take no for an answer and as soon as he had seen the news, texted me to say he was coming home. I almost cried with relief. He wouldn't be here until the morning, but I couldn't help watching out for him every few minutes.

It broke my heart to see the state of the house. It looked even worse in the daylight. All my hard work sorting and clearing ruined in a few hours. I went into the library, it was freezing cold as the wind whistled through the hole in the window. Making a note to get it mended, I began to move a few books from the floor but gave up within minutes. It all seemed so hopeless.

Mrs B was dying. I could see it in her face. She had that translucent, faded look my Dad had at the end. I was wretched with misery and guilt. The house felt hollow as I walked around, checking all the rooms. Most of them had been ransacked to a greater or lesser extent. I checked on Mrs B in the green room. She was fast asleep, her breathing heavy. I left the tea and sandwiches I had made her next to the bed, and sat with her for a while.

I felt so helpless. Keeping watch at a death bed reminded me so painfully of my Dad I couldn't sit still. Trevor was unsettled and gently whining outside so I decided to take him for a walk. I was desperate for fresh air.

Trevor, delighted to be outside began zooming around the garden on the way to the wood. For such a small dog he was pretty quick, and it made me smile to see him race away until he was only a dot, before shooting back and barking up at me, his face a picture of happiness. The wood was filled with birdsong and the cold was refreshing. I let my legs stretch and pushed myself until my breath was ragged. The ground was springy under my feet.

It was a relief to let my mind empty, thinking only about Trevor and the path in front of me. I was walking so fast it wasn't long before I reached the edge of the wood and I was heading down the path past the playground and towards the village. It was getting late and a bit damp so the playground was empty. My steps slowed as I reached the bench.

I knew he'd be there. It hadn't been a conscious decision, but my feet knew where they were going.

'Hello, lass,' my Dad said.

*

I was so tired, and so overwhelmed, and so sad. I collapsed onto the bench next to him in tears.

'Hello, Dad,' I said. And cried and cried, leaning against the rough cloth of his coat. I was worried he would smell strange and weird, so was relieved I could smell nothing.

He looked his old self. My lessons with Mrs B had developed my senses so each one was sharp and alert. I noticed the more I learned, the more substantial the ones became, and so it was with my Dad. I was grateful, as it meant it was as if he was really there.

Eventually, I stopped bawling my eyes out and reached the hiccupping, snotty stage. I wiped my nose on my jumper's sleeve and sighed. 'Ah, I've really missed you Dad,' I said. 'I'm sorry I haven't had the guts to talk to you before, I knew you were there but I just... couldn't bring myself to...'

'It's OK, Angie, love. You weren't ready,' he gave a deep chuckle. 'Though it seems like you've been doing pretty well on your own – I've been proud of you, girl.'

I swallowed back another wash of tears and blinked up at the sky. 'I know why you've been trying to speak to me,' I said. 'It's about Mum isn't it?'

He nodded and gave a sigh. 'I'm sorry, Angie. We should have talked about this a long time ago, I just felt so ashamed...'

'Ashamed?' I said, incredulous. 'Why? She loved you, Dad!'

'But I stopped her being all she could have been,' he said. He gestured up towards Pagan's Reach. 'That could have been hers, you know. All that stuff you're doing, all them spells – she should have lived that life.'

'She gave it up for you?'

He nodded. 'I didn't know,' he said hopelessly. 'I didn't know for years what she was. It was only when the old woman came to see me I found out.'

'Mrs B came to see you?' I said in surprise.

'No, not her. The lady who lived there before. Granny Wilson we called her. She was getting very old by then and came to see Kath. I'd come back from work early and there they were in the kitchen. I'd never seen Kath in such a state. She wouldn't tell me what was going on at first but I got it out of her in the end. I couldn't believe it!'

'What did she tell you?'

Dad looked uncomfortable. 'Well... you know, about her being a bit magic and all. Could do spells, talk to the dead, that sort of thing.'

'So why didn't she want to learn about it?' I asked.

'She wanted to marry me, have kiddies.' Dad shrugged.

'Couldn't she have done both?'

He was so quiet I looked over to check he was still there. He was looking across the playground and up to the wood on the hills. I couldn't read his expression. The sun had broken through the clouds and chased any that lingered over the horizon. Everything was bathed in a rose-gold glow; it felt like the end of a movie.

'Dad?'

He tapped the palms of his hands on his thighs, a gesture I found heart-breakingly familiar. 'Can we walk?' he said. 'I always think better when I'm on me feet.'

'Can you walk with me through the woods?' I said. 'I don't want to leave Mrs B alone for too long.' I had to rush to keep up with him as he took off at a trot. 'Dad? You haven't answered my question. Why couldn't she learn her craft and have a family?'

'Because I wouldn't let her, OK?' he said finally. I flinched at the anger in his voice but could hear the ache of sadness and guilt behind it.

'What do you mean? Dad? Slow down for God's sake, you're supposed to be a ghost not Usain Bolt.' I paused to catch my breath. He gave a laugh and slowed his steps. We made our way into the wood, falling into an easy rhythm.

'I didn't want her to do it,' he said at last, his eyes on the green canopy above him. 'I thought the whole thing was weird, I just didn't understand it. Everyone knew Granny Wilson was a freak, a scary old lady who lived on the hill. I didn't want my Kath ending up like that. I wanted her with me, with her family who loved her. And she loved me. I knew if I asked her she'd let the whole thing go. And that's what she did.'

'OK,' I said slowly, thinking hard. 'You can't blame yourself, Dad, she made her…'

'I shouldn't have asked her!' he interrupted, his face twisted with pain. 'I shouldn't have made her choose. It was my fault she died.' I was shocked rigid to see tears in his eyes. Dad never cried.

'Dad that's crazy! She had cancer! How can that be your fault?'

'Because I didn't let her be who she was!' His anguished roar set the birds racketing up into the sky in fright. 'I could see it, Angie, I could see how she withered, as if something died in her the day I made her choose. She told me over and over not to worry, that she was happy. She'd say her family were her whole world and she didn't want anything distracting her from that. Even then I knew that wasn't true. Well, not the whole truth. But I let myself believe it and never questioned her. It was only when she was dying I realised what a sacrifice I'd asked her to make.'

'But she was happy, Dad,' I said, stumbling up to him. 'I know she was, I remember.'

'Oh, aye of course. She loved being a mother – you hung the sun and moon for her. But I'd catch her reading her books and the look on her face... well, I used to hate it. I wouldn't say anything, but she knew. And the books disappeared from the house.' He stopped and bowed his head. He looked so hopeless I felt my heart turn over.

'She warned me, you know, Granny Wilson. She said I was only loving half of Kath, and pretending the other half didn't exist would kill her. When the hospital told us it was terminal I knew it was because of me. Because I'd made something important die in her. All the time I nursed her she never said one word, not once did she blame me, but she didn't need to – I know her sickness was because of what I had done.'

There was nothing I could say. I rested my hand on his shoulder.

'So that's what I needed to tell you. I didn't want you living a half-life the way she did. I wanted you to find out what you were capable of and by God you've done it already! Without me! Without even knowing about what your mother was. You're a marvel, Angie.'

'Ah, Dad,' I said.

'I can go now, love,' he said, turning to me and taking both my hands. 'I might have known you didn't need me to see the light.' I looked up into his face, it was like looking into the setting sun – his smile almost blinded me.

'You're going to Mum now, aren't you?' I could hardly speak for the lump in my throat. He nodded.

'It's been too long,' he sighed. 'I need to tell her I'm sorry.'

'Send her my love,' I said in a choked voice.

He was fading. Too quickly. I don't want him to go. My eyes stayed fixed on his face. His voice sank to a whisper. I leant close to hear him.

'Be careful, Angie. The man is coming... I know you can fight him... you're as strong as an ox, girl. Don't let me down...'

And he was gone.

*

I returned home feeling like a wrung piece of cloth that had been twisted back and forth so many times every drop had been drained. My phone bleeped as I reached the kitchen. Gary. He hoped to arrive early the next morning. It seemed like the best piece of news. The one bright spot in what had been a very dark few weeks.

It was nice to think, just for a second, about what I was going to wear and whether I had time to wash my hair. Some light relief from worrying about a dying old woman, a second goodbye to my Dad, and how long we had before Marroch arrived to destroy us all.

I hated seeing Mrs B flat on her back and as white as her pillow. Meekly she swallowed her tablet and fell back, looking wiped out.

'Is there anything I can get you?' I said. 'Anything from your cupboard? Is there anything that could help?'

She shook her head. 'I just need to sleep Angie, dear.'

I wanted to tell her about my Dad, but didn't want to burden her. I longed to hear her yell at me for making the floors too slippery, or smacking my hand away when I reached for another slice of one of Maeve's cakes.

Mrs B's eyes flickered. Charlie and I stood watch from either side of the bed. Every part of me railed against sitting passively, waiting for her to slip away. On impulse, I took her hand. I let it warm between mine and I closed my eyes. I pictured the length of her body and concentrated.

It was like looking into a river. I could see rocks and stones and flowing reeds that coiled and pulsed in the flow of water. Her bones were crooked branches snagged against the rocky banks. At the centre her heart bloomed open and shut, a huge blood-red peony.

I frowned to see rippling pools where the river had snagged on matted black threads. Leaning forward I dipped my hands into the water and pulled at them. Slowly, they unknotted and I rubbed the hair like yarn between my fingers until they dissolved, and were washed away.

Some petals in the flower had tightly furled and blackened. They felt like velvet under my hand as I smoothed them out, one by one. As each unfolded, flecks of black and yellow matter loosened, and they too were washed away like sand by the clear water. The peony bloomed more easily now, each petal joined the others, unfurling to their fullest point with only a few shadows remaining of the black spots.

With a crash I was back beside Mrs B's bed, holding her hand and feeling like someone had hit me over the head. Again. But no. The room was silent and still, it was me who has pushed something too far in my brain and my body has pushed back. I was dizzy and shaken but I looked at Mrs B and knew I had done something good.

The colour was racing back into her face as I watched. The slightly blue tinge around her mouth vanished, and her lips reddened. I felt for her pulse and instead of the rapid, thready beat I was used to, it throbbed strong and slow. I smiled in delight. I knew full well I hadn't cured her heart condition, but I had certainly made her better than she was.

My body drooped as I stared at her. I didn't want to move a muscle. After ten minutes of marvelling at her easy breathing and good colour, her eyes snapped open.

'For God's sake, what are you looking at, girl. Go get some rest and leave me in peace.' Within seconds she was asleep again, but I'd heard enough. That was more like the old woman I knew. She would sleep well tonight, and I knew without a doubt would feel much better in the morning. I left Eldritch and Trevor, curled up in unusual harmony together, on her bed.

As I got up to leave, I realised Charlie was standing by the door.

'Thank you,' he said as I passed. My mouth fell open in surprise. I didn't realise he could even see me let alone talk to me. I was about to reply when I realised he was gone, returning to his vigil by Mrs B's bed.

Closing the door behind me I thought longingly of my bed. I couldn't wait to run a bath, using up all the hot water, then retire to my rooms with a hot chocolate and the last few pages of *Tess of the D'Urbervilles*.

It was only about eight o'clock but it felt like midnight. The police had called the locksmith to come and replace all the broken doors and I took extra care to make sure they were all locked tight shut with the keys hidden in a nearby bowl before I went to bed. I was just making my way back up the stairs when the front doorbell rang.

I stopped. Who the hell was that at this time of night? The thought it could be Marroch, trying again to seize what he had lost, nearly made me drop my mug. But then I reassured myself he would hardly come knocking at the front door.

Placing my hot mug carefully on the shelf next to the bannister I sighed as I went back down the stairs. I'd turned the lights out, so knew I could have a peek out of the side window to see who it was without being seen.

I padded across the floor remembering with a shiver the events of the night before. The bell rang again and I quickened my step. It was getting very dark and I had to squint my eyes to make out the figure standing on the top step.

'Gary!' I screamed in delight, running to the bowl to get the keys. The door took an age to creak open and I tutted, wondering why he didn't go round to the back door as usual.

Finally, the door swung back and we grinned in delight at each other. 'I didn't think you were getting back until tomorrow morning!' I exclaimed, feeling a bit shy all of a sudden.

'What kind of welcome is that?' he said in mock outrage, opening his arms wide.

I ran over and hugged him. He smelt delicious: Cold night air, petrol stations, and sweat, better than any aftershave.

'Oh my God I've missed you so much,' I said, burying my head into his chest.

'Me too,' he replied, kissing the top of my head. 'Now come on, I'm gasping for a cup of tea. Got anything to eat? Then you can tell me what the hell's been going on. I've been worried sick about you.'

I couldn't stop smiling. It was such bliss to have him here, in the house. He was someone I could lean on, someone who could take the strain, just for a moment while I had a rest.

'Come into the kitchen, I'll get the kettle on and we can have a sit in front of the fire.'

I flicked on all the lights and Gary sat at the table, prising his boots off and stretching his feet towards the fireplace. I was just about to summon up a spark into the kindling to get it started when I paused. I wasn't sure I was quite ready to talk about all of that just yet, it was too complicated. It took me an age to find the matches as I hadn't used them for weeks.

Eventually, the fire burned in the grate and I bustled around the kitchen, loving the feeling of making tea and food for my man. The domesticity of lifting the whistling kettle from the Aga and pouring it into the pot, was a welcome change from the dark insanity and fear of the previous night. It already felt like weeks ago. I really needed to go to bed, I thought. Would it be too soon to ask Gary to join me?

As I sliced bread and chopped up cheese, tomatoes and herbs for sandwiches I watched as he stared into the fire. I felt a liquid burst of lust. My mouth went dry and thought of just going over there and putting my arms around him, but then neither of us were particularly lightweight, and I imagined the chair doing the splits beneath us, so I went back to the sandwiches.

He was obviously starving. He wolfed down two rounds within minutes and refilled his tea cup twice. I wasn't really hungry so just watched him eat and sipped at my tea, enjoying its hot sweetness. I let the warmth seep through me, allowing my muscles to relax.

Finally he was finished and we sat in contented silence, listening to the crackle of the fire.

'That was lovely, thanks Angie,' he said.

'So how was the holiday?' I asked. 'Cold and wet by the look of things. How's Danny? Did you do lots of male bonding and mountain climbing?'

He shrugged, 'yeah he's fine. But I'm not worried about him, I'm worried about you. I couldn't believe it when I saw the news – a bloody break in! And not long after the last one. Do you think they were connected?'

'Yes I think so,' I said. 'The police reckon he'd been sent in to check the place out, you know, see if there were any valuables here.'

'Must have been terrible.'

'It was,' I said, thinking he didn't know the half of it.

'And there were three of them? How did you manage to fight them off?'

'Well, one of them had a heart attack,' I said. 'And the other two... We... I...' I stopped. I didn't know what to say. How was I going to explain what happened that night? Gary was wide-eyed with interest and nodded at me to go on. 'We just got lucky I guess,' I said eventually. 'Mrs B managed to trip one down the stairs, I think, and I whacked one with a chair and locked him in the cellar.' My cheeks blushed at the lie, but there was no way I could tell him the whole truth. Not yet anyway.

'Wow!' Gary said, his face open with admiration. 'Remind me not to get on your bad side,' he laughed.

'Yeah, you better watch it,' I said, teasingly.

'So what were they looking for, do you know?' he asked.

'No idea. There's loads of old things here, probably worth a fortune if you know what you're doing.'

'It looks like they turned the place upside down, surely they wouldn't do that unless they were looking for something in particular.'

'I don't think so,' I said, starting to clear up the plates and running them under the tap.

'Did the old woman tell you where it was?'

'Where what was?' I turned to him, puzzled.

'What they were looking for, of course.'

'I told you, Gary, they weren't looking for anything special. I think they thought it was a big house and that there would be some valuable antiques and paintings they could steal. Well that's what the police thought anyway...'

I was about to go on when there was a great thud from upstairs. I looked up, 'Mrs B!' I cried.

'I'm sure she's OK,' Gary said. 'Probably just knocked something over going to the toilet.'

I didn't hear him. I ran to the kitchen door.

'Don't be stupid, Angie. Wait here, I'll go and look.'

He was too late, I was already out and racing down the corridor towards the hall, switching on the lights as I went. I reached the stairs and looked up. At the top of the second flight, Mrs B was clinging to the bannister post; she was swaying wildly, her legs shaking beneath her.

'Mrs B!' I shouted. 'Stay there, What are you doing out of bed? What's happened?' I started to climb the stairs, I could hear Gary behind me and was reassured by his presence.

As I got closer I could see she was staring at me, shaking her head wildly. Was she sleepwalking? I thought.

'He's here!' she croaked down towards me.

'What?' I shouted. 'Who's here? Gary's popped over, we've just...'

Mrs B's face was full of horror as she looked behind me. She was terribly weak but finally she found the strength to speak. 'That's not Gary!'

*

'What? Mrs B? What are you on about?' I took a few more steps and stopped when she reared back in fright, her hands lifted. 'Gary's come back early, he read about us on the news and came back to see if we were all right...'

'No,' the old woman's voice was a desperate moan. 'Look at his eyes, Angie.'

I turned and looked down the flights of stairs. Gary was at the bottom looking up. Seeing me, he smiled and I relaxed. He started to walk up. 'Gary you'd better come and help, she's got herself into a bit of state...' I stopped. Something wasn't right...

I studied his face as he approached, his broad freckled face so kind and so dear to me. My body involuntarily took a step back as he got closer. Mrs B gave another incoherent moan. She was right, something about his eyes...

'Wait. Stop. Stay there,' I found myself saying. Gary looked puzzled. I watched him blink and a waterfall of freezing water hit me, turning my blood to ice. His eyes were black. Gary's were a warm hazel. As I stared, he took another step and in horror I saw his features begin to melt.

It was a monster who was pacing up the stairs towards us. A monster with insane, black eyes and a face carved out of bone. I couldn't move. My feet were nailed to the floor with fear. He kept swelling and growing like a swarming heap of rats. He shook himself – like a dog – and black hair sprung grotesquely like wires from his head. The rippling energy stopped and a thickset, towering beast of a man stood in front of me.

Marroch.

# CHAPTER 23: FRIEDA, AN ENDING

*The Arching Boughs unite between*
*The Columnes of the Temple green;*
*And underneath the winged Quires*
*Echo about their tuned Fires.*

Angie's screams tear at my ears. At my feet, inky streams are flooding past, wrapping around my ankles. The vile stink of hatred and violence is a red and black smoke that makes me gag. I can't help gibbering with fear. Already I can feel him sending his tendrils to knot into me, ready to drag my strength out like a rabbit being gutted. His presence is a foul, swelling, solid muscle that stretches and throbs, filling the house with its dense, heaviness. All is lost. All is lost, I think in despair.

I can't see anything, the smog of fear presses against my eyes and mouth. I fall to my knees, tears spilling. A great bellowing roar splits the air. Angie hauls me up from the floor, pulling me behind her. She is summoning a sparking, crackling wind of fury that surrounds us like a tornado. She is grabbing handfuls, rubbing it onto my skin and mashing it into my hands. I have never felt anything like it.

Surges of power zip down my arms, it is drawn from a deep, lava-liquid core of rage hiding deep within Angie. I can see her draw on it, summon from it. It burns away our fear with a flame that sears. We both grow tall.

But Marroch is still smiling. He continues to draw near, with his relentless pace. He can no longer grow fat by feeding on our fear, but a wave of his hands sends Angie's scorching fire-coals of fury to the floor, where they sizzle into the wood.

'There you are, Frieda,' he says through the electric storm blasting around our heads. It is as if he walks inside a globe of space within which the air is still. He ignores Angie – his focus is entirely on me.

'You can't run anymore. This golem of yours can't protect you. Nobody can.'

'She's not a golem,' I say as I take Angie's hand. 'She's my friend.'

We glance at each other and begin to speak. Our words wriggle and burst from our mouths like butterflies. Mine and hers, silver and gold, begin to weave in and out of each other. They flicker as bright as stars, chains of the old language cascading like music down and around Marroch.

I see him pause, his head tilted to the blinding shimmer of the spells. He cannot step forward, and I see he is struggling to move his head. His eyes widen in surprise. My heart lifts in exhilaration, I have never seen him look uncertain. Maybe the two of us are enough to defeat him, I think with sudden joy.

But with an exclamation he breaks free and Angie gives a scream of horror as, quick as a cobra striking, Marroch darts forward and grabs me, pulling me off my feet. Angie lunges to stop him but it is too late, he is dragging me down the stairs. Fingers fumbling, I jerk at my necklace, unhooking it and flinging it to the floor as I crash painfully against the edge of a step. He is so fast we are in the hall within seconds. He carries me as carelessly as an old suitcase.

Angie hurries down after him, Marroch hisses and a stream of black ice hits her like a wall. She shakes her head, sending frozen crystals flying. Recovering quickly she stands straight and lifts both her hands.

'You do anything and it will kill the old woman,' he warns her, lifting me up in front of him. Angie's hands fall and she looks at me, agonised.

Marroch turns back to me. 'So, you old bitch. Where is it? It's deep isn't it? I can sense it,' he bends, shoving his face in mine. 'Show me,'

I shake my head.

'You know what I can do, Frieda. That friend of yours doesn't stand a chance. Want to see?' He spreads his fingers wide and then turns his hand flat as a knife, pointing it at Angie. I see her gasp, hands flying to her throat. She looks terrified.

'Angie!' I croak. 'The necklace…' I have distracted Marroch and he looks down and shakes me to shut up. It takes only a second, but it is enough for understanding to flash into Angie's eyes and she scans the ground, seeing the gold puddle on the stairs just in time. She snatches it up and gathers it around her neck.

Marroch growls in exasperation and tugs me towards the library door. He slams it behind him and topples a shelf of books to block it shut.

'It's here somewhere isn't it?' He is panting, eyes bright. Roughly, he pushes me towards the middle of the room and I stumble. 'Show me!' he commands.

I open my mouth to refuse and my heart sinks as I see the expression on his face change. He cocks his head and gives a dreadful smile. He spins round to face the huge, stone fireplace.

'No wonder they couldn't find it,' he says. 'Well done, Frieda – you hid it well.'

I hear a thudding sound and realise it is Angie, throwing herself against the door. Marroch hears it too and makes a decision. He pulls me hard, snapping my head back, and pushes me towards the fireplace. It is so tall I can stand inside it easily.

'Open it.'

Without my necklace I am weak, but I am determined not to give up without a fight, if I could just hold him here until Angie...

'Open it, or I snap your friend's neck,' Marroch interrupts my train of thought. His face is implacable.

I unhook the clasp holding the inside wall and push it away from me. The stone sinks with a gravelly whisper and a crunch. A gust of cold air blows into my face. Marroch pushes me forward, holding me tight in front of him. I nearly fall as it is pitch black. I know the way but refuse to help him.

The stone is slippery beneath our feet, the tunnel no bigger than a small man. I can't do much, but I can muster up enough energy to flick slicks of oil under his feet and I smile as he curses and slips, banging his shoulders and head against the jagged walls. We jink slightly to the right then the path tips sharply downwards. It is getting very cold.

We are walking right under the living cloak of the wood. I know exactly where we are. The mulch of green leaf, and the damp, crumbling darkness of the earth fills my senses. It is as refreshing as a tall glass of cool water. Marroch's dark power of ice and fear has no place here.

We emerge from the tunnel into a huge vaulted room. The stone roof soars overhead, and the roots of the majestic trees in the wood above us grow down through the ceiling. They knot around the beams, stretch from arch to arch, and sink into stone walls.

A strange light glows in the air, creating a green gloom – just enough to see by. An unseen stream bubbles and trickles across rocks, and water drops plop into puddles with a deep, plangent sound. There are many things hidden here, but Marroch is interested in only one.

With weary resignation, I watch him scramble across the cracked and crooked flagstones to the round depression in the centre of the floor.

'It's here, it's here,' I can hear him hissing to himself. In his craven excitement he has forgotten all about me. He is determined to smash the place open to find what his heart so desires. He holds no fear for me now. I am too close to death to worry about dying. No. My only wish is to keep the box from him and to save the house for Angie.

The ancient well in the centre of the room is securely locked and bolted with a round wooden door. Marroch has found a lump of broken stone and is smashing at it, sending splinters flying.

To my utter astonishment, I see Charlie at the tunnel entrance. He leads Angie behind him. As she moves into the room her mouth falls open and she cannot help gazing around. She sees Marroch crouched over the little door and disgust ripples over her face.

Suddenly he stands with a shout of triumph. He has the box in his hands, it is locked and he begins twisting it, his face fierce with concentration. Angie looks horrified but I shake my head and smile to reassure her. Before he has a chance to remember we are there, I step quietly towards Angie and move with her a little way back into the tunnel.

My heart is tip-tapping and a headache is threatening to split my brain in two, but I am filled with exhilaration and delight. My body sings with it. Marroch has been the demon on my shoulder for decades. He has pressed and compressed my spirit for too long; seeing him hunched over that box he is suddenly as ridiculous and inconsequential as a child drooling over toffees in a sweetshop window.

'Use the comb,' I say to Angie.

'It's the last one,' she warns. My elation is reflected in her eyes which shine green and bright as freshly washed silk.

We hold hands and turn towards Marroch. He is growling in frustration. The box is empty. He hurls the pieces across the floor. Just as he raises his head to find me, Angie pulls the last comb from her pocket and throws it into the centre of the room.

I want to dance like a dervish and howl at the moon as I watch the comb bounce once, twice, across the stone floor. Within seconds it begins to transform. Each prong fires out threads, lengthening and unspooling quick as a thrown ball of wool. They branch, and branch again bursting up from the floor. Angie and I watch Marroch scream in terror as the prongs darken and thicken from twigs, as thin as my wrists, into huge trunks that turn and twist with a tremendous, cracking roar.

It is so loud we have to cover our ears. Two trees shoot out of the ground right beneath Marroch's feet. The speed is indescribable. They lift and tear him apart as they grow, his shrieks of pain are muffled by the great rustle of a leaf canopy sprouting faster than a man could run.

At last there is silence. My ears ring with it. Angie looks dazed with shock and I can't help chuckling, despite feeling like I have been run over by a truck. She has clearly never seen anything like this happen before. I hope she spends the rest of her life seeing extraordinary and wonderful things like this. Using the trunks of the trees to hold me up I limp through the trees to the clearing at its centre. Angie follows me.

'Where is he?' she says in a hushed voice, she cannot take her eyes from the trees that tower around us, stretching so high we can no longer see the roof.

'He's gone,' I reply.

Angie is moving from tree to tree touching each trunk and pulling a leaf from a low hanging branch. 'It's a real wood!' she exclaims in wonder. 'Look! It stretches all the way down there, I can't even see the end.'

She finds the wooden circle on the floor, the one that marked where Marroch stood and cranes her neck looking up. She holds onto the tree for balance as she squints into the branches. 'I can't see him.'

My legs give way, and I slide down to the floor, the tree behind me holding me up. I flex my hands as they feel strange and weak. A soft blackness keeps stealing up behind me and I have to work hard to stop myself sinking into it.

'Mrs B are you OK?' Angie slips down next to me, gazing into my face and taking my hands.

I smile at her. 'I'm fine, dear – don't you worry.'

She sits back with a sigh. 'God, that was… unbelievable. Thank goodness you knew it was him, I'd never have guessed. How did he do it? He was completely convincing. I had no idea he wasn't Gary. Christ! I'd better call him, I hope he's all right – would Marroch have hurt him?' Her voice is panicky.

'No don't worry, he didn't need Gary, he just needed to convince you – you saw what he wanted you to see.'

She shivers. 'I've never met anyone so terrifying. And to think I thought Mark was bad.'

'He deserved to die,' I say. 'When I knew him he was responsible for the persecution and deaths of hundreds of innocent people. God knows what he's been doing since then. I should have faced up to him years ago. I've spent so long running away and hiding from him. What a waste.'

'Sounds like me,' Angie says comfortably. 'Well, without the mad Nazi bit. I've wasted years of my life, and except for a package holiday to Spain, I've never left the village.'

We are silent, thinking our own thoughts and gazing at the wondrous forest.

'Will they stay here for ever?' Angie asks. 'These trees?'

'They look pretty solid,' I say dreamily. My mind is zooming in and out as the darkness steps closer.

'I'd better take you back upstairs.' Angie scrambles to her feet and offers me her hand. 'It's cold down here and you look done in. Is there a way of getting out of here without using that creepy tunnel?'

'If there is, I don't know it,' I reply.

As I stand, my feet knock something which clangs and clatters across the floor.

'It's the box!' Angie says, leaning down and picking it up. 'Well half of it.' She starts to search through the undergrowth, which is creeping across the flagstones, swallowing the grey slabs and coating it with a skin of moss and bracken. 'Here it is. Gosh. It's beautiful.'

With great delicacy she fits the two pieces together. The box glows, very slightly as the top and bottom connect with a soft click. I reach for it and hold it heavy in my hand. It shows no sign of damage. The jade is the same deep forest green it was when I found it. It is cool to the touch and as I run my fingers over the surface, the mottled fire within curls and turns, lazy as a cat. The jade pieces are rimmed with thick frames of solid gold.

'You have it,' I tell Angie, passing it to her. 'It's no good to me now.'

'Mrs B, no, it must be worth a fortune!' she protests, but her eyes shine. I know she will appreciate its beauty for the rest of her life.

We enter the mouth of the tunnel, leaving the rustling underground wood behind us. As we step into the shadows I am happy to see Charlie waiting for me. His eyes are bright in the darkness.

'Take it carefully, Mrs B.' Angie instructs. 'I don't want you falling again.' Her hand under my arm is strong, I lean heavily on it, grateful for the support. My headache is painting blossoms of yellow and blue that dance before my eyes.

We both struggle as the floor tilts upwards. Without speaking we take one step after the other, focusing on our breath and taking care not to bang our heads. At the top the library is a welcome sight, despite the mess. The light, warmth and colour couldn't be more different to the scene we left behind us. I trip and almost fall as we climb over the grate and Angie manoeuvres me into the big armchair. 'Thank you, Angie,' I say with a relieved sigh. 'Just give me a minute to catch my breath.

Angie pulls the fireplace wall shut with a slam and collapses into the armchair opposite me. 'So what was in the box?' she says.

\*

We were on the train. Rattling through the darkness across Europe heading for London. I was in a carriage on my own, my husband choosing to drink himself into a stupor at the bar. I had been sickened all day by the sight of desperate people streaming away from the advancing Fascist tide. The contrast between their shabby clothes and drawn faces and the luxury of my pampered existence was obscene.

I was still reeling from the horrors of Berlin. But at least I had the contacts and the money to escape; I knew I had left plenty of people behind who had not been so lucky. As I pressed my head against the glass, seeing nothing beyond but my dark reflection, I remembered the box. It just about fitted into the deep pockets of my sable coat.

I remember drawing it out, marvelling at the richness of its colour and the way it was so beautifully crafted I couldn't make out the joins. It took a long time to work out how to open it. I was back in London, preparing my desperate journey to see Lilith, when I finally discovered its secrets.

Inside the box rolled a glass flask. It was made from a glass blower's single breath. So fragile I hesitated to touch it, worried it would shatter in an instant. The surface shimmered with the iridescence of the inside of an oyster shell. A tiny, beautifully crafted glass stopper sealed the top, its collar of golden oil the only heavy touch in the whole bottle.

I daren't pick it up but held it close to the light. Inside the bubble of glass, a pool of liquid hung. As I titled the bottle it moved - but more like a cloud than anything fluid. I had no idea what it could be, I'd not read of it in my books, and had never seen a bottle like it on Lilith's shelves.

It was the last time I was to see Lilith alive. She knew I had come to her out of fear and desperation, and she helped me with her typical grave calm. It was much more than I deserved. Once we had made the charm to protect against Marroch I brought out the jade box.

Lilith was sitting in the garden, the moonlight gleaming on her silver hair, her strong profile turned away from me as she looked across the meadows. Age had not crippled and curled her body as it has mine. She had led a more blameless life.

I placed the box in front of her and opened it. I still hadn't touched the bottle that lay within. Lilith had no such qualms. Without hesitation she dipped her hand into the casket and lifted the flask, holding it on the flat of her palm. I watched her face, expecting her usual measured response, but she surprised me. Her eyes flashed fire and after a moment or two she replaced the bottle and closed the box, waving her hand to seal it tight shut.

'What is it?' I asked her.

'With the bottle closed and the lid of the box sealed it is a powerful charm that will bring luck and good fortune to those who hold it close.'

'And if the box is unsealed and the bottle opened?'

'It will bestow immortality and unimaginable power.'

I felt a shiver of dread. Her voice when she spoke those words was so full of warning and danger. But what made my hands shake and my fingers fumble to hide the box was the note of desperate yearning in her words.

With the box hidden the tension holding Lilith's muscles rigid, relaxed. 'Frieda…' she began. 'People who know you have this will hunt you until they find it. The temptation is too overwhelming, even I can feel the tug of its power. You must destroy it, or use all your power to hide it beyond the reach of all who search – it will be a heavy burden.'

*

'Mrs B? Mrs B?' Angie is staring at me, The shift from memory to the present is disorientating and I struggle to work out where I am. I frown at Angie trying to work out what I'd said.

'Now you know everything?' I ask, confused. I can't remember… I remember the wood… 'Marroch's gone?' I say, a black hole is spreading in my brain. Angie doesn't seem to hear me.

'You must have fallen asleep! What am I supposed to know? Goodness, you were away with the fairies then – got me quite worried. Come on, let's get you to bed. You look done in.'

The lights are sparking on and off and I look around wondering what is wrong. My hands are far away but as I look down they zoom large in front of my eyes before stretching away again. Angie is talking to me but her voice is distorted and echoes in my ears, bouncing around my aching brain.

Charlie is close, he bends over me and I feel the whisper of his lips against my ear. I smile at him and raise my hand to touch the side of his face, noticing with mild curiosity it is shaking and twitching like a dying fish. My eyes roll into the back of my head.

*

I groan as I wake to the antiseptic sting of the hospital on my tongue. My mind plays tricks on me. Did I never leave? The white heat of a headache blinds me and I have to focus hard to make out the ward. I ground myself by placing my hands flat on the cool of the sheets, my mouth is dry but there is nobody there to bring me water. I am tired of this, I think.

Charlie sits next to the bed, to my irritation he is beaming with good humour.

'Here we are again, Freddy!' he says cheerfully.

'Oh God, Charlie,' I say, struggling to make sense of everything. Have I dreamed everything? I try to remember what happened before I came to the hospital but my head feels full of yawning emptiness. 'Why do I feel so strange?' I ask Charlie querulously, my tongue is thick in my mouth.

'You're going to be operated on,' he says confidingly, and lights a cigarette.

'For my heart? I told Angie I didn't want any treatment!' Anger slices through my confusion, sharp as a knife and I try to sit up. 'I want to go home,' I say.

'You can't, Freddy,' Charlie says, and when I see how my legs and arms collapse under me I stop trying to move.

'They found something here,' he touches the side of my head gently. 'And they have to cut it out.'

'Well they can't,' I say crossly. 'And I don't know why you're so bloody cheerful.'

'Freddy, darling, I'm cheerful because you did it. You destroyed Marroch, and you saved Will, and you learned to stop being such a self-absorbed bitch. You even made a friend. A proper one.'

'Where is Angie?'

'Signing some forms somewhere. Lover boy turned up in the morning and she's been with him while you were being treated.'

'Good. I'm pleased. She will need him after I'm gone.'

'Ah, now that's the thing! You aren't going anywhere.'

'What do you mean?'

'You've got a few more years in you yet,' he smiles. He is almost completely reduced now, just a few sketched lines that move the air, but his voice is still clear. For the first time since he returned to me, Charlie moves and lies next to me on the bed. I turn to face him and we look at each other, as close as we were when we used to lie on the hot sands of Margate beach. His eyes are gentle and sad.

'You're not going to see me anymore, darling Freddy.'

A terrible sadness constricts my throat. He reaches for my hair and curls a ringlet around his finger. I am my sixteen-year old self again, the girl who loved Charlie with every bit of her being.

I swallow and nod, tears running into my pillow. 'I will miss you, Charlie. Very much,' I say at last.

'I'll still be there,' he whispers. 'I'll be close, and I won't take my eyes from you.'

'But I won't know you're there?'

He shakes his head.

'Will I ever see you again?'

His lips curve. 'One day.'

The night passes with the most vivid of vivid dreams. Charlie's parting gift. Instead of fragmented glimpses, this time I dive into flowing streams of blissful memory. Years seem to pass as I swoop and glide through those long-ago days. It is a joy to see the faces of my mother and father, the dust of time and failing memory wiped clean so they live for me again.

I understand why it is Charlie who came to me. My heart, which had turned to a diamond hard ball of coal when he died, has bloomed again and my friendship with Angie was the right tribute to Lilith, acknowledging all she had given me.

Finally, as I could sense the dawn coming, bringing with it the knives and needles of my morning operation, I fly through the sky to Pagan's Reach. No need now for the canopy of light sheltering the house from Marroch's prying eyes.

The house preens itself, hiding a forest deep within its heart. A forest which will shield forever a breath blown glass bottle that must never be found. The books and paintings and beautiful things I have collected over a lifetime will eventually belong to Angie. It makes me happy to think of them as hers; she will look after them well.

The woods, and the beauty of my garden, gilded by the dawn, lifts my heart. I smile to see Will, tangled in the sheets of his bedroom with a girl who loves him. Downstairs, his father and mother pretend to fuss about him bringing a girl home, but they share a quiet joy their boy has been returned to them.

Even that pig Andy, who packs up his van ready for an early job, has brought beauty into the world with his most beloved daughter, Emily. She has lit up his life and made him a better man. If he hadn't followed his heart, Angie would never had followed hers, and we would never have found each other.

I awake to a body strange with weaknesses and tremors, but a peace steals through me. I summon a nurse to my side and ask for pen and paper but my hand won't work and I can't write. She agrees to write for me, and I speak for a long time, watching her golden plait swing round her neck, glowing as the sun brightens.

When I am done it is time. The white-suited children come, and ask if I am ready.

## CHAPTER 24: ANGIE, A BEGINNING

Even though I'd touched the forest with my bare hands, felt the roughness of the bark and cut my nail through the green of its leaves, I never quite believed it was real. Later, I learned the word 'improbable' from an old travel book, and immediately I thought of that wood - sprouting out of the ground at a hundred miles an hour.

Christ, the relief of seeing Marroch impaled and torn apart was indescribable. I'd never thought of myself as a violent person, but that night I discovered I could get pretty bloody angry when pushed. I was so sick of being attacked by brutal men, having that beautiful house invaded over and over again. And when that bastard went for Mrs B, dragging her about as if she was nothing, it made my blood boil. A good job too as it taught me rage was the antidote to fear. I dread to think what would have happened if I hadn't unleashed the fury I didn't know was swimming around inside me.

Mrs B never failed to amaze me. At Marroch's end she capered about, delighted as a kid. It made me appreciate what a burden it must have been, having him constantly snapping at her heels. I still have the jade box she gave me that day. It sits next to my bed and even now, fifty years later I fall asleep watching the shades of green swirl and deepen like emerald clouds. It is the most precious thing I own. I still wonder what it had contained – it must have been something special for Marroch to chase it for seventy years.

Sitting side by side with Mrs B, in the middle of the improbable forest, slightly hysterical and giddy with relief, is still one of my favourite memories. But then everything went wrong. At first, I dismissed her slurred speech as exhaustion. The shaking hands a side-effect of an unbelievably stressful day.

It had taken an age to walk back up the stone passage. Usually I would have been beside myself with excitement at finding a secret tunnel, let alone seeing a forest from a fairy tale explode into life in a hidden cellar. But I could barely muster the energy to put one foot in front of the other.

Back in the library, I made sure the old woman was comfortable before asking her what the bloody hell was going on with the box. What had been inside? What was it that had driven that monster Marroch to hunt an old lady down in the middle of nowhere?

Mrs B looked dreamy, and I noticed her hand shaking badly as she pressed it to her forehead. She described escaping Berlin by train and her despair at leaving so many behind who would be ground into dust by the machinery of Hitler's regime. Her words slowed and I had to prompt her to continue when she lapsed into silence.

'I took it to Lilith,' she said. Her voice sounded like a 45 rpm record played at a 33 speed.

'You took what to Lilith?' I said, leaning forward. 'The box?'

She nodded, then stopped.

'Mrs B?' I said, patting her hand.

Her eyes were open but she wasn't looking at me. She was staring beyond that room, that house, to something long ago. Her lips moved, but she didn't make a sound.

'Mrs B!' I called to her, my voice was sharp with worry. It was weird, it was as if her body was there but everything else was gone.

I caught the edge of a whisper and got up to get closer. I knelt by her chair and bent my head.

'Forever...' she said on a fading breath.

'Mrs B. Mrs B?' I patted her hand. 'I can't hear you. Are you OK?'

Her eyes snapped back into focus and she gave me a strange smile. 'Well then,' she said. 'Now you know everything.'

I laughed, 'You must have fallen asleep! What am I supposed to know? Goodness, you were away with the fairies then – got me quite worried. Come on, let's get you to bed. You look done in.'

Creaking to my feet I bent to gather her up when, to my horror, she suddenly snapped back in her chair – her body rigid. 'No no no,' I moaned as she began to jerk. Her eyes rolled back and I could only see a strip of white.

In my panic I couldn't think where my phone was. I ran as fast as I could to the kitchen and then my room until I realised it was in my back pocket. Sobbing with frustration I called 999 and screamed down the phone that they must send an ambulance. 'Please hurry!' I shouted.

Dropping my phone on the floor I cradled Mrs B until the terrible shaking stopped. I held her to me crying incoherently. 'Don't die, don't die. Please...'

This time there was no question whether or not to send the old woman to hospital. This wasn't a slow slipping away, it was a terrifyingly violent attack.

She had another seizure in the ambulance and I watched, sick with worry, as her readings went crazy, shooting up and down. The paramedics were urgent and intent, one barking into his radio – I was too crazed with panic to take in anything they were saying.

I wanted to hold her hand, to dip into that river again to help calm her, but it was as if an iron wall had been built between us, she was locked in her body - a rigid prison - and I couldn't make any connection.

Instead, I whispered words of comfort and hope, anything to still the crazy, jerking movements. They fell, warm and gold and I saw, at last, Mrs B's body relax and grow pliant. The jittering beep of the machines slowed and calmed.

Then all was noise and light and movement as we arrived and they flipped Mrs B onto a trolley, racing her into the hospital where two Doctors were waiting. Without a backward glance they ran away from me, down the corridor and through a set of doors which crashed shut behind them.

It was as if I had been thrown into an airtight, soundless chamber. The calm, as sudden as a curtain falling, after all the noise and movement felt unnatural.

I squeezed into a hard chair with a red seat. The cloth had worn and rubber stuffing bulged from the holes. I had to swallow hard to stop myself from sobbing. Mrs B had looked so tiny, like a little bird. I wondered whether I'd ever see her again.

My phone beeped in my hand. Gary.

'Where are you all?' he had texted.

With a shock, I realised it was early morning. Gary must have gone straight to the house to find me.

Tapping at the screen, I texted to say Mrs B was in hospital. 'Some kind of seizure…' I wrote.

'I'll be there in ten, babe,' he typed back. 'Don't worry, she's as tough as old boots. xx.'

Sighing, I rested my head against the wall. I hoped he was right. Mrs B was so fierce and intimidating it was easy to forget she was well over a hundred years old.

Hours seemed to pass. I sat watching people moving back and forth. I wanted to approach one of the staff speeding around to ask what was going on; but a combination of not wanting to interrupt busy people, and a dread of what I was going to find out about Mrs B's condition, stopped me.

I was desperate for Gary to arrive, but as soon as I saw him at the end of the corridor I couldn't help a visceral kick of fear. I sat frozen as he approached, watching as he looked up and down and finally approached a nurse. He pointed me out and Gary nodded his thanks. He turned, his face lighting up when he saw me, and hurried down the corridor.

Finally he was in front of me, out of breath, his face puckered with concern. 'Angie!' he said at last. I couldn't move, just blinked up at him searching and searching until I saw the warmth and kindness in his hazel eyes.

'Gary!' I cried and threw myself into his arms. I burst into tears and he didn't say a word, just patted me on the back and held me tight until the storm had passed.

'How's she doing?' he said at last. 'Oh it's so good to see you, Angie – it feels like months since I left.' His stubble had grown to a beard since I had last seen him. I liked it. It was redder than I would have expected, but it made him look unruffled and reliable.

'I don't know. She looked awful when they took her away, even worse than when she had her mini heart attack. I should ask a Doctor but I'm too frightened they're going to tell me there was nothing they could do.' I wiped away the tears spilling down my face. Three or four ones were wandering the corridor, looking at me hopefully, but I ignored them.

'Come on, sit down Ange, I'll get you some tea.'

He disappeared for a moment, returning with something hot and brown in a thin plastic cup. I took a sip, but it was so awful I put it down. Gary sat next to me and patiently asked questions until he knew everything that had happened since he left for Cumbria. I didn't tell him about Marroch, or what I had been learning from Mrs B. I couldn't begin to think about how to put all that into words.

'Sounds like you've been busy,' Gary said dryly, his rueful smile making the horror of the last few weeks suddenly seem bearable.

'I'm glad you're here,' I said.

'Me too,' he pulled me to him and I allowed my head to rest on his shoulder, just for a moment. I still couldn't quite get over that I was allowed to be so close to this lovely, big man – close enough to smell his skin, which always made me feel a little giddy. He was such a comfortable sort of bloke I didn't even stop to worry about how bloody awful I must have looked.

I couldn't help yawning so hard I almost cracked my jaw. I couldn't remember the last time I'd slept. 'Christ how long are we going to have to wait?' I said, exhaustion sapping my anxiety leaving a bleak numbness. He shrugged, and we lapsed into silence. I was just contemplating whether I could fall asleep on Gary when a voice made me jump.

'Hello, are you Mrs Tully? Mrs Beaudry's carer?'

I was so zonked I hadn't noticed a man approach us. His expression was serious and I clutched Gary in terror. I opened my mouth but couldn't form the words.

Gary stood, pulling me up with him. He held onto me tight. 'Yes, this is Angela Tully, she looks after Mrs Beaudry.'

'I'm Doctor Nalini,' he said. He was young, much younger than me, with thick brown hair that stood straight up where he'd run his hands through it. His eyes were liquid mahogany behind heavy framed glasses. 'I am pleased to say Mrs Beaudry is stable…'

I sagged with relief.

'But we suspect she may have some kind of lesion in her brain. I need to ask you some questions, would you mind coming with me?'

I glanced at Gary, panicking, he took my hand. 'Can I bring…?' I said.

Dr Nalini gave a courteous nod. 'Of course. This way.'

He took us into a side room, empty but for a dusty pink, uncomfortable looking sofa and a coffee table. Gary and I sat side by side and the Doctor perched on the table, taking out a pad.

'Has she suffered headaches do you know?'

'Yes, quite often,' I said. 'But she…'

'How about trouble walking or speaking?' he spoke over me, his voice clipped.

'Yes, well, a little bit. Particularly recently, I just thought it was because of her age…'

'Any hallucinations? Visions? That sort of thing?'

'I… er…' his quick fire questions were unsettling.

'Well?' He looked at me over his glasses, his pen poised over the paper.

'Yes. Well… No.' I didn't know what to say. Did Charlie count as a hallucination if I'd seen him as well?

'Memory loss?'

'Actually, yes,' I said sadly. 'She sometimes gets terribly forgetful. She remembers loads about the past but I have noticed she will have forgotten conversations we'd had, or what we did the day before, that kind of thing.'

'OK, that's fine. Well it would seem pretty conclusive and fits in with what we've seen on the scans. We need to make a decision whether to operate. She has recovered extremely well from her hip replacement last year, but I'm worried about her angina,' he paused, tapping his pen on the pad.

He was talking to me as he would any carer. Professional and pragmatic. It tore a hole in my heart. I felt helpless, and so tired my brain was thick and heavy, my thought processes muddled.

After more hours of waiting and tests, the decision was made to operate in the morning. Dr Nalini took time to stress to us how risky it was. I realised with a lurch they didn't think she would make it, but if they didn't operate, her seizures would get worse and there was no way her heart would cope.

Gary and I left the hospital and he drove me back to Pagan's Reach. We didn't speak. I stared out of the window not seeing the sky and clouds above. I couldn't stop crying, it didn't seem possible I had any tears left in me.

Pagan's Reach was in mourning, I thought, as Gary and I walked round to the back door, no longer having to fight through bindweed and nettles as I had done that first day with Maeve. Trevor yapped fiercely at the door, his teeth bared, but he began to pogo up and down, feverish with delight, when he saw me at the window.

I opened the door to let him out and he zoomed around a couple of dozen times, licking my hands and leaning his shoulder into my shins, before racketing into the garden and peeing for longer than I thought possible. Eldritch picked her way around my feet, making it absolutely clear I was of no interest to her, before disappearing, a black streak into the woods.

I led Gary in silence through the house. He held my hand tightly, exclaiming in despair and outrage at the devastation the burglars had created. We went through room after room before finally he stopped.

'Angie this is ridiculous. You're dead on your feet. Seeing all this mess isn't going to help and you certainly can't do anything now. Where's your room?'

He was right. I was almost delirious with tiredness. My skin felt filthy and my mouth and eyes were dry and filled with dust. I noticed with surprise the black dirt under my fingernails, and the bruises up my arms.

Gently, Gary led me to my rooms and ran as hot a bath as the house could manage. I watched as he picked up a square glass bottle of oil Mrs B had given me for my fiftieth, and emptied the lot into the water. The room filled with the exquisite perfume of a hundred red roses. In a dream, I let him undress me and help me into the bath. I almost groaned with the pleasure of the heat.

Telling me he'd only be a minute, he left me to float in the scented water. I let my mind go blank. Soon Gary returned, and wrapped me in an enormous dressing gown I dimly recognised as mine. I hadn't worn it for months.

My living room was lit by the cheerful flicker of the fire and I was warm and heavy and deliciously lazy. If I could just close my eyes...

'Come on Angie, you need to eat and then I'll let you go to sleep,' Gary coaxed. He sat me on the bed and fed me with soup and the end of the bread I'd made what felt like ten years ago.

At last, he patted my hair dry and folded me into bed. He pulled the soft blankets high around my ears. I had never felt anything so delicious. My body sunk into the yielding embrace of the bed.

'This isn't quite how I planned the first time we went to bed,' I said with a massive yawn. Gary smiled, leaning down to kiss me. 'Next time,' I heard him say as I surrendered to sleep.

*

I slept, dreamless, for the whole day and on through the night. Eventually I woke, groggy with a banging headache, but felt better than I had in weeks. God I needed that, I thought before jumping out of bed, my heart thudding. Mrs B! She would have had her operation by now. I couldn't believe I'd slept through it.

I scrambled about through the pile of clothes by my bed searching for my phone. I moaned in frustration to find it was completely dead. Heart still racing I reached to drag on my clothes but dropped them in disgust when I saw how filthy they were. They stank of mould and damp, and were streaked with green muck. There were some clean clothes folded in a basket at the end of the bed and I pulled on my old, soft jeans and a thick jumper.

Was Gary still here? I wondered? There was a cup of tea on my bedside locker but it was stone cold. I didn't know if Mrs B even had a landline – there certainly wasn't one in my little apartment. My phone charger was in the kitchen, I couldn't do anything until I'd powered it up.

The most delicious smell of frying bacon greeted me, and I couldn't help a grin to see Gary was still there. He was standing at the oven, wreathed in clouds of smoke, and he beamed at me as I came in.

I opened my mouth and before I could speak he lifted his hand. 'She's fine,' he said. 'I phoned the hospital every few hours. The operation went well and they've kept her sleeping until the swelling comes down. You can visit her tomorrow.'

'Oh thank God!' I said.

'I hope you're hungry,'

'Absolutely starving!' I exclaimed. I'd never been so long without eating. I was hollowed out with hunger.

Gary grunted in satisfaction and started shovelling food onto my plate.

'A proper British fry up,' he said putting it on the table. 'There's some bread there, an' all.'

'Oh, Gary bless you,' I said. He had piled bacon, eggs, two sausages, hash browns, mushrooms, tomatoes and black pudding so high it was in danger of spilling all over the table. 'This is just what I needed.'

Trevor watched us, still as a statue, his little brown eyes never moving from Gary's fork. He had identified him as the more vulnerable of the two of us, and was proved right when Gary, moved by Trevor's puppy dog eyes, tossed him a lump of sausage.

I managed to scoff down every single bit and finally sat back, stuffed, discreetly unbuttoning my jeans under the table.

'Luckily I'm wearing tracksuit bottoms,' Gary said with a grin, having noticed what I was up to. 'Super stretchy.'

I laughed. 'That was lovely,' I said getting up to pour more tea. I felt deeply happy. Mrs B was in safe hands and recovering, I was strong and refreshed after a good sleep and a generous breakfast. I leaned against the counter, looking out of the window, marvelling at how much had changed since Andy had told me he was leaving. I remembered the chaos of the house with a bit of a wince, but I'd cleared it up before – I could do it again. And at least this time it wouldn't be so dirty.

'What are you dolly day-dreaming about?' Gary called from the table.

'Sorry, I was miles away,' I said. I walked over and wrapped my arms around him, resting my head against his. I loved the smell of his skin, the velvet smoothness of the nape of his neck. Nuzzling his ear I sighed in delight, he was so solid and warm.

Gary stood, and with a speed and grace I didn't know he had, gathered me up and pressed me against the counter. Within seconds his mouth was on mine and I thought I was going to pass out with the pleasure of it. Trevor started to yap and Gary pulled back, leaving me cold.

'Wait! Don't stop!' I said breathlessly. Stupid interrupting dog! I thought. Every inch of me was swollen with lust, my face tomato red from the fire that had ignited the second he started kissing me. It seemed I had managed to unhook my bra and loosen my trousers still further. I must have looked a right state.

'I want you to show me round the house,' he said. 'Plenty of time for that later, I never knew you were such a sauce pot, Ange.'

Grumbling, I followed him out of the kitchen fixing myself back into my clothes. 'I don't need to see the house,' I said. 'I know it's in a complete state. Those bastards trashed the place. But why do we have to tidy it now? There are so much nicer things we could be doing. Besides Mrs B won't be back for a...' I stopped.

Gary was standing in the hall looking smug. I looked around, the rubbish that littered the floor was gone. The pink daisy painting was straight, the drawers in the chest had been put back in place. I looked at him in astonishment.

'You've tidied it all up?' I said.

'Yup! Well it wasn't all me, I got some mates to come up and help. Most of the village came, actually. They wanted to do something when they found out what you'd been through. Come and see this.'

He pushed open the library door and I followed him in, open mouthed. Everything had been cleared. All the books and paintings were back in their place. 'Oh Gary!' I said, my hands flying to my mouth. 'Oh, that's brilliant. I can't believe you did all this. How long was I asleep?'

Gary laughed, his lovely deep laugh which always made me smile when I heard it. 'Not that long, there were so many of us it went in a flash. Mostly it was just putting things back where they belonged.'

I ran and gave him a huge hug. 'Thank you,' I said, choked. He rubbed my back.

'There's some incredible stuff in here,' he said walking to the end of the room. 'All these books! Do you think she's read all of them?'

'Probably,' I laughed. 'She's over a hundred, remember.'

'Blimey!' he exclaimed softly. 'And look at these paintings. They're beautiful – and so many of them!'

My eyes were drawn to the shelves at the end, the ones that hid the little door leading to the second level. Against them someone had propped a canvas I hadn't seen before. I couldn't stop looking at it. I took a step forward.

It was a stark, boldly drawn sketch of a woman. She gazed out of the canvas, her chin on her hand. Strong, dark eyebrows cocked sardonically above wide, bored eyes. Great, wild, waves of black hair whirled around her head, filling the entire canvas. It was breath-taking.

'That's Mrs B!' I said in astonishment. I knew this woman. I kept seeing her. In the woods, when we sat together and I saw that strange, queen like figure flicker before my eyes. I turned to Gary. 'That's Mrs B when she was younger!'

Gary stood next to me and we fell silent. It was if the painting had cast a spell on us. 'It's a Picasso,' he said in surprise.

'What?' I said.

'Look!' he jabbed his finger at the corner of the canvas. 'There, see? Picasso.'

'Bloody hell!' I said. 'She told me once she'd posed for him, but I thought she was joking.'

'She must have some amazing stories.'

'We'll have to ask her when she comes back,' I said. I looked at him, I loved how awestruck he was by the paintings and books. I remember feeling the same when I saw them. 'Gary,' I said.

'Yes, babe?'

'There's something I need to tell you,' I said.

*

It took all afternoon. Half way through he stopped me, asking if there was any alcohol in the house. I unearthed a bottle of red wine from the back of Mrs B's pantry and we worked our way through it as I spoke.

I didn't tell him about Marroch, or the wood hidden in the heart of the house, but I told him about my mum, and what Mrs B had been teaching me. I couldn't carry on seeing Gary without telling him. I didn't want to become my mother, amputating part of myself and pretending it never existed. All the time I was talking my stomach churned with nerves. I prayed this wouldn't be the end of us.

Finally I finished, and he looked into the fire for what seemed like hours. I watched his face, trying to work out what he was thinking.

'Gary?' I said at last, the suspense was killing me. He looked up, I couldn't read his expression.

'Show me,' he said.

'Sorry?'

'Show me something you can do,' I watched his mouth curl up, first one side then the other as a smile crept across his face. He looked like an excited little boy and I found myself grinning in response. I couldn't wait to show off.

'Stand up!' I commanded smiling.

'Yes sir!' He stood and waited.

It was so lovely to use what I had learned for fun instead of to defend myself I almost laughed out loud. I couldn't wait to see the look on his face.

Slowly I twined my hand in the air, feeling the sparks gather along my skin. When they were ready I opened my fingers and allowed tiny butterflies with green and blue wings to glitter into the air, whirling round Gary's head, settling briefly on his shoulders and cheekbones before fluttering to the ceiling. I clapped my hands and they dissolved into a shower of sparks which spilled soundlessly to the ground.

'Wow!' he said. 'Oh my God, Angie. That's amazing! What else? What else can you do?'

So, I lit fires, and summoned, and made golden nets of sparks which shimmered in the air and sang shivery music

Finally, we ended up in the hall and I turned to him with a smile on my face. 'I've saved the best until last,' I said.

'OK, I'm ready,' he said. He looked completely shell shocked, but at least he was still there - I hadn't sent him screaming down the road.

'Give me a minute.' I closed my eyes and remembered what Mrs B and the books had shown me. I had practised this numerous times, but never in front of anyone – I found it slightly embarrassing. I focused deep within myself and concentrated. I heard Gary gasp as my hair started to grow, my waist narrowed, my legs lengthened. My lips blossomed and my eyes widened, and my skin smooth and tightened. Not breathing with the tension of holding everything in place I slowly opened my eyes.

Gary's eyes were as big as saucers. I preened a little, I knew I was taut, toned and youthfully beautiful as any of those young girls you could find on Instagram.

'What do you think?' I said, trying not to move my lips, 'quick! I can't hold it for long.'

'I… er...well. I mean it's amazing but…'

'But?' I said, incredulous.

Gary scratched the back of his neck, ducking his head. 'It's horrible, you look like a weird wax work. Can you… stop that?'

I let out a great gust of air, my fat exploded back into place and my skin loosened. 'Really?' I said.

'Yeah, I like a bit of meat on my women,' he said lasciviously. He slipped his arm around my waist, pulled me towards him and kissed my neck 'It was gross, like you'd put on one of them filters, you know, like what you see on Facebook? Made you look like plastic. Don't do that again.'

'I don't think anyone has ever said anything so nice to me in my life,' I said, gasping as he began to dot kisses up towards my ear around to my mouth.

'Got any good tricks for the bedroom?' he said.

'Oh! Loads!' I said, and unhooked my bra again.

\*

Gary stayed with me in Pagan's Reach for two weeks until Mrs B returned. It was blissful. Fifty years later, with Gary no longer with me, I reach for the memory of that time often. It never fades. Whenever the loss of him is unbearable I close my eyes and I am there. Laughing with him as we marched through the woods with Trevor, talking into the night over good wine and his special roast chicken, and best of all, rolling around in my creaky old bed. It's all there, just at my fingertips.

We fell into a routine. He went to work and I visited the old woman who was making an amazing recovery. I took her armfuls of flowers, the last of the late roses with their heady perfume, as well as out of season tulips and dahlias – the most colourful I could find. The little moments of absence that I used to find so disconcerting had disappeared and her eyes were sharp and clear.

I'd told her about Gary and she was pleased, asking loads of questions including some very inappropriate ones about our sex life.

'I can't wait for you to get home,' I said. 'The house looks great and Gary's been sorting out the dodgy taps as well as front door - it doesn't stick anymore.'

'It will be good for the house to have a man living there again. I suppose you'll have to move out of your rooms, they're not big enough for the two of you. Why don't you take the top floor, there's plenty of space up there.'

'That would be fantastic, Mrs B thank you.'

'And when I'm gone, I've made arrangements so Pagan's Reach and everything in it,' she gave me a significant look. 'Will be yours.'

'Don't talk like that, Mrs B. The Doctors have said you're in excellent shape.'

'I'm not talking about dying!' she said crossly. 'I'd quite like to go back to India for a while. I never did get to see the Palace of the Winds in Jaipur.'

'Can I come with you?' I asked, stroking her bony little hand.

'Perhaps,' she shot me a look, 'if you can tear yourself away from Gary's bed.' I blushed. 'And you've told him about everything?'

'Yes. Well. Most of it, I didn't tell him about Marroch – I thought you could tell him, one day. He wants to hear all your stories, and so do I. How the hell did you end up getting painted by Picasso?'

She gave a wicked grin. 'It was just after the war, he used to call me Françoise – oh, he was an old goat but a genius, and very funny. I must have been in my forties; he thought I was 21. I remember going into his studio in Paris, you wouldn't believe the mess...'

# EPILOGUE

'I don't know why you're flapping about so much,' Gary said as we walked up to Mrs B's room. She was due back the following day.

'I just want everything to be nice for her!' I said, lugging a pile of sweet-smelling bedding. 'Careful with those flowers!'

'Does she really need so many?'

I hadn't been into the old woman's room since Marroch broke in. Gary hadn't wanted to invade her privacy so he and his helpers had left the door tightly closed.

My heart sank at the muddle that greeted us. A spurt of anger choked me at the thoughtless devastation those bastards had wreaked on her lovely room. I set Gary to stripping the bed while I bent to the cupboards and drawers, replacing their contents that were strewn across the floor.

Her beautiful jewels were dotted about everywhere, I picked them up one by one - each of them was stunning in its own way. I slowed to admire them, draping bracelets across my wrists and trying on rings.

'Stop dawdling, woman!' Gary panted as he worked his way around the bed.

'Sorry!' I said, blowing him a kiss. Closing the jewellery box, I started folding up the old woman's clothes placing them neatly into the drawers.

'Why does she need such a massive bed?' Gary grumbled. 'She's only a tiny little thing.'

'Oh stop moaning and get on with it,' I said. 'I'll make you a cup of tea when you're finished.'

Books were everywhere, looking like they'd been thrown down and stomped on. Gently I smoothed out the torn and rumpled pages. Mrs B would hate to see them so poorly treated, I thought. I slotted them back on their shelves while Gary started to make up the bed with the clean sheets.

The room was finally clear and I arranged the flowers so they glowed from every surface. Fresh air blew in from the window I'd cracked open, and I made sure the grate had enough tinder and logs so we could have a fire burning within minutes.

'Wow... what's this?' Gary said. He was bent behind the bed. I pulled the wrinkled top blanket straight and slipped a couple of springs of lavender under the pillow.

'What is it?' I said, looking round the room. It looked lovely, clean and tidy with a good, fresh smell.

'Here,' Gary held out his hand. On his palm rolled a glass bottle. I'd never seen anything so delicate. Its body was almost complete spherical and the light moved over its curves like liquid.

'It's like a soap bubble,' I said, marvelling. I ran my fingers over its surface, it shimmered like the inside of an oyster. I could see every colour of the rainbow in it.

'Do you think it's something magic?' Gary asked.

'Probably.'

He held it up to the light coming in from the window. 'I wonder what used to be inside it,' he said.

THE END

Printed in Great Britain
by Amazon

# READ ON FOR A PREVIEW OF 'FRIEDA' THE NEXT IN *THE WOMAN AND THE WITCH* SERIES

I'm flying across the sea. The wind is cold and fierce, buffeting my face and hands. It is delicious. My hair, dark again, and long, is pulled into a skein of black silk that tangles with the star embroidered night sky.

Dawn hurtles me forward. I skid on the rosy beams, revelling in the freedom, almost forgetting the gaol of elderly flesh and bone from which I have escaped. For a moment. The delight is such I don't question where I am or where I'm going.

Until the scene darkens.

My body dips, the ocean reaches to grab at my legs, lacy spumes whip into dangerous coils and I pull up. I climb the ladder of the clouds and frown to see them thicken and knot together. They roll into black curls under my fingers and my heart jolts as I realise where I am.

The cliffs are ahead; I am racing towards them. The pits and caves in the surface of the chalk yawn and grin and I am falling.

It's waiting for me. The glint of its face, wrapped in wire, stares at me, bloated and blind from under the water. My legs kick. Desperate.

'Frieda … What have you done?'

The houses fall. Brick by brick. The sea guzzles everything up. Driftwood and broken trees bob crazily on the churning waves.

I wake up screaming.

'I told you not to have cheese for supper,' says Angie, swinging the door shut with her backside and bringing me my glass of Petrus. An indulgence, but I can afford it.

Peering up at her and taking the glass I sigh to find myself back by the fireside, back in my knuckle of a body. As Angie picks up my fallen books, one by one, restoring order to my beloved library at Pagan's Reach, I shudder to remember the cliffs. They still haunt my dreams though fifty years have passed.

'Dreaming of the combs again?' Angie asks, plumping into the armchair opposite and flapping herself cool with a folded newspaper. She takes a greedy sip of her gin and tonic and sighs with pleasure.

'It's not a dream, it's a memory,' I snap. My hip hurts, and pain rattles along my rib cage - not that I'll tell her that.

'Oh, right,' she says.

'Help me up.'

She hauls me to my feet, and I hobble from one table to the other until I find what I'm looking for. Angie snaps on the lights and there are two books, both written by my goddaughter, now Master of an eminent Cambridge college. I've never read them. She specialises in a field of Physics so complicated and absurd, I glaze over whenever she speaks of it.

But it was the painting I'm looking for, one of my favourites. A simple wooden frame from which glows the colours of a county garden, filled with flowers. I fancy I can smell the drift of freesias on the breeze and hear the hum of the bees.

'That's pretty,' says Angie, looking over my shoulder. 'Where is it?'

'Brokkton,' I say. 'It's where I lost the first comb.'

# ACKNOWLEDGEMENTS

To my Mum, Penelope Larkman, who is the reason I fell in love with reading. She would read something like James Herriot and I would hear her laughing her head off, and it made me want to find out what was so funny. She still gets through a couple of books a week.

To my Dad, Peter Larkman, who is the best storyteller I know, along with my brother. I realise now the stories he'd regale over the dinner table were paving the way to me wanting to be a writer.

To Bill Browning, I couldn't have done it without him; my punctuation and adverb use is much improved thanks to his input (Any mistakes you find are my own - Bill tried his best). He has been a teacher and friend for forty years, and words cannot express how grateful I am for his support.

To Jayne, Rosie, Helena, and Stephanie: thanks for reading a very bulky and badly written first draft - your comments and responses were invaluable.

And special thanks to my lovely husband, Paul, who never did read 'The Woman and the Witch' to the end, but kept encouraging me and saying how much he loved Frieda.

To my gorgeous children, Joe and Emily, thank you for inspiring me, and writing the name of this book in the soil of every landscape we visited in the Lake District.

Thank you so much for buying this book and I hope you enjoyed it. Do come along and say hello on Good Reads. You can also find me on Facebook 'Amanda Larkman – The Middle Aged Warrior' and if you liked this follow my Amazon author profile and I'll make sure you know about the next things I write before everyone else! (If I can, I'm not quite sure how it works).

You can find me on Instagram @Amanda_Larkman and Twitter @MiddleageWar

# ABOUT THE AUTHOR

Amanda Larkman was born in a hospital as it was being bombed during a revolution. The rest of her upbringing, in the countryside of Kent, has been relatively peaceful.

She graduated with a Masters in English Literature and has taught English for over twenty years. *The Woman and the Witch* was her first novel, and it was followed by a collection called *Airy Cages and Other Stories*. A thriller, *The Bookbinder*, was published in April 2021. The second in 'The Woman and the Witch' series, Frieda, is to be published in 2022

Hobbies include trying to find the perfect way to make popcorn, watching her mad labradoodle run like a galloping horse, and reading brilliant novels that make her feel bitter and jealous.

She has a husband and two teenage children, all of whom are far nicer than the characters in her books.

Instagram: @Amanda_Larkman
Twitter: @MiddleageWar
Facebook: Amanda Larkman: Middle Aged Warrior
Blog: www.middle-agedwarrior.com